TRAILOKYANATH MUKHOPADHYAY

Tales of Early Magic Realism in Bengali

Translated by
Sucheta Dasgupta

THORNBIRD
NIYOGI BOOKS

Published by
NIYOGI BOOKS
Block D, Building No. 77,
Okhla Industrial Area, Phase-I,
New Delhi-110 020, INDIA
Tel: 91-11-26816301, 26818960
Email: niyogibooks@gmail.com
Website: www.niyogibooksindia.com

Editor: Upama Biswas
Design: Shashi Bhushan Prasad
Cover design and illustration: Pinaki De

ISBN: 978-93-89136-97-5
Publication: 2023

Printed at Niyogi Offset Pvt. Ltd., New Delhi, India

To Siddhartha

wind beneath my wings

Contents

Foreword

Trailokyanath Mukhopadhyay (1847–1919), or T.N. Mukharji, as the British Raj knew him, is an exemplar of that curious nineteenth-century invention: the Victorian Bengali. He was a contemporary of Michael Madhusudan Dutt, Bankim Chandra Chattopadhyay, Jagdish Chandra Bose, Toru Dutt, the Tagore brothers. Woven out of the twin strands of Bengali and English, these individuals reworked the contents of the national consciousness, first, in their own Bengal, and later, through myriad translation projects, the rest of the colonised subcontinent. First, that is, the Bengal Renaissance, and parallelly, the great Swadeshi project that spread to every part of the country.

These individuals possessed that dual consciousness so often found in an oppressed people who are resigned to the rationale of their oppression. As Trailokyanath wrote in an account of his travels, *A Visit To Europe (1902)*: 'We could scarcely realise our own individuality when on that chilly evening of the 7th of April (1886), we looked down from this magnificent bridge into the silvery water of the Thames beneath.' He was simply describing his reflection in the water, but perhaps it pointed to a deeper truth. Trailokyanath's account of his travels indicate that he identified most closely with his Bengali self while he was in England and most closely with his British self while in India.

Such dual selves are the norm, not the exception, in literature. When we read a story or poem by such an individual, to whom should we give authorial credit? When W.B. Yeats wrote an English poem, what was the colonised part of him, the one which had said, 'No people hate as we do in whom that past [the English oppression of the Irish] is always alive, and there are moments when hatred poisons my life', what was *this* W.B. Yeats doing?

One way to think of such works is to see them as inherently acts of translation. Of course, all authors are translators in the sense that they turn experience into expression. But when the experiential self is rooted in a world with a fundamentally different aesthetic from the expressing self, then we get a truly hybrid work that cannot be reduced to either aesthetic.

However, I do not believe Trailokyanath was wracked with such conflicts. The ability to compartmentalise and contextualise is necessary for survival in a pluralist world, and as A.K. Ramanujan has persuasively argued, it comes 'naturally' to Indians. We have one rule for Peter and another for Parveen and quite another for Parminder. By and large, Trailokyanath was a loyal British subject at work and a progressive traditionalist elsewhere. He was comfortable, I suspect, with both his British as well as Bengali self. A reflection in the water was simply a reflection in the water.

In his stories, therefore, I find little of the complexity or psychological subtlety we find in the works of, say, Bankimchandra, or a little later, Rabindranath Tagore and Jibanananda Das. When Trailokyanath sets out to write a ghost story, he writes it, and what we are left with is exactly what he set out to write. We get an honest-to-Durga*mata* ghost story filtered through the consciousness of a writer who has grown up in a native lamp-lit world with storytelling elders, banyans with their hag hair, and still bodies of water embanked by moss-covered walls. When Trailokyanath wrote, he was keenly aware of English fiction—indeed short fiction itself was something of a foreign import—but unlike the case with Urdu writers in the opening decades of the twentieth century, his style remained closely tied to the traditional oral tale.

In other words, Trailokyanath wrote for the entertainment of his living, breathing readers and not to provide fodder for critics or future academic groupies. I don't think he ever imagined, as Toru Dutt did, that his work would interest professional critics like George Gissing, or that their didactic value would extend to all people and not just his people.

These are all speculations of course. But then again, his very able translator Sucheta Dasgupta believes his works fits within the category of speculative fiction. I am less persuaded this is so. The context of a story matters just as much as its content. Take the category of magic realism. This category, I submit, makes sense only in its twentieth-century context. It is less justifiable, at least for me, to extend it to works from the twelfth century or in Vedic times. This is not because these early works don't have all the elements we associate with magic realism. What they don't have is the context. The twentieth-century context is completely different from the Vedic one. Thus, the Mahabharata performed for a post-classical Vedic society would be an entirely different story if it were performed in Carnegie Hall, even if it is replicated word for word, gesture for gesture. The Carnegie Hall audience might file it under epic fantasy; for the Vedic society, it would be a living reality. What we *can* say is that there is a magic realist reading of such-and-such work. The classification refers to the relationship between the reader and text, and not to some essence in the text itself.

Admittedly, this is a rather punctilious stance. Ultimately, what matters is not the classification, but the object itself. And we owe it to Sucheta Dasgupta that we have Trailokyanath's stories available in a new incarnation. Her introduction amply resolves the difficult task of having to do justice to the content and contextualisation of these stories. Borges remarked that a translation can only serve as its own apology. I do not think so. A translation is one of the greatest gifts a writer can offer to the world. If an apology is due, it is from the reader that they have left this burden of bridging worlds to a few brave individuals. We are in Sucheta Dasgupta's debt.

Anil Menon

Author, *The Inconceivable Idea of the Sun: Stories*

Translator's Note

I am indebted to my editor, Dr Nirmal Bhattacharjee, redoubtable literary scholar and the finest mind, for asking me to explain what spurred me to take up this project.

It was my husband, erstwhile Bengali writer and documentary filmmaker Siddhartha Samaddar, who reintroduced my adult self to Trailokyanath. As my senior author, Siddhartha was keen to bring to my notice that, being a fantasy writer myself, I ought to read the work of my more illustrious predecessor in the same genre. He also shared with me folklore about Trailokyanath's love for marijuana and *chandu*, citing their frequent mentions in his prose. Was substance part of Trailokyanath's process? Was it at the core of his visions about what it meant to be a ghost and how to be one, which he went on to relate to the reader by means of fantastical tales of love, adventure and laughter that never failed to somehow galvanise?

Up until that point, which was in the early noughties, I, who wrote what I self-identified as speculative fiction, was familiar with Trailokyanath Mukhopadhyay or Mr T., as I liked to dub him mentally, exclusively as a Bengali satirist from the texts I had read and been marked on during my school days. And it would not be before 2011, when back from Kolkata's storied Collegepara, Siddhartha would bring me my first copy of *Trailokyanath Rachanabali* (*Collected Works of Trailakyonath*), the first of which, *Kankabaty*, had been published in 1892. The name of the current publisher (2006) is Sri Shyamapada Sarkar, Nabin Chandra Pal Lane, Kolkata. There were at least three editions of the republished work until 2011, which happen to vouchsafe its extant popularity. The pages of this last volume are the space where I discovered, to my immense intrigue and wonderment, one of the world's first magic realists, nay, authors of speculative fiction, Trailokyanath. With the weight of the 850-page omnibus of stories behind him, was it he then who invented this genre?

The form of original, and not derivative, fiction writing can be broadly divided into two genres: realist and speculative. Speculative fiction is characterised, uniquely so, by the building of imaginary worlds. Subgenres of speculative fiction include magic realism ('Lullu', *Kankabaty*), surrealism ('Beerbala'), fantasy (*Kankabaty*), fable ('Shambhu Ghosh's Baby Girl'), science (*Domrucharit*), myth ('The Legend of Raikou: A Japanese Folktale') and supernatural ('Every Cloud Has a Silver Lining; Behold the Honest Woman That Is Smiling'); the last literary style referring, in plainer terms, to the good old Bengali tradition of the ghost story.

As illustrated by the examples of his works above, cited genre-wise within each pair of parentheses, with the exception of possibly hard science—because his science-fantasy leaned strongly towards fabulism—Trailokyanath's oeuvre cuts across all these subgenres. The thrilling aspect of this is, while the actual definitions of many of these genres and subgenres (magical realism, speculative fiction, and so on) would be coined only decades later in English literature, our man was already creating these genres and bending them in Bengali, in nineteenth-century United Bengal! When I came to discern it, it was a revelation. It inspired me in 2015 to write an essay titled 'Rereading Trailokyanath', in Contrarywise, my *Times Of India* blog, positing these facts.[1] It was not before many more years had gone by, however, that I would be pleasantly surprised and vindicated to find my theory echoed by scholar Boddhisattva Chattopadhyay (University of Oslo) in an essay and read another piece by him in an old favourite ezine, the highly reputed *Strange Horizons*, that argued for a non-Anglocentric vision of the world of speculative fiction.

It is no one's postulate, however, that Trailokyanath completely stayed away from straight-up realist narrative fiction. His novel, *Fokla Digambar* (*Gumsy Digambar*), for example, is a lovestory but also a 'serious' comedy of manners. *Paaper Porinaam* (*Sin and Consequence*) is a social drama and short story 'Lalit O Labanya' ('Lalit and Labanya') an intimate study of hardship in the Bengali countryside.

1 Dasgupta, Sucheta, 'Rereading Trailokyanath Mukhopadhyay', *The Times Of India*, 21 April 2015, https://bit.ly/3Ebn7Sa. Accessed on 16 February 2023.

Even the ghosts that pepper Trailokyanath's writing are of two kinds—'real' and metaphysical. The realist ghosts are spirits of dead men, women and children. They edit newspapers (in 'Lullu') and have magical powers (also in 'Lullu'). They haunt the houses of humans in Kolkata ('Chinese Spooks on Pous Sankranti'), a city which appears as a character in this and some of his other works (like *Kankabaty*, 'One-Shanked Chhoku', 'The Mysterious Ring' and 'When Vidyadhari Lost Her Appetite'). This is even as a majority of his pieces are set in the northern (*Kankabaty*), eastern ('Nidhiram Bengali', *Gumsy Digambar*), western ('Shambhu Ghosh's Baby Girl') and southern ('The Invaluable Tobacco and the Learned Snakes') Bengali countryside. The metaphysical ghosts of Trailokyanath appear in 'Lullu' and *Domrucharit* as subaltern characters living a marginal existence on the fringes of genteel Bengali society. They look and act like the wraiths that they are. Wraith-like, too, they fall in the ambit of the curious rules of ghostship that govern the ghostly lives of 'real' ghosts.

My egalitarian (and personally speaking, feminist) reading of his works has made it incumbent upon me to use the singular they as the third-person generic pronoun for many of Trailokyanath's characters as well as for the Great Unknown, personified by him as God. In its 14th edition (1993) of *The Chicago Manual of Style*, the University of Chicago Press explicitly recommends using the singular they and their, noting a 'revival' of this usage and citing 'its venerable use by such writers as Addison, Austen,

Chesterfield, Fielding, Ruskin, Scott, and Shakespeare'. By 2020, most style guides have accepted the singular they as a personal pronoun.

The style of Trailokyanath's prose is weighty and formal while its tone is wry and irreverent. Hence, I have consciously adopted a Victorian style while rendering it in English and, at the same time, tried to be as exact as I can so as to not miss the many cultural facts peppering it, which is another attraction of his works, as well as efficaciously capture the subtleties of his humour.

Why is reading Trailokyanath still important in today's climes and times? Here are five reasons.

Trailokyanath was a classical liberal thinker. His works show what it is to be a civil servant (a bilingual, well-travelled rationalist) as well as a socially invested libertarian in British India. He inhabited a unique, non-activist yet extremely clear-eyed, perspective. It lends a certain fineness to his works that makes them aesthetically timeless.

Trailokyanath is relatively unsung and underrated because his legacy fell on the wrong side of the post-Independence political establishment. But as a short story writer, his talent considerably exceeds that of even Rabindranath Tagore (whose aesthetic has become old-fashioned but whose sensibilities as expressed in the short story form still have the power to appeal and provoke thought) or Saratchandra Chattopadhyay. It is both a joy and comfort to read Trailokyanath's stories a century and more after they were written. Perhaps due to professional rivalry, Tagore is known to have played him down as a children's writer.

At a time when the rest of India was rooted in mind-numbing dogma that stank of soul-killing illiberalism, irrationality and inhumanity, Trailokyanath wrote magic realism, speculative fiction and science fiction, and was among the first in the world to write, masterfully, in these genres. It can be said that in India it was he who invented these genres.

Trailokyanath is also unique in that he, himself, was a nineteenth-century bilingual writer. His first works were travelogues in English. He was well-travelled and toured all of Europe as a curator for the world-famous Indian Museum, Kolkata.

We need more authentic Bengali icons in the mainstream, going beyond political certitudes and clichés. Fortunately, we have little dearth of them in our history. But we need to spread the word lest and before their legacy is diluted, or worse, erased and overwritten.

While selecting the pieces, my editor and I have taken special care to pick out a diverse palette to showcase the author's marvellous versatility and offer the reader a mind-expanding experience. Purposefully, we stayed away from the quirky but too overly known *Domrucharit*, which is a part of every college and school syllabus. Instead, our selection communicates a richer mixture of the many human moods.

Kankabaty is a magic realist lovestory of an adolescent girl and a tiger. 'When Vidyadhari Lost Her Appetite' is a look inside a high-caste kitchen, which doubles as a funny story about a get-rich-quick scheme and conspiracy. 'The Alchemist' is historical non-fiction. Not so, 'A Japanese Folktale' and 'Rostam and Bhanumati' which are folklore collected in the course of his travels by Trailokyanath. "Lullu" is a gently humorous tale following the general theme of how the maiden was won or the ghost conquered. Together, these stories cover 202 pages of the 850-page original *Collected Works*.

The author passed away in 1919 and the work is not copyrighted. The challenge for me, therefore, was to be accurate in my translation so that I could communicate as much of the Bengali idiom and history of the language to the reader while preserving the thrust of the dialogue and the thought process of the author. I fully intend my work to be the 'same text in a different language' and not a transcreation. It is for this reason that I have included a glossary at the end of each of the works to elucidate upon the idioms, customs, sayings and indigenous terminology used by the author.

Still, the process of translation involves the subjective exercise of preference and discretion. It also leads to the refinement of one's own understanding of people and their worldview. Better to say I am Bengali, rather than I am a Bengali, my father had once said when I was in school, preferring the adjective to the noun, as I bullishly cross-questioned the mickey out of the nuance. But is it wrong to say the latter? It is not incorrect, he had conceded, in one of his first exact and hence less absolute responses, which I failed to fully receive as a schoolchild.

I had completed over 200 pages of initial translations when I encountered, in 'A Japanese Folktale', the first of my political differences with Trailokyanath. Therein, he advances, diffidently but without the benefit of evidence, the possibility of ancient seafaring Hindus from Bengal having reached Japan, thus betraying the teeniest sentiment of Bengali exceptionalism that was not inappropriate in his time. In the same story, he is also vociferous about the ills of saké, the Japanese national drink. Perhaps, he had retained, notwithstanding his reputed affinity for *chandu*, a brahminical abhorrence of liquor. Hindus and Rastafarians are known to keep their senses virgin by avoiding all forms of intoxicants, including the theine (found in tea), with the sole exception of tetrahydrocannabinol. If as a personal habit, it is an unassailable choice.

Glib and convenient virtue-signalling by taking a high moral ground just because it is now to do so is a bane of our own times. Minds far greater than its combined self have been brought down to the dust by the cancel culture brigade using ideas gatekeeping and social media amplifications. Indeed, one can wonder, legitimately so, if those who persecuted the Renaissance men and women from the Right are now doing the same from the Global Left by deleting them from syllabi. But quick and dirty judgementalism in order to signal virtue is not the same as thinking and exercising one's judgement while doing a close reading of the works of an author.

As I have disclosed before, this translation is a feminist reading of Trailokyanath. Female readers are particularly sensitive to how women are portrayed in literature, directly impacted as they are by the world history of misogyny. Trailokyonath's women are often idealised; they don't have the anger and meanness, jealousies and worries that are intrinsic parts of the psyche of an ordinary woman. Trailokyanath fails to see through the helpless mother stereotype. In *Kankabaty*, for instance, the character Khetu's maw is only in her early twenties but shown as frail and having failing eyesight. Like an old woman, too, she never ceases complaining, but this last behaviour is cultural. A common adage every Bengali girl grows up hearing is '*meyera kuditei budi* (by the time she is twenty, a woman's youth is all but over)'.

Yet Trailokyanath does such a superlative job in capturing the inner child of women. Indeed, it is so good that identification is spontaneous. Many of the protagonists of his stories are female. Unerring, he lays his finger right on what proves to be the undoing of many Bengali girls and the foolish Kankabaty, the propensity to be an overconfident hero in order to save the day and impress the beloved, a tendency not entirely out of line with the urge to please others.

That said, my own concept of womanhood is incongruent with Trailokyanath's. This, I learnt, however, only when I came up against his descriptor of *tthunto* (cripple) for the 'overeducated' *bhadramohila* (well-born woman) who reads novels and gets het up over talking points and lies in bed in a blue funk, neglecting housework and lacking in gravitas. Such a characterisation of the turn-of-the-century

Renaissance Woman appears twice in his body of work, once in the story 'The Mysterious Ring' and the second time in *Gumsy Digambar*. For me, those are his only lines that rankle. Clearly, Mr T. does not have a public role for women in mind. They are, to him, only servants of the men as muse and helpmeet or agents of procreation. In any other setting, they are rendered crippled and pointless.

If he is uninterested in the woman as provider, Trailokyanath is also not altogether comfortable with women protecting themselves against danger and even walking at night. Notably, this habit among well-born women was not unheard of a century ago in rural Bengal and in freedom fighter circles in Kolkata. Jyotirmoyee Devi, a member of the Surya Sen–Ananta Singh–Pritilata Waddedar circle of revolutionaries who played a small but risky role in the Chittagong armoury raid, had, for instance, reminisced in 2008 that, on a regular basis, she would 'sneak out of home in the dead of night and ride her bicycle to the meetings of freedom fighters'. It was her mother-in-law who covered for her. But even though he creates Kankabaty, and Beerbala, who in the eponymous short fiction conquers hearts in Arabia as a young tomboy, and, in *Gumsy Digambar*, his narrative voice Yadav Daktar is quite enamoured of Kusee for finding his house in the night time in order to call him to take care of her husband, Trailokyanath goes on to reveal that the cause of the injury of said husband is a shot from the gun that he had illegally acquired to guard his young wife from rape during tourism.

This fact is kept a secret from Kusee but she is never really shown as being prepared to question it.

Despite being endowed with a fertile geography, for centuries together, the Bengali community witnessed terrible hardship, perhaps more than any other group of people in India. Recurrent cyclones, famines and malaria epidemics frequently wiped out entire populations while the average life expectancy of an Indian in 1910 was a little over 22 years. It is a premise of a hypothesis that I would now like to forward about the Bengali personality. From a nagging suspicion, it first crystallised into concrete form when I read 'Nidhiram Bengali'. The premonition arose: Do Bengalis, like Kashmiris who, too, have witnessed long decades of strife, suffer from CPTSD (complex post-traumatic stress disorder)? Exhilaratingly, Trailokyanath himself seems to have been quite free of the anxiety neurosis, personally. He was hardly a worrywart Nidhiram. One can take heart from his example.

The prospect of reading and the experience of translating Trailokyanath had been so mesmerising that when I first got the go-ahead from Prof. Bhattacharjee, I jumped into the project with a huge appetite. I ended up furnishing him with so many pieces that their combined dimensions became unmanageable. Depending on how well you enjoy this volume and the publisher's discretion, there will, perhaps, be a second edition of the immortal stories of Trailokyanath.

Lullu

Taken

'Le Lullu.' Little inkling did he have at the moment these words passed Aameer Sheikh's lips what disagreement they were just about to unleash upon his world. The words landed on Aameer's destiny in the way of a thunderbolt. Aameer's homestead was in Old Delhi; Aameer was a Muslim by caste. One dark evening, Aameer's wife had stepped unaccompanied out of doors. To pull her leg, with the sole purpose of scaring her and getting a laugh out of that outcome, Aameer piped up, proffering from indoors, 'Le Lullu.' Meaning, 'Lullu! Come, catch my wife and spirit her away.' Lullu is not the name of any fierce tiger, nor is it the name of a knife-brandishing miscreant with a missing ear. 'Lullu' has no meaning other than the sound it makes; you would not find it in any dictionary, purely in jest had Aameer put the sounds of its syllables together and uttered that word.

But when trouble comes, it arrives without notice. The surprising news is this that Lullu was the name of a ghost. At that moment, on that same night, Lullu was sitting on the terrace of Aameer's house, swinging his cheerful feet from the parapet. Suddenly, someone called him by name. He started and listened: someone was asking him to take something; he looked and found a beautiful woman before him. She was whom he was being requested to take and leave. If you are set to get hold of such gorgeous goods, even the gods would go about performing the nikah in a minute, so you can leave aside thoughts of how a ghost is wont to behave. In the blink of an eye, the unfortunate woman was whisked through the air and flown away to such a place as to no one could say wherefore.

From inside the house, Aameer was of a mind that his wife would walk in anytime. He waited and then fidgeted, as time stretched forth, but she did not turn up. He began to feel afraid, called out to her; there was silence. The darkness was deep and impenetrable. Here, there, everywhere he looked, but he could not find her. Still, he hoped—that his wife was pulling a prank on him by hiding herself. He returned to the house and searched it thoroughly—no trace or whiff of her ladyship. What was a bit strange; the gates of the house were still locked. Just as the wife had locked them at dusk, so they remained. Then where did she go? An honest wife, faithful to her husband, would not step out of the gates. And even if such an ill-advised plan had come to possess her mind, she could not have passed through them without having opened them first. Greatly distressed, Aameer began analysing these odd bits of information. Tears flowed continuously from his eyes and down his bosom. Not seeing the angel of his hearth made him sensible to a huge emptiness in his hearth, heart and world—his bosom burned like sand in a desert in summer. 'I gave away the jewel among womankind with my own hands. Harkening my words, whether a djinn or a ghost or Satan himself took her, I cannot understand. Alas, and alack,' he cried. Finally, he wiped his eyes, opened the gates and called over his neighbours. They came in haste and searched the house once again. Then they searched all the houses in the neighbourhood. Lanes, bylanes and alleys, no spot in the locality was overlooked. But they still did not find Aameer's wife. Whispers started going around—Aameer's wife has certainly left with a man. How long can a young and beautiful woman like her live with an opium-eater? Aameer was an aficionado of clarified opium; that was the only weakness in his character. Lost as his wife was, being a user notwithstanding, hearing word of this scandal hurt his feelings. He thought, 'Enough. I have no use of this society anymore. Won't show my face to anyone, will become a faqir and travel the world. If ever I get back my dearest Layla, I will return, or else I would give up my life like Majnu once had.'

So thinking and donning the faqir's colourful garb, Aameer left home. He did not take with him any possession save a small tin container, a bamboo pipe and an iron scalpel. Aameer was somewhat of a dandy. The tin container had glass atop its lid, and he could see his face in it as in a mirror. Sometimes, he would actually do it, especially after eating a betel leaf stuffed with condiments, just to see if it had reddened his lip. The bamboo pipe was his favourite thing. He once accompanied a British sahib as a chef to the hills; it was there that he bought this dainty object. It had several black markings etched on it. Aameer liked to think that those weren't mere adornments, that they were letters in the Chinese language. The words said, 'Close to the Great Wall of China, lies the City of Lingty where lives a craftsman by the name of Moping who has fashioned this pipe. In fashioning pipes, Moping has no peer, worldwide this pipe would cost 25 *anna*. Whoever requires a pipe may contact him for procuring one and not waste his hard-earned money by approaching poor makers. If anyone is unsatisfied with Moping's pipe and returns it, Moping will give him back its worth immediately.' For all you know, it had been fortuitous that Aameer had liked the pipe. Else, he would have had to get back its worth. Taking the road that Yudhistthira had travelled to enter heaven, crossing over the snow-clad mountains and the plateau of Tibet, walking through the Tartars' cold desert, Aameer would have had to reach Lingty on China's northern frontier. Once he reached there, he would have met Moping; only then would Moping have given him back his coin. Hence I say it was fortuitous that Aameer liked his pipe. With a great deal of care, he would oil it every day. Having soaked in so much oil, the pipe had turned a reddish hue. In the container, lay Aameer's beloved opium, which is referred to as *chandu* in the common man's language. Aameer would inhale the *chandu*'s smoke through the pipe. With the scalpel, he would pick the opium from the container and place it on the end of his pipe.

The Exorcist

With all these articles, Aameer left home. He passed the borders of Delhi and crossed many rivers, villages and meadows. A mendicant by day, he would spend his nights under a tree or in the moors, praying to the Almighty so harm may not befall him past twilight. Hope of reuniting with the wife had slowly begun exiting from his heart. Soon he became distraught at the thought of the two options lying before him—marry an elderly woman or be a faqir for the remainder of his life. One day, he came upon a village where a sizeable number of people were gathered in front of a large house. Enquiring, he learned that the village was a frontier settlement to the west. The house in question belonged to a jaan. The head of the house was an eminent occult reader. Future, present and past, nothing was unknown to him; no news of the world was a secret and the writing on people's destinies he would read as easily as one could see their own reflection in water. In nautical studies, he was more proficient than no other than Hanuman. Forehead or the palm, wherever the Fates had left their scratches, whatever be their native tongue, English, French or Devbhasa, or the demons' patois, all would be rendered fluently by Jaan, thievery or scam nothing would escape his notice. While it was true that the ignorant government had never given him title nor penny, people would cross great distances to be in his company, in exchange of five paise or five ounces of atta flour, they would gain an insight into what lay in store for them and what had taken place in the times gone by. Aameer said, 'Let me go to Jaan's house, inshallatalah. He will make his calculations and tell me who has taken my wife.' Aameer took his place in front of Jaan's house. When everyone had left, very humbly he went before the astrologer and told him his tale. The astrologer reflected for a moment. Then he took four pot shards in his hands, chanted a prayer as he blew into them severally, and then cast them about in the four directions—north, west, east and south.

Following a few moments' silence, he spoke, 'Faqir*jee*! A ghost has spirited your wife away. But what can be done? I am not an exorcist. I have no control over spirits. If I did, I would have restored her to you long ago. But I tell you her whereabouts. Please look for a good exorcist. If you find a good exorcist, you would definitely be able to rescue your wife from the ghost's clutches.' Hearing his words, Aameer felt considerably reassured. The thought that his wife had not left home under the spell of an evil lecher became a source of comfort for him in these trying times.

Now, an exorcist is required. But under the influence of the British, all our traditional trades have gone extinct. Forget all other trades; the trade of ghostship as practised by ghosts has vanished. The citizens of this hapless country have become so anglicised that if someone falls under the spell of a ghost or to the charms of a witch they pronounce that they have been struck by hysteria. Such words boil the blood of one of flesh and bone, let alone the spirit. Thus it was that the entire caste of ghosts said in unison, 'Ruin it! We won't possess anybody anymore.' The caste of witches said in unison, 'Wreck it! We won't eat anyone anymore.' India's castes of ghosts and witches are morose and silent today. The cremation grounds are quiet. At the dead of night, in the empty fields, feet raised heavenward, tongues dangling, witches would roam and seek their prey. But no more. Alack, and alas. One by one, every glory of India has died its death. In such circumstances, how can an exorcist ply his trade? That, too, is now moribund. In all places, at hundreds of homes belonging to the Ganga Mairas of the world, there is no food in the kitchen. Those who would put up their feet and deck themselves in gold and jewels now live in penury.

Aameer understood it would be no mean task to find a good exorcist. But Aameer was not a fellow to be easily disappointed. He decided, 'If I have to scour the earth and turn it over in search of a good exorcist I will do so but I will not rest before finding the same.' So thinking, he restarted his travel. Wherever he reached, he would say, 'Pray, tell me if your village has a good exorcist.' He even met a few small-time ones. Some of them were Musalman by faith; he also met the ones who wrote tabeez and incantations to drive away demons and spectres. But he could find no one to his liking, no one could promise him that yes, he would kill the ghost and return his wife to Aameer. At last, after a long journey, Aameer reached a village. There, the first soul he met was an old woman. Aameer enquired of her, 'Pray, tell me if your village has a good exorcist.' The old woman answered, 'Yes, my son. Our village moneylender's daughter had lately been possessed by an intrepid ghost. The moneylender's wealth is endless. So many doctors, so many vaid, so many roza and hakim came and left, I cannot even enumerate, but none could do what was required of them. In the end, an indigent brahmin from our own village uttered a spell and she was cured. The brahmin and his wife were wanting for food and habiliment—today there are camels, steeds and elephants tied to their wicket gate.'

The Weaver

It does not beggar mention that Aameer did not waste time in reaching the brahmin's door after he had heard the old woman's words. He met the brahmin, curtsied before him and narrated from start to finish his tale of woe. The brahmin said, 'My dear man, I can only rescue one who is possessed. What can I do if someone is spirited away? How can I guess if the spirit has hidden them in the mountains or the deep sea. It is beyond my powers, Faqirsahib, to bring back your woman.' Aameer bowed his head and dropped to the ground. Teardrops welled in his eyes and fell onto the earth before him. Durbasa's tribe, it is said, is as gentle as it is indifferent to mortal concerns. It was those teardrops that wet the brahmin's heart and melted it. The brahmin said, 'Look, faqir*jee*, let me tell you a secret, do not share it. If you do, I will lose what prestige and influence I have acquired as an exorcist. The plain truth is that I am not a genuine exorcist; I know not a single spell to drive away spirits. I even do not know how to say the *gayatri mantra*, and I have not even learnt the alphabet. However, what I can vouch for is this:

I am a very faithful brahmin. Seated on a four-legged low stool is how I eat my meals. Unlike today's English-educated fellows.' Aameer exclaimed, 'How so, sir? How then did you heal the moneylender's daughter?' The brahmin replied, 'Of that I can give you a full explanation. But repeat it to none or ill fate will befall me.' 'I swear on Allah Almighty that not a word of your story shall pass my lips,' Aameer said.

The brahmin said, 'In a village lived a weaver. The weaver wove cloth on a handloom; there was no trouble at all. But one day, he had a brainwave and he hummed a tune to himself as he worked his loom. The tune rang sweetly to his ear. He sang it again, softly; it was sweet, indeed. The weaver thought, "I am a true singer. I have been wasting my talent. Such is the way of the world, else why would diamonds and precious stones not shine unconcealed but lie encumbered in rock or under water? That be, I will sing to enchant the world, ceaselessly pour my sweet music like nectar into the world's ear. For now, let me acquaint my neighbours with a small sample of my talent." So determining, the weaver began his performance, progressively raising the volume of his song. A day went by, and then another. The villagers became hyperactive. In a matter of days, they had lost their sleep. They began to feel as if they were losing their souls. Presently, they arrived at the weaver's doorstep, women, children and elderly included, and beseeched him: "Son, for ages we have been dwelling here with our families and relatives. But we can no longer rest for the power of your song. If you say so, we are ready to leave our homesteads and migrate, or else, fall silent, put a stop to your song." The weaver said, "Sirs, desist. What a thought! Why would you leave the village? If, owing to not having an ear for good music, you do not enjoy my song, I won't wish to disturb your peace. From hereon, I will sit in the meadow and sing my song. Whoever is a connoisseur may visit me, and I will give him a cowrie as a token of my appreciation." Thus relieved, the villagers returned, each to their homestead. The weaver went to the meadow and set up his loom under a fig tree. Seated there, he began singing to his heart's content. The only regrettable matter being there was no one to hear him, no man or animal stepping his way. Even perchance, the crow or another bird never flew in that direction.'

The brahmin continued, 'Faqir*jee!* I was very poor in those days. In the entire village, no one was as penurious and miserable as I was. I cannot even count the days the lady of the house and I spent in fast. I did not care for my future, but my heart wept at the sight of the brahmani's gaunt face and lean frame. Having no recourse, I would dry my tears inside my eyes and put out the flame of disgruntlement in my heart before it burnt the next person. One day, the brahmani said to me, "Today, there is no flour in the kitchen. The weaver has said if you become his audience he will give you a *pana*'s worth of cowries. Why don't you go to meadow and hark him for a while? If we get those 80 cowries, there will be rice in the house, and the two of us will survive." Said I, "Look here, Brahmani—please don't ask that service out of me. Ask me to sit atop a spike, and I am willing; burn myself alive, and I can bring myself to attempt it, but don't ask me to listen to the weaver's song; I don't believe I can brave that scorching of my spirit even for one minute." The brahmani and I discoursed for a bit on this topic. Then the brahmani pushed me outdoors, with the words: "Go forth, listen to the weaver sing and bring home a *pana* of cowries." Hitting the street, I thought to myself, "What can I do for myself? How can I help listening to the weaver's song? Yet none will be worse than the brahmani if I return without the cowries. Dying is preferable to listening to the weaver's song. What is the point of this miserable life any way? Let me kill myself by hanging." So determining, I borrowed a length of rope from a neighbour. Then I walked two *krosh* in the opposite direction, to a field different from the one in which the weaver was singing, set up the noose on a different fig tree and tightened it. Just as I was about to pass my neck through the noose, at the very moment a ghost appeared from inside the tree. The ghost said, "Hey, Brahmin! What are you up to?" I narrated my entire predicament to him. The ghost said, "Brother, don't tell me. You know of the fig tree under which the weaver is singing, don't you? For eons I have been living on it. The tree was very dear to me. But that came to nought for the day the weaver began his song from under it. I have had to abandon the tree and the field and run away. I see that the both of us are under the greatest of threats. But you do not worry and return home for the time being. I will go to your village and possess the moneylender's daughter. Whatever they do, I won't leave her alone until you come along and whisper in my ear, 'I have come to see you. I am the poor brahmin you met under the fig tree.' That's when I will depart. The moneylender is a rich man and has only one daughter, no doubt, he will reward you with gifts. Your days of hardship will be over."' The brahmin said, 'Sheik! Now you know I am no exorcist. I have no spells. By dint of good fortune I met a ghost; what I have goes to his credit. After I exorcised the moneylender's daughter's ghost, I got myself quite a reputation as an exorcist. People began to say there was no other exorcist as powerful as me. Whenever anyone was possessed, I got a call and was taken to heal them. But I don't have to do much; I just bend down and whisper into the ear of the patient, "Go quickly if you like, for if you don't, I will bring the weaver's song to you." As soon as I mention the weaver, all ghosts become petrified and cannot but wait to depart.'

Initiative

Aameer replied, 'Sir! If what you recount is the truth, then why don't we go to your ghost and request him if he will be kind enough to restore my wife to me? Evidently, a ghost will know another of his tribe, for one must have met the other at a feast, function or marriage event, and if this gentleman speaks to the ghost who has taken my wife, it might prove to be of great assistance. Else, he can advise me of a way in which I can get back my wife.' The brahmin said, 'This isn't a bad suggestion; I am quite sympathetic to you in your plight. Alright, let's take the walk, see what transpires.'

The brahmin and the Musalman thus began their journey together, respectively uttering the names of 'Durga!' and 'Bismillah!' for their protection. Presently, they reached the meadow where the ghost was at. They made their way to the tree on which this ghost resided, stood under it, and, with upturned faces, began their praises and entreaties to the yet-unseen spectre. The brahmin said, 'Dear ghost, your rescued brahmin has again come to your doorstep. It was your mercy that saved his life. It was your mercy that dispelled his indigence. Among all the ghosts in all the world, you are the best. O king of ghosts, I beseech you, please make an appearance!' The Musalman said, 'Ghostsahib! Hearing the name of your honour, I have come to kiss your feet. Please grant me my wish. I will bring sweet *sinni* to this tree and treat you to it.' Even as these paens were thus sung, the tree began to sway in the wind, its branches swinging noisily from side to side. Next, a spot of darkness appeared at one corner of the treetop. It was the second hour of noon and the sunrays shone brightly, illuminating all objects everywhere else save that one spot where the darkness deepened gradually. The mass of deep darkness shape-shifted into an enormous figure. The figure descended from the tree and stood by, a little to one side.

Here, let us digress to a pertinent observation. Scientists, particularly those specialising in theories about ghosts, might do well to ponder this hypothesis. Let me posit that it is darkness that coagulates into ghosts in the same manner as water freezes to form ice. The Europeans have invented machines that create ice, can't they devise one that will freeze darkness and produce ghosts from that energy? There is no dearth of darkness in nature. It is more or less dark outdoors at night. Furthermore, speaking of the darkness residing in the human mind, there is no limit, neither end to it. If one excises that darkness with a spade and shovels it all into a place, one can beget darkness by the basketfuls making way for mass production. This will lead to very reasonable pricing of ghosts—a *ser* of ghosts could be bought at a pice or two, or at most four. If ghosts come cheaply, the poor and the oppressed can buy them as per their respective means.

The ghost standing by the tree spoke a bit angrily. He said, 'Yo Brahmin! What brings you here again? A died-in-the-wool brahmin such as yourself is not beyond my powers to kill. I can twist your neck right away if I so will it. The ones I cannot kill are the English-educated babus. I fear them, and I also hold them in some esteem. The fear is, lest they lurch into me or barf on my person. The esteem, well, after having consumed this, that and the other, their thoughts flow without inhibition, they attain shiva-hood while leading their mortal existences, their minds are not at all filled with twists and turns like a pretzel unlike their neighbours.' The brahmin said, 'My lord! I haven't come here to seek my own benefit. Thanks to your generosity, I don't want for anything. This man is in deep trauma, it is for his sake that I have come to see you.'

The ghost was somewhat pacified by his words. 'Who is the man with you then?' he asked the brahmin. The brahmin narrated Aameer's tale. Having thus updated him, he entreated, 'Sir! It is up to you to devise a solution. Otherwise, this man will die of grief. You are kind. You had saved my life once; the time has now come for you to save his.' The ghost said, 'I am certain it is Lullu who has taken his wife. Lullu has newly been given his job of ghostship; he is super-devoted to his assignment and quite intrepid!' The brahmin asked, 'His job of ghostship! But sir, what is the meaning of these words?' The ghost smiled and explained, 'You humans are unaware of these matters. People are wont to say, so and so has died and become a ghost. It is not fully accurate to say so. When a man dies, he does not become the ghost of himself. It is one of us who is awarded his ghostship. There are many lakhs of ghosts present in this world. Some of them have secured the job of being a ghost; others are lobbying for that position, while still others are sitting unemployed. It is our boss who hands out these assignments. He says to the ghost, "Go and stay with this person, when he dies, be his ghost, I award his ghostship to you." From that day forward, that ghost accompanies the man. His joy knows no bounds, for soon as the man dies, he will be able to begin his ghostship.' The ghost's mood changed. He said, 'For your destiny that I thus described it is you, yourselves, to blame. The *desi*, nationalist newspapers impart so many good lessons. Had you but followed them body and soul you would not have brought yourselves to this predicament. For instance, the economy of the country is crashing, foreigners are robbing it through sale of foreign textiles. Granted. But have you pondered, what is the need to wear clothes? If you don't wear them, no one can rob your wealth. Next, the British are transporting your wealth away on the railways. Well, do not ride the railway, walk to Kashi, Vrindavan et al., can't you? If you do so, the foreigners will build no more railway tracks in your country, and the wealth of the land will remain in the land. But no! It is the same principle we follow when we observe your ghostship. We network and lobby amongst ourselves for ghostship. If only you humans stopped dying, no one would come along for performing your ghostship. I say, stop dying, and put an end to this. But no, you will be the ones to die, and we will be the ones to get the bad name. All we have done is performed your ghostship.

'Now while that is very well the case, Lullu had long applied for a ghostship in writing. He had not got a good ghostship anywhere till that point. Finally, the boss appointed him as Dukhiram Chandal's apprentice ghost. Though Dukhiram was an old man, he was capable and still going strong. He wasn't one to die soon. Poor Lullu was saddened by his attitude. It has been a few days since Dukhiram has expired, and Lullu has, at last, got his ghostship. He is now a legitimate, civil and modern ghost. That he is devotedly doing his job having earned it after such long and dedicated work is commendable. I am so pleased by this news.' The brahmin was nonplussed. He exclaimed, 'Is that what you think, sir? Why, you are pleased by the work of evil Lullu when we came here to complain to you about him. We have come to pray to you to rescue this gentleman's wife from him.' After much discussion, the ghost offered: 'Well, I have presently become an ascetic and detached from worldly affairs. I do not know where Lullu has kept his wife. Neither do I have the time of day to look for her. But you could try one tack. About 10 *krosh* from this place, in the middle of a meadow is a well. A ghost named Ghyanghon lives inside it. He is the gazetteer of ghost society. If you go to him, he will tell you where to find what you seek. There is only one catch. It has been a few days since Ghyanghon has developed high fever from his depression. He is sitting inside the well and refusing to speak to anyone. See if you can make him talk to you.'

Ghyanghon

The brahmin and Aameer, what recourse did they have within their means? The two had no choice but to start their walk in search of Ghyanghon. Their walk took them to the glade on which Ghyanghon resided. Together, they approached the edge of the well, and began their exhortations directed at Ghyanghon. The brahmin called: 'Dear sire! Mr Ghyanghon! Ghyanghonbabu! Are you home?' The Musalman called: 'Ghyanghonsahib! Are you home?' They called until their voices cracked under the strain, but Ghyanghon did not emerge from the well, did not even do the courtesy of answering them. The two men wondered, 'What a nuisance! How do we resolve this problem?' The brahmin thought for a while and suggested to his mate, 'Let's go to the weaver.' Disappointment writ on their faces, the two departed. They went to the village again and found the weaver. The brahmin addressed him: 'Brother! You have a service to perform. There is a ghost. Ghyanghon is his name. He is a dear friend. He is suffering from earworms and is struggling to get rid of them. In terrible pain, he has gone and taken shelter inside a well. He is not taking his meals or resting; when called, he won't come out. Many an expert vocalist can rid a man of earworms, but a ghost's annelid won't emerge save your out-of-the-world music. Therefore, if you deign to accompany us for a performance beside the well, we will be most grateful to your largesse.' Until this point, no one had heard the weaver of their free will. Yet now he had an audience appealing to him to sing. The weaver was delighted. There was no way he would deny his guests their request. Overjoyed, the weaver said, 'I will go at once. Just let me dress up for the occasion.' Right away, the weaver dressed and left his hut. The three men walked in the direction of the well. Upon reaching the well, the weaver sat himself down by its side. Assuming the lotus pose, he began his song. The brahmin and Aameer put their fingers in their respective ears and waited at a safe distance. The sound waves began flowing into the well. Ghyanghon thought to himself, 'Sick with depression, I gave up company and isolated myself in this well. Now, what might be this dreadful event transpiring on this very spot? Despite having heard the songs of Kabir and Chaitanya of yore, I had managed to sustain myself. But now I see my soul thrashing about in a bid to escape.' To his credit, though, Ghyanghon had not come out of the well easily. But presently, as he realised that his soul would leave his apparition, he was left with no alternative. Willy-nilly, he came crawling out of the reservoir. Ghyanghon is a short, plain-looking, bony and middle-aged ghost. The depression had struck him hard. His fever was so high that fiery sparks were being seen exiting his nose, mouth and eyes.

Once out of the well, the ghost prepared to take to his heels. Just then, Aameer and the brahmin appeared before him. The brahmin said to the ghost, 'Ghyanghon, my dear son. Don't run. You need have no fear anymore. Behold, the weaver has stopped his song. But if you do, pray, whence will you run to? Wherever you go, the weaver will follow you. Why don't you let us ask you a question and answer it truthfully instead? If you do, we will depart and take the weaver with us.' Ghyanghon glanced upon the brahmin's face, then cast another glance at the weaver. He saw the weaver clearing his throat in preparation of beginning a fresh song. The essence of him shrivelled at that sight. He said, 'Agreed. Well, then, go ahead. Say your piece. Ask me your query.' The brahmin said, 'A ghost named Lullu has taken Aameer's wife. Where has he kept her? Do you have a clue as how to restore her?' Ghyanghon replied, 'It has been many days since I am sitting inside the well, immersed in my heartache and sorrow. I have not kept up with the news of the world. But I could go on a fact-finding mission and inform you if you promise not to have the weaver sing his song.'

'Don't take us to be simple. You say, you will go and fact-find, but you might well seize this chance to give us the slip. What if you don't return, and we never see you again,' the brahmin retorted. Ghyanghon replied, 'But you just convinced me I have no place to run. Wherever I go, the weaver will reach and begin his song. Besides, how can I truthfully tell you where Aameer's wife is without finding out first?' 'Promise us you will return quickly,' the brahmin hazarded. Ghyanghon said, 'I promise to return.' Thereafter, the brahmin said, 'Go then, godspeed, as we wait on the spot for you.' Ghyanghon said, 'Hold on, let me put on my big pair of *naagra*. I can fly like the wind when I put on those shoes, travel all Bharat momentarily.' So saying, Ghyanghon returned to the well and emerged in a pair of floppy *naagra*, was next seen race-walking on the air and was soon gone. The brahmin, the weaver and Aameer remained seated on the ground staring at the firmament in his wake. When will he return, they worried and they fidgeted. After a while, Aameer let out a cry, 'There, there he comes, look north, see the small dark line up in the sky.' The line deepened and expanded, and when it was large enough, everyone said, 'It's Ghyanghon alright; oh look, it is Ghyanghon, indeed, in his pair of *naagra*.' Ghyanghon was much feted and received with fanfare. All said, 'Ghyanghon, you are a truthful ghost. Although you were depressed and had a fever, you kept your promise. Tell us, do you have good news?' Ghyanghon responded saying it was good news indeed, for he had found Aameer's wife.

Everyone then said, 'Then tell us quickly, where is the lady? We trust that she is well.'

Ghyanghon said, 'In Himachal Pradesh, lies a lake. Its name is Bheemtaal. In the mountain inside the lake, Lullu has built a small room. One has to dive inside the lake to enter the room, for there is no other route to reach it. Lullu has hidden Aameer's woman inside that room. However, I won't say that Aameer's wife has been weeping like Seeta had during her days in Ashok Vatika. Lullu is our legitimate, genteel and modern comrade. Why should she weep when she has been picked up by such an eligible ghost? Lullu has given her a one-year deadline. If she does not calm down and marry him in that timespan, he will slay her. The question is no human can enter the lake, and having entered the lake, reach the room where Aameer's wife is located. Being a ghost, I can't act against another; if I do so I may be boycotted in society. Nevertheless, this piece of advice is important for you. If you can catch a plump and healthy ghost and extract his oil, then smearing that oil all over yourselves can bestow on you the power to enter the lake and reach Lullu's room. Subsequently, you can hatch a plan for carrying out the rescue. Here I must warn you, do not try to catch me and extract my oil, just because I told you this secret. Over and above being depressed and sick, the weaver's song has left me so weak and listless that not a single drop of oil will you obtain. One more thing: At the end of this glade, there is a tree. On that tree lives a hangman ghost. Gongon is his name. His occupation is to abet suicides by hanging in the nearest village. Whoever falls for his inducements hangs themselves from that tree on which Gongon lives. To hasten their demise, Gongon assists their suicide by swinging from their legs. It will afford me much pleasure if you can catch this ghost and extract his oil. For, that evil spirit is my great enemy. Wherever my marriage alliance is made, he goes and fouls the arrangement. *Petini, shankhachoorni, chudail,* I had had prospective brides of various kinds. I had even seen one or two of these women, given my heart to them; but this evil ghost fed rumours about me to their parents. What can I say of my ill fate? A ghostship holder, I have begun to age, but I am yet to marry anyone. I am but half a ghost in this world; I could never become a whole Ghyanghon. This, when so many others marry 10 and 20 women, and become more than a full 16 annas. Remember, it is never easy for a human to catch a ghost. You do not find these days an exorcist like one from the days of yore who could make a palanquin bearer of a ghost or make them draw their coach. Hatch a plot to catch him.

'Speaking of marriages has made me wistful. There had once been a marriage alliance fixed between a *bhootini* of unparalleled beauty and your humble friend. I am at a loss for words to describe the *bhootini's* beauty. Suffice it to say that one glimpse of her nose was all it took for me to become entranced by her. Oh, Nakeshwari of the great nose! How can I live without the sight of you? Let me cast my eyes on your image in order to calm my soul. Allow me to bring it and look at it. You, sirs, you, too, look, and partake of her inhuman beauty.'

Oil of Ghost

Gazing at Nakeshwari's portrait for a short while did go some length in restoring somewhat the unruffled disposition of old Ghyanghon. One by one, he shook the hands of his newly formed acquaintances and then he went his way. It was now Aameer's turn, and he addressed the weaver and the brahmin: 'Sirs, though inadvertently, my company has led you to undergo much hardship. But you have steadfastly supported me, and have been walking with me, leaving behind your families. I have no wish to put you through any more trouble. Please go home, let me answer the call of my destiny.' But the weaver and the brahmin were in no mood to leave Aameer's side. In the end, after much pleading and entreaties, they agreed, said their goodbyes, and left, unhappily. Post their departure, Aameer sat by Ghyanghon's well and wept for a while. Then he consoled himself, thus: 'What is the point of weeping bitter tears? If I don't brainstorm a solution to the riddle of how to catch a ghost, how ever may I rescue my wife?' Much cogitation performed, he unravelled his turban from his crown. Twirling the length of the turban to form a makeshift rope, he prepared a noose at one end. Thus geared, he made for the mango tree on which lived the hangman ghost, Gongon. Having reached, he began climbing the tree. Having climbed quite a distance, he tied the other end of his turban onto a high branch and made as if to pass the noose around his neck. This was the moment when he looked before him and spotted the hangman ghost, sitting on a nearby branch of the tree smiling at him.

The ghost spoke. 'Come now, hurry up, put on the noose and hang quick, I, too, will pull your feet from below, then you will die right away and my grandson-in-law will be able to secure your ghostship.' Without saying a word, Aameer slowly put a hand into his pocket and came out with his small opium can. He opened the lid and held the can before the ghost. The ghost peered and puzzled for a bit, then said, 'Who's that moving inside it?' 'A ghost,' said Aameer. 'A ghost,' repeated Gongon. 'Indeed? Please afford me a good look.' Having looked at the can to his heart's content, Gongon felt certain that there was a ghost inside it. 'Why have you kept a ghost inside the can,' he asked Aameer. Aameer replied, 'I desire to open a newspaper. I need an editor and an assistant editor for it. The one inside the can, he will be my assistant editor. And I am planning to appoint you the editor of my paper.' 'But I don't have an education. How can it be,' wondered poor Gongon. Said Aameer, 'Are you crazy? What do you need an education for? You know how to curse, don't you?' Gongon informed Aameer that delivering all the various curse words in use among ghosts was well within his acumen and abilities. Aameer seemed pleased. 'If so be the case, then what more do I need? Heretofore, people would catch hold of humans and make editors of them, but all the curse words known to man have been spent or gone stale from overuse. From now on, I will serve ghostly abuse to the masses of this country. I will make a lot of money, I am sure of it,' he said. For the very first time, the ghost was confused. He asked Aameer, 'If that be your intent, then are you not going to die by hanging? What then was the turban for? And the noose?' 'I am not crazy that I will hang myself to please you,' Aameer snapped. 'The turban and the noose are bait, you wretch. Bait to catch you. Tell me, had I not devised this ruse, would you have come out of the tree? Now quick, enter the can.' So saying, Aameer showed the ghost his *chandu* smoking pipe. 'What now,' asked the ghost. Aameer replied, a tad sarcastically, 'It is called bamboo. Now step inside.' The ghost hesitated, and Aameer noticed his demeanour. He fished out the stopper of his pipe and brandished the stone pyramid menacingly before Gongon. 'What's that for,' asked Gongon. Aameer said, 'Its common name is *aatkhille.* But it is called *thok* in chaste Bengali. Now, if you don't enter that pipe, I will gouge out your eyes with it.' As a matter of fact, at that very moment, the *thok* caught the rays of the sun and began glinting wickedly. It looked as if for ages, it had been gouging out the eyes of countless, nameless ghosts, as if without having performed that job of eye-gouging, it never even accepted a drink of water as a matter of principle. And it also seemed as if that the *thok* would do the job of its own initiative even if Aameer should perchance change his mind. Glimpsing at the terrible apparition of the stopper, the ghost was quite overcome by fear; and his body trembled under its spell. 'Why be a hero,' the ghost decided. 'Better be in service of man as an editor than be a blind man!' So contemplating, he contracted his form and quietly entered the pipe. Aameer put a wax seal to the mouth of his pipe and climbed down the tree.

Having come thus far in his quest, a small measure of optimism buoyed Aameer's heart. Whistling a tune under his breath, he walked in the direction of the village; and once having reached, asked the people there, 'Good folks, is there an oil press man in your village?' The people replied in the affirmative. Aameer reached the house of the oil press man and knocked on his door. 'Brother,' he said. 'I do need a special favour. In this bamboo pipe, I have captured a ghost, if you are so kind as to press the ghost in your wheel and get me the oil from him, it will benefit my interests greatly.' The oil press man replied, 'That's easily done! I could do it right away. Sesame, mustard, flax or Oriental poppy, I have extracted oil from all these sources; today I get to try a new component, what's the big deal in that? Bring it on.' The two men walked to the oil wheel. Aameer took the ghost gently out of the pipe and placed him in the press bracket. The oil press fellow wasted no time in starting his machine. The bullock began its languorous walk, the wheel revolved, and the ghost's bones started crunching noisily. 'Mercy, oh dear Madhusudan, help me, oh dear Madhusudan,' cried the ghost. He said to Aameer, 'Is this what you had in mind? Is this what you meant when you said I would edit a paper?' Aameer smiled and replied, 'Don't you know, mister? Why, this is how I get my articles out of my editors. How are you feeling then, mate? Don't you have the choicest abuse, sharpest catchphrases passing through your mind at this moment? Mister Gongon, have you not even been read to in childhood that old Aesop's fable? That one about a deer? The one in which it is written, "Welcome to the westside. First swim or sink in this swirling tide, then do your business or not, I can hardly mind.'" Soon, big globules of oil began to drip from the wheel. Once collected, the liquid almost filled up a small glass bottle. Only when the apparition's essence did become dry and wholly desiccated the bullock stopped its perambulations. The wheel moved no more. Aameer set free the shrivelled shell of the ghost. Suffice to say that had he been human, he would have been long dead by then.

Mission

Glass bottle in his pocket, Aameer began his journey. He walked non-stop, covering great distances, until he found himself at the foot of the Lesser Himalayas. Aameer continued his trek. Countless peaks and valleys behind, at long last, he sighted Bheemtal. Circumbulating the tarn, Aameer remembered Ghyanghon's instructions and found the exact spot from where he was to dive into the lapis-blue waters. Lullu's chamber was located right underneath it. Aameer took out the glass bottle from his pocket, opened it and smeared its contents all over his body. The oil imparted to his muscles a demonic strength, and his aches and niggles disappeared. He felt light as a bird, as if he could take flight if he so wished it. Massage completed, he stood up, exclaimed 'Bismillah!' and dived into the lake. Aameer began an uninterrupted descent towards the floor of the lake. He did not have to quite reach the netherworlds in his mission, but he went a long distance before he could spy a hole on the side of the mountain. He entered the hole and stepped on dry ground. There was no lack of illumination about him. In fact, there was plenty of daylight inside the cave. A few footsteps ahead, he spotted a line of grottos on the mountain wall. But he could not see their inhabitants, human or ghostly. It's still daylight, Aameer thought to himself. I should not move about so publicly. Let me proceed with my investigations after nightfall. So saying, Aameer secreted himself in a small grotto on the side of the cave.

Do not be surprised to learn that one can enter a dry chamber underground after diving into a lake. Lest people form the notion that what I am writing is a fairy tale, I had to present some historical references to substantiate my story. In the time of Akbar's reign had lived a man who had prepared such a chamber in Lahore that could not be accessed without diving in water. The badshah Jehangir had also witnessed a similar boudoir in Agra. In the book titled *Waqiyat e-Jahangiri*, he writes, 'Just like a water-house that was built in Lahore in the time of my father's reign, so also a water-house exists in the residence of Hakim Ali which I visited with the purpose of surveying it. A few of my courtiers accompanied me; they, too, had never seen such a house. The area of the waterbody was approximately 6 *guz*, 54 square feet. There was a chamber next to it in which there was plenty of light and to reach inside which there was no route save through the body. But the marvellous aspect of it was not a drop of water was present inside the chamber. It could accommodate about 10 seated people. Inside the chamber, Hakim made a gift of money and some precious articles to me. Having surveyed the chamber, I returned home. As a prize, I appointed Hakim to the post of a *do-hazari*.' Thus with historical evidence have I established the truth of my story. There are such geological and architectural marvels in this world that might take even the most cynical mindset by surprise.

Aameer spent the remainder of the day in the mountainside grotto. Dusk fell, and the night was young. Suddenly, a storm appeared in the cavern. In a while, there came a lashing noise from the lake. Aameer listened carefully; it was the noise of someone ascending through the waters. Night has fallen; the ghosts are leaving for their business, thought Aameer. He waited until the lashing stopped, and soon it was quiet once again. Aameer emerged from his hiding place and began exploring the underground cave. He looked inside every nook and cranny of the cave. Soon, he spotted a dim light shining at a considerable distance. He followed the light and so it was from a clay lamp shining in a larger, inner chamber of the cave. Next to the lamp sat a glum-faced young woman in rags, with her cheek resting on her palm. Aameer approached her and realised that the woman was no other than his dear wife. His heart started hammering wildly. His first thought was to jump right into her arms, with the words, 'dearest mine', on his lips. 'Dearest mine, I know. Fear no more, I am here. Your Aameer is here for you,' he wished to say. But he desisted. 'Why not fear some more,' he thought to himself. 'We are still in the clutches of these ghosts. I have yet not been able to rescue my wife. I see that my wife is despondent and has lost weight. It is possible that she has not been eating and sleeping well. It will be injudicious to appear at once. I will bide my time for the opportune moment.' Aameer's wife had been crying. Tears fell incessantly from both her eyes. From time to time she wiped them. Often, a sigh escaped her lips as she muttered her regrets. She said, 'Alas! What did I do to deserve this fate? Having fallen in the clutches of Satan himself, I have endangered the good name of my caste and family. But for her virtue, a woman has nothing of value to herself. Come ghost or the devil, I will not allow it to be destroyed by anyone. The wicked one has promised he will not disturb me for one year. In that one year, will not the Almighty, who is the saviour of the weak and the helpless, come to my aid? Dearest Aameer, wish you were here to see my sorry predicament.' Aameer spoke. 'Fear not,' he said, 'for the Almighty has been merciful. He has sent me to your aid.' Surprised, Aameer's mate raised her eyes. But they had been flooded with her tears, so she could not see him. She thought, perhaps, it was a fantasy, after all, conjured up by her feverish imagination, but it had filled her with hope, even if momentarily, and she was afraid to wipe her eyes and look upon reality for fear of losing it. Reading her mind, Aameer stepped forward and stood in the light. He said, 'Look. It is indeed I. Fear not, for with God's grace, surely, we will rid ourselves of this grave peril.' So saying, Aameer reached out and put his arms around his wife. His wife did the same, and the two shared a long and tearful embrace.

Minutes lengthened into the quarter of an hour. At last, Aameer wiped his eyes, and he said, 'Weep no more. Inform me about the details of this place. First, tell me how the ghost brought you to it.' Aameer's wife replied, 'I do not know. When I stepped out into the garden, I heard you call out some words from indoors. The next moment, a great storm lifted me off my feet and carried me some distance. In fear, I fell in a faint. I cannot say I had been unconscious for how long. When it was morning, I opened my eyes and saw a monstrous demon stood before me. I fainted again at the sight. When I regained consciousness again, it was dark. I was in this chamber and there was no one else. The lamp was burning softly, and in the weak light, I could see various foodstuff lying about me. But I did not partake. I determined to fast unto death. The next morning, the monstrous apparition returned. This time, I didn't faint. I did feel quite frightened, and I almost did lose my consciousness, but I mastered my fear with the thought that, come what may, I had to find out who it was, why I had been brought here and to what end. The apparition addressed me, and said, "My beauty! You are no longer Aameer's mate but the lady of my household. Your husband, himself, made a gift of you to me. This home and hearth belongs to you from this day on. Let me call the *qazi* if you so permit, he will formalise our union by marriage." Hardening my heart with my resolve, I asked him, "But who are you? When did my husband grant me to you?" The apparition said, "I am but a ghost. My name is Lullu. I am a humble ghost. And this cavern that you see and its riches all belong to me. I am performing the ghostship of Dukhiram Chandal. My reputation of being the valiant one precedes me in ghostly circles, and I am well-respected." I said then, "I do not believe the lie that my husband has granted my ownership to you. Besides, there is no precedent of a human mating with a ghost. I am a faithful Muslim woman, and not a comrade of Satan like some idolaters are. The *khuda* will certainly punish you for torturing me."

'Thus did I daily discourse with the ghost. But he dare not lift his hand on me. I had forgone food and sleep for the first few days. But when I noticed he was not making any special demands of me, I began to take my meals. There are spells available with the *alim* scholars using which one can govern ghosts. I believed you would bring such a spell with yourself to rescue me. Every day, the ghost comes to me, and says, "Well, shall I call the *qazi* today?" Seeing him everyday has dispelled my thrall of him. Most days, I shoo him away contemptuously. One day, however, he angered terribly. His volume doubled; had he not been a ghost, perhaps, he would have exploded to bits. Sparks began being emitted from his orifices. After thrashing his arms and legs about, he extracted his eyeballs from their sockets and began juggling them about the way wrestlers do with dumbbells. Then he unfastened his whole head, held it in both his hands and said, "O beautiful one! If you do not consent to marry me, I will chew up and eat my head." Now, try as I might, I could not fathom as to how anyone could eat his own head. But that aside, I told him, "I do not care if you eat your head or if anyone else eats it, why would I want to marry a ghost? Take me to my home, if you wish well for yourself." Thereafter, the ghost said, "Alright! Today, I let you be. From this date until a year has gone by, I will leave you to your wits. If, after one year has passed, you do not marry me, then I will kill you. Your husband has given you to me; I will do what I like with you. Do not believe for a moment's sake that I will return you to him." Since that the day, the ghost disturbs me no more. When night falls, he goes out on his business, returns at daybreak and sleeps all day there, in that big grotto. All day I hear his thunder-like snores, but he does not approach me. He only comes to my chamber every three to four days to leave foodstuff, and asks, "So, have you calmed down? Shall I bring the *qazi*?" The last he came, he said, "Have you noticed I have begun using soap?" He pronounced the word as *shoap*. He said, "I use it daily. My complexion is turning light. Soon, people will be unable to recognise me. Wherever I go, they will say, 'This is no Lullu. It is a white man's ghost. Maybe, he is the son of a rich aristocrat.' You will see then you will have no peace of mind until you marry me. I will hear you saying, 'Where is my Lullu? Whence has he gone to?' You will say, 'I can't wait anymore, bring the *qazi* quick, marry me!' But I won't bring the *qazi*. I will procrastinate. You will beg and beseech me, and I will derive pleasure out of your entreaties. I will think to myself, 'Look, how she loves me. I am the goal of her entire existence.' All the ghosts say that I am a legitimate, urbane and modern ghost. Elder brother Gente and I, we are both legitimate, urbane and modern ghosts.

You can see for yourself we don't come home until dawn. Let me go put some shoap." So saying, he has departed. He will return in a day or two's span.'

Aameer asked his wife, 'Is this a ghosts' mess or a vagabond's lodgings? By saying so I mean, does Lullu live here alone, or are there several ghosts living next to one another on these precincts?' Mrs Aameer replied that she had seen none there save Lullu and that she believed Lullu lived by himself. Aameer said, 'Now I get the full picture. God has been kind. Nevertheless, at this time, I do not know how we can save ourselves. I am hungry. If you have anything to eat, please share it with me.' Aameer's companion said, 'There is no dearth of food here. The ghost brings food in copious amounts and gives it to me.' So speaking, she brought forth *pulao*, *kalia*, *qorma*, *kopta*, kebab and curry and served them to her husband.

Chandu's High Merits

After his meal, Aameer lay on the bed for a post-prandial smoke and plotted on how to rescue his wife. Smoking a ring, he addressed his wife, 'I have devised a way out of this mess. What do you say? Lullu is a civil, gentlemanly and modern ghost, yes? Even as I have gained demonic strength by smearing ghost oil on myself, I do not see myself defeating him in combat hand-to-hand and face-to-face. Especially seeing as Ghyanghon has advised that I resort to tricks and strategem. Hence I say to you, flirt with Lullu for a bit. Encourage him to smoke *chandu*. By and by, we will know what is required of us. One can lose one's heart to the Banka Kalachand of Gokul and live to tell the tale, but one can never be safe after losing one's mind to the Kalachand of opium; have him form a bond of affection for *chandu*. I will leave my opium box and all my contraptions with you. For this sake, I am ready to subsist on raw opium for the next few days.' Mrs Aameer opined it wasn't a bad idea.

Their parleys continued almost until the night's end. Then Mrs Aameer said, 'Stay no more. It is time for the ghost to return home. When he leaves tomorrow, please visit at night. Leave the apparatus for smoking with me. Let me see what I can do. Take some foodstuff with you, have during the day.' Aameer said goodbye to his wife and went back to his small grotto.

As soon as it was dawn the ghost appeared and first went to his own grotto. Snoring loudly, he slept there for the longest time. Then he rose and took a bath in the lake waters, rubbing himself over thoroughly, first with stone, then with burnt brick dust, subsequently with sand, and, lastly, with soap. He rubbed until his skin broke in places, and blood began to flow. Then he put on his clothes and called on Mrs Aameer. 'Hi, my beautiful! Can you see? How I am fairer by the day? Like milk and roses,' he exclaimed. 'Indeed!' Mrs Aameer responded. 'Verily, you are a modern, urbane and legitimate ghost!' 'In that case, should I call the *qazi*,' the ghost came straight to the point. 'I have no problem with your calling him,' returned Mrs Aameer. 'Except that you happen to be a ghost, and I happen to be human, and I wonder how the two of us would meet. If I see you behave even a bit humanely, I may persuade myself that we can be affectionate towards each other. For instance, so many foodstuffs you are wont to bring me each and every day, never have I seen you break off a piece and try it yourself. I have no idea what you eat if at all you do so. Can't say if you eat frog or snake. Perhaps, one day you will eat a rotten corpse and appear at my doorstep. Smelling your breath, I will choke to death. Humans, on the other hand, eat betel leaf. They smoke tobacco and marijuana, and various other substances. Oh glory be! My husband, for instance, would smoke the *chandu* opium. I would sit by his side and prepare his smoke. When the smoke entered my nostril, I would be on cloud nine, seventh heaven. I always carried his smoking apparatus about with me in my handbag. I used to keep it close whether I sat or lay. Oh glory be! That bag is still on my shoulder.' Said the ghost testily, 'Really? Well, I, too, can smoke *chandu*; bring it, I will smoke it right away.' 'If you can indeed manage it, it will be an extremely happy ending,' Mrs Aameer said. 'To ghosts and the wives and sisters of ghosts, you may surely be legitimate, urbane and modern; but our human noses detect an odour on your person, and it is not pleasant. If you smoke, you will no longer carry that unpleasant smell and, on the other hand, will smell human.' 'So give it to me. I will smoke,' the ghost repeated. Mrs Aameer instructed, 'Be it raw opium, resin or *chandu*, one should not consume a large amount at once. If you do you will be ill. And if you are ill, won't I be miserable? For, is this gift nothing but a token of my new affection for you? That question aside, the horizontal position is the correct way to smoke a pipe of *chandu*. Fools believe one puff of *chandu* is sufficient to render a man unconscious, and hence one must lie down while having it. The real reason is different. If you lie down and smoke, you can easily enter the private garden of your mind.' Mrs Aameer produced the apparatus for smoking *chandu* and prepared a smoke for the ghost. She made him lie down beside the lamp and showed him how to smoke the pipe. After the ghost had smoked a small while, Mrs Aameer said, 'That's enough for today. Come to me again before you leave. Incidentally, did you feel anything?' The ghost replied that he felt nothing save for some itches and a tiny spot of nausea. Mrs Aameer said, 'That then is the measure of the gratification it has provided, it is what's called a trip, by the way.' Come evening, the ghost called on her again and smoked a pipe of *chandu*. When night fell, he left on his adventures, and Aameer returned to unite with his wife.

Release and Restoration

Aameer was much amused to hear from his wife the full account of the ghost's encounter with *chandu*. Just like before, the two chatted the night away. By dawn, Aameer was in his grotto, which was now his private accommodation. The couple stuck to this routine for the next few days. Twice every day, the ghost would come to his wife for his quota of diurnal smoke. The nocturnal hours Aameer would spend in the company of his wife. Once Aameer noticed that the ghost had formed a vigorous habit that would be hard to let go, he suggested to his wife, 'Why don't you withhold your supply tomorrow? Tell the ghost, your stash is over, it has to be replenished from the mortal world.' Next morning, when the ghost returned for his smoke, the wife said to him, 'Look, I have exhausted the stock of *chandu* I had carried with me; you will have to bring some more from civil society.' The ghost felt despondent. Still, he was yet innocent of the catastrophe that had befallen him. Nevertheless, however, he returned gloomily to his own grotto. As the day progressed, he began to feel various curious aches in his mind and body. First, he began to yawn ear-to-ear, next his eyes watered. His muscles became taut and inflexible. Then his heart started palpitating and sleep eluded him. Late afternoon, he took the empty pipe near the flame of the oil lamp and pulled on it once for a long drag. It was pointless. Now his only thought was when dusk would fall, so he could go out amid civilisation and beget some of the drug to save his life. Soon as it was dark, the ghost left. He emerged from Bheemtal's waves. Single-mindedly, he engaged himself in the pursuit of *chandu*. Yet, even after scouring city after city and region following region all across Bharat land, he did not score. Little had he known that as soon as evening falls, the excise department closes all shops selling any form of the drug. By now, Lullu had trouble breathing. His stomach, too, began to roil and he started having motions. His body felt like an awful burden, he could not walk nor fly. He thought his hour of death was near. 'What's the purpose of travelling anymore? Let me take myself home. At least then I can die after enjoying the glimpse of my dearest's face for the last time. I can guilt her, saying, "O beautiful one! I have given up my life in the quest for your love."' Who knows, then, perhaps, she can even find a way to save it. Thus agonised, the ghost returned home long before his allotted hour. Aameer had had an idea that something similar would transpire, so he had said an early goodbye to his wife and returned to his hidey-hole. But the ghost did not go to see her; he went directly to his own resting place, crashed there and began to moan. His whole body had turned cold. His nerves slackened, ligaments loosened, joints fell apart and the muscles became disparate and spaced far apart from one another. He had no strength to raise himself. He lay on the spot in great anguish and serious pain. When it was morning, Mrs Aameer arrived there smiling, with her husband hand in hand. Aameer said, 'Ahoy there, you civil, legitimate and urbane ghost! Haven't you heard that old saying? "Partake of me but in a small measure; I am bitter, my friend, so don't try to be brave: or else, you will sell your cattle and your chattel, all for my sake, and be my beholden slave."'

'Who is this weirdo mocking me in my hour of distress,' the ghost admonished, but his voice came out in a whisper. 'It is Aameer, the husband of this lady and the man to whom you have imparted tremendous grief; no doubt am I pleased to witness your torment,' Aameer replied. The ghost responded, 'Oh please do me the favour of reclaiming your chattel. I have neither need nor desire for enjoying it. And what a chattel it is, I swear! I had been a happy ghost, fulfilling my duties of ghostship; now has anyone ever heard of a ghost smoking? She is the one who hooked me on it. If you have any opium or *chandu* with you at this moment, please let me take it and save my soul. When I feel a bit better, I will return you and your wife back to your house. And not only will I take you to your house, I see that I will have to be your slave for life. For, I can no longer rest a day without having a smoke; it is but for a smoke that I must do your bidding. If you let me smoke twice a day, I will work in your household all hours like a ghost.' Aameer was very well experienced in the effects of *chandu*. At once, he could discern that the ghost was speaking the truth; that there was no deception behind his words. He produced some raw opium from his pockets and allowed the ghost to swallow a bite. As a result, the ghost was well again, his muscles finding their connecting ligaments and joints. He was, once again, a whole ghost. Lullu fell at Aameer's feet. 'Sir, I have sinned against you. I have made a terrible mistake. Please forgive me. You have released me from a great affliction. I will never be able to repay your kindness. All the time I have I am prepared to spend at your disposal serving you and the dear madame. Please have an early lunch. Tonight, I will fly you back to your house.' Aameer and his wife then left the place.

In the evening, the ghost appeared at their chamber. The couple climbed onto his back. Emerging from the lake, Lullu took to the skies. Like lightning, he began to speed across the firmament. It was about two in the morning when the three beings reached Delhi city. The ghost deposited the two humans on the terrace of the mansion. When Aameer had left home in the guise of a faqir, he had locked the terrace door. He reopened it, and man and wife re-entered the house. Aameer showed Lullu his room. He said, 'This is all yours. You can stay here. Opium or *chandu*, whatever you need, we will provide you.' Lullu said, 'Why, sir, I will never leave your side. Besides, even if I wish to, I have little recourse.' Next morning, Aameer called his neighbours over and gave them a blow-by-blow account of all that had transpired. Everyone was pleased that he had returned home.

Bengali Flatbread

After everyone departed, Lullu and Aameer lay on the master bed side by side and smoked a pot of *chandu*. Thus did man and ghost bond and draw close to become intimate. One morning, over a pipe, Aameer said, 'Dear Lullu, dear champion of the secret club of *chandu* users, I nurse a wish—of seeing again my friends who rendered me special help in the matter of my wife's rescue. Back in those days, you used to be my enemy; don't you think they deserve to now see how good a friend you are to me? The first among them is the astrologer, who informed me that you had spirited my wife away. Next is the brahmin, an exorcist par excellence, the likes of whom the earth has never seen nor ever will. Then there is our brother, the weaver. No musicologist of his calibre has ever graced the face of the earth. Then we have the oil press man fellow, an extractor like whom the country has not produced or ever will. And if you can bring along the ghostly brigade, my joy will know no bounds. The ghost of that great brahmin pundit and transcendentalist, the super-spiritual lover Ghyanghon, and the aspiring editor-in-making, Gongon. I have also longed to meet your Gnete*dada* personally and get to know him. I do have one more request. Alas, Ghyanghon is still unmated and unmarried, if you could invite his beloved Nakeshwari and somehow unite them, I will no doubt be most pleased.' Lullu said, 'I am ready and able to fulfil all your orders. I will bring everyone here by tonight.' Come eventide, Lullu exited his room. By one in the morning, he had brought over to Aameer's mansion the astrologer, the brahmin, the weaver and the oil press operator. As per custom, Aameer made each feel very welcome. The guests were indeed pleased to hear that he had got his wife back. In a short while, Lullu again took flight and this time he returned with the brahmin's spirit, Ghyanghon, Gongon and his civil, legitimate and urbane Gnete*dada*. Ghyanghon's Nakeshwari, the one of the enchanting nose, whose beauty bewitched the universe, was also flown in. She stepped to the inner wing to meet Aameer's wife. The male humans and the male ghosts made themselves comfortable in the outer wing of the house. After all the guests had acquainted themselves with one another, Aameer begged and beseeched them, 'Gentlemen! Each of you has bestowed a great kindness on me by deigning to step into my poorly lodgings. At this moment, a desire beats strongly in my heart. Please fulfil it. I yearn to see performed the rituals to formalise a union by marriage between Ghyanghon and Nakeshwari. The lie that was told by Gongon about Ghyanghon, that resulted in the maligning of his name, has been laid bare before Nakeshwari's aunt by my wife. Gongon, too, has now confessed. Nakeshwari's aunt has agreed to their marriage union, now what is your opinion?' No one wasted any time saying, 'Granted. No need to delay an auspicious occasion.' Aameer then asked Lullu and the other ghosts to invite to the wedding every ghost on earth. But all the ghosts present on the spot kept pin-drop silence. No one came forward to comply with his request. Aameer asked, 'Have I asked you people to perform the impossible? Isn't inviting all ghosts to the wedding your objective and intent?' Speaking for the others, Lullu then answered, 'Sir, you are such a generous man that every wish you make is our command. However, we are Indian ghosts; there is no going abroad permitted for us. If we cross the sea, we will lose our caste and family. Our faith is somewhat underdone. Just as a pot made of unbaked clay dissolves in the contact of water, so also our faith dissolves immediately at the touch of the air from across the sea, every sign of it vanishes, even its odour, too, abandons our person. Not only that, thenceforth whoever comes in contact with us, be he god or ghost, human or ape, will also become an outcast of his own community and faith. To each his own arrangement —and so, from then on, they will either have to spend all hours of their remaining days partaking of the five sacred nectars or reading the *kalma*, depending on their respective injunction, then they will have done just enough to keep their hold of it. I have shared with you all information, now it is up to you to make known your will.' Aameer said, 'In that case, there is no need for a party on such a large scale. Send an invitation only to the Indian ghost society.'

Various chewable, suckable, lickable and drinkable beverages and foodstuffs were also arranged for. Within moments, the ghosts collected enormous quantities of Bengali flatbread, sandesh-cheesecake and curd. Many citizens, too, were called over by Aameer to attend the wedding. When all arrived and the feast was ready, Ghyanghon and Nakeshwari's wedding rituals took place amid greatest fanfare. Aameer himself gave away the bride while the brahmin performed the priestly ceremonies. Though he was innocent of the marriage incantations, he sported the long, white sacred mark on his forehead, made the right onomatopoeic noises and generally put on a good show for the night. The nubile and passionate Nakeshwari's resplendent grace bewitched all minds. Committedly and unblinkingly, everyone gazed at her singular beauty. The longer each person looked upon her, the higher the flame of desire burned in their heart. The bridegroom was told, 'Ghyanghon, you are indeed a lucky ghost. You have acquired an invaluable gem of a wife.' In reply, Ghyanghon would roll his eyes and smile. Being a bridegroom, it was not becoming to say much, he held. But the meaning of his eye roll and smile was, 'Didn't I tell you before that after witnessing such beauty who can stay composed and calm?' All invitees also had their fill of food and drink. The guests picked up as much flatbread and sandesh they could carry, tied it in a bundle and took it home. The wedding bed was set up in the marriage hall itself. In unison, everyone requested the weaver to perform the wedding song. Delighted, the weaver happily sang before an audience numbering hundreds and hundreds that night. The audience watched him intently and clapped at his mannerisms. Not a note of song had entered their ears. At Aameer's request, each had stuffed their ear with cotton wool. That night, there was dancing too; the ghosts formed troops and performed so many dances that they cannot all be listed. The party broke a little before dawn. Lullu took the astrologer, the brahmin, the weaver and the oil press man home. The citizens returned to their respective abodes.

Writers, Beware

Before the ghosts left, they addressed Aameer, 'Sir, your good conduct has impressed us immensely. Let us know if we can come of any use, we will be very pleased.' Aameer said, 'If you really want to be useful to me, then I will fulfil your desire. Four *krosh* from this spot on the side of the Yamuna there is land that belongs to my forefathers and the income of that land was enough to keep us in princely airs. But the topsoil of that land has been totally eroded by floods and replaced with sand. I will benefit much if you can pick up the sand and replace it with topsoil.' The ghosts said, 'Thank you. We will do it right away.' So saying, the ghosts reached the land and within a short while, picked off the sand and put back topsoil. The land became fertile and abundant as before. The ghosts then returned to Aameer's mansion, said their goodbyes and went back to their respective places. But Aameer asked Gongon to stay. He told him, 'Gongon! Don't leave. Your bones and muscles are shattered and you are in poor shape. Milk and opium—just these two items can help you rebuild your health again. The marvel of opium is such that one does not age after one forms its habit, one's body stops losing cells. Malaria and other fevers also cease to afflict them. Ghost or man, using opium is beneficial to all. Hence, stay in Lullu's charge. Learn to smoke the *chandu* under his tutelage.' Gongon acquiesced to that plan. Thus Aameer and his wife prospered and thrived.

Within a few days, Lullu became a favourite among all eminent citizens. The aficionados of *chandu* were taken by his qualities. All women, Lullu addressed with 'ma'am'. No longer young, he indeed was a civil and urbane ghost. Having milk and ghee in conjunction with *chandu* had given him a fair complexion. However, he never spoke to anyone save a user. Be that the case, Lullu had become so tame that Mrs Aameer mixed freely with him and would never hesitate or fear in his presence. Even when Aameer became prosperous, he did not let him purchase a carriage. Wherever he was required to visit, Lullu took him there on his back. Countless a time, he had taken Mrs Aameer on his back to visit her parental home. Seeing as he had to go out often, Mrs Aameer had called the goldsmith and got made for Lullu a pair of golden wings. He put on these wings on his flights; they became him and the buoyancy afforded reduced his labour. Once, Mrs Aameer had desired to go to the seaside. Lullu said, 'Why worry? Climb on my back. Hold fast to my head, I will show you there and back.' Thus did Lullu take Mrs Aameer to the seaside.

Shortly, Gongon regained his health. Aameer said, 'Gongon. I will keep my promise to you. I will open a newspaper, and you will be its editor.' When the time was right, Aameer indeed took out a newspaper. Having a ghost editor, a user at that, meant business was fantastic. The good name of the newspaper spread all across the globe. Selling it, Aameer began to make a tidy profit.

But Gongon doesn't sit quiet after producing his own newspaper. To every newspaper office of the world, he has invisible access. When other newspaper writers begin their essays, Gongon goes forth and possesses them, if he so wishes. Once possessed, there is really no accounting of what goes out in the paper. Hence do I say, writers, beware.

Glossary

1. Ganga Maira: A confectioner named Ganga
2. *pana*: A denomination of currency dating back to Turko-Afghan rule in undivided Bengal; one *pana* equals four *budi*s equals 20 *ganda*s equals 80 cowries; 16 *panas* equal one *kahan*; 10 *kahan*s equal one tanka or rupee.
3. *krosh*: Variously referred to as *kos* and *krosha*. Dates back to *Arthashastra*. A unit of distance measuring 2,060 metres or 1.9 miles.
4. Bengali flatbread: Known as the fluffy *luchi* in parlance and literature, it is made of refined flour, is white in colour and is best enjoyed with deep-fried brinjal circles and sautéed mutton as sides.

Treks of Kankabaty

PART ONE

The Old Wife's Tale

Who doesn't know of Kankabaty? As a child, everyone has heard her story.

Kankabaty's brother had brought home a mango for himself. Placing it on the kitchen sill, he issued a warning: 'None may eat my mango. Whosoever does, I will marry that person.' Kankabaty hadn't known about the portent. A mere child, she was. Not having understood the price entailed by the act, she who had eaten the fruit.

Consequently, the brother said, 'I shall marry Kankabaty.'

The parents did their best to dissuade him: 'Is it right for a brother to marry his sister?'

The young man paid little heed. Said he: 'Why then did Kankabaty eat my mango? No doubt, I shall marry her.'

Kankabaty was overcome by shame. Fear, too, entered her psyche. With no recourse at hand, she built herself a small boat. Seating herself in the boat, she floated right to the centre of the pool in her backyard. The brother could marry her no more.

Thus begins the story of Kankabaty. Yet it is an incredible story. Can someone truly propose to marry their sibling for just a mango only? Let me provide you with a credible story.

Kusumghati

Not in the suburbs but in the forest districts lies the village of Kusumghati. It has a largish population, though, and there is a moor right next to it. In earlier days, many people passed through this moor. Whenever they got a chance, miscreants from nearby villages waylaid them and took their lives, and then removed their money and other belongings. Thereafter, the villains would dispose of the corpses in the water. The lakes on the moor do still give up human skulls and other remains till this very date.

There was one other means of disposing the bodies. Having murdered a traveller, the miscreants would carry the body over to a different village and leave it in its precincts. After dropping the dead body on the ground, they would call out a shrill, whistle-like, halloo, going, 'kooh'. They would then forthwith make themselves scarce from the spot.

The village guard who heard the sound immediately knew that a corpse had been dropped in his jurisdictional area. He would worry: 'If a corpse has been dropped in my jurisdictional precinct, then tomorrow there will be enquiries.'

So thinking, he, too, with the assistance of his associates, would take the dead body and leave it in a farther village, whistling 'kooh' in his wake.

Thus would the body travel a 10-20 *krosh* distance in the span of a single night. Whence the man came and who did away with him would become impossible to investigate, let alone find out.

Kusumghati was forest country for one, and then there were the murders to boot. On no account, could there have been in these tracts a dearth of ghosts. Folks there believe in various types of ghosts who reside in the sacred fig, banyan and Bengal wood apple trees. At eventide, the elderly keep indoors and tell themselves stories of ghosts, hearing which the children start shivering.

There is no scarcity of witches, too, in Kusumghati. Grandparents frequently warn the kids: 'Do not step on a stray branch on the road. They are witches who have shifted shape. You will be eaten alive by them if you do.'

And so it is that for the villagers, the fear of danger unknown lurks at every step on hard land. Yet they hardly feel safer in water either. A brook flows by next to the village. Descending from the hillside, it gurgles past the settlement, going '*kool kool kool*' towards the great ocean. While there is no shark or crocodile in the brook, it is, however, filled with other perils. Aside from the ever-present dreadlocked old woman who waits, shackle in hand, there are plenty of living stones in the water. Should they get half an opportunity, the stones bestride a man's chest while he is underwater. Thus it is that danger lurks in the water.

Not far from Kusumghati passed the mountain range. The mountains are forested. Tigers and bears live in the forest. Villagers frequently lose their cattle to these beasts. Oftentimes, a tiger learns to eat men. Then the tiger won't have anything else. Oppressed, the people hatch a plan and slay the tiger.

Yet, there are exceptions. Sometimes, a tiger is so clever that none can hunt him. People then opine that it is no tiger but a former human being. There is a herb in the forest that, if worn on the head, lets a man shift his shape. If anyone quarrels or has a dispute, they use the herb to become a tiger and vanquish their enemy. Then, they remove the herb and are human again. But some of them fail to unfasten the herb. They must live out as a tiger the rest of their days. These tigers are the ones that trouble villagers the most.

The people of Kusumghati hold many such beliefs. But nowadays these fears are gradually being dispelled from their minds. Many from the village collect tussar pupae and proceed to Calcutta city. Some of them live there as well, in rented houses. A few have even done studies in the English language. They don't believe in ghosts and witches. If someone speaks of ghosts before them, they smile and they say: 'There is no ghost on earth and in heaven. And if there are, what can they do to us?' Seeing their example, the modern generation is feeling somewhat braver than before.

Tanu Ray

The Eminent Mr Ramtanu Ray His Grace puts up at Kusumghati. No one calls him by his given name, 'Ramtanu Ray'. He is referred to as 'Tanu Ray' by most people. Being a brahmin and advanced in years, he fulfils all of his caste obligations. Thrice a day he prays and he pays obeisance to his ancestors. He is pious towards the gods and the family masters. Thus he is seen duly engaging in disputes and contentions with other schools of brahmins as well. That the humans of today do not follow perfectly all the rites and rituals as per the medieval scriptures no doubt causes him great pain.

Says Tanu Ray, 'The boys are atheists nowadays; one shouldn't accept water from their hands.'

He himself observes all rules, and performs all ceremonies, especially the ones related to family and pedigree.

Being a brahmin by birth, he believes that since the Almighty has caused him to take birth in his particular family, he must do his best to abide by its way, or else it will be counted as a slight of the Great God and a sin for which he must suffer damnation. At this point, it is legitimate to ask: What might that way be that pertains to this family? The way is this—'While giving away the daughter in marriage, one must accept a token of wealth from the groom. Or else, one risks perdition and loss of faith. One becomes a fallen brahmin. So is written in scripture.' Because he followed the scripture in all his activities, the people of the village had great regard for Tanu Ray. He was the first to be invited by womenfolk to perform priestly duties. Everyone opined, 'A brahmin as faithful as Ray*mahashay* is indeed hard to come by.' This repute was the strongest in the Shudra community.

Tanu Ray is a high brahmin. Those jealous of him are given to jibe, 'It is not customary for the Rays to get married. The respective marriages of the father or the grandfather, too, are questionable.'

The truth is that there had been trouble during Ray's own marriage. He had decided on a bride, having promised a dowry of five hundred rupees. To fulfil the dowry, he had sold land inherited from his paternal family. When the day of the marriage arrived, he went to the bride's home with the money. The bride's father received the money and counted it. Yet when the ordained moment arrived for tying the knot, he made no move to give away the bride. No one could figure out as to why he was dragging his feet.

Subsequently, the man himself dispelled all anxieties. He said, 'That the bridegroom is so advanced in years I had not factored earlier. It was why I had readily agreed to give my daughter at five hundred rupees. As of now, for less than one thousand rupees I cannot agree to the match.'

The word of the bride's father set off a terrible crisis. The auspicious hour went by; the night, too, almost ended. When it was about dawn, the elders mediated between the two parties and came up with a solution, 'Ray*mahashay* must furnish another fifty rupees.' Writing an undertaking, Tanu Ray borrowed fifty bucks and paid it to the bride's father to take her home. In order to satisfy requests from his new relatives, Tanu Ray had taught himself quite a few tunes to perform at the reception party. But there was no party, as by the time the rites got over, it was already morning. The pain of this unfulfilled wish remained with Tanu Ray lifelong.

Today, Tanu Ray is the father of three daughters and a son. As per the way of his family line, he has given away two of his daughters to suitable husbands. The sons-in-law had upheld Tanu Ray's honour. That's so because they had coughed up one thousand, or five hundred, respectively, in cash on the spot. Hence they can certainly be deemed as suitable husbands.

In the hope of being a bit more honoured, Tanu Ray had raised both daughters to reach the age of majority before marrying them. He would say: 'If they are married young and widowed thereafter, who will atone for that sin? Raise your daughter before you marry her. If you are a brahmin by birth or of high lineage within that caste, you will not draw punishment. This is how does the scripture advise.'

And for this reason when the law of the wedding sleep was passed in 1891, Tanu Ray saw it as redundant. Said he: 'What is the need of a new law when I have practised this all my life?' It became the basis of his reasoning for taking up cudgels to oppose the law. He called a meeting and raised subscription, then pocketed the monies.

Tanu Ray's sons-in-law were no spring chicken. As it stood, their father-in-law could hardly bear to look upon a childish groom, seeing as they liked to marry for a hundred bucks or so. Hence he had selected men who were a little mature for his girls. One of them was seventy years old. The other was seventy-five. If the girls in the neighbourhood raised their eyebrows, Tanu Ray would say: 'Shush, girls. Listen to a secret. If the man is mature, he loves his wife.' Nevertheless, the sons-in-law were perhaps a tad too mature, as post the marriage, a year had not gone by when both girls were widowed.

Tanu Ray is a learned man. Grief has not overwhelmed him. His words of consolation to himself are: 'It is the Fates. Who can counter what is ordained by them? So many marry their five-year-olds with twelve-year-old boys; why then do their daughters get widowed? What is lotted can't be blotted. None can wipe the writing on one's forehead.'

Tanu Ray's son takes after the father. At this moment, he is no longer an infant; he has crossed twenty-five years of age. His education fell through, but he is familiar with the scriptures just the way the paterfamilias is. The man has saved money by marrying his daughters. That has cheered, not saddened, his heart. For, he is the only successor of his father. In any case, no one mentions the word 'widow' nowadays eventhough he always praises this demographic.

Says he: 'Our widows are living Saraswatis. Always serving the Lord and doing good is their life's motto. They are constantly ensuring that I eat well and so does our father. Three days of fast notwithstanding, they cook five recipes for the family. My sisters are like Ahalya-Draupadi-Kunti-Tara-Mandodari, names to be recalled at the start of day.'

Sometimes, he feels sorry that *sahamaran* has been abolished. For, had it been in place, the sisters could have ascended to heaven at a moment's notice. Then they would not have had to sit unoccupied and consume their beloved father's rice in vain. Why do the British block thus the doors to the heavenly abode?

Tanu Ray's wife, though, is a different kettle of fish. At every wedding feast in the neighbourhood, she carefully notes the good looks of the groom and then bursts into bouts of loud weeping. Then Tanu Ray scolds her much, and says to her: 'Just remind yourself what your father himself had done to you.' With more taunts in similar vein, he succeeds in consoling her. The marriage of their daughters is a bone of contention between man and wife. Gazing upon the faces of her widowed daughters, the mother sheds copious tears. Along with them, she, too, observes the widow's Ekadashi ritual fast, only swallowing a sip of water so that the Fates do not cast the evil eye on her own husband. Following worship every day, she bumps her head in obeisance at the foot of each deity in her gods' room. To one god after the other, she prays: 'Oh dear Ma Kali! Oh dear Ma Durga! Oh dear God! May my little Kankabaty get a husband after her wish.'

Kankabaty is the youngest daughter of Tanu Ray and, in this very moment, no more than a mere infant only.

Khetu

In Tanu Ray's neighbourhood, lives an impecunious brahmin wife. She is addressed as 'the Mother of Khetu' by all people.

The mother of Khetu is doubtless impecunious, yet once upon a time had she lived prosperously. Her husband, Shibchandra Mukhopadhyay, literate and well-read, then worked in Calcutta and provided for his family.

However, Shibchandra lacked the knack of holding his money. Another's grief disturbed him immensely, and he would do his level best to dispel it. Thus it is that he provided for a considerable number of people and bore the expenses for the education of several young men. No doubt, a man such as Shibchandra could not hold on to his earnings.

Late into their marriage, his wife bore them a son. He named the boy Kshetra, hence the origin of the moniker, 'Mother of Khetu'.

When the boy was born, Shibchandra said to himself, 'The time has arrived when I must teach myself to be careful with my expenditures. I need to make sure that in my absence my wife and son do not despair for meals.'

The intention was born but it never got acted upon. No doubt this world is full of sorrow, yet the one who makes getting rid of it his own responsibility will never know opulence.

When Khetu turned four, his father suddenly passed. His death rendered his wife and baby penniless. Khetu's father had come to the aid of many. Several of them were now wealthy men. But in this hour of need, they were conspicuous by their absence. Not one of them enquired after the family's well-being. No one asked the lady: 'Khetu's Mother! Do you have arrangements for your widow's meal?'

In this time of sorrow, only Ramhari Mukhopadhyay supported the family.

Ramhari is a distant relation of the family. Khetu's father had got him appointed to a petty job through his good offices. Since there is no guardian to protect his wife in the village, he needs must live in Calcutta with his family. The little income he makes is spent fulfilling their needs.

How could he then bear the funeral expenses? Nonetheless, he did his best and covered some of it while he went door to door to raise subscription for the rest. Many an excuse, objection and slight did the men whom Khetu's father had once supported mention while parting with one or two subscription rupees. With the money thus raised, the funeral rites of Khetu's father were performed with the sanctioned gifts of gold and sesame seed. The remainder of the subscription Ramhari spent on buying rail tickets to send Khetu's mother and Khetu home.

Thenceforth, he would bear the expenses of their rice only as he could do little else. The brahmin wife spun sacred threads and sold them to make ends meet. There were no comrades in the village. Save Niranjan, who made regular enquiries and stood by them in times of crisis.

Khetu's mother began spending her days on the borderline of penury. Yet her son began growing serene and respectful, while brave and powerful physically. Witnessing his talent, love and beauty, the mother forgot her misfortunes. When the boy was seven, Ramhari visited the village.

He addressed Khetu's mother: 'It is time for Khetu to begin his formal studies. We can no longer keep him in the village. I desire to take him to Calcutta with me. How do you opine on this?'

Khetu's mother responded, 'Oh dear! How can I allow it? I can't be without my son. Even if he is out of my sight for a moment's timespan, I cannot live without him. No, dear, I can't send him anywhere else while I am living.'

Ramhari reasoned, 'Hear me. If he stays here, Khetu will grow up without an education. I am sure you are aware of what happened to Mathur Chakrabarty? Only by performing priestly duties at the annual Gajan could he support his family. Everyone despised him. They called him the "Gajune Brahmin". His young son, Sandeshwar, was employed as a cook at your rented accommodation in Calcutta. Seeing him, your kind-hearted husband put him in school. Today he is a lawyer and a rich man.'

Khetu's mother answered, 'Shut up now. If my son goes to school in Calcutta and turns himself out like Sandeshwar, I'd rather not have him acquire such learning.'

Ramhari said, 'It is true that Sandeshwar drinks alcohol and is served by his Muslim horse carriage driver various proscribed meats, but he also participates in singing the name of Hari every evening. Yet, does everyone turn out the same way? If a male child does not get an education, how will he fend for himself? The way a human has a right to live their life the way they deem fit, if male, so, too, is unassailable their right to an education.'

Khetu's mother said, 'Perhaps, you are right. The right of a son to his education is in fact superior to his right to live as he pleases. The parents who deny it to him are his greatest enemies. Yet consider: I have a mother's heart, I have no guardian nor assistance. There is no one in the world for me; I only live in this home with my tiny grain of a son beside me. I miss him momentarily. If he is late coming home from his evening games, I cannot bear speaking of the ills I anticipate have happened to him. I fear he has drowned, or burnt himself, or fallen from the tree, or been beaten by the neighbourhood's children. When he sleeps, I rise at night and place my hand near his nostril to feel his breath fall on my fingers. Consider if I send him away how my heart will go on beating. Hence do I cry, hence do I say, "no".'

Khetu's mother said again, 'Ramhari! My son, Khetu, is very bright. He has been going to kindergarten only for two years, yet in these two years, he has finished learning to inscribe the alphabet on the *tal* leaf and is now writing on the banana leaf. The master says, "Khetu is the best of all the boys in class." And, hear me, Ramhari. Khetu is a very agreeable child. Whatever I ask of him, he carries out. What I forbid him to do, he does not. Once, the Dases' daughter came to me and said, "Ma'am, the boys in the neighbourhood have ganged up on Khetu and are beating him." Breathless, I ran. I saw six boys piled up on Khetu. Khetu did not show fear, neither did he cry. I ran up to him and picked him up in my arms. Then Khetu wiped his eyes and he said to me, "Dear Mother, I did not cry before them, so as to not let them think that I am afraid. Alone they cannot overcome me. They were six and I only one, so I was beaten. When I find them by themselves, then I, too, will give them a good beating." Said I, "My dear, but if you fight every day, who will you play with?" Khetu heeded my warning. Many a time thenceforward has he met the boys alone; he could have thrashed them if he wanted to. But because I forbid him from so doing, he hasn't.

'Another day, did I say to Khetu, "Khetu, don't throw stones at Tanu Ray's mango tree. Tanu Ray is an irritable man; he will abuse you." Khetu said, "Mother dear, that tree does bear very sweet mangoes. One luscious mango was beaming at me from behind the leaves. I had a stone in my hand. Hence I thought, let me see if I can bring it down." I said to him, "Dear, the mangoes of that tree may well be sweet, but that tree itself does not belong to us. If you throw stones at others' trees, their owners will be angry. When the mango falls to the ground by its own accord, pick it up and eat it. Then no one will admonish you."

'And then, another day, Khetu ran up to me and said, "Dear Mother, the fruits have ripened on the fishermen's velvet apple tree. All the boys in the neighbourhood had climbed on it and were eating the fruit. They called me over, and they said, 'Khetu! Come on up here. We can't reach the farther fruits.' But, Mother, I did not climb the tree. The tree does not belong to us, does it, Mother? So, I stood under it. The boys threw down a fruit or two. Oh, Mother, the fruit is so tasty I cannot tell you. Here, Mother, I have brought one for you, why don't you taste it and see? I wish we had a velvet apple tree." Said I, "Khetu, my dear. The elderly don't eat velvet apples; you can have it yourself. And there is no wrong in climbing others' velvet apple trees. The fishermen will not admonish you. But take care, don't climb to the top and don't step on thin branches or else they will break." How happy my dear son was to receive my permission to eat the fruit, I cannot even narrate.

'And hark, a man had come to our village one day from somewhere else to sell sandesh. The boys of the village stood around him in a circle. Their parents bought them the sweet as per their respective means. I spotted Khetu standing along with the boys with an ashen face. I quickly went up to him and picked him up; my heart broke and tears burst forth from my eyes. Wiping my eyes at the end of my garment, I came home with my son. Khetu was mum, there were no words on his tongue. What was passing through his child's mind, I cannot say. After a while, he touched my face and asked, "Dear Mother, why do you weep?" Said I, "My little one! There was a time when my kitchen counter overflowed with sandesh; the servants and employees, too, had their fill and still a lot remained. How can I forget that today I could not buy you a penny's worth of the sweet? Why did you take birth from the womb of an unfortunate soul like me?" Now wait until you hear a seven-year-old child speak. Said Khetu, "But Mother dear, that sandesh is not sweet. Did you not see that it had gone sour? And, Mother, you do remember that I fall ill if I take sandesh. Remember the time I went to the feast given by the Chowdhurys. I had taken sandesh there, and the very next day, I fell ill. We should not eat sandesh, Mother, but we should eat puffed rice. If you have it, please serve it to me."'

Thus could Khetu's mother only struggle to finish recounting Khetu's exploits. Ramhari heard her out as she narrated his many qualities and sang his praises.

At length did Ramhari say, 'Madam, do not fear needlessly. I will care for your son more than I care for my own. I have eaten Shib*kaka's* rice aplenty. It is owing to his graciousness that I today feed my family. That his son will grow to be an ignoramus I cannot in good conscience abide by. How Khetu is feeling, how he is faring in his studies, all this I will keep you posted on through mail. When Khetu will learn to write, he, too, will do the same. Every summer and Durgapuja, I will send him back to the village. Each year, he will spend two to three months with you. Let me take my leave. Today is Friday. Wednesday is a good day for me to return and collect Khetu for taking him to Calcutta to live with my family.'

Niranjan

Tanu Ray hardly converses with Niranjan Kaviratna, who is his neighbour nextdoor. That's because Niranjan has said, 'Mr Ray, I beseech you not to accept money in exchange of giving your daughter away in marriage, for it is a grievous sin to do so.'

It is the reason why Tanu Ray dislikes Niranjan. Nay, he harbours a grudge against him. On the days of his daughters' weddings, Niranjan leaves the village and spends the time elsewhere, saying, 'It is a sin to be present at a human being's sale. One should not witness nor abide by it.'

Niranjan is a great scholar. He has studied many scriptures and texts. As there are no limits to research and scholarship, day and night, he is to be found immersed in books and manuscripts. He does not prefer to show off his erudition, so his reputation is not wide. Not too long ago, he was teacher to numerous boys. He gained a huge deal of satisfaction in giving lessons to them. He even supported them with meals and clothing as if they were his own children. If invited himself for meals, he did not stay on and haggle for gifts. He was affluent, seeing as he had been left ownership of some ancestral estate.

A few wires had been crossed regarding a portion of this land between the village landowner, Janardan Chowdhury, and himself. One day, in the second hour, the zamindar sent over a watchman to his house.

The watchman arrived and said to Niranjan, 'Lord, the landowner has summoned you. Come with me forthwith.'

Niranjan replied, 'It's past the second hour now. I have just taken a break and the rice is ready. Let me have a quick bite to eat and I will accompany you. If I don't have my meal, the housewife won't, and the boys, too, will remain unfed.'

The watchman said, 'That won't be. You must come at once.'

Niranjan said, 'Oh yes? At once should I proceed? Let's leave then.' Watchman by side, Niranjan appeared at the zamindar's manor.

Janardan Chowdhury spoke, 'I had sent for you since an hour I cannot recollect, yet you seem to have little time to spend at my behest.'

Niranjan said, 'You speak verily, mister. For I have taken some time arriving.'

The zamindar said, 'The fifty bighas you own at Bamunmaari moor has been found to measure fifty-five bighas following government survey. Your deed is authentic, so I will spare you. But I lay my claim to the excess.'

Niranjan said, 'You speak verily. My papers are authentic. Why don't you look over them and confirm it?'

Janardan Chowdhury accepted the document and said, 'Yes, indeed. I have seen this document before. I don't need to look again.'

So saying, he returned the paper to Niranjan. Niranjan took it from his hands and dropped it into the shisha tobacco bowl. The flame flared up as it caught fire and within minutes it had turned to ash.

'Stop, what have you done?' said the zamindar.

Niranjan said, 'Why claim just five bighas! From this date, my estate is all yours. The one who has created life will feed Niranjan.'

Fearing that he will incur a brahmin's curse, Janardan Chowdhury said, 'No matter if the deed is gone. You continue to enjoy your estate; I won't seek any of it.'

Niranjan said, 'No, sir. The one who has created life will feed all living beings. It's best to contemplate that friend of the needy and spend your time at his behest. If plots of prominence and property disturb that programme and divert the disposition, it is better to sacrifice them. Isn't it just because I owned land that I had to listen to the cruel speech of your west-born watchman? Therefore, I have no use of that land. Only the one without desire can behave justly with poor and rich, and pauper and king. As a propertied gentleman, you can hardly understand that. Yet if you do, you are so thoroughly trapped in the web of society that you have no choice but to follow that mirage. Alas, you will fail to free yourself from the reaches of the hot desert that is this world. Now bless me so that never ever do I have to depend for anything material on anyone.' On this note, Niranjan departed.

From that day onwards, Niranjan came to be blacklisted. Hardship befell his household. One by one, all his students left his tutelage and joined Gobardhan Shiromani's college.

Gobardhan Shiromani is the chief scholar in Janardhan Chowdhury's court. He provides meals to several students. He has no time to give them lessons. For, he must register his presence at Mr Chowdhury's residence each morning and night and attend various scholarly conferences besides. Hence the students learn their lessons on their own.

Yet no one has any regrets. It's hard to be angry with Gobardhan Shiromani. To hold a grudge it's harder still. That's because he has a silver tongue, and he wins hearts by dint of his polished speechmaking. Particularly when he is in the presence of barons and those with deep pockets, this talent of his acquires a special dimension, and like

Shravan rain, he rains on them the manna of his quicksilver speech. Like parched Jacobin cuckoos, they soak up the gifts.

One day at Janardan Chowdhury's manor, Tanu Ray was confabulating on scriptural injunctions. Niranjan, Gobardhan, etc., were present there.

Tanu Ray said, 'The brahmin will be served some respect in the form of material gifts in exchange of his daughter. Do the scriptures bar this custom?'

'Why don't you cite the Mahabharata?' whispered Gobardhan.

Tanu Ray misheard him. After a pause, he said, 'It is mentioned in the story of Daata Karna.'

Hearing his words, Niranjan smiled. His smile annoyed Tanu Ray to no end. Niranjan said, 'It is a sin to take money for marrying one's daughter. If you wish to commit sin, please do, but do not blame the scripture, do not taint its name. You do not know the scripture; you have never studied the scripture.'

Tanu Ray flew off the handle. Calling Niranjan various derogatory names, he at last said, 'So you think I haven't read the scripture, do you? Well, then, give me one good reason why I should read the scripture. If I so wish, I can write so many of them. Why should the one who can write scripture read it?'

At this, Niranjan had to accept defeat. He had to admit that the one who could produce his own scripture had no need for studying it.

Goodbye

On the night of the same afternoon the talks took place between her and Ramhari, did the mother of Khetu place her warm hand on her son's arm and say: 'Khetu, my dear son! Hark, for I have news.'

Khetu said, 'Yes, Mother?'

The mother answered, 'Dear child, you must accompany Ramhari, your elder brother, to Calcutta.'

'And where's that, Mother?' Khetu asked the woman.

The mother said, 'Why, but don't you remember? It is the place with constant traffic.'

Khetu said, 'Aah, I remember now. Won't you come with me, Mother?'

The mother said, 'No, my dear child. I won't come with you. I will stay right here.'

Khetu said, 'In that case, Mother, I won't leave either.'

The mother said, 'You have no choice but, my child. I am a woman and so I am not supposed to go there. Ramhari will be with you, so what are you afraid of?'

Khetu replied, 'Why, Mother, but I am afraid of nothing on this earth. Yet I will think of you and wish for your company, so let me stay.'

The mother said, 'My dear, am I sending you away to please myself? I have no recourse, my dear, and so I shall send you there. For, you have grown, my dear, you must go to school. If you don't, you will be an ignoramus. No one cares for an ignoramus; no one pays any attention to them. If you go to school, on the other hand, and do your lessons well, you will be loved. What's more, my sorrows will come to an end. For instance, see, I can't prepare sacred thread of finer dimensions anymore, for my vision is fading. It is possible that in the coming days I will no longer be able to make the coarser ones either. In that case, advise how I shall pay my bills. But if you can learn enough to earn, I can give up my job and spend my time in prayers. I will say to the deities, "My Khetu is a good son. Please give him a long life."'

Khetu said, 'But, Mother, if I leave you, won't you cry?'

The mother answered, 'No, my dear. I won't cry.'

Then, Khetu said, 'There, Mother. There, I see you.'

The mother said, 'Right now, I want to cry. But later on, I will not. Now, then, Khetu, you don't have to stay there all twelve months a year. During a holiday, you will sometimes come home. I will wait on your arrival, reach the Duttas' fishpond early on, pick you up and bring you home. If you work hard, you will learn to write letters. I will keep all your letters safe and not let anyone open them. When you come home, you will read them aloud to me.'

Khetu then asked his mother, 'And, Mother, shall I find beads over there?'

Khetu's mother said, 'What beads?' and Khetu replied, 'The ones you had wished for one night when you had said you cannot sleep, so if you had them, you would have counted them.'

The mother said, 'Yes, dear. You can get many beads over there.'

After a pause, she spoke again. She said, 'Why, that's a nice idea. You can bring me a string of those beads.'

Having settled on this plan, Khetu went to sleep with Calcutta on his mind. Next morning, he arose and he said, 'Mother, from this day forward until I go, I will not go to the kindergarten. I won't play with the boys either. I will spend all my time with you.'

The mother responded, 'That's fine by me, but pay your uncle, Niranjan, your respects before your departure.'

Khetu said, 'Certainly, I shall do that. Now, I have one more request. During these last days, I will eat out of your plate once you have finished your meal. The reason being… well, do you know why I have stopped eating lunch from the lunch plate, dear Mother? It is because I have noticed that you forgo all that you enjoy merely in order to serve them up to me. Hence, did I say to you, Mother, that I don't feel hungry at midday. Yet, I do get those pangs, Mother, that's when I pick jujubes and quinces fallen from neighbours' trees on the ground. The reason being…Mother, you don't get to pick them up and eat them as I do, do you? That's why I would not prefer eating lunch from the plate, Mother, for I fear that you will go hungry for my sake.'

The brahmini took Khetu in her arms and, weeping, carded her fingers through his hair. Then she said, 'My dear, I am not weeping for sorrow. What sorrow can befall a woman who has given birth to a moon of a son like you? Only, hearing your heavenly words, I fear if destiny will not lead me to losing you.'

When dinner ended, the mother took out her needles and began darning worn clothes.

Khetu said, 'Mother, let me hold fast the edges of the tear and you can begin stitching it up from the other end. This way, we can work faster. When the strand is used up, I will thread the needle. You can't spot the hole, and that takes up time.'

Together, the two chitchatted and finished the work. Then the mother soaked the clothes in washing salts and cleaned them. And this is how preparations got underway for Khetu's starting of school in the city of Calcutta. The next evening, Khetu visited Niranjan's home. He touched the feet of Niranjan and his wife and paid obeisance to the two of them. Then he informed him of the upcoming trip. Ramhari had already intimated Niranjan about the matter.

Niranjan gave Khetu his blessings. Then he said, 'Dear Khetu, in all that you do and say, try and be truthful. Give up cruelty and pettiness. Be kind to living beings. Help one and all when they are in need, it is the eternal dharma. Confide in Ramhari, your brother, when you are in trouble. Don't keep secrets from him. There will be many boys in your class; some naughty, others quiet. There are bound to be arguments. Never hit anyone who does not deserve it; don't strike a weakling; don't gang up against any boy and throw your weight behind someone who is being wronged. There is no shame in being defeated while helping an underdog. When you go to bed each night, count your good deeds of the day. If you have committed a bad one, make a promise to yourself not to repeat it.'

Thus did Khetu bid his farewell to his Uncle Niranjan.

Mother and son could not sleep on Tuesday. All night, they stayed up, speaking to one another. Often, Khetu's mother would say, 'Go to sleep, Khetu. You will fall ill if you don't.'

Khetu would reply, 'No, Mother. I won't sleep tonight. Tomorrow I won't be talking to you. I will have gone far away. When I think of it, I want to cry.'

Khetu's mother said, 'It is not long before Durgapuja arrives. These few months will fly by. Then you will return to me again.'

At dawn, Ramhari arrived. Khetu's mother put a mark of yoghurt on Khetu's forehead. She tied quince leaves to the end of his linen wrap. Without a word, she placed Khetu's hand in Ramhari's and held back her tears.

At last, she spoke. She said, 'I, an impecunious woman, give over to you my only belonging.'

Said Ramhari: 'Khetu! Touch the feet of Mother.'

Khetu bent to touch his mother's feet. So did Ramhari, and the duo said goodbye and left.

Till the time their figures were visible, Khetu's mother stood by the cart road gazing into the distance. Khetu, too, kept looking back to see Mother. When he disappeared, Khetu's mother lay down on the dust of the cart road and wet it with her tears.

Kankabaty

As Khetu's mother lay on the cart road weeping, Tanu Ray's wife came upon her. She took her by her hand and helped her up from the ground. Presently, she said, 'Calm down, my Sister. Your tears will bring obstacles in your son's path of progress.'

Khetu's mother replied, 'I am aware of it, my Sister. But how can I help it? The tears flow of their own accord. Today I am bereft, what shall I do by returning home? Today I have chores no more. Today, Khetu won't come running home all dirty and dishevelled from his lessons in the kindergarten. By now, he must have travelled so far away. He must be lonely by now.'

Tanu Ray's wife said, 'You are right, Sister, but let's go indoors anyway. There we can relax and speak of Khetu. Aah, Khetu! He is a gem of a boy. If only he has a long life, else all your sorrow will be in vain.' So saying, Tanu Ray's wife took Khetu's mother by the hand and led her to her tenement. There, the pair conferred about Khetu at length.

Khetu had had an early lunch, and Tanu Ray's wife washed his used plate. She swept the floor and cleaned all utensils. His mother would have to eat a meal at noon, so with that purpose in mind, she chopped vegetables and minced spices.

Khetu's mother said, 'Let it be, Sister. To what end shall I feed myself a meal today? Today, I shan't eat anything.'

Tanu Ray's wife then said, 'My dear Sister, should you fast on no account? Won't it bring adversity in Khetu's way? Can you, as a mother, abide by that?' 'Adversity in Khetu's way'—these words had always had the power to silence the mother. A deed that would bring adversity in Khetu's way: could she, as a mother, indeed abide by it?

Tanu Ray's wife again said, 'Here I have arranged it all. When it is forenoon, put the pot on the stove. When my chores get over, I will stop by in the evening.' She kept her word. In the evening, Tanu Ray's wife returned. She had brought her baby girl with her. Khetu's mother looked at the infant and she said, 'What a beautiful baby! What features, what hair, what complexion!'

Tanu Ray's wife said, 'Yes. Everyone tells me: "This daughter of yours is a beauty by birth." Yet, Sister! I wonder why they choose my womb to take birth from. If a daughter is born, the man in the family is beside himself with joy. And I fight the urge to poison them in the crib with brine. Every summer on Ekadashis, when the girls' faces become all parched and drawn and they silently wish for a sip of water, tell me, pray, what goes on in a mother's heart? The wretched rules won't allow them a drink. If I had the means I would take a broomstick to the one who has made these rules. Had he issued an injunction that would let them drink water, I may not have done that.'

Khetu's mother said, 'Whoever sinned in their previous birth will be punished in the present. What they sow in the present they will reap in the future birth.'

Tanu Ray's wife said again, 'Yet, very often do I think, if the Vidyasagar Act is followed in this village, I would offer *sinni* to the deities.'

Khetu's mother answered: 'Shame on you, Sister! Do not even utter such reprehensible words. If the British sahibs fall for Vidyasagar's argument and say there can be no more widows in this land and everyone has to marry, then imagine the disgrace. Where will I go in my advanced age? I will have no option but to hang myself or drown.'

But Tanu Ray's wife only smiled and said, 'Dear Sister, you have been to Calcutta and lived there, but are clueless about important happenings. The Honourable Vidyasagar has not wished to catch hold of all widows and get them married, notwithstanding their senility or reduced physical prowess. He has spoken almost exclusively of girls who are widowed at a tender age. Even so, he has left the final decision with them and their guardians—whoever wishes to may remarry, who doesn't needn't.

Khetu's mother then said, 'Who knows if you are right? I certainly do not.'

Tanu Ray's wife was the mother of two young widows, and moreover, she constantly felt sorry for them. Hence she kept up with the news, and what Khetu's mother had missed as a former resident of Calcutta, she didn't.

As mentioned before, Tanu Ray was a learned man. He latched on to Vidyasagar's opinion as soon as it arrived in the public domain. He said, 'Only because it is in the scriptures do you disregard this injunction. It is a great sin to disobey the scriptures. Why only two marriages? A widow can have ten remarriages if she so pleases. And there is virtue in facilitating such marriages. But this darned country is full of superstition, no good will ever come to it.'

At first, the locals were surprised to hear a faithful brahmin such as Tanu Ray speak in this manner. But soon they surmised, 'It must be the father's heart speaking. Seeing not one but two of his daughters suffer so abjectly, he is being emotional.'

Only Niranjan remarked, 'Oh yes, if widow marriages get underway, Tanu Ray's business will indeed flourish well.'

At this comment, everyone started cursing Niranjan. 'His heart is filled with envy. If not, why else would he meet such a fate? He owned two hundred bighas of ancestral land, yet today he is a pauper. If he gets his rice today, he fails to obtain it the next,' they said.

Thus did progress the conversation between Khetu's mother and Tanu Ray's wife. Khetu's mother asked her: 'Is your daughter now a year old?'

Tanu Ray's wife answered, 'Yes. She will soon be one and going on two.'

Khetu's mother said, 'Kankabaty! What a lovely name. The lilt in the name suits the lissomness of your daughter's looks.'

Thus came about a bonhomie between Khetu's mother and Tanu Ray's wife. Whenever she had time to spare, she would bring Kankabaty over and leave her in Khetu's mother's care.

The girl has not learned to walk but she crawls about the house. Sometimes she sits up and amuses herself, often she holds onto a cupboard and stands upright. Khetu's mother goes about her chores and speaks to her frequently. When spoken to, the girl beams at her. Her smile is radiant. The girl is very calm and she never cries.

The Children

Once in Calcutta, Khetu immersed himself in his lessons. With his innate composure and intelligence, he came to earn the affection of everybody.

Ramhari had just had a baby boy; his name was Narhari. But in three years' time, he would become the father of a daughter, too, and her name was Seeta.

Ramhari and his wife loved Khetu more dearly than their own son. At school, the teachers were pleasantly surprised at his sharp mental acumen. Khetu can grasp any lesson and he can remember it as well. Whichever class he is in, he tops it. No one can outshine him. Whenever he reads a set of books, it becomes hard to stump him with a question based on their content. Thus did Khetu progress from one class to the next.

Each morning, Ramhari gave Khetu a penny to buy lunch with. Khetu would buy it on some days; on other days, he would skip it. As it would turn out, one day, the matter came to Ramhari's knowledge.

He asked Khetu, 'Khetu, why don't you eat your lunch? What do you do with the pennies?'

Caught unawares, Khetu blushed involuntarily and took a moment to gather his wits. Presently, he said, 'Dear

Brother, sir! I do have lunch the days I am so hungry I cannot go without my meal. On other days, when I can do without, I don't have it. The pennies I have saved are safe in my care. When I left home, I had told my mother that I would buy her some beads. To that end, I am keeping aside the money.'

As Khetu was speaking, he stood close by Ramhari. Ramhari put his hand in Khetu's hair and began moving the locks in front to the back of his head. Khetu understood his brother had not been annoyed; he was being affectionate.

In a while, Ramhari said, 'Khetu, my dear, let me know when you plan to buy those beads. I will help you make a good purchase.'

The Durgapuja holiday drew close. Khetu said, 'Big Brother, it is time to buy those beads that you promised.'

Ramhari said, 'Oh yes, bring me your pennies.'

Khetu brought over his stash of pennies and handed them over to his big brother. Ramhari counted them and saw they amounted to more than a whole rupee. He got a nice string of stonefruit rosary beads with fifty annas and returned the rest of the money to the boy.

Khetu said, 'Big Brother, what shall I do with this money? You better keep it.'

Ramhari replied, 'No, Son. This is not my money. It is yours. Give it to your mother, she will be very pleased.'

The day to return home drew closer. Hither in Khetu's heart and thither in his mother's there was no more space left for joy's bounty. The tussar and lead merchants were also homebound for the holidays. Ramhari let Khetu accompany them and wrote to his mother to inform her in advance of the date and hour at which he was scheduled to arrive.

Not at the Duttas' fishpond but Khetu's mother had gone way past that landmark to stand watch for Khetu. Catching sight of his mother from afar, Khetu, too, covered the remaining distance in a run and reached her. The two embraced, and Khetu's mother's heart was filled with heavenly pleasure.

Khetu said, 'Oh Mother, stop, Mother, let go. I have forgotten to touch your feet.'

The mother said, 'It's too late for that. I bless you all the same, live a long life and write from a golden inkpot with a gold pen.'

Khetu said, 'Mother, I had thought you would be waiting by the Duttas' fishpond. I did not expect you to come so far up the road.'

The mother said, 'My dear, had I the means, I would have gone up to Calcutta and collected you. Khetu dear, you have lost weight.'

Khetu answered, 'No, Mother, I haven't lost weight. I'm just tired from the journey, that's why I am looking pale. But, hark, Mother, I can walk so far now that you can hardly carry me the same distance.'

The mother said, 'That may very well be, my dear, but I will carry you the rest of the way.'

In his mother's arms, Khetu quietly tied his stash of pennies to the end of his mother's sari.

Perplexed, the mother said, 'Why, what's this? Khetu, have you tied pennies to my sari?'

Khetu laughed out loud and said, 'Hold on, Mother, let me do something to amuse you.' So saying, Khetu fastened the rosary around his mother's neck and said, 'See for yourself, Mother. I did remember my promise.'

The mother tapped his cheek and said, 'You are indeed a naughty boy.' At her remark, Khetu laughed again, and, this time, his mother joined him in laughter.

The next morning, Khetu found a little girl come from nowhere in the house. He asked his mother, 'Mother, who does this girl belong to?'

The mother said, 'Don't you know her? She is the youngest daughter of your Uncle Tanu. Her name is Kankabaty. Tanu Ray's wife comes here daily. I prepare the sacred thread, and she and I chat in the meanwhile. Sometimes, she leaves her daughter here with me. The girl amuses herself and never causes any trouble. She likes being here.' Tanu Ray is no relative of Khetu but a neighbour; it is only out of good manners does he address him as an uncle. Khetu called over to Kankabaty, 'Come now, come here.'

Kankabaty began tumbling forward in the direction indicated. Khetu said to his mother, 'Look, Mother, how she toddles.'

Khetu's mother said, 'The legs have not gained strength yet.'

Khetu produced a leaf and said, 'Here, take this.'

To accept the leaf, Kankabaty held out her hand and smiled.

Khetu said, 'Mother, see how she smiles!'

The mother answered, 'Yes, my dear. The girl smiles a lot and does not know how to cry. She has a fine disposition.'

Khetu said, 'Oh Mother, had I known she would be here, I would have brought a little doll for her.'

Khetu's mother said, 'Bring it down the next time around.'

Cat

When the holidays got over, Khetu left for Calcutta. Once there, he put all his attention into his lessons. Twice a year, when school closed for holidays, he visited home. That's when he would bring one or another article for his mother, plus a doll or a toy for Kankabaty. Kankabaty was always to be found with Khetu's mother, who loved her no end.

When Khetu turned twelve, he began giving lessons in private to a rich man's son. The boy's father paid him a monthly fee of five rupees.

Khetu handed Ramhari his first month's salary and then said, 'Big brother. From this month onward, you need not pay for mother's rations; just give her this money. I have come to learn of your debt, therefore, I took this initiative to earn it.'

Ramhari said, 'My dear Khetu, you have done well. Initiative, enthusiasm and courage are must-haves for every human being. I will send this money over to your mother. I will write her that you have earned it yourself. And tell everybody that our twelve-year-old Khetu is taking care of his family.'

The next time Khetu went home, he brought for his mother a wrap with the name of God inscribed all over it and for Kankabaty a little red sari. When she received her gift, Kankabaty was delighted. She ran to her mother to show off her new possession.

Khetu said to his mother, 'Mother, why don't we teach Kankabaty how to read and write?'

The mother said, 'What can I say, my dear? Tanu Ray is an unpredictable man. There is no telling what he is going to say.'

Khetu said, 'But what can he say, after all? So many girls go to school in Calcutta. It is no sin to go to school!'

The mother said, 'Let me speak to the mother of Kankabaty.'

When Tanu Ray's wife came over, Khetu's mother broached the subject. She said, 'Khetu says, "When I come home this time around, I will bring a book for Kankabaty and teach her to read from it." I told him, "Khetu, my dear, let it be. Perhaps, your Uncle Tanu will be annoyed."'

Tanu Ray's wife replied, 'Why should he be annoyed? It is the trend. Every girl nowadays reads books and wears blouses. Since we live in the hinterland, we don't get to know that.'

Tanu Ray's wife went home and told her husband, 'Khetu has come home. He has brought Kankabaty a red sari.'

Tanu Ray said, 'Khetu is a good boy. He is studious and diligent. He will be able to support his family. Only I hope he doesn't turn out to be foolish like his father.'

His wife said, 'Khetu has been saying the next time he comes home he will bring a book and teach Kankabaty to read from it.'

Tanu Ray said, 'Why should a woman learn to read? A woman has no use of learning.'

With no forethought, Tanu Ray uttered these words. But then he paused to reflect and he found that learning had a lot of merits. Most particular among them was that husbands today preferred wives who were literate. They respected these women and also valued them. Yet a woman's learning was supposed to be disallowed by the scripture. And if that were the case, Tanu Ray could not be seen to let his ward take lessons. So Tanu Ray began debating the scripture in his mind.

After much contemplation, Tanu Ray decided that though a woman was disbarred from learning as per scripture, this injunction applied to the three eons, Satya, Treta and Dvapar, but not for the ongoing Kali eon. What was done in past is banned in the present, one instance of it being human sacrifice or the Narmedh Yajna. Today if one performed it, one had to go to the gallows. Another instance was that if one went to sea today, one lost one's caste. This was why when Tanu Ray's mother was living and had once expressed a wish to go to Sagar, the confluence of the Ganga with the Bay of Bengal, he had refused to arrange the trip.

He had explained to his mother, 'Dear Mother, one should not travel to Sagar. Going to sea is proscribed. The scripture and the sea are not on talking terms with one another. It is sin to see the sea; it is also a sin to touch it. Why, Mother, will you spend money to buy a burden of sin to carry on your shoulders? Why, Mother, will you sacrifice your caste and family?'

At this point, Tanu Ray concluded that what was done earlier should not be done in the present. Thus what was not permissible in the past could conveniently be indulged in now. Since it was forbidden for women in the past to study the texts and scriptures, it was no longer a sin to do so in the present time.

In this way, Tanu Ray broke scripture and reformulated it. Once he had suited and finetuned it perfectly to his liking, he told his wife, 'I agree with Khetu's proposal. If he teaches Kankabaty to read a little, I do not have any objection.'

Tanu Ray's wife relayed this to Khetu's mother, and Khetu's mother, in turn, posted Khetu of the green light. When Khetu came over this time, he got for Kankabaty a copy of the *Varnaparichay Pratham Bhag (Introduction to Alphabets Part One)*. At first, Kankabaty was overjoyed at the opportunity to navigate her way through the world of books, but soon she realised that learning wasn't all fun and games. To her eyes all the letters seemed like one. She would say one letter when she meant another.

Khetu grew annoyed with Kankabaty. He said, 'Kankabaty! You are not teachable. You will remain an ignoramus all your life.'

Little Kankabaty burst into tears of pique. She said, 'What can I do if I can't remember it!'

Khetu's mother said, 'How can one scold a little child? They must be cajoled with sweet words. Come, dear, come sit by my side. You don't have to learn anything.'

Khetu said, 'Mother! Kankabaty spends all her time with Cat every day and night. Has she any time to spare for learning?' Cat was the name of Kankabaty's cat. Cat was loved and treasured, and never left little Kankabaty's side.

Kankabaty said, 'Old Aunt! I teach the alphabet to Cat. But Cat is as stupid as I am. Aren't you, Cat? The way Cat can't read, neither can I. I am a child, and so is Cat. When I grow up, I will learn to read, and so will Cat. Won't you, Cat?'

Khetu burst out laughing. He said, 'Kankabaty! Have you lost your mind?'

That may have been the case, but presently, Kankabaty completed reading *Varnaparichay Pratham Bhag*.

Khetu said, 'I will leave for Calcutta. I finished the *Pratham Bhag* in a hurry, did not go into detail. In these months, learn the book by heart. I will bring with me *Dvitiya Bhag* (*Part Two*) when I come again.'

Khetu came home again and then Kankabaty completed *Dvitiya Bhag*. She did not require lessons anymore. She began reading books on her own. Khetu had brought Kankabaty an arithmetic book, too. Kankabaty learned to solve sums from it. Only once in a while, Khetu would clear her doubts and answer her questions.

Kankabaty loved reading. Sitting in Calcutta, Khetu would send her various books and newspapers. Kankabaty would even read the advertisements on the newspapers.

The Brother's Wife

At age thirteen, Khetu passed his first state exam. Upon passing the exam, he won a scholarship. Upon winning the scholarship, Khetu appointed a domestic employee for his mother. Khetu's mother was by now advanced in years, and he did not wish for her to exert herself. He would also bring gifts and clothes and pitch in to help Ramhari's family.

When he was fifteen, Khetu passed another exam. The amount he received as scholarship got appended. At seventeen, Khetu passed yet another exam. His scholarship got appended once again. As Khetu began receiving money, he commenced to put it to use with the objective of eradicating his mother's hardship completely. Now, whenever his mother wished for anything, he would fulfil that wish. No longer did Khetu's mother want for any article or means.

Once, Khetu's mother had not been able to obtain flowers for Shiva's worship. When Khetu heard it, he planted a beautiful garden near her house. He brought over various plants from Calcutta and placed them in the soil. The garden would beam with flowers of every colour all twelve months of year.

By this time, Ramhari's daughter, Seeta, had turned seven. Since his mother lived alone by herself, Khetu obtained Ramhari's consent to send Seeta over to his mother. Khetu's mother was overjoyed with Seeta's company.

Kankabaty, too, enjoyed Seeta's company greatly. Every evening, the two girls would go to sit in the garden. Kankabaty no longer appears frequently before Khetu. She now feels shy in his presence. Yet she likes speaking of him and hearing stories of him. She is too shy to seek these from just anybody. Seeta is her source. In the evening, they go to the garden and string flowers to make garlands. They also fashion flowers into various ornaments. Kankabaty then makes Seeta wear those on her neck, wrists and head. In return, Seeta tells her stories of the various exploits of Khetu.

Khetu, on the other hand, has not forgotten Uncle Niranjan. Whenever he comes back to the village, he brings a gift for him. As is customary, Niranjan and his wife shower him with blessings. When Kankabaty grew older, Khetu would bring her other articles, too, aside from newspapers and books. The chemise and the petticoat, and the other women's wear in vogue in the city, Khetu would take them all home for Kankabaty's use.

Though Khetu had been pitching in to run Ramhari's household, Ramhari had not easily accepted his assistance. Once, Khetu had brought home for Narhari a pair of wraps for the legs and the body. When he learnt the news, Ramhari had told off Khetu. Khetu had been highly piqued at the reprimand. He did not say a word to Ramhari but took his complaints to his wife instead. As per convention, Khetu addressed her as Boudidi, meaning the sister who is also a bride.

Seeing Khetu's temper, Boudidi said, 'You could not stand up before your big brother and now you have brought the battle to me, haven't you?'

Khetu answered, 'Boudidi! You have reared me as a son. To you I must be the same as Narhari. If not, I am an outsider. In which case, there is no battle between us. Since Big Brother thinks so, you may follow suit. Say so, and there is no battle between us.'

The boudidi said, 'How can I say so, dear Khetu?'

Khetu answered, 'Of course, you can. And then I will stop looking for means to earn money. Neither will I speak to you or ask after your well-being. Nor will I live here anymore. I will think to myself, they saw my mother as a mendicant and gave her alms. My body, my bones and my flesh have all been constituted from alms only. I am not fit for polite society; I will no longer mingle with its members. The one whose body has been created from alms has no place to stand here.'

The boudidi said, 'Shame on you, Khetu! How can you say so? You may be my brother-in-law, but I love you as my own son. You are a suitable son; all will be as you decide, why fret and fume?'

Khetu said, 'To keep my mother happy and keep you happy has been my goal. Now that I have acquired the power and means to fulfil it, if you do not let me do so I will become demoralised.'

The boudidi said, 'Yours is a successful mother. I bless you, Khetu, with a pretty wife.'

That afternoon, Ramhari and his wife had a long talk. The wife said to Ramhari, 'Look here, my good man. Seeing our hardship, Khetu feels very sorry. He has now begun to earn for himself. He says, "Since they have reared me as a son, it is my duty to help them." If Khetu pitches in for the budget, do not refuse him. If you do so, he feels defeated.'

After giving an earful to his wife, Ramhari summoned Khetu. When the latter arrived, Ramhari said, 'Are you angry, dear brother? The world is a cruel place. When you reach my age you will know how people hanker for money and what they can do to get hold of it. That's why, Khetu, I had asked you not to put money into the running of our family. My hardship is never to end. We will never have the means to fulfil all our needs. Why should I make you party to that misery? It has been many days since I have had a full breakfast. When I fall ill, I fast to get better instead of seeing a doctor and buying syrups and pills. You are of tender age, is it right for me to share with you that sorrow? It's only for this reason I asked you not to spend money on our account. I did not think then that you carry the genes of your father within you. Dear Khetu, no words are sufficient to convey the greatness of his heart. He was just like a god, your father was, my Khetu. I bless you, little brother, so that you may become a god as he was.' Ramhari began shedding tears, and his wife, too, wiped her eyes with the end of her sari. Khetu blinked back his own tears.

Now that Khetu had passed three exams, those burdened with daughters began making rounds of Ramhari's doorsteps. Everyone wished for giving their daughter in marriage to Khetu. Someone said, 'I will give you gold and so much money.' Another said, 'I will give you property.' A veritable auction began in Ramhari's drawing room.

Ramhari explained to one and all that till the time Khetu finished his studies and began drawing a regular government salary he would not arrange his marriage to anybody.

But the fathers of the daughters would have none of that. They began begging Ramhari for Khetu's hand. In the end, Ramhari had had enough. He surmised, 'Let me give my word to someone, so that the others stop disturbing me.'

With this idea, he inspected a few prospective brides and settled on the daughter of Janmejay Bhattacharya. Janmajay was affluent and well-born. Yet Ramhari could not make a final promise in the matter. How could he, since he hadn't consulted Khetu's mother for her opinion?

The Match

As the years went by, Kankabaty grew more and more beautiful. Her beauty lit up the ten directions, and she dazzled so that one could not cast for long one's eyes upon her mien. Her skin was fair and luminescent, and radiance sprung forth from it: it gave one the illusion that if she drank one could spy the water pass down her throat. Her figure was not thin, nor fat, perfectly proportioned as it was like a doll's body. But her face was the best—and it was as if the great creator themselves had sculpted it with their own, personal hands. The nose was thin; the eyes were drawn up at the ends; the eyelashes long, lush and very dark. If she looked down, the shadows cast by the lashes made up a marvellous sight. Such a set of eyes would be well served by a pair of slim, dark and luxuriant eyebrows, and Kankabaty had been blessed with just those. Her cheeks were not full, yet they dimpled as she smiled. Upon seeing that spectacle, the worst enemy was disarmed. The lips were soft and full. Their owner need must not chew betel leaves to redden them; they were rosy always. When opened to speak, moon-white teeth were seen within, and they shone as pearls. Kankabaty had lavish curls, dark as the night; when let down the tresses covered her back. The front parting of her hair was as slender as if it had been drawn by a paintbrush. In short, then, Kankabaty is a true beauty; a crowd-stopper she is, verily, whom onlookers can never get enough of. When seen dashing around at playtime with other girls of her age cohort, she looks like lightning streaking through the courtyard.

Now that Kankabaty is older, she does not dash around as before. Yet one day, she had hurried home on a particular errand. Her face had turned pink with exertion, her skin glowed and the blood throbbed in her cheeks; in that moment in all the world, there was no one as beautiful as Kankabaty.

One look at her, and the mother said to Tanu Ray, 'Do cast a glance upon your daughter. Do not throw this golden goddess into the deep waters. Why, Kankabaty is Laxmi herself! Have you ever seen a girl with such propitious qualities as her? Find a Narayan to her Laxmi to wed with her. Heed my word, I beseech you, but this time around.'

Tanu Ray looked in the direction of Kankabaty, and his heart skipped a beat. Such had never occurred before, but he thought, 'Wherefore is this? Is this what is called filial love?' Tanu Ray refrained from commenting on his wife's words.

It was another day when Tanu Ray's wife did say to her husband, 'Mark my speech. The time has arrived for Kankabaty's marriage. But you must fulfil this entreaty of mine. Will a human life go by without the fulfilment of even one of its wishes?'

Tanu Ray said, 'Well, then, what is your wish?'

The wife said, 'My wish is that I spend my days in mirth and merriment with my daughter and son-in-law. You married two of my daughters, but that wish of mine was not fulfilled. Instead that became a constant source of grave sorrow. Be that as it may, now find Kankabaty a good husband. Her sisters, too, have said, "We have suffered what destiny has ordained; our solace lies tied to our kid sister's fate."'

Be it wife, son or daughter, none is dearer than money to Tanu Ray. Nonetheless, his heart stops beating whenever he remembers his youngest daughter. He does not know if it is born of affection or guilt. Indeed, to suddenly sacrifice his goddess of a daughter is something he rather dreads to commit to. And yet, his rapaciousness is indomitable. All this while he has been hoping to sell his enchanting daughter and make a tidy sum; how can he give up that dream completely? Today Tanu Ray swings on the horns of a dilemma. Never before has he been visited by such perplexity.

Having reflected for a while, Tanu Ray said to his wife, 'Fine! Say, I do not accept money in exchange of Kankabaty's hand in marriage. Yet, I cannot, in all rightness, let the other party have my money instead. Nowadays, it is hard to find a suitable boy in the market without dowry. So, I am left with little recourse.'

The wife responded, 'Oh yes? If I find you a suitable boy who will not accept dowry, will you marry Kankabaty to him?'

Tanu Ray asked her, 'Where is such a boy? What is his name?'

The wife said, 'Indeed, when one grows very old, one loses both eyesight and cognition. Haven't you seen the one who is right under your very nose?'

Tanu Ray said, 'Tell me yet who it is.'

The wife answered, 'Why, haven't you known Khetu?'

Tanu Ray said, 'How can that be? He has no powerful friends, neither connections, nor property. How can I place Kankabaty in the care of his family? Even if I don't accept money from him, I must, in the very least, assure myself that the girl will have a prosperous future wherein she gets to wear a few gold ornaments.'

Tanu Ray's wife replied, 'Do you think Khetu will never get ahead in life? Don't you yourself also say, "Khetu is a good boy, he will certainly take care of his family"? If it is so destined, Khetu himself will gift plenty of ornaments to Kankabaty. Yet I am not concerned about whether there will be ornaments or not. My wish is that the boy be a responsible one. Tell me, where on earth will you find a boy more suitable than Khetu? If my daughter is a genuine Laxmi, so is Khetu a rare husband. It is as if the great creator has fancied the two of them as two flowers on the same stalk.'

Tanu Ray said, 'Ah, well. We shall see that then. There is no hurry.' A few more days went by. Then, a letter arrived for Khetu's mother from Calcutta. She had Tanu Ray read it aloud to her. The letter had been written by Ramhari. It could be paraphrased in this fashion.

'Many gentlemen are calling on me asking for Khetu's hand in marriage. They have kept me on my toes. My plan is to marry Khetu only after he has completed his studies. Yet the fathers will not listen to me. They say, 'Let the bride be decided, we can wait for the ceremony.' I have inspected a few young women. Of them, I liked the daughter of Janmajaybabu. The girl is pretty, responsible and calm. The family is a reputable one. The parents and siblings are all present. The daughter's father is a prosperous man. He can conduct the ceremony with gifts for the groom and ornaments for the bride. If you convey your opinion to me, I will let him know my decision.'

For Tanu Ray, the letter was a huge surprise. The boy he had shunned as a match for his daughter, thinking him to be impecunious, was being sought after and wooed by one and all for the same station.

Khetu's mother wrote to Ramhari, 'I am a woman, why count my opinion? What you will shall prevail. Yet I had a wish. Now that I see it won't be fulfilled, it is pointless to express it.' Having received this letter, Ramhari informed Khetu of the matter and asked him how to proceed.

Khetu said, 'Big Brother, I do have an inkling of my mother's wish. Till the time there is a chance of it being fulfilled, do not promise my hand to anyone else.'

Ramhari said, 'Yes, that's the right thing to do. I will not give my word regarding your match to anybody.' Meanwhile, hearing that Khetu would be married to someone else, Kankabaty's mother fell apart. All day and night, she wept and complained before her husband.

Tanu Ray was seen vexed and apprehensive. He thought, 'I am an old man. I have to provide for two widows. My son, too, is an ignorant boor. I need someone who can take care of my family. Since Khetu is learned and responsible, he shall advance in life. Even if he cannot give me any money right away, I can take some from him every month at a later stage.'

With this mind, Tanu Ray said to his wife, 'I have no objection if you fix Kankabaty's marriage with Khetu. Only I will not be able to spend on the ceremony.'

Khetu's mother said, 'I have forever wished for Kankabaty as my son's bride. Yet, Sister, if you had spoken sooner, I would not have written to Ramhari to fix Khetu's marriage somewhere else. If he has done so, he will not break his promise. Oh dear, my heart fills with dread at the thought of it.'

Tanu Ray's wife said, 'My Sister, if only you give your consent, Khetu's marriage will be performed with none else but Kankabaty. Prepare a letter. I will have it couriered.' The next day, the two women sent a courier to Calcutta. Khetu's mother had written to Ramhari.

Khetu's mother wrote: 'My wish is that Khetu's marriage is performed with Kankabaty. Tanu Ray and his wife have approached me with the proposal. If you have not fixed

Khetu's marriage elsewhere, please write to Tanu Ray asking for Kankabaty's hand.'

Having received this letter, Ramhari, his wife and Khetu were delighted.

Ramhari put the letter in Khetu's hands and said, 'Your mother's wish is my command.'

Khetu said, 'So it is with mine. Yet there is no rush. It is well-known that Uncle Tanu raises his daughters to an older age than others before giving them in marriage. He can easily keep Kankabaty for another two or three years. In the meantime, I will complete my exams and avail my degrees. I will also get myself a job. Please write to Uncle Tanu and inform him of my intent.'

Ramhari complied and wrote Tanu Ray. Tanu Ray gave his consent. He was not unhappy in the least for the delay. On the other hand, he was gladdened.

He said to himself, 'It is only under pressure of my wife's tearful complaints that I gave my consent to Khetu's family. Let me see in the meantime if I can find a better match. If I do, I will think about it presently.' Khetu's mother had confided in Niranjan. 'Tanu Ray has discovered morality in his old age,' Niranjan said to himself.

Kankabaty had been gloomy in the past few days. That morning, everyone saw her sunny face. During the day, she took Cat aside and spent uncounted hours conferring with her. Cat is no longer a baby; she is a grown adult cat. It is no wonder then that Kankabaty would choose her to share with her all her deepest secrets.

Sandeshwar

On the way to Calcutta, days before the Durgapuja holidays were to commence, Khetu should meet whom else but Sandeshwar. Sandeshwar called, 'Hail Khetu! When will you make your trip home? I have arranged for a motor car to drive me home; if you like, you can accompany me on the ride.'

Khetu answered, 'As of now, my college has not closed for the pujas. It is not certain when I will depart.'

Sandeshwar said, 'Why, Khetu, what is that in your hand?'

Khetu said, 'That's a lion throne. My mother makes a Shiva out of clay everyday to worship it. So I have bought her a stone Shiva. This is the throne for the Shiva.'

Sandeshwar said, 'Oh, but do you have it with you? Show it.'

Khetu slipped the Shiva out of his pocket and handed it to Sandeshwar.

Sandeshwar smiled. 'Did you keep the Shiva inside your trouser pockets? It sure looks like you have a lot of piety,' he said ironically.

Khetu answered, 'It has not been worshipped yet, so there is no sin.'

Sandeshwar said, 'Since you say so.'

So saying, Sandeshwar returned the Shiva to Khetu's safe custody.

The two walked a few steps together. Then, Sandeshwar said, 'Why, here is the house of the padresahib. You are well acquainted with him, aren't you? Why don't we stop by and see him?'

Khetu and Sandeshwar went to see the padre.

After exchanging pleasantries and talking about the news, Sandeshwar said, 'Why, do you know, sire? To help his mother better worship her deity, Khetu has purchased a stone Shiva phallus. In this moment, he is carrying it in his pocket.'

The padre said, 'Why, Khetu! Is that true? What a shame! I would not have dreamed that you could do such a thing. Alas, all our efforts at opening schools for you and educating you for your benefit have gone in vain. Didn't a famous litterateur once write that Bengalis are a hypocritical, defrauding, cheating, cowardly race of slaves?'

Khetu said, 'Hark! How sweetly your teachings fall on my ears like heavenly nectar! It cools my body like the breeze in springtime. I wish to take the Christ's name and enter his kingdom right away. Do you have some holy water at home? Why delay? Bring it and baptise me. The way your ilk has cornered the Bengalis and has been showering them with your heavenly teachings, their minds are tender with devotion to Christianity. Wait no more to collect your blessings. Watch them about to receive the holy word one after another. And when they come to learn of your fraternal feelings towards your black brethren in America, and when your kindness to the unarmed African peoples comes to be known, not one living being will be left out of its reach, all will be Christians thenceforth. Have a good day.'

With these words, Khetu left the place. Smiling, Sandeshwar, too, accompanied him. As they walked, Khetu asked Sandeshwar, 'It is well-known that everyday you take part in songs of praises sung in the name of Hari, the Lord. Why then did you poke fun at me before the padresahib?'

Sandeshwar said, 'I really did not. Let that be, it is evening and time for the Hari paeans. Why don't you join us? You will be blessed even for attendance.'

Sandeshwar's rented accommodation was not far. The two young men reached there. Khetu saw that the paeans had begun on Sandeshwar's porch. Yet Sandeshwar did not stop and went straight to the sitting room. He asked Khetu to take a seat and proceeded indoors.

Presently, Sandeshwar returned and said to Khetu, 'Khetu, let's go to a different room.' Khetu entered a room upstairs and found two young men, friends of Sandeshwar, seated there. They were preparing to be served a feast.

Downstairs, the paeans were in full flow. Sandeshwar was a pillar of the Hindu religion and society in Bengali-speaking circles.

Soon, the feast began. Two Muslim waiters served it to them.

Khetu said, 'Why don't you enjoy your meal? I am off.'

Sandeshwar said, 'But tarry a while. Even your attendance counts as blessings. The broth we are eating is called a soup. Why don't you taste a little of it?'

Khetu said, 'These are foods I do not partake of. I never have any wish to partake of them.'

In a while, Sandeshwar said, 'Khetu, what I am eating now is the bekti fish. There is no sin in eating fish. Why don't you have a little of it?'

Khetu said, 'Mister! Don't you ask me to do so. Please have your meal. I will sit here.'

Sandeshwar said, 'In that case, please have a drink. This is good brandy. If the words of the padre had hurt your sentiments, it will take your grief away.'

Khetu said. 'Mister! I join my hands in entreaty. Please don't ask me to. Permit me to go home.'

Sandeshwar's friend then said, 'If that be the case, have a ham and chicken sandwich. This is not Indian pork. It has come from England. The rural pork is not eatable. It is no sin to eat foreign pork. And the chicken, too, is the great foul, the Lord's bird. It is bought from Hogg Market and is no ordinary chicken.'

Sandeshwar's other friend said, 'And now we shall have veal cutlets. I am sure Khetubabu will now have a bite.'

Let us talk no more of the dish brought in by the chef at this point. Downstairs, the paeans had reached their crescendo. Hear them and let peace be upon your souls.

Some time passed. Sandeshwar's friends brought their heads together and conferred in whispers. Then one of them caught hold of Khetu while the other made a bid to pour brandy down his throat.

Khetu was a powerful man. With a heave of his arm each, he felled the both of them. He upended the dining table and flung what utensils he could find, glasses and glass bowls, to the floor, breaking them. Leaving thus a trail of destruction behind him, Khetu left.

Three years passed in a jiffy. Khetu was twenty now. All the degrees and scholarships that were there to be won by anyone were picked up and collected by Khetu. He also won a few international degrees. Having done so, he felt he would soon achieve an important posting with the government.

Ramhari and his wife then supposed that the time had at last arrived to organise Khetu's wedding. To fix the date of the wedding, they wrote a letter to his mother.

The Broken Word

Replying to the mail, Khetu's mother asked after everybody's health and concluded saying, 'I have been unable to speak with Tanu Ray and set the date. He seems to be busy lately; he is hardly around. The zamindar, Janardan Chowdhury, has lost his wife. Janardan Chowdhury's wife is a fortunate woman. Leaving sons, grandsons and grandnephews all around her, with her head resting on her white-haired husband's lap, she did breathe her last. What greater prize for her good deeds can there be for a woman? When they were taking her away to cremate her, I went to bid her goodbye. Her head was covered with holy vermillion put there by relatives and neighbours. She had been dressed in a fine cotton sari with a bright carmine border. It was a dazzling sight. Be that as it may, as soon as Tanu Ray can spare me a moment, I shall speak to him.'

In a few more days, Khetu's mother wrote again. What she wrote could be paraphrased as follows:

'What I hear is terrible news. For Tanu Ray's word there is no guarantee. He has no compassion, nor a sense of the scriptures. I hear that he will marry Kankabaty to Janardan Chowdhury. What a terrible decision, I must say. Has Janardan Chowdhury, too, gone off his rocker, himself? Any which way one looks, his sons, grandsons and grandnephews are present. There is no count of how many years he has accumulated. With every step he takes, he shakes from side to side. His mien is that of a corpse lying in the cremation ground. Why should he harbour this evil wish? Does money and property have to induce one to behave as such? He may well be a rich man, a land shark, a king even. Does that have to mean that he has no use of judgement? Doesn't the old man stop to think that death is near? He cannot take a step but with the aid of stick. What a terrible idea! And what of Tanu Ray? Is he a devouring parent? How can he give away his innocent, milk-fed child to a shrunken, white-locked husband? Did Kankabaty have such a life partner written in her fate? My heart breaks to look upon her honey-sweet face. I hear her mother is weeping constantly. I had called her to come to my place. She did not. She said, "I have lost face. I no longer have the courage to stand before my big sister nor appear before other people. My heart is breaking at the thought of this marriage that I cannot prevent." She has the heart of a mother. I cannot imagine what it has gone through.'

Ramhari showed the letter to Khetu.

Khetu said, 'Big Brother, I will go to the village this very moment.'

Ramhari said, 'Janardan Chowdhury is a rich man. You are a boy without any help. What can you change by going to the village?'

Khetu said, 'Perhaps I cannot but taking no step is unconscionable. It is also about helping Kankabaty, who is in danger. What else must I do even if I fail?'

Khetu returned to the village. From his mother and neighbours, he informed himself. He was told that at first Janardan Chowdhury had not been agreeable. It was only his scholar-in-chief Gobardhan Shiromani who had so persuaded him.

Does it matter if Janardan Chowdhury is an old soul? He is charming and a romantic at heart. Rosary beads made of five-faceted stonefruit forever cover his neck and chest. He being phlegmatic, for the purpose of keeping away the cold, a peaked cap always rests atop his head. When, thus geared and outfitted, he sits aside with Gobardhan Shiromani and shares with him his confidences, the heavenly deities, Indra, Chandra, Vayu and Varun, all hide their face in shame at the sight of his exquisiteness.

Khetu was told Janardan Chowdhury had turned quite impatient to marry Kankabaty. He could bear to wait no more. The twenty-fourth day of the coming month of Baishakh had been assigned for the wedding. Janardan Chowdhury was counting the days to the date. His children's wish was that the marriage would not take place. Yet no one speaks up owing to lack of courage. Only the oldest daughter had taken the pains. Janardan Chowdhury no longer speaks to or of her.

To give Janardan Chowdhury his daughter, Tanu Ray, too, had had some early hesitance. However, when Janardan Chowdhury said, 'I shall gift the new bride shares worth ten thousand rupees, a taluka of land and gold ornaments covering her entire body, and I shall give her father two thousand rupees in cash upfront', Tanu Ray could not overcome his avarice. Even so, looking at Kankabaty's fair face, he had hesitated. But his son jumped at the chance of acquiring the money. He scolded his father until he gave his acquiescence. For the present, *both* father and son are crazed by Janardan Chowdhury's promise of money.

Nevertheless, Tanu Ray hadn't had the courage to break the news of his decision to his wife. Then the son said, 'Let it be. You don't have to intimate her of the news, I will.'

So saying, the son went to see the mother. He said, 'Mother, our sister will be married to Janardan Chowdhury. Our father has made arrangements for the wedding.'

It was as if a bolt of lightning struck his mother. She said, 'What did you say? Why, how can that be? Why, Janardan Chowdhury is an ancient man. There is no count of the number of years he has seen on earth. How can he be wedded to our Kankabaty?'

The son said, 'No doubt, he is old, isn't he? Why, would you have preferred a youth instead? Or would you have preferred a boy? Well, does Janardan Chowdhury suck his milk from cotton balls? Or, play with a rattle, say? It is as if our mother is a madwoman. Our mother doesn't see any sense. Kankabaty will get ten thousand rupees, gold ornaments for every part of her body, taluka and land; our father will get two thousand rupees on top of it, what else would you prefer to desire? When the old man dies, all of Kankabaty's money and jewellery will be ours. The groom's extreme elderliness is precisely the reason to rejoice. Had he been able and strong, there is no telling how long he would have lived. Oh, Mother, now you have no judgement, have you?'

There being no answer to this line of thinking, the mother fell to the ground. Tears flowed incessantly from her eyes down her breasts. 'Let the earth break asunder,' she imagined. 'Let me enter your bosom.' The two daughters, too, wept a copious amount, but the plan remained unaltered. Kankabaty was silent. How could the one shed tears whose heart burnt as a raging pyre?

Khetu heard this account from his mother and the neighbours.

Foremost of all, Khetu saw Tanu Ray. For a while, he reasoned with him. Then he said, 'Good sir. Do not marry Kankabaty to this ancient man. If you do not want to marry her to me, do not. But give her to a suitable man. If the kind sir cannot search for a suitable match, I will find one for him.'

Upon hearing his proposal, Tanu Ray and his son were enraged. Showering various abuses on him, they turned Khetu out of the mansion.

Khetu sought the company of Niranjan. Accompanied by him, he then went to the manor house of the zamindar.

Folding his hands in prayer before him, he humbly begged Janardan Chowdhury not to go through with the wedding. Initially, Janardan Chowdhury laughed away his entreaties. He began shaking in anger by the time Khetu had made a mentionor two of his advanced age. Being phlegmatic, his anger resulted in a tumultuous coughing fit. Everyone around him thought that he would asphyxiate and that would be the end of him.

In-between coughs, Janardan Chowdhury said, 'Why don't you take this boy by the scruff of his neck and throw him out of the house?' Having got his go-ahead, his cohorts ganged up on Khetu.

Khetu picked up Janardan Chowdhury's big wooden stick. To the gang of aides, he said, 'None of you must lay a finger on my body. If any of you so much as touch me, I will smash his head on the spot.'

Seeing his fearsome appearance, everyone present was overcome by terror. No one stepped forward to throw him out of the house.

Niranjan rose from his seat, consoled both parties and sent Khetu along his way. Khetu departed. But Janardan Chowdhury would hardly calm down and neither would he stop coughing. His whole body still shuddered with unspent anger, and coughs delivered a juddering impact to his substantial frame.

Said Gobardhan Shiromani, 'No, my dear Zamindar, who says you are old? Whoever calls you old is himself old.'

Sandeshwar happened to be on the spot. He said, 'Is it possible the boy had been under the influence? Did you see his eyes? They were red as hibiscus flowers.'

Niranjan said, 'Don't speak so. Whoever consumes liquor does so on their own responsibility. Everyone knows who drinks and who takes chicken meat. Don't cast false aspersions in others' name.'

Said Sandeshwar, 'Hear one, hear all. This gentleman says, "I take drinks and chicken meat." I will file against him a defamation suit in court. I will assure that his bones rot in jail.'

Gobardhan Shiromani then said, 'Whether Kshetrachandra drinks alcohol or does not is not in my knowledge. I do know, however, that he drinks the water of the foreign invader. Gadadhar Ghosh has seen him partake with his own very eyes.'

Janardan Chowdhury spoke then. 'What was that again?' he said.

Sandeshwar said, 'Gracious me! Does he take ice? Ice that is made of the blood of the cow by the British men? I see now that everyone is soon to lose their faith in no time. Alas, and alack! The Hindus are about to be extinct from the face of this earth. Oh, woe betide him.'

Niranjan said, 'Mr Sandeshwar! Reflect for a moment how Khetu's father had helped you when you were a lad. Do not try to harm him.'

Janardan Chowdhury said, 'Stop this idle chat at this very moment. Send for Gadadhar Ghosh.' The watchman ran out in search of Gadadhar Ghosh.

Gadadhar's Report

Gadadhar Ghosh reached the manor house. Joining his hands and turning them upwards, he then touched them to his forehead to greet the zamindar, then retreated to the far corner and sat on his haunches before the assembly.

The chowdhury said, 'How now, Gadadhar? What is this I hear now? What is it that was consumed by that chap, Khetaa, son of Shibchandra? What did you witness before your own eyes? What did you hear him say? What did you say to him yourself? Tell all, don't secret anything from the council of the village.'

Said Gadadhar, 'Sire! I am an unlettered man, not learned like yourself. I will narrate what happened before myself.'

He said, 'The other year, I had been in Calcutta. I had no place to put up, so I went to Ramhari's address. As I rested in his parlour that evening, I spied a man walk up the road with a pot on his head, emitting a strange cry. Hearing that cry, Ramhari's son ran out of the bedrooms and called out to Khetu, "Uncle! Uncle, where are you? The kulfi-seller goes by, please buy me a treat." Khetu got him two paise's worth of the sweet. I said to Khetu, "No, young master. I do not take kulfi." Ramharibabu's son then asked after Khetu, "Uncle, won't you have some?"

'Said Khetu, "No, my dear. I am thirsty, it does not quench thirst; I will directly take some ice instead." So saying, Khetu exited the house. Presently, he returned with an object that looked like a white stone knotted in his cotton towel. He broke that stone to pieces and put them in water. Then he drank it all.

'I asked him, "Young master, what is that object?"

'Said Khetu, "This is ice. When one is thirsty on a hot summer day, one can put this in his water to cool his drink."

'I asked him, "Young master! Does it mean you can put any glass in water for the purpose of cooling it?"

'Khetu replied, "This is not glass, it is ice. It comes about when you freeze water. It is no different from the water you find in the river, it's only frozen, that is all. It is the same as the hailstone that falls from the sky. The British prepare it in their ice-maker machines. Come now, hold it in your hand and see."

'Without giving me a chance to decline, he then placed some on my palm. As soon as he did, I felt as if my palm was being sawed in half. Try as much as I did, I could not keep it on my palm and dropped it on the ground. Khetu said, "Gadadhar! Try having some of it now. There is no sin in eating ice."

'Said I, "Young master! You have learnt to read the English language, you must eat all kinds of food; there is no sin for you in so doing. Yet I have not read the alphabet. If I take a product made by the British with their machines, it will go against my faith, and I will lose my caste."'

Addressing the chowdhury, Gadadhar again said, 'My Lord! I have said to you what I have seen. Next, Khetu asked me many questions about the old times, we spoke at length about the old ways, but it will be of little import to mention them.'

Janardan Chowdhury said, 'Be assured it will not. Tell me all. Do not keep any secret.'

Addressing Gobardhan Shiromani, Gadadhar said, 'Master Shiromani! It is about those cloth merchant brahmins. Should I go on?'

The shiromani said, 'It is loose talk. You don't have to go into that detail.'

But Janardan Chowdhury said, 'Be assured that I need to hear all the words that were exchanged between Khetaa and yourself. I have heard of the account of the cloth merchant brahmins, indeed, everyone in the village knows their story. Nevertheless, I wish to know what Khetaa enquired of you and how you responded to him.'

Said Gadadhar: 'Well, then, next Khetu asked me, "Gadadhar! Is it true that in the olden days men were killed on our moor? And that you were one of the leaders of that band of brigands?"

'I replied, "Young master! Many an indiscretion have I committed in my juvenescent years. Is there any point in harking back to them? There isn't. The Company's stringent rules are observed everywhere today."

'Khetu said, "You are right, Gadadhar. Nonetheless, I desire to know more about the thuggees of the old days. Since you performed those acts with your own hands, you can give me a first-person account. Hence I ask of you this question. There is only a handful of old men like you living today, when you are gone, these stories will die with you. Consider, too, that your being a leader of that gang is an open secret."

'I replied, "Young master. In the presence of your kind, how can we be the leader of any project. You are brahmins, and our lords and masters. You are the leaders of any and every project."

'Khetu asked me, "In that case, who was the leader of your gang?"

'I said, "Sir, the name of our leader was Mr Kamal Bhattacharya. Since he was our colleague, we called him by his first name. He is dead today."

'Khetu then asked me, "Well, Gadadhar, has your gang ever killed a brahmin?"

'Said I, "It was our protocol to bump off anyone we found in the middle of the moor. There was no sin in doing so. We could not very well make our introductions and ascertain the antecedents of our victims before we targeted them. That's not the way to do the job. We had to finish them off first. Subsequent to that, we would find a sacred thread and decide if they were a brahmin, or fail to find one and label them to be from the Shudra caste. As for the loot, it depended on what had been lotted by the fates for us on the day. Many an unfortunate traveller we have murdered but not received a penny's worth for our effort. Not from the pouch fastened to the drawstring, nor in the recesses of the groin, neither in the pleats of their dhoti. Those fellows were gamblers, wicked and fallen. If they have to cover great distances, they ought to carry some money! Yet they had been walking empty-handed. Pray, tell me, young master, what an injustice to have done so on their part! Was it so easy to kill a human being? By going empty-handed they put paid to all our hard work.

'Still Khetu asked me, "Really, Gadadhar! Do people die hard? Is it not easy to kill a person?"

'I answered: "Everyone is not the same. Some die as soon as the stick strikes their head. There are some others who will take three to four blows, or even up to fifty of them. There was an occasion when it had been really hard to kill a brahmin."

'Khetu said, "How so?"'

At this point, Gobardhan interjected. He said, 'Master Chowdhury! Why listen to such sinful natter! Let us confer upon what to do with Kshetrachandra. Having drunk the water of the British masters, no doubt he is now one of them.'

Still Janardan Chowdhury said, 'Be assured I would like to informed of the whole conversation. If he hadn't any evil intention, why else would the bloke ask Gadadhar so many queries?'

Gadadhar began speaking again, 'Khetu asked me why it had been hard to kill the brahmin. Said I, "Young master, it so happened that three cloth merchants had appeared from somewhere to sell garad, or white silk, in our village. They were brahmins, all three of them. They could not find a boarding place and had been roaming the streets of the village. I chanced upon them, when I was walking the streets with a leaf in my hand, looking for a brahmin to collect the dust oftheir feet. I do not take a sip of water before tasting the dust of a brahmin's feet each morning. When I saw the brahmins, I collected the dust, and I said, "Come to my home, I will give you space to stay.' They put up in my residence. They stayed in our village for three days, sold their ware, made a whole lot of rupees. I gave their lead to Kamal. 'All three must be knocked off,' Kamal and I decided. We did not breathe a word to the other members of the gang or else we would have to share the prize. I said to Kamal, 'Go to the moor ahead of me and hide yourself. At the crack of dawn, I will take these men there myself. Once on the moor, together, we will hit them.' The next morning, I took the brahmins to the moor, accompanying them on the pretext of seeing them off and guiding the way. That it had been a foggy dawn had been sheer providence. The Almighty had been so merciful that one could not even see the face of the one in their lap. When we reached the appointed spot, Kamal came out of his hiding and struck one of the brahmins with his stick on the head. I, too, struck the other on the head with mine. The both of them fell to the ground. The third brahmin took off while we were busy terminating them. Kamal went after him. I stayed back to finish my job and then followed suit. The brahmin re-entered the village.

'Reaching Master Shiromani's house, he cried, "Ahoy! A brahmin is murdered anon. Save from murder this poor brahmin", and took his refuge. Tenderly, Master Shiromani took him in his arms and rested his head on his chest. Ever so gently in his ear he whispered, "Life is fragile and it is transient. It is but a drop of water on the lotus leaf. On account of that life, why are you so desperate, honey?" So saying, he raised the brahmin in both his arms, dropped him out the door and closed it with a resounding bang. Kamal chased the brahmin back to the moor.

'When he saw that there was no recourse, that Kamal was about to catch hold of him, the brahmin suddenly turned around and pounced upon Kamal. The two men were locked in mortal combat for a while. But Kamal was as mighty as an elephant, so the brahmin could not overpower him. Kamal felled him to the ground and delivered blow upon blow to his head.

'Yet that brahmin-lord's spirit was so resilient that he would not die, nor lose consciousness. "O Madhusudan, save my life. O Madhusudan, save my life," he repeatedly cried out. I had fallen back in the chase and lost my way in the thick fog. I hadn't been able to make out which way the brahmin had fled, nor discern Kamal's trail. Now, hearing those cries, I ran in the direction whence they came from. Presently, I came upon the brahmin lying on the ground, with Kamal on top of him. Both his arms were pinned down by Kamal's one of whose feet rested on the ground below them. The other was planted on the brahmin's belly and Kamal was trying to force his big toe into the brahmin's navel. From his position on the ground, the brahmin was letting out loud exhortations.

'Seeing me appear, Kamal said, "What a lowly brahmin bloke this is! This bloke does not die at all, does he? Gadadhar, quick! Do something at once. Or else, people will come running hearing his cries." I had lost my stick, but a big stone lay nearby. With the help of that stone, I crushed the brahmin's head. That's when he died. Whatever it was, it had been hard work killing the brahmin, but the pickings from that operation made it worthwhile. We obtained a lot of money and a load of silks. How Nishiram Sardar, leader of a different gang, came to know of the job we do not know of. He demanded hush money. We said, "Since you did not take part in it, why should we give you any?"

'The argument had escalated into a dispute between Kamal and Nishiram. As per custom, Kamal tore his sacred thread and spelled a ritual curse on Nishiram. Kamal Bhattacharya was a brahmin. His curse was not to fail. In five or seven years, Nishiram vomited blood and passed away. Whatever it was, from that loot of silks, we had gifted a pair to Master Shiromani. When Master Shiromani walked the road wearing the cloth, with the wrap swung from his shoulder and the sacred mark adorning his forehead, everyone said, "Behold, there goes the god of love." Who would not then take the pleasure of gazing at his pulchritude. Am I not right, Master Shiromani?'

Master Shiromani said, 'Gadadhar! Gadadhar! You should not utter such words. I know not of what you say, so I can't corroborate your account. Your pains have robbed you of your senses; I will offer basil leaves to Narayan on your behalf. Then your sins will be expiated.' Niranjan had been listening to the discussion, and he had been sighing and murmuring, 'Dear Madhusudan! Dear, gracious lord, friend of the humble.' Janardan Chowdhury was silent for a while; then he said, 'And what happened next, Gadadhar?'

Gadadhar answered, 'That is nearly all. Khetu was quiet; then, forgetful, he asked, "Will you have a little ice,

Gadadhar?" Said I, "No, young master. I will not have ice. If I do, I will go against my faith, and lose my caste."'

Janardan Chowdhury said, 'So you are certain that Khetu has taken ice himself?'

Gadadhar replied, 'Yes, my lord. I have seen it with my own dear eyes. You are the divine brahmin. I could swear it touching your holy corpus.'

Delirium

Hearing Gadadhar's account, Janardan Chowdhury proceeded to send for Tanu Ray and other gentlemen of the village.

When all arrived, Janardan Chowdhury said, 'Today, I have been unfortunate to learn of the great damnation that is only about to visit us. Our castes, clans, religion and deeds will soon become extinct. Even for serving our forefathers in heaven two palmfuls of water there is no means left. The most intense Kaliyuga is upon us.'

Whereupon all said, 'Wherefore, Master?'

Janardan Chowdhury replied, 'It is Shibchandra's son, that bloke called Khetaa, the one who stays at Ramhari's residence in Calcutta and studies the English language. He eats ice. Ice made by the British, the water of the British themselves. Can you beat that? Master Shiromani has decreed that whosoever takes ice, and whosoever associates with the British or with people having British ways, becomes British themselves. Having associated with Khetaa, we all stand the risk of turning Britons.'

Having heard this pronouncement, the entire village ducked their heads under their palms and fell to their haunches in the deepest of despair. 'What perdition! Oh no! What damnation! Eating ice? For sure, we will all lose our religion and our castes!' went the cries on all sides.

Sandeshwar was indeed the most worried of the lot. Though he did not break into loud lamentations, his religious sentiment was in tatters. On many an occasion did he express his regret through various phrases and exclamations.

Whatever sense it might have made to the reader, the fallout was this: the village consensually ostracised Khetu; he became an outcast, a one-family parish. Only Niranjan disagreed with the villagers. Let it be a two-family parish then, he opined.

But Niranjan spoke more. He said, 'Master Chowdhury! Having witnessed what I have since morning, I indeed agree with you that the most intense of Kaliyuga is verily upon us. Today I heard of terrible murders of brahmins and men. Master Chowdhury! You are ancient, learned and Lakshmi's blue-eyed boy. Towards you, destiny is gladly disposed. This conspiracy does not behove you. There is no valour in robbing anyone of their caste; it is one's duty to rescue the fallen instead. It is because the lord, Vishnu, saves the sinners that he has been called Patitapavan, purifier of souls, by the grateful multitudes. In the mortal world, gentlemen are the manifestation of his Patitapavan form. Yet little does one expect the likes of Sandeshwar who is immersed in drink and toxic pleasures, Tanu Ray who is tainted by the charging of levy on his offspring and Gobardhan who has committed the sin of sins of murdering a brahmin—hardly does one hope for these molten worms from hell's inferno to appreciate the true meaning of dharma.'

When Niranjan left, Gobardhan Shiromani said, 'The peer just abused our young lord Sandeshwar, yet our young lord Sandeshwar is a valiant man. No one can reside in this village having slighted our young lord Sandeshwar.' To amplify the news of the ostracisation of Khetu, Janardan Chowdhury began to host a monthly funeral for his departed wife to which were invited the society heads of seven villages. Word spread like wildfire that Kshetra, the son of Shibchandra, resident of Kusumghati, took ice and converted to the Christian faith.

That night, Sandeshwar got four bottles of drink made from fermented mahua fruit. He secretly ordered chicken meat to be cooked at Tareef Sheikh's home. Then he collected four friends, and the five of them enjoyed the feast merrily. Only once was the merriment interrupted; it was when it had occurred to Sandeshwar that Tareef Sheikh might have put ice in the meat. He had put up his hands, and said, 'I could not finish my meal. I shan't consume meat with ice and lose my caste, shall I?' Everyone had reasoned with him saying the meat had not been prepared with ice. Only then had he returned to his meal. After the feast, everyone went to Niranjan's and, secreting their persons in the dark, cast upon his house cattle bones and stones. Thus it was every night that Niranjan's house began to be showered with cattle bones and stones. Driven out of their wits, a weeping Niranjan and his wife left their ancestral abode.

Khetu said, 'My dear Uncle! Do not fret. I will join you shortly.'

The maid who worked for his mother resigned thereafter. She said, 'My lady! How can I be with you any longer? The others won't accept water from my hands.'

There were other ways Khetu's mother was tormented. At whichever hour she went to the riverside to take her bath, she found herself alone. The womenfolk kept a vigilant distance, whispering about her and covertly ogling, lest they accidentally touch her or she them.

One day, the widow of Kamal Bhattacharya, the man spoken of by Gadadhar, said to Khetu's mother, 'Dear, if one knows how to take care, one is not spoken ill of. If one knows how to stay, one need not leave either. Since your son has taken ice, you have lost your caste. What have we done to merit the same? Why destroy the power of our good deeds? You, for instance, I have seen for myself prefer no other spot but this. The other day, you ascended the steps with your precious clay pot nestled in the crook of your arm and drops from your hair fell on me. I had to throw away the water pot I had got for myself paying three full pice and, on top of it, take a fresh bath. What have we done to you, my dear, that you are after our peace?'

Khetu's mother did not reply to her query. Weeping, she made her way home.

Khetu said, 'Mother, do not cry. We won't stay here for long. We will leave the village.'

Khetu's mother said, 'Dear, I do not hurt from the utterances of those unfortunate souls. Yet, I look upon your face and my heart burns in my chest in sorrow. You do not eat, neither do you rest. You aren't at peace even for a moment. Your body is thin and your face pale. For my sake, at least, be at peace yourself.'

Khetu said, 'Oh Mother, tarry another seven days. Today is the seventeenth of the month. On the twenty-fourth, Kankabaty's wedding will be hosted. That day, my hope will be uprooted. That is the day we will leave the village forever and ever.'

Khetu said, 'The daughter of the Dases told me it is difficult to recognise Kankabaty nowadays. Her beauty has vanished, so has her colouring and the brilliance of her smile. Oh dear! Yet she is unhappy for her mother's sake. The poor dear is occupied by her mother's unhappiness, forgetting her own sorrows! It is Kankabaty's mother who weeps all day and Kankabaty who consoles her.

'They told me that Kankabaty says to her mother, "Mother, do not fret. If the father stands to gain by selling a handful of my bones, then so be it. There are many such bones seen lying about on the cremation ground. Who pays to take them? If my bones are valued thus, and the father and brother get to live well on that account, why should we not be pleased about it, Mother? Yet Mother, I have become weak lately, and listless. I pray I do not die in the next few days. If father does not get his due and I die nonetheless, he will be angry with me. I will be ash, but he will be berating me whenever he thinks of me."'

Khetu's mother then said, 'I do not disclose to you what I hear of Kankabaty. I fear you will become impatient and act in undue haste. Yet, what I hear of her state, she will not live long in it.'

Khetu said, 'Mother! I said to Tanu Ray, "Master Ray! You do not have to marry Kankabaty to me, but marry her to a suitable groom most definitely. Brother Ramhari and I will find a wealthy groom for her. Yet, Mother, Tanu Ray did not hear me; he abused me and sent me on my way. However, we do not stand to lose, Mother, for we will go and stay in a different village. But what of Kankabaty? Her fate will be sealed, and that is my regret. That I could not be a man and find a recourse, that is my regret too. Mother, if you hear any news of Kankabaty, do share it with me, do not keep it secret. Oh how I wish I had not sent Seeta back to Calcutta at this critical hour. Had she been around, she would have given me correct daily updates.'

Presently, Khetu's mother said to Khetu, 'I hear that Kankabaty is in high fever today. Oh dear! That she will fall ill out of worry is only to be expected. I only hope her life is saved, the poor darling. Janardan Chowdhury has sent the *kabiraj* to her with strict instructions: In four days' time, Kankabaty should be well.'

Khetu said, 'Now what, Mother! All we can wish for is that her life is saved. Mother, if Kankabaty's Cat comes by, please feed her well. Give her all the milk and the fish. For, when we go, Mother, Cat won't come with us, will she? She will prefer a rich man's residence, will she not, Mother? Then she will forget all about us.'

The mother did not reply to Khetu. She only wiped her eyes with the end of her raiment.

Thus, day by day, did Kankabaty's illness build up. Seven days passed and it was time for her marriage.

That was the day when Kankabaty's body broke out in hives and itched with shame. Her thirst was massive and unassailable. She could not rise from the bed. Every illness visited her. She was deeply delirious. Kankabaty had no sense, no consciousness. She recognised none. Every single individual moment could well be her last.

PART TWO

The Boat

Oh, the hives, the thirst!

Said Kankabaty to herself, 'Let me go to the river, sit on the steps leading down to it, drink by the bellyful and pat water on my integument. Perhaps then I will obtain some relief.'

Seated by the river, Kankabaty was massaging water onto herself when a little voice piped up, 'Who sits there? Is it Kankabaty?' Kankabaty looked about her, but did not see anybody. There was none to be found. Unable to see anyone, she could not decide who it was that had spoken. All she saw was a *kaatla*, a carp, sinking in the water at a distance and then floating to the surface.

Someone spoke again, 'Who sits there? Is that Kankabaty?'

This time, Kankabaty answered the voice, 'Yes, my dear, I am Kankabaty.'

The voice said again, 'Has your body broken out in hives? Are you enormously thirsty?'

Kankabaty replied, 'Yes, my dear. I have hives. I have a great thirst.'

Someone said again: 'In that case, why don't you come to the middle of the river? In the middle of the river is a cold chamber, if you enter it, your thirst will be quenched and your body soothed.'

Kankabaty returned back, 'Yet the middle of the river is far away. How can I reach it?'

The voice said, 'See the fisherman's boat. Why don't you sit on it?' Kankabaty went and sat on one of the boats belonging to the fishermen.

In that very moment at home, her family missed her. 'Where did Kankabaty go? Where did Kankabaty go?' A quick search started. Someone said, 'Hallo there! We saw Kankabaty walk in the direction of the riverbank.'

Kankabaty's relatives gathered that to escape her marriage with Janardan Chowdhury she had run away. In order to persuade her to return, first of all, her eldest sister ran towards the riverbank. Upon reaching there, she spotted Kankabaty seated on a boat and gliding away. The sister called:

Kankabaty, sister dear, come now, return,
I am your older sibling, don't you love me in my turn?
Three sisters are we, two of us widows,
Kankabaty, being the youngest, you are precious the most.

Sat in the boat, Kankabaty rejoined:

Below the waves I have been told to assume
There's a blissful, peaceful, underwater room.
There's where I am headed, my sister, don't stop me pray:
Away, Kankabaty's little boat, away, away.

At these words, Kankabaty's little boat slid into deeper waters.

Next, the brother arrived and entreated Kankabaty:

Kankabaty, come back home, don't spoil your family name.
Your father is enraged and he will say the same.
You are but a girl, what do you know of society's more;
Come back home, my dear, do not tear his heart apart and make this sore.

Kankabaty reparteed:

What you say, dear brother, I know not about;
I am on fire, I can't put it out.
Be a king, my brother, I bless you, go your way:
Away, Kankabaty's little boat, away, away.

Sooner than she had said these words, Kankabaty's boat swung farther down the river.

Then Kankabaty's mother arrived. She said:

Little goddess Kankabaty, come home to me,
Your mother's heart weeps, don't make her wait for ye;
The rice grains harden, the curry goes stale,
Having fasted for seven days, my darling Kankabaty is frail.

But Kankabaty made this revert:

So much thirst, Mamma, nary can I bear,
My body is ablaze as a paddy husk fire,
Mamma, I go to put it out if I may,
Away, Kankabaty's little boat, away, away.

And Kankabaty's boat sashayed some more yards away on the distant waters. The father came and addressed her:

> Kankabaty, come home, you are about to be wed,
> Come home and survey the arrangements made;
> Much gold you will don, and a satin blouse,
> The figure you will receive is that I cannot pronounce.

Kankabaty said to her father:

> No use have I of cowrie, satin and jewels,
> Alack, I burn in a flame most cruel;
> Release from the pain, father, is what my soul craves
> Down, Kankabaty's little boat, go down under the waves.

And like a small stone, Kankabaty's boat sank on the very spot, leaving no ripples in its wake.

Underwater

Kankabaty sank with the boat and went underwater. Down and down she descended, traversing a great distance. The fish in the river gathered to watch her fall. A hue and cry ensued—Kankabaty has arrived.

The *rohu* said, 'Kankabaty is here.'

The *punte* said, 'Kankabaty is here.'

Everyone did say, 'Kankabaty is here.'

Slowly, Kankabaty arrived at the spot where all aquatic

animals had collected, gazing unblinking to see her entry. Everyone welcomed Kankabaty.

Everyone said, 'Come on, Kankabaty. Come hither. Take your place.'

The children of the fish said, 'We want Kankabaty to be our playmate.'

The old *kaatla* grandmammy rebuked them. 'This is no time for Kankabaty to play,' she remonstrated. 'Seeing the poor dear suffering so from hives, it was I who called her over from the riverbank. Just for my sake, what a distance she has travelled. Her face has paled in exhaustion. Come, my dear, come sit with me. Rest a little, then the rest can be figured out at length.'

Kankabaty approached the *kaatla* and sat by her side.

Whilst Kankabaty rested, the aquatic animals called a big conference with much pomp and splendour. Seeing as the tapasvi fish wore a beard, he was voted the chairman. There was a long debate regarding what to do with Kankabaty. After countless speeches had been made, the sly baata fish proposed, 'My dear brothers, let us make Kankabaty our queen.'

The proposal went down swimmingly. The hall broke into loud cheers.

The joy, thereafter, in the fish community was limitless. They said, 'Dear brothers, if Kankabaty is the queen, we will have no more worries. If someone fastens us to their rod, Kankabaty will cut the line. When the fishermen cast their nets, Kankabaty will pass her knife through them. When Kankabaty is queen, there will be nothing to fear. Let us all now go to Kankabaty and say to her, "Kankabaty, you have to be our queen."'

Said Kankabaty, 'I cannot be your queen at this moment. I have become weak, my heart is sick to boot. Therefore, I cannot be your queen at this moment.'

Then Grand Lady Kaatla said, 'Have you prepared her royal robe? If she doesn't get a robe, why should Kankabaty want to be queen?'

Hearing her suggestion, the fish said, 'Now, now, we see. Without a royal robe Kankabaty will nary be a queen. A rosy gown, a dress fit for a memsahib, will make her change her mind.'

Kankabaty answered, 'No, my dears. I don't wish for a rosy gown. I don't fancy clothes and jewellery. I only wish to be left alone so I can shed my many tears.'

But the fish did not heed her words. A huge commotion arose. At last, Kankabaty grew tired of the commotion and she said, 'Alright. I will be your queen now. What is it that I have to do?'

The fish said, 'Is that all you ask? Why, that's simple. You have to go to the tailor's house, give them your measure and wear your outfit.' Everyone then told the green crab, 'Green Crab sire! You can walk both on land and water, and are an intelligent animal. When you bat your eyelids, the glow of your intellect shines forth from your eyeballs. Take Kankabaty with you and go to the tailor's abode. Give the tailor the correct measurements and tell him to use the best fabric. Take the bundle of mohur loaded on the back of the tortoise. Money is no matter, give the tailor what he asks for but make sure the gown is exquisite.'

The green crab replied, 'No doubt, I will go. If Kankabaty gets a pretty gown, who shan't rejoice at it? If our queen is not well turned out, it is our repute that will be at stake. While you load the mohur on the tortoise's back, let me make a quick trip home. I will put on my Sunday best, part my hair and comb it to one side nicely.' The mohur was loaded onto the tortoise's back. In that interval, the green crab put on his best suit, combed his hair and arrived looking all sharp and ready to go forth and win the world.

The Royal Vestment

There was no recourse left for Kankabaty except to oblige the others and depart in their company. Master Crab led the team, with the tortoise bringing up the rear and Kankabaty forming the middle rank. First they traversed the waterways; then they walked on land a great distance. Over the hills and mountains they went, and over forest and woodland, until they arrived right at the tailor's doorstep.

Scissor in hand and spectacles perched on his nose tip, the old tailor was stitching fabric when he looked up from his work and spied some figures descending the mountain trail. 'Who might these customers be?' he wondered to himself. When they drew nearer, he recognised some of them.

'Hail Brother Crab,' the old tailor greeted.

'Hail Brother, are you well?' the crab returned.

The tailor said, 'What can I say! We are so old that all will be well only when we go to our graves. Yet you are a man about town and nattily dressed. For you, it is by no means the same. Tell me, my dear man, what brings you to my place?'

The crab replied, 'See Kankabaty here? We have made her our queen. For her coronation, we need a new dress.'

The tailor responded, 'Really? Well, I have many beautiful dresses. I have some made from the famous Patna burlap. It is a bright carmine whose colour will not run, and it will not tear seeing as I have basted it all over. If your queen Kankabaty is *semal* cotton, let her wear it; it will well behove her. It won't be too hard on your pockets either. Now, have a feel, won't you, and tell me if your queen is *semal* cotton or not?'

With its walking legs, the crustacean probed Kankabaty's body, then looked at the tailor and returned the verdict, 'Indeed, she is not as soft.'

Kankabaty interjected, 'Are you all planning to put me in a burlap case and make a pillow out of me? Didn't you just decide to make me queen? In that case, why are you all plotting to make me pillow?'

The tailor piped up: 'Really? Doesn't this little girl have a big mouth on herself? Do you want to be a bolster then that you refuse to be a mere pillow?' Hearing the tailor's heartless words, Kankabaty burst into tears.

Master Crab spoke. 'You are but a child. Please don't speak unless you are spoken to. We are doing what's best for you, so be quiet and watch us. Be quiet, for you mustn't cry.'

Saying these kind words, Master Crab took out one of his spiny legs and wiped Kankabaty's face for her. Kankabaty's face got lacerated from the spines.

The old tailor said, 'Really. I don't have a dress for her. I know not how to design that dress; neither do I know how to stitch it.'

The crab said, 'Then what is to be done? Where do I get a pretty dress?'

The old tailor said, 'Don't worry. Why don't you go to the khalifa who is a good craftsman? He has many different kinds of fabric, too, wearing which the flat-faced can grow a nose on themselves.'

These words angered Master Crab very much. He said, 'Are you laughing at me then? Maybe you have a long nose. Maybe I have a shorter one. Is there anything to laugh about that?'

The old tailor said, 'Not at all, not at all. Little do I have such temerity. Why, there's nothing wrong with your nose, is there? That it cannot be seen is regretful indeed.'

The pleasantries calmed Master Crab who said, 'You are right, indeed! My nose is fine, only that it cannot be seen. Where it is at even I can't find myself. Yet, had it been visible it would surely have been praised by one and all. It would surely have been said, "Oh what a beautiful, flute-shaped nose." The poets would have sung the ode, "Sesame flowers are a-sprout, behold this snout. It is the very beak of the shuk." You may say what you like, but I certainly do have a beautiful nose.'

Kankabaty said to herself, 'What is the matter with him? I see that I have landed in the clutches of madmen. This one should certainly be locked in a loony bin.' Yet Kankabaty refrained from speaking aloud her thoughts.

The trio began their trek again. Master Crab was in the lead, Kankabaty in-between and the tortoise was the rear. Thus walked the three. They walked a great distance. Upon reaching the khalifa's home, they learned that he was in his inner quarters.

'Khalifasahib, Khalifasahib,' Master Crab called from outdoors.

From indoors came a voice, 'Who calls?'

Master Crab answered, 'This is Crabchandra. Please step out for a moment, I have come on a special commission.'

The khalifa appeared. Seeing Crabchandra, he welcomed him heartily. The khalifa said, 'Welcome, Crabbabu. Hail Tortoisebabu and welcome to you. Why don't you sit on this stool; and Crabbabu take this chair. Oh where do I seat this girl? She is very easy on the eyes, Crab, is this your chattel then?'

Crabchandra answered, 'Oh no, she isn't, for I haven't tied the knot. I have come here on her behalf. We have made her our queen and we need a royal gown. That is what brings us here. You must sew a beautiful royal gown for her.'

The khalifa replied, 'Perhaps, I could sew a royal gown. I have silks, furs and satin, and I have kingkhap from Benaras. Yet it is not easy to prepare a queenly raiment. One must sew diamonds to the fabric, and pearls, too, and embroider it with zari and lace. A lot of money it will take to make. Will you be able to provide it?'

Crabchandra smiled and said, 'What financial stress do we suffer from? None. For, the money from boatwrecks and ship capsizes all come to us by rights. You only mention the amount you would like to charge.'

The khalifa replied, 'If you can give me two bunches of currency, I can prepare a majestic garb of excellent quality.'

The crab picked up two pouches of mohur from the tortoise's back and dropped them before him. For many a king, gentleman and bridegroom had the khalifa stitched garments but never had he been paid two bags of mohur all at once in a single business deal. Seeing the gold, Kankabaty begged pitifully, 'My darlings! Give the mohur directly to me. Let me take these home. My father loves money so dearly, how happily he will celebrate if he begets these. I will be your queen in these shabby clothes; I don't need nice dresses. I fall at your feet now, give me the mohur for to give to my parents.'

The crab snapped at Kankabaty, 'You are a very disobedient girl. Haven't I asked you not to interrupt us while we are talking? Be quiet and watch what we are doing.'

What recourse did Kankabaty have but to stop speaking? She did. When he received the mohur, the khalifa's joy knew no bounds. He said, 'Let me keep the money aside safely and return with fine fabric. I will make you a queen's costume right away.'

The khalifa went to the inner quarters with the mohur. Overjoyed and displaying two full sets of teeth, he began to show the mohur to his wife.

The wife was astonished. What a surprise, she thought. Whose face had we seen first today upon arising that such good fortune should come by our door? At last, she spoke, and she said, 'This time, my dear, you absolutely must buy me a gold armlet cut like the suit of diamonds.'

Presently, the khalifa accompanied Kankabaty inside the house. He said to the wife: 'This is the queen. Her name is Kankabaty. It is for her use we must sew the gown. Please do take her measure very carefully.'

The khalifani collected the measurements. The khalifa employed an assembly of men and very quickly got ready the dress. The khalifani gently helped Kankabaty into it. Wearing the royal dress, Kankabaty dazzled and ravished.

The khalifani said, 'Glory be!'

The khalifa said, 'Glory be!'

All said, 'Glory be!'

Once dressed, the crab and tortoise took Kankabaty on the return trip. Traversing a lot of land, they entered the river once more. Once they reached there, everyone was enchanted by Kankabaty's charming gown and her beguiling beauty. Each sang her praises. Everyone said, 'Are we not fortunate that we got a queen just like Kankabaty!'

But now a new dilemma presented itself. The aquatic animals began debating where their queen would reside. For she was no ordinary queen but Kankabaty herself. She required a well-appointed, beautifully decorated abode as entrancing as her captivating self. In the end, they decided that a *motimahal* was the only befitting place. What is *moti* is also known as a pearl. Where it originates is the pearl palace or the *motimahal.*

Rohu and the other fish folded their hands and addressed Kankabaty, 'Your Majesty, o' queen of queens! The motimahal is the perfect home for you; go to the motimahal yonder, and reside therein.'

Having spoken these humble words, the fish showed Kankabaty an oyster shell. Since the oyster shell gives rise to the pearl, motimahal is by rights its name. Kankabaty entered the oyster shell as indicated. From inside the shell, she began dispensing her queenship duties to the community of fish.

The Milkmaid

Some days passed. Then a milkmaid came to the river for a bath. While washing herself, her foot touched the oyster shell. Diving underwater, she picked it up and saw that it was indeed quite handsome. She took the shell home and slid it atop one of the roof rafters.

Fastening the door with the big bolt, the milkmaid would make the rounds of gentlemen's homes dispensing milk and curd. Kankabaty would then emerge from her shell. The very first day she stepped out and placed her foot on the ground, her queen's gown had magically disappeared and she had found herself in her old wear. Kankabaty herself was much surprised at the transformation. Every day, emerging from the shell, Kankabaty would complete all of the milkmaid's chores. She would sweep the floor and clean the vessels, cook rice and greens, eat some herself and leave the rest served on a platter for the woman.

Finding it and her home in order upon her return each day, the milkmaid would no doubt be puzzled. She would wonder who it was that did her chores seeing as the door remained locked from the outside.

A few more days went by. At last, the milkmaid thought, 'I must catch the one who does all my chores.'

So determined, the milkmaid returned home early the next day. Quiet as she could, she unfastened the door, and what should she find there, but a beautiful girl washing her vessels vigorously.

Seeing the milkmaid, Kankabaty rushed to hide in her shell, but she caught hold of her. The milkmaid saw that it was none other than Kankabaty.

In astonishment, the milkmaid asked her, 'Why, Kankabaty, didn't you drown in the river? How come you are here then? And how did you find your way?'

Kankabaty replied, 'Yes, Madam. I am no other but Kankabaty. I had drowned in the river. While in the river, I lived inside that oyster shell. You brought the shell home and put it on the rafter overhead. That's how, Madam, I am in your home.'

The milkmaid thus comprehended all. There was no question of being astonished anymore.

Kankabaty spoke again. She said, 'Please, Madam, do not tell my mother and sisters that I am here. My father will scold me if I go home empty-handed. Underwater, there is a lot of money that I have seen with my very own eyes. They gave it to the tailor but not to me. I cried a lot, yet they refused to give it. Let me try and persuade them to give some of it to me, then I can give it to father, in turn, so he won't scold me and my brother won't curse me.'

The milkmaid said, 'The poor dear. To think that the scoundrel wants to sell this dear young thing to Janardan Chowdhury. Just you wait and see. As soon as I meet the man I will curse the mickey out of him.'

Kankabaty answered, 'No, Madam. Do not curse my father. You just don't know how sad he is. There are many mouths in our family. If he doesn't sell me, how can he feed them?' With this discussion, it was decided that Kankabaty would live with the milkmaid for the next few days. Kankabaty said, 'Madam. Since you go to the village every day, update me with the news upon your return.'

Kankabaty took up with the milkmaid. The milkmaid briefed her everyday with the happenings in the village. One day, the milkmaid came home from work, and she said, 'Oh dear! Khetu's mother is so sick that she may not live more.'

In a quavering voice, Kankabaty asked her, 'Why, Madam, what's wrong with her?'

The milkmaid replied, 'I am told she is delirious with fever. Khetu had gone to fetch the naturopath, but he would not come. He said, "I do not wish to lose my caste by treating your mother at your home."'

Kankabaty said, 'Madam, the lady loves me so. She is a mother to me. Yet in her hour of need, I could not stand by her.' So saying, Kankabaty burst into tears.

Very early the next morning, Kankabaty said to the milkmaid, 'Madam, could you go to the village right away? Please go by her house and find out how she is doing.'

The milkmaid began her rounds before the appointed hour, returned early and said to Kankabaty, 'Dear me, what can I say! Khetu's mother is no more. Khetu's mother is dead. To take her to the cremation ground, Khetu is going door to door, but no one is ready to accompany him. Everyone is saying, "Since you took ice, you lost your caste. If we take your mother to the ground, we shall lose ours as well." The trio—Sandeshwar Chakrabarty, Gobardhan Shiromani and your father—are going about dissuading everyone from participating.'

Hearing the news, Kankabaty lay down in her bed and began weeping incessantly. The milkmaid tried to reason with her. She said, 'Kankabaty, you must stop weeping. You must feed yourself.'

But Kankabaty did not rise; she did not cook that morning, nor did she have a meal. She spent the day in bed weeping.

In the evening, Kankabaty said, 'Madam. I request you to go to the village once more. Please observe what is happening there and bring me the news.'

The milkmaid left. When it was night time, she did not return. Nor did she return when it struck the first *prahar*. Lying in her bed, the weeping Kankabaty waited on her return.

It was past the first *prahar* in the night when the milkmaid came home.

Said the milkmaid, 'Dear me, Kankabaty, what can I say! No one came by to take Khetu's mother to the cremation ground. So what did poor Khetu do? When it was evening, he carried the firewood and fuel on his head to the ground himself. Yet how would he take all the wood at one go? He had no choice but to make three trips. Right now, he is taking his mother to the ground. He is all alone and is carrying his mother in his arms. When a human dies, they become heavier. And the ground is not nearby either. Thus every few hundred steps, he is stopping to lay his mother on the ground and rest before picking her up again and proceeding forth. I hid myself under cover of darkness, kept my distance and watched his progress.'

Hearing these words, Kankabaty sat in contemplation for a few moments, then arose slowly, opened the door of the house, passed through it and then took to her heels.

'Where are you going?' the milkmaid called behind her. 'Kankabaty, my dear, where are you going?'

But there was no reply. Today, Kankabaty was no queen of queens nor princess but a mere madwoman. She was not clothed in an enchanting gown but a milkmaid's shabby raiment. Her face was not glowing and impressive but dark with sorrow. Emerging from the house in the milkmaid's clothes, hair flying, Kankabaty ran in the direction of the cremation ground. 'Kankabaty, wait! Kankabaty, tarry a little!' cried the milkmaid as she chased after her, and yet Kankabaty paid no heed to her call, did not even cast one glance behind her.

The full moon entered the eclipse and pitch darkness befell the earth. The milkmaid lost sight of Kankabaty. Weeping, she returned home.

The Cremation Ground

The madwoman dashed towards the cremation ground paying scant regard around her. Having covered some distance, she saw Khetu seated on the ground with his mother's head on his lap. He gazed at her face intently as tears flowed uninterrupted down his own.

Quietly, Kankabaty went and stood by him. Because of the cover of darkness, Khetu failed to see her.

Khetu said, 'So, Mother, even you have left me now. When Kankabaty left, I thought why prolong this unfortunate life? But one look at your face and I resolved to continue. Now, Mother, you are gone, too. In that case, Mother, wherefore do I live and to what end? For whom should I sustain my life? The world holds no temptation for me. Here, there is much sorrow and sin. You did the right thing, Kankabaty, by leaving this world. You, Mother, you, too, did right. Let's go, Mother. I, too, will join you anon. From this day forth, heaven, earth and sea for me is nought but a cremation ground. There is no one in this world who is mine. Anon, mother, I come.

'When I join you, I will stop hurting inside. Mother, tell Kankabaty, I will see her soon.'

Kankabaty emerged from the darkness and eyes cast downwards stood before Khetu. Khetu started, unable to recognise her in the dark.

Kankabaty seated herself at the mother's feet. She took the feet in her lap, placed her head on them and wept silently.

Greatly astonished, Khetu stared at length at her face.

At last, Khetu said, 'My dearest Kankabaty. Since the time I have made sense of this world, I have never wished ill of anyone, only wished them well. I have never lied intentionally, nor deceived anybody. Never have I engaged in any kind of wrongful conduct. In that case, what is the great sin that I have committed for which I suffer this perdition, this hellfire? For no fault of mine have I suffered and borne it. The neighbours tortured me per custom; I bore that too. My soulmate, you, Kankabaty, you drowned and I bore it. My mother who is more precious than my soul died today, and I bore it too. Yet I never ever imagined that in this hour of crisis, you would come seeking to be my enemy. Alone, I can no longer carry my mother's body. Owing to her illness, I have had no food or sleep for three days. Not a drop of water have I taken during these days. There is no strength left in my body and I am exhausted. I can't take one more step and worry about how to proceed. And yet, Kankabaty, you thought to appear as a spectre before me at this juncture only to scare me? My sorrow is now four cupfuls. I can nary bear it.'

Eyes cast downwards and in a quavering voice, Kankabaty said, 'I am not a spectre for I am not dead. I am still alive.'

In amazement, Khetu asked, 'Are you still alive? When you drowned, I searched for you so. Yet I could not find you. I decided to drown, then. For that purpose, I dove into the water. Even though I knew how to swim, I stayed under water until I fainted. The fishermen picked me out of the water and saved my life. When I came to, I saw my mother weeping. Seeing her tears, I decided to continue living. Kankabaty, who saved your life?'

Kankabaty answered, 'That is a long story. I will narrate it later. I was with the milkmaid recently. When I heard of your calamity, I could stay there no longer and came running. Let us take Mother to the ground now. You take one end, let me take the other.' Thus did Kankabaty and Khetu take the mother to the ground. Once there, they built the pyre, gave the mother a good bath and dressed her in a new garment. They placed her on the pyre and, holding fast to her feet, wept.

Khetu said, 'Dear Mother, you are bound for heaven. Bless your wretched son so he never stray from the true path. Let truth be my goal, my light and my deed. May I never leave that path for the sake of money, pleasure or glory. May I never falter in my duty for fear of being frowned upon by the unenlightened, hypocritical human society. Dear Mother, at pain of death let me never be less than a man.'

Kankabaty said, 'Dear Mother, you are ascending to heaven, so cast a glance of benevolence toward your luckless Kankabaty. In sleep and wakefulness, and in my dream, my Mother, may I be true and may I meet my true fate. What more can I say, dear Mother, for you know the desire that lies in my heart of hearts. Whether or not I live, my truth I shall abide by. Even if the sun rises in the west and the apocalypse come about, Kankabaty will remain an honest woman, no one will be able to make her falter. This I have promised myself all along, today I touch your feet and give you my spoken word. Dear Mother, your little Kankabaty is a madwoman today, so forgive her transgressions.'

Khetu said, 'Kankabaty! Tell me how I will light the pyre. How will I say goodbye forever to my dear mother? I won't see her anymore, will I? Come on then, let's look at her for some more time.'

Standing by her head, Khetu carded his fingers through her hair and pushed them away from her face. Kankabaty stood beside him and incessantly wept.

Khetu said, 'Behold, Kankabaty, how calm she seems and how at peace. It is as if she were fast asleep and dreaming happy dreams. Do you remember, Kankabaty, when you were a child and played with kittens? You could not read the *Introduction to Alphabet*. I would get furious, and Mother would scold me instead. My mother loved you just as much as she loved me. Gracious me, Kankabaty, what a lady have we lost to ourselves, you and I in this world.'

Thusly, and with many a regret, after circumambulating the pyre thrice, Khetu performed the rite of lighting the pyre. The flames burned furiously.

Kankabaty and Khetu sat nearby and wept, spelled their regrets and also spoke of other matters. Kankabaty narrated to Khetu how she was saved from drowning. Khetu thought to himself that her misery had caused Kankabaty to lose her grip on reality. It was a fresh sorrow that appeared in his heart. However, he did not make it apparent to Kankabaty.

Once the death rites got over, the two took a bath in the river.

Then, Khetu said, 'Kankabaty, let me walk you home.'

Said Kankabaty, 'How can I go back home again? Father will disapprove of me, Brother will abuse me. Let me go to the fish, or stay with the milkmaid.'

Khetu said, 'Dear Kankabaty, you mustn't think after that fashion. You must return home. Whatsoever distress that entails, you must stay there and bear it. Listen to me carefully. It won't do anymore to speak like a girl. We are like two small boats that have been thrashed about by the waves of the ocean of sorrow that is called society. Hence we must speak with judgement and discernment and act similarly. I want to hear you speak the way you did when you made your promises touching mother's feet. One may not have complete control over future events, but can influence them to a large degree. Why else would the farmer and man sow the seeds of grain and karma, respectively? Ignorance is what makes the difference in the outcome. Hope is the thing with feathers. With this hope in my heart, I say my goodbye to you. Go home, Kankabaty, I will accompany you to your doorstep. Because you stepped out of doors, Janardan Chowdhury will no longer marry you. Bear all the ignominy for a year's period. I have heard there are jobs in the west that pay one a bigger salary. I will go west, and complete mother's funeral ceremonies in Kashi. Then I will look for such a job. Armed with the savings, I will return thereafter and offer them to your father. I am certain that your father will thereupon gladly fulfil my prayer and give your hand to me. It is only one year that I beg from you, Kankabaty. It will pass before you know it. Be it in happiness or in sorrow, just wait for a year for me.'

Then, Kankabaty said, 'I will do as you bid me.' The two then walked slowly to the village. It was not yet morning when they reached Tanu Ray's doorstep.

Khetu said, 'Kankabaty, I take your leave. Take care of yourself.'

Yet, Khetu's feet were fastened to the spot and he hesitated. Tanu Ray's door became wet with the tears of the pair.

Gathering himself, Khetu departed but before long returned and said, 'Kankabaty, I forgot to explain something. It is that you must take good care.'

The two spoke some more. Then the sun rose, and people could be heard awakening.

Khetu said, 'Kankabaty, I will certainly go now. Be very careful. Do not cry. If I live, I will return in a year surely. Then our sorrows will be dispensed with. Say all to your mother, but there is no need to say anything of this to anyone else.'

This time around, Khetu went for good. As long as he could be seen, Kankabaty gazed after him. Then her tears clouded her vision and, fearing that she would faint, she leaned against the wall next to the door. Khetu turned around and saw his beloved Kankabaty stood like an image in a portrait. Then he saw her no more.

Khetu thought, 'Dear God, have you built the human heart out of stone? Why is my heart still beating after having left behind this golden goddess bereft of any care, influence, means and resource?'

The Tiger

Khetu having departed, Kankabaty stood leaning against the wall for a while, weeping copiously. For the longest time, she did not dare to knock on her father's door. In the end, she gathered courage and began knocking.

Having arisen from bed, Tanu Ray was having his morning smoke inside the house. He answered the door. Opening it, he found Kankabaty stood before him.

Seeing her, he said, 'Good heavens, but isn't this Kankabaty! Aren't you dead, Kankabaty? Hence have I been saying, is Kankabaty going to die, after all? Where were you all this time? And where are you coming from today? Indeed, why don't you go back whence you came from? In my home, there is no more space for you.'

Kankabaty did not enter the house. Wearing her soiled and wet garments, she stood by the door weeping her tears.

She did not reply to her father's questions. Hearing the father's loud admonishments, the son quickly appeared on the spot.

The brother said, 'There, the sinner has come here again with her blackened face. No doubt, she has nowhere to go. Yet she can't stay here—from this home, her plate of rice has been taken away. Don't also think that Janardan Chowdhury will marry you either. Indeed, before any of the neighbours comes to know, let us send her on her way.'

Hearing the argument, Kankabaty's sisters appeared at the door. At last, their mother joined them as well. The mother saw poor Kankabaty dressed in shabby old garments weeping by the side of the door. Father and son were abusing her thoroughly and driving her away.

Kankabaty's mother did not say a word, nor did she cast a single glance at her son or husband. Embracing Kankabaty, she only said in the tendermost tones, 'Come, my dear child, welcome home. Where were you all this time having forgotten your poor mother?'

Resting her head on her mother's chest, Kankabaty felt an indescribable peace. The fire that had been burning in her chest was extinguished to a large degree.

Then, Kankabaty's mother took Kankabaty by one hand and her sister by the other. Addressing her husband and son, she said, 'Are you going to turn Kankabaty out? Will you not give her a place in her own home? Really? What misdeed has this innocent child committed that even her parents cannot forgive? Here, take your honour and respect, good karma and religion, and live happily and in style. We, the four unfortunate ones, say goodbye to you. Come on, my child, let us all leave this place. We will beg a living door to door but shan't eat a grain from these savants and saints.'

Only when the three women and their mother did actually begin preparing to leave the house did fear enter Tanu Ray's soul.

Tanu Ray said, 'Wife! Stop it. Are you mad just like Kankabaty? Contemplate this seriously. What am I supposed to do with this girl? Will she be ever married to anybody? That's why I say, let her go where her view takes her; we have little say in what she does hereafter.'

Tanu Ray's wife said, 'Really? Kankabaty will not marry? Well, you need not burden yourself on this account; I will take care of that aspect of matters. In any case, that is none of your concerns, is it? You are concerned about having to let go of your claim on Janardan Chowdhury's money, are you not? And even if it is not so, we will no longer depend on you. Wherever our view takes us, the four of us will go there. Holding the hands of my daughters, all three of them, I will beg my meals from door to door.'

Witnessing the rage of his wife, Tanu Ray thought to himself, 'This is frightening.' He began saying sweet words of consolation to pacify her. When she had calmed down to a large extent, he rudely said, 'Don't talk like a madwoman. Go indoors. Kankabaty, my dear child, you, too, go indoors.'

Mother, Kankabaty and the sisters proceeded indoors. Kankabaty began living with her parents once again. All that had happened post leaving home she recounted to her mother fully, and the mother did not mention it to anyone else. Frequently, Tanu Ray would slight Kankabaty. Kankabaty never replies to the slights, with her head bowed low, she hears them silently.

Tanu Ray says: 'With a kingly groom did I fix your marriage. How can I help if you aren't destined to be happy? How I pleaded with Janardan Chowdhury to accept you. Yet he has refused. Now what do I do with this daughter? No one will even pay fifty rupees to marry her.'

Man and wife would often dispute on this count. The wife would say, 'Little do you need to worry for the marriage of Kankabaty. Hold your horses for one year's timespan. I will fix Kankabaty's marriage myself. If you don't abide by my words and try anything funny, I will take my three daughters and walk out of your house.'

Tanu Ray is an old man now. He is frightened of his wife and no longer dares to reprimand her recklessly. Thus one year did go by in relative peace. There is no sign of Khetu, nor is there any news of him. Kankabaty's mien grew paler by the day and her mother began to deeply worry. Whenever her husband broached the subject of her marriage now, she no longer had the confidence to scorn him. As more and more days went by, Tanu Ray's insults grew in power and intensity. Kankabaty's mother grew perplexed before them and could not supply repartees. A day arrived when post eventide Tanu Ray said, 'With such a grown daughter on my hands, what do I do with her and what not? Forget a suitable boy, it is hard even to find an unsuitable match for this girl.'

Kankabaty's mother replied, 'Since you have waited a year, why not wait a few more days? A suitable groom you will certainly beget.'

Tanu Ray said, 'This is what you have been saying for one whole year. I don't see from where such a groom will arrive at my doorstep. Certainly, listening to you has landed me in this predicament. Had I turned Kankabaty away on the very day she came to my door, I would not have had to see this day. I see now that I have to do as the kings did in earlier days. If I don't find a willing brahmin, I have to marry her to an undertaker instead. If not man, an animal should suffice. My whole body is burning in fury. I speak the truth and the truth is that if a tiger appears in this very moment and asks for Kankabaty's hand, I shall give it to him. If, in this very second, a tiger walks by and says, "Mr Ray, open the door," I will not waste time in doing his bidding.'

As soon as he spoke these words, there was a roar outside the door. Then a deep voice said, 'Mr Ray! Will you open the door in that case?'

Hearing the noise, Tanu Ray took fright. He had no idea who it was that was roaring at his doorstep. To check their identity, he slid it open ever so slowly and to his immense consternation saw a large tiger stood right outside it.

The tiger said, 'Mr Ray. Just now I heard you promise that if a tiger walks by and asks to marry Kankabaty, little would you hesitate to wed her to him. Hence have I arrived and if you do not wed me to her in this very moment, I will make a meal of you.'

Verily it might be said that while Tanu Ray had been frightened—indeed so frightened was he that he had nearly lost his wits—he had not forgotten his business interest in the deal, and he said, 'Doubtless shall I keep my word seeing as I have given it as once it exits my mouth it doth not budge, and yet, you may be aware of my principle, aren't you? If you can preserve the ways of my family line while marrying my daughter, I do not have any objection to the match.'

The tiger said, 'How much will it take to preserve your family way?'

Tanu Ray said, 'I am an honest brahmin. Without completing my evening exercises, I do not take a sip. It is fortunate indeed to be the son-in-law of such a man. If you wish to be my son-in-law, then you have to keep my honour. You have to loosen your purse strings, that's what you must do, indeed.'

The tiger replied, 'Well am I aware of it. How much money will you take to marry me to your daughter at the moment?'

Tanu Ray said, 'The zamindar of this village, the respected Mr Janardan Chowdhury had deigned to marry my daughter although it was divine will that the ceremony could not take place. Mr Chowdhury had been willing to give me two thousand rupees in cash. He is human, a brahmin and a man of my own caste. You do not fulfil any of these criteria, hence you must top that amount.'

The tiger said, 'Proceed indoors. Trust me, I will give you so much money that you have never seen with your human corporeal eyes nor in your dreams, not in your mortal lifetime.'

Thus speaking, the tiger roared and entered the household. Tanu Ray took fright again. He thought he was about to be devoured with family. But he had no choice but to follow the tiger inside the house.

Hearing the roars, Kankabaty, her mother and her sisters had been almost scared to death. Not Tanu Ray's son, however, for he was out visiting friends. Being talented and special, he did not find it appropriate to return before late night.

The tiger arrived at the room where Kankabaty and the others were present. Before all eyes, he dropped an enormous pouch of coins within Tanu Ray's reach.

The tiger said, 'Open the pouch and see what is in it.'

Tanu Ray opened the pouch and saw that it was filled with mohur. He took them in his hand and saw that they were made of real gold. Unable to believe his eyes, he put on his glasses and held them under the light. Yet all his efforts confirmed that these were indeed gold. Everyone was amazed. How did a tiger come by so much wealth? Tanu Ray was beside himself with joy.

Tanu Ray said to himself, 'At long last have I got myself a suitable bridegroom.' He pulled the lamp close to him and began counting the mohur.

Seeing his chance, the tiger sidled up to Kankabaty and her mother, and said, 'Have no fear.' Kankabaty and her mother both started in surprise. In a fraction of a second, they had recognised the voice. Hearing it, they felt emboldened. An unspeakable joy pervaded their hearts. The mother spoke in soft tones, 'Dear God, let it be so.'

The tiger, having spoken to the women, returned to Tanu Ray and sat on his front paws. Tanu Ray had found three thousand coins of gold inside the pouch.

The tiger said, 'Well then?'

Tanu Ray answered, 'But of course. Since I have given you my word, I will marry my daughter to you this very night. There is no need to be anxious on that count. Do not think that I think any less of you because you are a tiger. Oh no! I am no bigot. I know very well whom to respect and in what manner. Leave Janardan Chowdhury aside, I will not marry my daughter to him even if his father comes and begs before me.'

Next, Tanu Ray spoke to his wife, 'Do not second guess my decision. Or else, all will be spoilt. I will certainly give my daughter to him. For, I won't get a more suitable groom in all the world. I won't hear of any protests. If you and your daughters fret and weep, I will complain to Mr Tiger and he will gulp you down.'

Tanu Ray's wife said, 'Do as you will. I have no wish to speak to you.'

What's to worry for the rich? Within the hour, Tanu Ray had sent for his son, and the neighbourhood women, too, had appeared at his gate. The priest and the barber arrived as well and all arrangements were completed.

That night, the marriage ceremony between Kankabaty and the tiger took place and since anyone would be glad to have relations with the king of beasts Tanu Ray was happiest indeed. To the neighbours, Tanu Ray said, 'Indulge in all merriment with my bridegroom and ensure that he feels neither slighted nor disappointed.'

To the bridegroom, Tanu Ray said, 'Son, you must sing at the wedding reception. Your growls will not cut it with my guests. If you don't, your sisters- and brothers-in-law will box your ears most vigorously. Being a tiger won't spare you from their excesses.'

Like a disgraced thief caught red-handed, the tiger spent the wedding with head firmly bowed and steadfastly silent. If he sang in the waiting room post the wedding, only the sisters- and brothers-in-law and the grandaunts can tell. We, writers, have no clue as to that soiree.

Before daybreak, the tiger said to Tanu Ray, 'Mister! I must leave human society and return to the jungle while the night is still darkest. Hence dress your bride and bid her farewell. Do not waste more precious time.'

The neighbourhood women did Kankabaty's coiffeur while her mother began picking out her best garments.

Seeing her mother at it, Tanu Ray said to his wife, his eyes red with rage, 'Never have I encountered such a fool in my life as yourself. With a wife as unlucky as you, who can do well? Tell me this, is there any want in the tiger's home? All he has to do is simply walk into the clothier and roar. In fright, the clothier will run out of his outlet and the tiger will take his sack of fabric and walk away. At the goldsmith's he will enter and roar. The goldsmith will run for his life and the tiger will rob his gold ornaments. After much interviews and investigation did I find such a suitable groom for your girl, yet how did you deem fit to give away her best saris? Hence I say, in all of India, there is no one as foolish as yourself.'

Tanu Ray is a lucky man, and a worshipper of the goddess of wealth, wastage being something he can little tolerate. When his own mother met the divine, she was lying in bed. As her breathing slowed down, he picked her up and laid her on a bedraggled mat. She was wearing a garment that was still in the original condition. When her breath caught in her throat, Tanu Ray disrobed her and dressed her again in a threadbare, tattered cloth. Engaged as he was in pulling at her limbs, he had not even found a moment to place a sip of water on his mother's lips. When he was done, he placed her gently back on the mat and found that she had long departed.

Scolded by her husband, Tanu Ray's wife tied a bundle out of a couple of fraying and well-worn garments. Weeping bitter tears and invoking the deities, she bid farewell to Kankabaty.

In the Forest

Bundle in hand, Kankabaty stood before the tiger with bowed head. In tender tones, the tiger said, 'Kankabaty, you are but a girl. You will be unable to walk great distances. Climb onto my back. I will carry you. It will be no trouble.'

Kankabaty tucked the end of her sari into her waistband and sat astride the tiger. The tiger said, 'Kankabaty, hold fast to the fur on my neck. Make sure you don't fall off my back.' Kankabaty did as bidden. The tiger ran in the direction of the forest.

Arriving in the middle of a lonely forest, the tiger spoke again. He said, 'Kankabaty, are you afraid?'

Kankabaty said, 'What is to fear so long as you are here?'

No doubt, Kankabaty had said these words but it would be inaccurate to report that she was not in the least bit afraid. She had never ridden a tiger. This was a first. Therefore, she had a right to be scared.

The tiger said, 'Kankabaty. I will explain to you why I am a tiger. You need not worry though, for I will soon be free from this state. Yet don't ask me any questions at this moment.' Chatting in this way, the two proceeded until they reached the foothills of a very high mountain.

The tiger said, 'Kankabaty. Close your eyes and keep them shut for some moments. Do not open them until I say so.'

Kankabaty closed her eyes. The tiger sped through the forest. Very soon, a horrific cackling noise pierced Kankabaty's eardrums. Kankabaty said, 'What a grotesque way to laugh? Who is it who laughs in this manner?'

The tiger replied, 'You will know soon. Not at the moment. Open your eyes—there is no cause for fear anymore.'

Kankabaty opened her eyes and found herself inside a wonderful castle. It was made of white marble and studded with precious stones. The rooms were large, clean and well-appointed with all comforts and luxurious objects. Silver, gold, diamonds, pearls, rubies and other costly jewels lay in shining heaps about her and she marvelled at their sight. The castle, however, was located inside the mountain. It was invisible from outside it. It was accessible only through a dark tunnel leading from a small hole on one of its sides. The light inside the chambers came from the top of the mountain. Yet the path of the light, too, was so cleverly designed and well concealed that no bird or beast could discern and follow it into the interiors. No one can reach the interior of the castle. Inside the castle, there is no dearth of garments and furniture. What is missing is food.

Having reached inside the castle, the tiger said, 'Kankabaty. Alight now from my back. Sit here for a while and await my return. But beware. Don't touch any object you find here, and don't take it in your personal custody. Take only what I hand over to you, and touch nothing else.' Thus warning Kankabaty, the tiger left the spot.

In a while, Khetu appeared before Kankabaty. Khetu asked, 'Kankabaty. Can you recognise me?' Kankabaty kept her head bowed steadfastly low.

Khetu said again, 'Kankabaty. Are you feeling scared having come here inside the jungle?'

In soft tones, said Kankabaty, 'No, I am not. I am only thinking if I should cover up before you now that you are my husband and feel shy. But I don't want to. So I worry if you will mind that.'

Khetu said, 'No, Kankabaty. You do not have to cover up in my presence, nor must you feel shy. You do not have to worry whether I will be worried for I do not mind. Since there is none here but you and I, whom do you have to perform shyness for? Yet even so, we are not completely safe. There is a good chance that we may be struck by jeopardy.'

Kankabaty asked, 'What jeopardy?'

Khetu said, 'You need not learn that detail yet. Don't ask me to spell it either. All I can say now is that if you do not touch any object here, there is nothing to fear and no danger will strike us. What I hand you take it, don't put your hand on anything yourself. We have to observe this rule and stay here for a year. After a year, all these riches will be ours. We will take the riches back to the village. Yet Kankabaty. When I married you, did you know me for myself?'

Kankabaty answered, 'Of course, I did. I waited for you a whole year. When the year went by and you did not return, mother and I began to lose heart. How can I tell you how copiously mother cried and so did I? When father said last night he would marry me to a tiger, and you responded from outside asking him to open the door, even through all the growling I could make out that it was you who was speaking. I became sure when you came in and whispered in my mother's ear, "have no fear". Then I knew you were no tiger.'

Khetu said, 'We have overcome many a difficulty, Kankabaty. You have faced many a difficulty, as have I, myself. Another year we must tide over, and then, God willing, happier times will present themselves. One year will go by in no time. Then all this wealth will be ours. Alas! Mother is gone, and so I have no need for wealth. Had she been present, I would have taken her on pilgrimages and got her to conduct charities. Yet there are many impoverished and unfortunate people in this world. Kankabaty. It is but you and I now, and together we will spend our lives in their service.'

Kankabaty asked, 'Where did you go after cremating Mother and leaving me at my door? What did you do and why were you late returning? How did you shift your shape into a tiger's? Won't you inform me?'

Khetu said, 'No, Kankabaty. I won't speak now. You will know in one year's time.'

Kankabaty asked no more of the mystery.

Khetu and Kankabaty began living inside the hidden castle. Kankabaty did not touch anything inside the castle. She only accepted what Khetu handed to her himself.

There was many a comfort inside the castle and every utility, but no comestibles. Consequently, Khetu would go out every morning into the forest and bring fruit, nuts and greens. Thereafter, the two would consume the eatables. Khetu never stepped outside without assuming the tiger's form. Only once he was in the castle he would take the human shape. Why ever would he not go out in human form is something Kankabaty cannot figure out. And yet since Khetu himself has forbidden it, she cannot ask the question. Ten months passed in this way.

One day, Kankabaty said, 'I have not seen my mother in a long time. I wish to see her. She has no news of us either.

Perhaps, she is anxious after our welfare. As it is, she has no idea where we went, what we did or where we stay.'

Khetu replied, 'I have not sent them our news since we would be returning soon anyway. Every time I go into society, I must take the form of a tiger, which is why I have not felt like visiting myself. One can't say when danger will strike and from which direction. However, since you want to see your mother, I will fulfil your wish. I will take you to her in the evening tomorrow. Kankabaty. There are only two months to go before a year is completed. If you wish, you can spend these two months with your parents.'

Kankabaty said, 'Oh no. I have no wish to stay there. I will not leave you alone surrounded by dangers in this forest. My heart is sick for the sight of my mother; one glimpse of her face will make me well. We will exchange our news and I will return forthwith.'

At the In-Laws

The next day, at eventide, Khetu turned into a tiger and asked Kankabaty to mount him. Collecting a lot of gold coins from the castle, he handed them over to Kankabaty, and said, 'Give these to your mother, father, brother and sisters.'

The two left the castle and entered the dark tunnel. While exiting the tunnel, Khetu said to Kankabaty, 'Kankabaty, close your eyes. Do not open them until I tell you to.'

Kankabaty closed her eyes. Once again, she heard the terrible laughing. Hearing the laugh, she shivered in fright.

Having exited the tunnel and entered the forest, Khetu asked Kankabaty to open her eyes. Then he sped in the direction of the village. It was nearly the first *prahar* of the night when the daughter and son-in-law reached Tanu Ray's threshold.

To Kankabaty's mother, it was as if she had reached out and caught hold of heaven. The sisters, too, were delighted. With plenty of dough, the tiger paid his respects to his father-in-law. The brother-in-law, too, was gifted money and riches. He was treated with the greatest regard. The mother fed Kankabaty a meal with five dishes. Tanu Ray had a sudden wish to do the same for his son-in-law but was at a loss as to what meal to serve.

After much thought and contemplation, Tanu Ray said, 'My dear son, you have come a long way and are hungry, that is certain. Yet in our home we have nothing save boiled rice and cooked dishes. Boiled rice and cooked dishes are not your diet, are they? So I wonder what to feed you. Why don't you take my advice? There is an old cow in my stable. Once she was a milch cow. Now she no longer bears calves, and no longer yields milk for us. In vain does she sit and eat our fodder. Gulp down our cow. You will fill your belly and I will fulfil my obligation towards you. No longer will I have to feed the cow.'

Said the tiger, 'No, Mister. I have had a heavy lunch. Now I am no more hungry and plead inability to feed on the cow.'

Tanu Ray said, 'Right. If you do not wish to feed on the cow, then take my advice. Gulp down Niranjan Kaviratna.

He is my eternal enemy. He does not know scripture, yet dares to argue with me. I cannot stand the sight of him. He has left the village. In a different village six *krosh* away from this one, he lives now with his maternal uncle. I will give you his address. You proceed at leisure and devour him.'

The tiger replied, 'No, Mister. Tonight I am not a tiny bit hungry. Tonight I will be unable to devour Niranjan Kaviratna.'

Tanu Ray then said, 'Right. If you are unable to cross the distance, then I will fix a meal for you right here in this village. In this village, there lives a milkmaid. What a wicked broad she is I cannot say. Twice a day she comes by just to quarrel with me. Because I have married my daughter to you, she says to me, "You short-lived rascal, you old rogue, you. You went and sold your daughter to a tiger and ate lavish meals from the proceeds, now didn't you?" Being my son-in-law you are obliged to find a solution to this nuisance. Why don't you break her neck and drink her blood? It is healthy blood, plentiful and free of disease.'

The tiger said, 'No, Mister. I cannot eat anything tonight. I am not hungry.'

Tanu Ray reflected, 'Sons-in-law are wont to be bashful. One must coax them to take every single bite. Once served a meal, they must be guided through the entire process, and through every helping, or else they don't partake and leave their plates unfinished. With hunger burning up their insides they say outwardly, "I am hungry no more, I can hardly eat." It is the custom of sons-in-law to say so.'

With this thought in mind, Tanu Ray said, 'Once you come to your in-laws, is it good form not to eat? People will badmouth me. What can I say of the ones in our neighbourhood? Suffice it for you to know that, woman and man alike, each is a museum specimen after the other. Ever ready to relish a family drama. Yet cannot tolerate others' good fortune. You have become my son-in-law. Whatever that might mean, it is apparent that you are prosperous. Your prosperity has triggered their jealousy to unfathomable limits. As certain as the sun will rise will they say, "Tanu Ray's son-in-law had paid a visit. Tanu Ray did not take care of him, he did not even offer him a glass of water." It is the reason why I ask you to have at least a bite. Come on, let me show you the milkmaid's hut. She eats ghee and drinks milk. Her flesh is tender. You will savour the taste of it. You will even enjoy it. As your father-in-law, will I ever offer you a bad meal?'

The tiger replied, 'Mister, forgive me. The next time around, we shall see.' Tanu Ray felt a little offended. The son-in-law is an object of care. If they cannot care for them to their heart's content, the parents-in-law are aggrieved. While he did name three good treats, the son-in-law did not accept one of them. Taking offence was justified.

Tanu Ray said, 'One shouldn't visit the in-laws' home with a full stomach. Why shall the parents-in-law abide by that? If the son-in-law doesn't break bread, their parents-in-law feel sad. Do you know how I will be censured by your mother-in-law on this account? She will say, "You did not speak nicely to your son-in-law, hence he did not eat with us." When you come again, do not come having eaten a meal. Eat once you are here with us. I am assigning these three treats to you. The next time around, you must eat all three of them. If you do not, I will not let you depart to the jungle. I will hide your umbrella and wrap. Well, not really, seeing as you do not own an umbrella and a wrap. If you do not, I will feel very offended by that.'

Kankabaty spent the night in conversation with her mother and sisters. Before her mother, she disclosed the tiger's true identity. That she would come by enormous wealth in just two months' time she also confided in her mother.

At one point, Tanu Ray beckoned Kankabaty over and, in a whisper, said, 'Kankabaty. It looks like the son-in-law is not a true tiger. Aren't there stories of people placing roots of herb on their heads and turning into tigers? It is likely he is one of them. I offered him different treats. I asked him to eat the old cow in my stable, Niranjan and the milkmaid. Yet he did not touch one of them. Had he been a true tiger, could he have abstained? Hence I have the suspicion that he is not a true tiger. Why don't you take my advice and look up something? Why don't you see if he has the root of any herb on his head or not. If you find one, burn it up. If he is cursed, then the spell will be lifted upon burning the root. Whatever be the reason behind his attaining his present state, burning the root will cure him of it. Then he will be human and return again to society.'

When Kankabaty returned to her mother having received her father's advice, the mother said, 'What did he whisper in your ear, pray?'

What her father had told her, Kankabaty narrated to her mother.

Hearing her report, her mother said, 'Kankabaty. Do not do this job. You will certainly come to a bad end. Khetu is steadfast and prudent. If he has a plan, it is for the best. Do not go against his bidding. Take care, Kankabaty. Remember my warning and see that you heed it.'

When the night was almost over, Khetu and Kankabaty journeyed to the forest. When they arrived at the mountain, Khetu asked Kankabaty to close her eyes just like before. At the entrance to the tunnel, Kankabaty heard the same chilling laugh. Once inside the castle, they began to spend their days in the earlier fashion.

The Root

Another month passed by. Then Khetu said, 'Kankabaty. There is but one more month to go. One month on, and we will sing our freedom. After one month is past, we won't be obliged to stay forest dwellers anymore. With this enormous assembly of treasure, we will go home.'

As each day ends, Khetu says to Kankabaty, 'Kankabaty. Now twenty-nine days remain. Kankabaty. Just twenty-eight more days are left to spend. Kankabaty. Only twenty-seven to go.'

Thus did twenty days expend themselves. There remained only ten days to go before the deadline. Thinking that he would be taking Kankabaty back to the village after ten days, Khetu grew excited beyond words. All the time, he would be seen smiling.

Khetu now said, 'Kankabaty. I assign you this task. Take a piece of coal and make ten marks on this yonder wall. When you rise each morning, wipe off a mark. This way, you will always see before you how many days are left for you to achieve freedom.'

Kankabaty said to herself: 'The dear husband is so impatient to return to the village. I have done his bidding and placed ten marks on the wall that I will be removing one by one every day. And yet, can't I wipe all ten of them in a single day? Can't I rescue my husband in one day only? Why don't I heed father's advice and do as he says? If he can go to the village today or tomorrow, how happy would my husband feel!'

Several times in the past couple of months had Kankabaty recollected her father's words. The suspicion that evil men had cast a spell on her husband had come to her again and again, yet seeing as her mother had forbidden it she had not tried anything on that count. Now, witnessing her husband's eagerness for freedom, Kankabaty began to feel restless.

Kankabaty thought, 'Father is male. He knows about hills and mountains, woods and forests, tigers and bears, roots and herbs, and hymns and spells, as well. Mother has not had a chance to access this knowledge. She, being female, is wont to stay at home. How will mother know how to break an evil spell? Father has said if only I burn down the root all dangers will be dispelled. There are still ten days left to go home, and my husband is counting the days. If he can go home tomorrow, how happy would he be!'

Kankabaty spent the entire day lost in thought. Sometimes, she would reflect, 'Perhaps, I am about to commit a blunderous mistake. Let me close my eyes and ears to my husband's exultations and spend the remaining ten days. After all, mother has forbidden me to do what father says.'

Yet again she would go, 'The evil men have harmed my dear husband. I will save him from their wicked intentions. Will he not be pleased with me if I free him from their clutches?' The day went by, yet Kankabaty failed to reach a decision. She carried her cogitations into the night. Kankabaty recollected the tale of Maiden Tilaksundari and the Giant Potato.

The Prince had fallen in love with Tilaksundari's beauty and had desired to marry her. Tilaksundari's stepmother placed a root on her head. Tilaksundari became a bird due to the spell of the root. She took flight and perched herself on a bough. The stepmother hatched a scheme and got her own daughter, Giant Potato, married to the Prince. The Prince began to shower his affection on Giant Potato. Beholding the sight, Tilaksundari called out from her perch: 'Giant Potato is on your knee. But Tilaksundari's on the tree.' The Prince wondered, 'What does the little birdie say?' He beckoned the bird over. The bird flew over and sat on his fingers. When the Prince stroked her head, the root dropped to the ground. Tilaksundari was restored to her original form. The Prince figured out the stepmother's trick. He buried Giant Potato in a bed of thorns and spent the rest of his days with Tilaksundari.

Kankabaty recalled the tale of Tilaksundari at this juncture. She was also reminded of *Arabian Nights* that contained similar accounts. She thought, 'The evil use this exact means to perpetrate their plans. Why not check and see if there is indeed a root in my husband's hair?' So decided, she went to a different room and lit a lamp. Returning with the lamp, she stood beside the bed and began investigating. Khetu was fast asleep and had no clue as to what was happening around him.

Behold and alack! Hunting for the root, Kankabaty spied it half-hidden in Khetu's hair. 'Father was right,' Kankabaty thought. 'To contemplate the evil of men! It is fortuitous that I conducted this search tonight, or else what calamity would have transpired who can say?'

Kankabaty tried to uproot the herb from Khetu's crown. However, it was tied fast to his hair, so she failed in her attempts. Anticipating that he would be aroused from his slumber, she did not exert herself further. She slipped away into the next room again and returned with a pair of scissors. These she used to snip out a portion of Khetu's hair and the herb came away in her hand. Wasting no time, she held the herb to the flame of her lamp and burned it.

The vapours given up by the burning herb spread a heavy, noxious smell that entirely filled the room. They nearly asphyxiated Kankabaty. Fear overcame her and she lost her wits. Kankabaty's body began to shiver.

Khetu awoke with a start. He put his hand to his head and found the root no longer there. He then saw the quaking, insensible Kankabaty stood before him. Just as she fainted and collapsed to the ground, Khetu got up, caught her in his arms and broke her fall. He took the lamp from her hands and seated her carefully on the bed. Patting her face with water, he began doing his best to revive her.

Kankabaty came to, and said, 'I realise I have committed a grievous error. Please forgive me.' So saying, Kankabaty lowered her head and began to cry.

Khetu said, 'It is not your fault, Kankabaty. Foremost, it was ordained by fate. Else, why would such a mishap occur right at the very end of our ordeal? Then, too, it is my fault. Had I told you my story and not kept secrets from you, you would not have done as you did. This mishap would nary have taken place. Kankabaty. Have you burned the herb to ashes?'

Nodding, said Kankabaty, 'Yes, my husband, so I have. I have gutted the herb and it is no longer present.'

Khetu said, 'In that case, Kankabaty, you have to take courage. No longer can you afford to weep like an incompetent woman or a little girl. Amidst this deep and deserted forested you are alone by yourself. I grow concerned thinking of your welfare. Kankabaty. The valiant never fear to die. They only worry about the welfare of their dependants.'

Growing concerned herself, Kankabaty asked, 'What do you fear? What kind of danger do you anticipate?'

Khetu answered, 'Kankabaty. If there were time, I would have kept this secret. There isn't. You will have to travel back alone to the village. Go north after emerging from the tunnel. When the sun rises in the morning, keep it to your right and walk home.'

Kankabaty said, 'And yourself?'

Khetu said, 'I have no option. I have touched the objects that belong to this place and partaken of its wealth. Hence I can leave here no longer. I need must stay back in this place. This was the reason why I had forbidden you from touching any object belonging to this place. Wait no more. Do not waste any more seconds. Leave the castle and enter the tunnel. Find a tree and spend the night beneath it after leaving this cave. When the sun rises in the morning, take your bearings. Go north and reach the village. Kankabaty. Wait no longer.'

Kankabaty said, 'Do you expect me to go away leaving you here all by yourself in this strangest of places? For, I wonder why else you would bid me do as such. While it is true I have committed an offence and am doubtless a sinner most unfortunate, does it behove you well to turn me away? Being a girl and ignorant, I have committed an error even if I wanted to do good to you. Can you not forgive me? Is there no way I can atone for my mistake?'

Khetu replied, 'But, Kankabaty, I am not angry with you. I did not turn you away. How can I tell you of the danger that awaits you? You have to leave, Kankabaty, and you have to leave right away. You cannot wait any longer. After you reach your father's house, collect the neighbours and return to this spot when ten days have passed. There will be nothing to fear after ten days. Take all the treasure lying in the castle. No one will say a word. Divide the treasure into four equal parts. Give one part to your father, one to Brother Ramhari, one to Uncle Niranjan and claim one part yourself. Spend your days in fasts, rites, worship, pilgrimage and charity. A human lifetime is not very long and will pass presently. After that, you will go to where I am now bound for, and we shall unite again.'

Kankabaty said, 'My heart is breaking hearing your words. I am feeling frightened as well. Alas, what have I done, my love. What is the danger that awaits us? Where are you headed? And what is the terrible secret? Tell me all this very moment.'

Khetu said, 'Listen well. The treasure you see in this castle is guarded by a terrible ghost called Nakeshwari. She sits by the tunnel at the entrance of the castle. Whoever touches the treasure is devoured by her at once. I have touched her riches. So far I had been protected by the root that you just burned to ashes. Had it not been so, I would have been devoured long ago. Perhaps Nakeshwari has not yet cottoned on to the fact that the root is absent. But she will in a moment. As soon as she comes to know it, she will arrive and finish me off. There is no way I can save my life or leave this castle. Even if there had been a way, it would be to no avail. Whether I go to the forest or the sea, the city or the village, Nakeshwari will find me there and take my life.'

Hearing these terrible words, Kankabaty held fast to both of Khetu's feet and prostrated herself before him.

Khetu said, 'Don't cry, Kankabaty. Tears are of no help. What is lotted cannot be blotted. It is divine will, not else. Arise, Kankabaty, and proceed towards the tunnel. Depart quietly through it. It is time for Nakeshwari to arrive. Seeing her, you will feel frightened. Go to your mother, Kankabaty. If you see her, you will feel a little better.'

Kankabaty said, 'Do you really expect me to leave you and run for my life in fear of Nakeshwari? Well, if I do so, woe be upon me and shame on my life and soul. I may be a foolish girl who has ignored your bidding, yet I am no hellworm. I will save you from the clutches of Nakeshwari. And if I am unable, I will simply share your fate. Kankabaty is not afraid to die. And Kankabaty does not want to enjoy the pleasures of the world without you by her side. This is Kankabaty's promise and she will certainly fulfil it.'

Khetu gazed at Kankabaty's face and noticed that her promise was unbreakable. There were no tears in the young woman's eyes, and all traces of fear had vanished from her face. Said Khetu to himself, 'It is futile to ask Kankabaty anymore to leave this place.'

The Theft

Thereafter, Khetu said: 'Kankabaty. Since you shall not leave, let me narrate to you my circumstances and how we came to live here. You being a girl staying by herself in a godforsaken jungle with the fierce Nakeshwari at her door, I earlier surmised you would take fright hearing my story and hence withheld it. Listen well. Only I hope I finish seeing as

Nakeshwari will soon inhale the fumes from the root. Then she will guess what transpired and enter the palace to take my life.

'Following the completion of cremation rites for mother, I departed for Kashi. I went westward instead of to Calcutta following the plan I had explained to you earlier. Upon reaching Kashi, I performed her funeral. Then I began looking for work. Fortuitously, I found a good position and took it. It involved a lot of hard work but also paid me a significantly high salary. Inspired by the hope that I would be able to save substantially inside the time of a year, I began putting away money for your father, spending only as much as I perforce had to in order to sustain my life.

'Oftentimes in the evening, after having spent all day hard at work, I would be on the verge of fainting from hunger pangs and yet would skip my dinner nonetheless. Instead of a light meal, I would drink water to fill my stomach. It helped somewhat, refreshing my senses and soothing my pangs. Then I would go to bed and sleep would overtake my appetite. I did not pay anyone to bring water for me. I had bought for myself a large *lauta*-pitcher that I used to fetch water for myself from the Ganges every evening under cover of darkness, so people would not know me for who I am. The steps on the riverbank in Kashi are rather high. One night, I had lost my footing in the dark, fallen down and hurt my foot and hand. Raising myself with difficulty, I had then sat down on the steps and wept copiously.

'Said I to myself, dear God, what is the sin I have committed that I am thus being punished for? Is this why people leave the worldly *samsara* and choose the life of an ascetic? For, only the one who depends on oneself and no one else for one's happiness is the one who can hope for peace. The one who lives with others will have his happiness become contingent on their affairs. How can such a person ever reach that carefree state? Conversely, how am I expected to know what misdeed a loved one will commit so that I can otherwise influence them? Verily, I don't have any right over their decisions, yet my heart will weep when I see them in grief.

'Indeed, even if such a loved one commits no sin, wrongdoing or crime, they may be tortured and suffer the consequences of the misdeed of another. Now since I love them, I still have to bear witness to their pains. For instance, could I stop your parents from mistreating you? When I saw the ascetics' bonfires burning all around me, these were the thoughts that arose in my mind. And yet, I persisted. Said I to myself, the *samsara* is a battlefield. Of it sin and sorrow are a legitimate part.

'It will be a shame if an enlightened human such as myself who has armed themselves with skill and confidence by navigating various temptations should turn away from this battle. For the sake of my honour and others' well-being should I fight the good fight. Kankabaty. Thus did I vacillate between duty, escape and whatnot.

'Presently, I rose and took my pitcher home. The year circled by. By this time, I had collected close to two thousand rupees. Said I to myself, perhaps your father will pleased to receive this money and give me your hand. So decided, I prepared to travel home. The money I took in coins and not currency notes seeing as our villagers do not have faith in the latter format.

'Placing the money in a bag, I boarded the train. The bag I kept in close custody of self. For fear that someone would purloin it, I did not, for even a moment, alight from the train. When it was evening, the train stopped at a large junction. It was going to be a long halt. I was hungry but fearful of leaving my seat to buy a snack. There was no one save a single stranger in my vestibule. He got down from the train to buy himself a bite. Before leaving, he said to me, "Mister. Do you need me to get you anything from the station?" I answered, "Indeed. If you do buy me something to eat, I would gladly accept it." So saying, I gave him some money for a snack. Having eaten the food he brought me, I began to feel dizzy. Said I to myself, it must be hot inside the train. With this, I lay myself down on my bunk and fell asleep immediately. It was the deepest slumber of my life.

'When it was early morning, I began to awaken in stages. I found myself with a splitting headache, unable to sit up. When I did, I saw there was no bag. Looking around, I could not find the man either. A bolt from the blue struck my skull. Immediately, I rose and began a methodical search through the compartment but could find neither man nor bag. I realised what misfortune had befallen me. The money that I had starved myself to earn over one entire year was gone.

'Contemplate for a moment, Kankabaty, what heartrending, unbearable pain I had suffered at this point. How could a human being be so cruel, I thought. And is not suffering such cruelty not living in hell on earth? Why does man do thus to fellow man and does it not pain them the least to do so?'

After a long while, tears welled up in Kankabaty's eyes, and Kankabaty began weeping. Said Kankabaty, 'Then so be it. Let us leave samsara. Let us depart together. Nakeshwari is hardly our enemy; she is our friend in disguise.'

Khetu said, 'Just concentrate well. Can you hear any moves by Nakeshwari?'

Kankabaty listened for a while, and said, 'I cannot. Not a pin drop.'

Khetu said, 'Well, then, let me continue with my story. When I realised that I had been robbed, said I to myself, today, all my hopes of marrying Kankabaty have come to an end. The man in the train travelling in my compartment had been a thief, dear Kankabaty. He had put a narcotic in my meal. When I lost consciousness having eaten that meal, he fled with my money. How was I to know which station he had disembarked at and left? Hence there was no chance of anyone catching him. Even so, I informed the railways staff. With me by their side, they conducted a thorough search of all the carriages.

'Gradually, any residual hope that I had had of recovering my bag faded away. I was in despair. I wondered if I should return to Kashi, go to Calcutta or proceed onwards to the village. Then I become aware that for belongings I only had my ticket to Raniganj and a few pennies. Appreciating that you would be waiting on my promise to return in a year, I finally thought that going back to the village would be the correct decision.

'I worried about the torture and humiliation you might have faced at the hands of your parents in the meantime. Said I to myself, let me fall at the feet of Tanu Ray and sign a bond for two thousand rupees. I will work every hour to pay the money from my salary every month. It pains me to talk thus of your father, Kankabaty. After all, he has brought you to this world. Yet whenever I talk of him, the words take on a critical tone.

'I had thought that I would show him so much money that he would begin to tire of it. What a world we do live in, Kankabaty! Here, everyone is running madly after riches, yet how much do we require even so we can serve a lavish meal to ourselves?

'How much finery could one desire to wear, Kankabaty, to seek wealth in such a craven fashion? Yet money is important as a means to dispel hunger and suffering. With it you can help a friend, fulfil duty to your family, shelter the needy and assist the deserving. The one who sacrifices their pleasure to earn money for a better society or achieve knowledge is supreme indeed. Why should such a one seek money so covetously? Why waste one's precious hour divinely allotted in fruitless pursuit of petty rivalries? It is ludicrous to contemplate even at such a desperate hour.

'And so contemplating to return to my village, I disembarked from the train at Raniganj. From Raniganj, one can take one of two paths to our village. One is the high road, which is well travelled; the other is deserted because it goes through a forest and its takers stand the risk of being mauled and eaten by tigers, bear and other wild beasts. Yet the forest trail is shorter because it takes you to the village in five days. Taking the highway, you won't reach home in six days. When I got down at Raniganj, I had only four pennies in my pocket. To reach the village quickly I took the road through the forest.

'I spent all four pennies on the first day. Crossing hills and valleys, forest, river, spring and dale, I advanced, eating fruit and leaf to survive. Nights I would camp out at the doorstep of anyone in the nearest village. On days there lies no village a canopy would suffice. Said I to myself, let a tiger or bear take my life, an unfortunate soul like myself has no right to live on this planet.

'Thus did go by four days. At last, I was at the foot of this mountain, which is the one visible from our village inside which we now reside. From here it is a day's journey to the village. Not having eaten well those past few days, I had become feeble-bodied. Thinking I would tire more if I hiked during the day, I began to cover the distance by night sans stoppage. About one *prahar* it was when the moon set and the whole forest got enveloped by darkness. Suddenly, I found myself surrounded by great trees and I lost my way. To my right and to my left, to the front and back, there was only bush and arboreal foliage. I spent a lot of time searching for the foot trail but to no avail.

'At last, I became quite exhausted. At this point, a temple appeared in sight. Seeing the temple boosted my morale. There must be someone about, I surmised. Even if they cannot feed me, they can certainly spare a drop of water. So thinking, I began advancing quickly towards the temple.

'It was my cursed fate that upon reaching the temple I found that there was no deity in the shrine which was ancient and broken down and overrun by vines. It had been long since anyone had stepped into that space. Putting it down to another one of the good God's tests, I sighed and cleaned up a spot where I lay down to take some rest.'

Ghost and Company

Khetu said, 'It was almost the second *prahar*. Against my will had I but given in to the silken embrace of slumber when there came a steady thumping sound from the direction of the temple stairs. Opening my eyes presented me with a marvellous sight. The white head of a corpse was bouncing up the flight of stairs up one step from another. Kankabaty. I do not take fright easily but must admit I felt goosebumps. I rose from my supine position. The corpse head got to the top of the portico and then came rolling towards me like a great ball of fire. Proceeding nearby, it leapt into the air, suspended itself right in front of my face and gazed at me for a few long moments. Then its opened its mouth up to the ears and grinned at me, presenting a full set of white teeth.

'Still grinning, it addressed me: "Babu! It has been said you do not believe in ghosts, yes?"

'Replied I, "Spare me, sire. I am a much-tormented soul, persecuted and beset by many troubles. I hardly wish to add you to my list of adversaries. Desist from your antics, sire, and go home."

'Hearing my words, the head became angrier. It yelled at me, repeating its earlier words, "Babu! It has been said you do not believe in ghosts, yes? Having read the English language, you no longer believe in ghosts, is that correct?"

'Said I, "Are you annoyed seeing as the English-educated babus do not believe in ghosts? Do people disbelieving in the existence of ghosts annoy you?"

'The head replied, sarcastically, "Do you imagine their doubt would soothe me instead? Aren't ghosts slighted by this mistrust or are you suggesting it raises their prestige? Why would anyone say there is no ghost on the face of the earth? What harm have we brought upon English-educated babus that they should deny us our rightful due? Having denied gods the same, it is now the turn of the demigods to lose their respect, you say, yes?"

'I was amused despite my plight. I had been told so far that the gods, if they go unworshipped, take umbrage and go into sulking fits, yet no one had ever mentioned that ghosts, too, feel slighted if they are not expected. I wanted to smile, but could not for fear of offending my guest. So I said, "Indeed, sir, it is very unjust of the English-educated babus to deny your rightful existence."

'The head seemed somewhat pleased at my speech. It said, "You, young man, on the other hand, seem to be sensible. You are neither a nihilist nor an atheist, unlike the English-educated babus. Do you bear the sacred ponytail?"

'I said, "No, sire. Indeed, I do not sport one."

'The head said, "Never you mind. Grow one when you go home. And hear me well. We shall not let the English-educated babus go easily. In order to have them acknowledge us, arrangements have been made. We shall solicit their audience. We shall go to town, printing pamphlets, producing newspapers and delivering speeches. For the purpose of accomplishing these tasks, we have opened a company. We have named the company, 'Skull, Skeleton & Co.'"

'Kankabaty. You may remember from your biology lessons that the osseous tissue of the human head is known as the cranium or the skull, and the same with respect to the rest of the body that verily forms its structure and form is the skeleton. What the head said could be paraphrased thus: in order that English-speaking Bengalis acknowledge and accept the existence of ghosts and fear them, the spirits have organised themselves to spread a message to the same effect.

'Skull, i.e. the head of the corpse, said to me, "We have opened an enterprise and named it, 'Skull, Skeleton & Co.' We had good reason to pick an English name. The reason being in so doing we will be able to do brisk business. Had we gone forth as 'Khuli, Kankal and Company' in the vernacular, it would have been impossible to build trust amongst our clients. Have you not noticed when the Mukhopadhyays,

Chattopadhyays and Bandopadhyays trade in shoes or drinks or ham, they call their outlet, 'Longman & Co.' Or else, they call it 'Goodman & Co.' Having been fleeced by their native brethren, people trust each other no longer. Even the Vedas and scriptures gain in regard if they are recommended by the Caucasians. What Indian scholars think no one cares. Taking these facts into consideration, we have named our company, 'Skull, Skeleton & Co.' At this moment, Brother Skeleton is standing at a distance, listening to us confer. Come hither, Brother, come, join our conversation."

'Jingle-jangling its bones in a loud beat, Brother Skeleton approached. Even though a skeleton by definition comprises all bones of a human body, the specimen before us was missing its head. The Skull then insisted again, "Well, my dear, do you now believe us completely?"

'I answered, "I have always believed in ghosts. For it is the result of their conspiracy that I am suffering such grief, seemingly interminably. Yet it is a different category of ghost that has brought that about. Henceforth, I will also acknowledge your kind of ghosts. For, how can I not believe what I see before my very eyes? There is no need to worry for you on that count, and you can go home in peace. Your family must be worried for you. I, too, must take some sleep. Come morning, I have to hike a great distance."

'Skull addressed Skeleton, "See that? This is the benefit of opening a company. This babu's English education had all but warped his mind. Just a word or two from us brought him back to his true dharma. Come, let us now go in search of other warped babus. Let us find a way to generate regard and respect within them for our kind."

'Skeleton rattled its bones. I listened carefully and realised there was more to the noise than the clink of bone on bone. Having no mouth, it could not speak but it could beat a tattoo to mark its words. The strange aspect of it was that I could understand every one of them.

'Skeleton said, "If this gentleman has turned into a ghost lover, it is our duty to reward him. One way to turn people into devotees is by giving them gifts of money. If people get hold of money, they turn into super-pious great men. Hence, donate this gentleman riches. This way, he will go back to his village and sing our praises, and thousands will become our followers."

'Said I, "Lately, I have been in dire need of money. Yet I am not a greedy man. You don't have to bribe me to beget my respect. I shan't accept your money."

'Hearing my words, Skull became even more pleased with me. It said, "Come along with us. Let us give you this gift. You clearly deserve it and will doubtlessly put it to good use. For this reason, we will give it to you. If you accept it, its purpose will be served. While we were alive, we never used our collected riches well. Now the same shall be done by your hand; yet we are the ones who shall be rewarded."

'Skeleton, too, made the same earnest entreaty. To honour their request, I travelled with them through the forest. While the skeleton went on foot, the skull bounced ahead or rolled down gradients. Foremost, they took me to a grove of fruit trees where mango, persimmon, banana and almond had grown and ripened. They bid me feed on them and I obliged them. Next, they pointed to me a scenic little waterfall where I quenched my thirst before we left the place. Soon we reached the foot of the mountain. The skull said, "We must make for us here a clearing. For a thousand years, the forest has grown as no one has stepped into this spot." The three of us did our best to clear the foliage. Once the foliage had been removed, I spied a tunnel on the mountain wall. I saw Nakeshwari, the dreadful monster, at the mouth of the tunnel. Nakeshwari laughed her terrible laugh. But she fell quiet as soon as Skull gave her a death glare with those empty sockets of its grim visage. Through the meandering tunnel, we entered the castle. I was astonished to glimpse the enormous riches lying about me.

'The skull spoke then. It said, "It was almost one thousand years ago that we were kings of this entire region. We defeated all neighbouring kingdoms to amass this huge wealth. While alive, we never spent our time in any pious or charitable activities, being fully occupied in warfare and building our treasury. We had no offspring, yet were completely satisfied since there would be zero expenditure on that account. We derived our happiness from counting and handling the wealth we had assembled together. To guard our wealth and keep it safe when we pass over to the other realm, we fixed a 'yak' to it, which means we appointed a ghost to look after it; we had not tasked a living man or woman belonging to the Austric *yaksh* race, a true *yaksh* or *yakshini*, that is to say, with the work. These people are known as *yaksh*, too, but it is not their job. Be that as it is, for the purpose of fixing a *yaksh*, first of all, we designed a beautiful castle inside the mountain, then we transferred all our gold, finery and jewellery inside it from the palace. As per rite, we conducted a yajna, paying homage to the god of fire, upon the completion of which we sacrificed a nine-year-old virgin at the site and told her to stand guard to the treasure for a thousand years. 'If anyone tries to steal it, you must liquidate them,' we said to her. 'After a thousand years have passed, you are free to go where you please, while the one who is so destined will enjoy this wealth.' Passing this order to the girl, we lit a lamp inside the castle, pushed her into the tunnel and sealed its entrance. When the lamp went out, the girl died and turned into a large, long-nosed monster. Because of this one feature of hers, she is known among ghosts as Nakeshwari, or She of the Long Nose. She is the one you saw guarding the tunnel and heard laughing with a terrible cackle at its entrance. There are others who appoint a boy instead of a girl to thus guard the tunnel. The boy dies and transforms into a demon. After a few days, we died in battle. The enemy's sword severed our head from our trunk. In life, we were but one person, but in death we are a pair of ghosts. I, Skull, am the head, while the trunk is he, Brother Skeleton. Nine hundred and ninety-nine years ago, we fixed the *yaksh* to our treasure. In the last month of Pous, Nakeshwari was duly wed to a ghost named Ghyanghon. When another year goes by, Nakeshwari will relinquish her post. She will go to live at her in-laws' home. If you claim the treasure after that time, no harm shall come upon you. But if you touch just a tiny bit of it within this time, Nakeshwari will gobble you up and you will dispense with your life. The two of us are the true owners of these assets and we hereby bequeath them to you. Beware, do not touch them in the meanwhile."

'Said I, "Dear sires, I am much obliged to you for your kindness. Yet find me a route so that I can make use of a small portion of this wealth right now. Lately have I experienced a dire need for money. If I am able to procure it, I will be benefited, even my life will be saved. On the other hand, if I am not, I may not be alive in a year."

'Hearing my submission, the skull and the skeleton conferred for a very long time. What words were exchanged between them, I was hard-pressed to understand.

'Finally, Skull turned around and said to me, "Come along, let us leave again." All of us left the castle and began roaming the forest. Skull began searching for something in the forest. At last, he showed me a herb and he said, "Uproot this herb." I complied. At Skull's instance, Skeleton fixed the root of the herb with the sap of another plant to my hair. Then the three of us returned to the castle.

'Inside the castle, Skull said, "Listen and listen well. Take what you need from here and fulfil your purpose. The virtue of the magic herb fixed to your hair is this: as long as it is on your person, Nakeshwari cannot touch you inside the castle. Once outside, the herb cannot protect you. The magic herb has another power to it. If it is on your head, you can shape-shift into any animal you wish. The tiger is Nakeshwari's revered deity. When you go outside the castle, take the form of a tiger and she will not harm you. Once you are inside the castle, you can be human again. There are two other things to remember. First, for this period of one year, do not let the herb fall from your head, or else it is certain death for you wherever you may be. Next, do not leave the castle without taking the form of the tiger even for a second, or else death is equally certain. After a year has passed, burn the root, collect all the wealth and go to your village. Had you not required money before a year, all these arrangements would be needless. If you do not take the wealth, Nakeshwari will not harm you, nor can she do so. After a year is gone, Nakeshwari will leave to her matrimonial home. Yet, ere her wedding, people had spread so many evil rumours just to prevent it from taking place."

'I asked then, "Wherefore had they spread rumours, sire?"

'Skull said, "You are a naïve fellow, aren't you, to ask such a silly question? Don't you know what fun it is to spread rumours and spoil an alliance? Nary as much fun can be had from any other dalliance. Say, you find a groom or a bride. You share the news with your friends and family. They go, 'Most certainly, go ahead, won't you, with the match? And yet...' That single word, 'yet', carries a shipload of meaning. Be that as it may, when Ghyanghon's alliance was being made, a clever rumour nearly ran it to the ground. What a clever rumour it was! Its originator does deserve unstinted praise."

'I said, "How ever could a rumour be clever, sire?"

'Said the skull, "Why do you, as the saying goes, having read the seven parts of the book that must not be named, ask of me such a silly question? Be quiet and listen. When Ghyanghon's alliance arrived, Nakeshwari's maternal aunt sent forward a ghost to inspect the groom. Ghyanghon received his guest most cordially and got prepared a lavish meal for him. When it was time for lunch, he sent him to a nearby lake for to take a bath. At the lake, some neighbours met the visitor ghost. Said the visitor ghost, 'Live I in the Land of the One-Legged on a mango tree called The Wife Seducer.'

"''And what brings you here,' asked a neighbour.

"'The visitor said, 'I have come to see Ghyanghon.'

"''Are you a doctor then?' asked the neighbour.

"''Why do you say so?' asked the visitor. 'Ghyanghon does not suffer from any long-term illness, does he?'

"'The neighbours looked about embarrassedly. Then one of them said, 'Oh no, not really. He only has a persistent cough, and the phlegm he spits out has spots of tar in it. In the evening, he sports a slight fever. It is nothing. It must have been brought on by the heat, nothing like a good bath to cure it.'

"'The visiting ghost was shocked out of his senses. His eyes bulged with consternation. He never returned to Ghyanghon but went straight to the far end of the Land of the One-Legged to the residence of Nakeshwari's aunt, where he spilled the beans. The alliance was broken. Nakeshwari is a good-looking monstress. Her beauty had enchanted Ghyanghon. For several days, Ghyanghon wept migrating from one tree to the next. Then he took a vow of silence and sat inside a dark well. That, finally, that alliance has been revived is the good news and nought else."

'I said to the ghosts, "What is it about spots of tar in phlegm?"

'Skull said, "You have blood in your veins. We have tar in place of blood. If tuberculose, our lungs emit that tar."

'I asked them, "Do ghosts then also die from illnesses? Humans, when they die, turn into ghosts. In that case, what do ghosts become after demise?"

'"Why," replied the skull. "Ghosts become marbles, don't they, when dead? Surely, you have seen the small fiery glass balls that boys play with!"

'I said, "Marbles! Why on earth should they become marbles of all things on this planet?"

'The skull looked annoyed. Said he, "Why, we are sorry. We should have consulted you before dying. From henceforth, that can be the idea."

'I said, "Forgive me, sirs, for I was ignorant. If you kindly permit, may I ask yet another question. If ghosts become marbles upon death, is it not dangerous to play with them?"

'The skull answered, "What is the trouble with playing with dead ghosts? Had they been live, it would certainly be different."

'Then he said, "We really cannot waste time talking nonsense. We have started a company, and must get to work. We are the Skull, Skeleton & Co. We are no ordinary ghosts. Take care, and remember our words. If you don't, you will be in trouble. We go now. We will not see you again."

'So saying, the skull and the skeleton departed. I was left all alone inside the castle. From thenceforward what I did, you have already guessed. Hence I need not repeat it. Kankabaty. This is my story and you are now abreast with it.'

Kankabaty said, 'In that case, perhaps I should go and take some of Nakeshwari's money. Then she will surely kill me and you and I shall depart together. For a devoted wife, what destiny could be more ideal?' So saying, Kankabaty prepared to rise to her feet, but at this very juncture, a terrible yell rent the air. The entire castle shook and the doors and windows reverberated with the impact of the cry. A great darkness descended inside the castle. The lamp inside the room did not get extinguished but its flame grew small. Khetu said, 'Kankabaty! Here comes Nakeshwari!'

For so long, Kankabaty had been seated by the bedside. She rose quickly, shut fast the door and stood against it, pressing her full body weight onto the wooden barrier. She was determined not to let Nakeshwari enter the room.

A horrible smell, deep darkness and the intermittent banging of windows and doors overtook the room.

At last, the noises receded, so did the darkness and the room was again filled with light. Kankabaty saw Khetu lying with eyes closed, as if he were dead, on the bed. Next to him stood a giantess—Kankabaty ran forward and fell at the feet of Nakeshwari.

Said Kankabaty, 'My dear, do not kill my husband. I am poor Kankabaty. I have gone through immense hardship to get married to my husband. He is as precious as my life to me. Indeed, I have no one in the world save him. My dear, why don't you take my life instead of my husband's? I fall at your feet, do not kill him. I do not want your money neither your riches; only give me my husband, let me go home with him. What I have taken from you I will return. If you want to taste human flesh, I offer you myself, drink my blood and be pleased. Do not hurt my husband, let him go.'

Holding fast to Nakeshwari's feet, Kankabaty wept and made various entreaties. They were so pitiful as to even melt a heart of stone, but the monstress remained unmoved. She did not even pay Kankabaty the least bit of her attention. The more Kankabaty wept and beseeched, the higher she raised her left palm, and uttered, 'Shoo, shoo!'

Kankabaty said, 'My dear, I won't leave here without my husband. Give me my husband, and I will leave immediately. Rise, dear husband. Let us go from here. Dear husband, rise, please.' The more Kankabaty wept and the more she spoke, the more Nakeshwari said, hand raised, 'Shoo, shoo!'

At last, Kankabaty stood up, her eyes red with anger. She wiped her face and haughtily addressed Nakeshwari: 'So you won't give him to me, will you? Nor eat me either? You have nothing to say save "shoo, shoo!", haven't you? Well, then, I nary care if you are Nakeshwari or any other, today will be the end of one of us—you or me.'

So saying, Kankabaty rushed madwoman-like to take Nakeshwari by the shoulders. Without saying a word in reply, Nakeshwari simply let out a breath and the draft carried Kankabaty right to the entrance of the room. She rose again and went at Nakeshwari. Nakeshwari cast another breath, and this time Kankabaty fell right outside the castle.

Then Kankabaty arose slowly to her feet and entreated, 'My dear, I will not wrestle you, I will not hit you. I don't even want my husband back anymore. All I want is not to be separated from him. Let me die holding his feet. If you have to kill, kill us both. If you have to eat, make a meal of the pair of us together. Nothing else I want from you. I only make to you this prayer. Do not deprive me of my destiny.' So saying, Kankabaty ran towards the bedroom. Without a word, Nakeshwari then exhaled again, and Kankabaty found herself outside the mountain in the middle of the forest.

Frog Sahib

As if departed, Kankabaty lay prone in the middle of the forest, bruised and bleeding from her frequent falls. It is pointless to rise, she reflected, seeing as Nakeshwari would literally blow her off soon as she entered the castle. Kankabaty wept inconsolably at what she thought was her misfortune of not being able to join her husband in death. She said to herself, 'Better to breathe my last out here contemplating his beautiful feet. Perhaps, the Great God will have mercy on me and we will be reunited in heaven.'

So decided, Kankabaty began meditating on Khetu's rosy feet, which had shapely toes bearing the likeness of champak flowers.

When Kankabaty had thus entered her trance, the seed of a fresh idea germinated in her mind. The thought went thus—

'Aren't there antidotes and remedies to the harm wrought by the ghosts, witches and monstresses of this world? There are wizards and medicine men who know chants that can break their spell, surely they will successfully restore my husband to me. And if they cannot, at least I will be given his dead body in which case I will gladly join it in the pyre to obtain some peace. Either way, I shall attempt to rescue my husband from the clutches of Nakeshwari and will not rest sans initiative. I may be a woman who is not expected to do so, but I fear none when the stake is the welfare of my husband.'

Kankabaty wiped her eyes and sat up. Then she rose from the ground resolved to hike her way to a human colony.

However, Kankabaty did not know the way to a human colony. Khetu had asked her to hike north but in the deep darkness it was impossible to make out which direction it lay in. And Kankabaty was afraid that if she waited for the sun to rise, it might be too late for her husband. She decided to walk steadfastly in a single direction and in whichever village she reached contact the medicine man and bring him back to Khetu. Time being of essence, she knew she must not waste a bit of it.

Crossing cavern and forest, hill and vale, Kankabaty went, unwavering from her mission, true as a lodestar. Morning dawned, and soon it was midday, yet she spied neither town nor village. Let alone a hut or a cluster of houses, she did not even spot a single human soul in her milieu.

She had just begun to worry and formulate plans as to what to do next when Kankabaty came across a frog in her path. Seeing the strange appearance of the frog, Kankabaty was perplexed. The amphibian had a hat on its head, sported a waistcoat on its chest and belly and wore a pair of trousers over its legs. In short, it looked like a pucca British sahib. Indeed, its get-up was such that it was almost unrecognisable. Only its complexion stayed green as of a frog, notwithstanding the liberal use of soap, and it had not yet purchased a pair of shoes to complete its ensemble. With both hands in its pockets, the frog strode along the foot trail with a swagger matching its bold image.

Accosted by this unforeseen sight, Kankabaty smiled even in the midst of her troubles. She decided to ask the frog the way to the nearest village.

Kankabaty said to the frog, 'Master Frog! Which way is the village? Which way should I go to reach the village?' Then she said, 'Master Frog! I did not hear you. Could you not repeat what you just said? I said—which way should I go in order to reach a village—any village?'

The frog said, 'Sheesh. Fish. Damn.'

Kankabaty said, 'Master Frog! I gather you are English spoken. I do not speak English, if you could repeat what you said in the Bengali language, I shall be most grateful to you.'

The frog looked about itself. It realised that there was no one in the vicinity. Its concern was that if it was heard speaking in Bengali, then it would lose its caste and people would begin to refer to it as a mere 'native'. When it found it was alone and had no witnesses, it felt brave enough to speak in the language.

Looking daggers at Kankabaty, it angrily said, 'What a country bumpkin you are. Don't you see I am a pucca sahib? Why do you still call me Master Frog? What do I have to do to have you address me as Frog Sahib?'

Said Kankabaty, 'Dear Frog Sahib, forgive me my trespass. Now please do me the favour of telling me which way to take to reach the village.'

Curiously enough, the frog grew more annoyed at Kankabaty's words. It snapped at her, 'Death be upon you, you unfortunate wench. Just hearing your words scorches my epidermis. Even after reasoning with you, you are unbothered. Why would you keep referring to me as a frog? Don't I have a name for myself? Are you too high and mighty to bring it to your lips? Mister Gumish is my name.'

Kankabaty said, 'Sire! I was ignorant, hence forgive me. Now, Mr Gumish, would you mind telling me the way to the village? My name is Kankabaty. I am in distress. I have lost my beloved husband. I am looking for a medicine man to cure my husband. I do not have time to lose. Please take pity on this unfortunate soul and tell her the way to the village.'

That Kankabaty called him a sahib and addressed him as Mr Gumish somewhat calmed the frog. In fact, it became quite cheerful. It said to Kankabaty, 'Do you know the story of my turning sahib?'

Kankabaty said, 'No, sire. I do not know that story. How do I get to the village? How far is it from this location?'

The frog said, 'Look here, Lankabaty! Did you not say your name is Lankabaty? Well, listen well, Lankabaty. One day,

I was seated inside the forest. The elephant had been coming up my way. I thought that out of regard for my prestige and fear of reprisal the elephant would sidestep me and proceed ahead. Now hear me relate the account of his impertinent audacity. Without so much as a warning or request, the wicked elephant passed right over me. While so doing little did it hesitate. I trembled in anger and swore to teach the elephant a lesson. When angry, I lose control over my senses. It is one reason why people fear me. Said I to the elephant, "You camel-browed, comb-toothed mammal, did you think nothing of crossing me?" Didn't I speak well, Lankabaty?'

Kankabaty said, 'My name is Kankabaty, not "Lankabaty". You did well. But you have not yet told me about the way to the village. Let me take your leave then. I can wait here no longer.'

The frog said, 'Tarry, what's your big hurry? Let me finish my tale. The elephant was frightened by my rage. So he said, "Speak no more, you flat-nosed one, only my goodness has kept you alive and pain-free." Well, Kankabaty, tell me this. Is my nose flat after all?'

Kankabaty thought here is an issue on which the green crab, too, had taken umbrage. And it certainly does very much look to be the case with this fraud of an amphibian. So she said, 'Not at all, not at all. Who says your nose is flat? You have an aquiline nose. Is this the way to the village?'

The frog seemed immersed in deep thought for a while. Kankabaty hoped it was ascertaining the way to the village in response to her question. Thinking that it would speak suddenly and she would somehow miss it, she gazed at its face hopefully.

After spending long moments in solemn rumination, the frog spoke at last. It said to Kankabaty, 'Perhaps it is then that the elephant said so in order to rhyme his repartee to my remark. Here, listen for yourself:

'"You camel-browed, comb-toothed mammal, did you think nothing of crossing me?

Speak no more, you flat-nosed one, only my goodness has kept you live and pain-free."

'Here, Kankabaty, don't you think it is a nice idea to publish this poem in a newspaper? Yet it contains my criticism and references to flat noses. Better not publish it in a newspaper then. Well, now you know the tale of the elephant's exceptional audacity. It made me reflect—don't people always respect the sahib? Henceforth I will dress as one. I do look like a pucca sahib, don't I? From now on, people will curtsey before me, and fear me. When I board the third class of the Indian Railway, others will not board the same carriage. I will don my hat and stand at the door, and the passengers will say, "This carriage is reserved for sahibs. We shall not board this carriage." Well, Kankabaty, is it not a grand idea?'

Kankabaty said, 'It is certainly a grand idea. Now please show me the way to the village. Or else, let me know, and permit me to take my leave.'

The frog cupped a forepaw behind its ear and it said, 'Pardon me, but what did you just say?'

Kankabaty said, 'I asked you, which is the path that takes me to the village? How far is the village? How long will it take me to get there?'

The frog said, 'Right, please help me with this one calculation. How can I show you the way when I am in grave distress? I had an *aadhuli*, half a rupee, in my personal possession. I have lent it to somebody. This person and I have come to an agreement that everydayhe would pay me one half of his debt. On day one, he will give me four annas, which is the quarter of a rupee, on day two, two annas, on day three one, on day four two paise, on day five he will hand over one paisa or five *kada*. The next day, he would give two-and-a-half kada, and the next day one kada and a quarter, the next, a half of that, and the next a half of that, too.'

In a fine soothing croon, the frog now began to weep aloud. It went, 'Oh dear, oh my. This debt I see will never be repaid. I will never get the full value of my half a rupee, my dearest. Here I die in its grief. A fraudster has cheated me in a confidence trick out of my very belongings. Oh dear, I have nothing in the world save this half of a rupee. Yet people think it is a joking matter and jeer, oh dear. What shall I do? Where shall I go? Oh dear, I have lost everything, I have nowhere to go.'

The frog sniffled and sobbed. It crooned, 'Oh dear! All I had hoped for was for you to sit with me for a while and ask after my well-being. Yet now you will depart, leaving me all alone. Oh dear, it breaks my heart to little smithereens and triggers oceanic waves of sorrow. Oh dear, what shall I do? Which way do you go, my dearest? You would reach the village by that way, though, even if it lies far ahead. Indeed, it is so far you cannot reach it today. You cannot leap like a frog, can you, my dear? You can only take small paces. Indeed, my dear, your gait amuses me so. Oh dear, oh my, your gait makes me weep. My dearest, you are a good soul. Even if you are educated, you are not a superior woman, my love. You are steadfast and responsible, discreet and devoted to your husband. Oh dear, you don't act all high and mighty, do you? Alas, I have lost my half-rupee forever. What shall I do now? Oh dear, what shall I do?'

Stale Waters

Said Kankabaty to herself, 'Oh dear, what a pain on top of my own! Let's see, now he has stopped crying, it is time for me to go.'

Kankabaty walked as the frog had indicated. Soon it was eventide but the forest still loomed about her. When it was dark, she felt exhausted. Seating herself on a rock on the forest floor, she began to weep at her bitter fate.

As she wept, a tiny voice buzzed softly in her ear: 'What people are you, my dear? Whose daughter are you then?'

Kankabaty looked about herself and saw nothing but a little mosquito flying by her ear. Inspecting it carefully, she found it was just a girl of a mosquito.

She replied to the mosquito, 'I am a human woman, my dear. My name is Kankabaty.'

The girl mosquito said, 'A human woman? Then you are food, aren't you? Whose blood our father brings to us every night? I do drink it, but I have never seen a human before. Being genteel and all, we have not been told of such matters. Show yourself to me then. Let me see how humans are.'

So saying, the little mosquito began circling Kankabaty in order to see her from every angle.

Having seen her to her heart's content, the little mosquito then said, 'You are not a big human. You are little, aren't you?'

Kankabaty replied, 'Not really, but I am still considered a girl.'

The mosquito girl asked, 'What is it that is your name you said?'

Kankabaty said, 'My name is Kankabaty, I am the Bangled One.'

The mosquito girl said, 'Great. My name is Raktabaty, I am the Bloody One. When I was young, my belly would be tumescent with freshly drunken blood seeing which my father gave me this name. Kankabaty and Raktabaty. Our names rhyme together, now, don't they? Come on, then, let's exchange a friendly vow.'

Kankabaty said, 'I have been aggrieved and am in great distress. Now is not the time for me to exchange vows and celebrate.'

Raktabaty said, 'You are an honest woman who has lost her husband. But do not worry. As soon as Father comes home, I will tell him about you. He will find you several husbands. Now come along, Sister, let's exchange a vow.

Yet what vow should be exchanged? I like stale waters a lot. Wherever there is stale water, I come out to play and fly there without a care or worry. Let's name our vow Stale Water. From today, you are my Stale Water and I am your Stale Water; now then, is that a good vow after your liking?'

Kankabaty thought there is no point arguing with this individual. If an old man like the frog could not be made to see sense, here is only a slip of a mosquito who is yet to get a grip on the world. Let it do as it pleases, I will not enter any disputation.

So Kankabaty sighed, and, in a resigned tone, said, 'As you please. I am your Stale Water, and you are my Stale Water. Dear God, dear god of my heart, where are you? Where am I? How are you faring wherever you are? Well, such is how I am.'

So saying, Kankabaty sighed and wept. The little mosquito said, 'Dear Stale Water, where are the other two legs of yours? Have you broken them? Is that why you weep? Don't worry, Stale Water. One day, I, too, broke a leg while playing. See, that leg got regenerated. Your leg will grow back, too, don't cry anymore.'

Kankabaty said, 'I have not broken my leg. Humans don't have as many legs as mosquitoes. I was not crying from losing my leg.'

The little mosquito resumed buzzing all around Kankabaty. After examining every part of her body, and organs as well, it finally settled on her nose, and said, 'Oh dear, Stale Water, what misfortune! Where is your nose?

Who cut it off, Stale Water? Now, how shall you have your dinner?' Kankabaty was at a loss to make sense of what it said. At last, she figured out that the mosquito was referring to the proboscis.

Said Kankabaty to herself, 'This mosquito girl is a mere infant. It has still to learn so much about the world.'

Kankabaty said to the mosquito, 'The human nose looks the way you see it. It is not as long as the nose of the mosquito. We do not eat through the nose but through the mouth we perform that function.'

Raktabaty said, 'My poor Stale Water. You are so unlucky you don't have a long nose. Don't I look so pretty in mine? When I see my face reflected on water, my heart is filled with joy. My mother says, when I grow up, I will be a true beauty. Sister Stale Water, I will make you out into a beauty, too! When Father comes home, I will ask him to pull your nose and extend it.'

Kankabaty said to herself, 'Not again! What a big deal these animals make of the nose. All they can think of is the nose. Truly, they spend the larger part of their lives thinking about it. The green crab mentioned the appendage, so did the frog, now the mosquito girl is also talking about it, and then there is Nakeshwari of the Long Nose. How unbearable!'

She reflected, 'Indeed, I have landed in some trouble even amidst my plight. Here I am trying to reach a village to bring the medicine man to my husband, and first the frog, next the mosquito, all of them are chewing my brain in concert. It is as if I landed from the frying pan right into the fire. If the mosquito's little daughter can exercise me so, I have no idea what it will take to put up with its father's jokes.'

Said Raktabaty, 'See that leaf yonder, Stale Water? The one which has its corner all curled up. That's our home. My mothers are inside it. I have three mothers. Father has gone on his foray, he will return with treats and food. Let me fly to my moms and let them know that my Stale Water has arrived.' So saying, Raktabaty flew off. She returned in a minute to say, 'Come on, Stale Water! Mother has summoned you. Come, meet my mother.'

Kankabaty had no choice but to rise. She followed Raktabaty to the curly leaf. A young woman mosquito looked out from inside it and said, 'Hello, my dear!? Are you my daughter's friend? Very well. Raktabaty is a very dear daughter. The husband is a rich man with assets, and she is our only heir. Raktabaty told us you have lost your husband. Have you? What happened to him?'

Kankabaty began weeping anew. She said, 'My lady, I am in distress. I have suffered a great sorrow. I cannot see nor think clearly. If I don't get my husband back alive and well, I will certainly give up my life. Nakeshwari has gobbled my husband. I am headed to a human village to save his life. I will meet the medicine man there and bring him to my husband. Hence I can wait no longer. I will walk the forest path again, and walk through the night. But I don't know the way, and besides, I will be unable to see in the dark. If you give me an idea ofwhich way to go, I will not forget your kindness.'

The mosquito missus said, 'You are young, and hence very naïve. You do not know society's ways. We are married women and, moreover, we are respectable wives married to a mosquito of high repute. On top of that, we observe the purdah. We do not step out to avoid being humiliated. How are we supposed to know the way to the village? Do not weep, though. Just you wait. Let the boss come home. You are our relative now, being Raktabaty's Stale Water, aren't you, now? The boss will certainly devise a solution to help. Just you wait.'

The mosquito who had been speaking to Kankabaty was the mother of Raktabaty, the mosquito's youngest wife. Now, the mosquito's oldest wife peeped out of the leaf.

The older missus said, 'Is that a human child over there? I will adopt it. Seeing as I don't have a child of my own, long have I wished for a pet. It is as well that this human child has stopped by. I will keep it. It is a bit old but not too old to be trained. Don't humans eat sheep, goats and pigeon and yet keep them as pets? If we adopt this human, we will begin to love it. Then we will no longer get the urge to feed on it, will we?'

Now, the middle wife of the mosquito appeared on the other side of Raktabaty's mum, and she said, 'Come on, Big Sister. Talk sense, will you? If you will keep this young human as pet, do it in a way that is useful. Take a lesson from the humans who keep cows as pets for the sake of their milk. We can do the same with this child. The boss travels such long distances to procure blood that it is stale by the time it gets home. If we keep a human at home, we get to drink fresh blood anytime.'

Raktabaty's mum interceded, 'The two of you are exasperating, indeed. Why do you interfere with every affair? Raktabaty is a mere child, she has found this human by the wayside and taken a liking to it, why should she let you adopt it or drink its blood? Do you want to rob a child? Is this the quality of your judgement? Let the boss come, I will definitely complain. I don't want to live here anymore. Let him escort me to my parents'. My brothers and father are still in this world. I have nothing to worry. Besides, my family is not poor. Everything shines brightly about me.'

The oldest missus then said, 'Woe betide you, just hear the girl speak. So proud is she of her brothers and father that she won't walk on her own six feet. Oh, woe betide her relatives.'

Thus, a loud quarrel began amongst all three, as Kankabaty stood by aghast at them. 'Wow, these creatures duly want to keep me as if I were a four-legged pet animal,' she said to herself.

The quarrel of the wives-in-law paused for recess. Kankabaty sat on her rock and waited for the mosquito male. A long time passed, but it did not return home.

Kankabaty asked the mosquitoes, 'My dears, why is your boss so late?'

The youngest queen of the hearth replied, 'The bamboo is slashed, the baskets are stashed, for to bring home the blood by the sires.'

Meaning, the boss has come upon a lot of blood today. It is unable to bring it home all by itself. So it has hired porters to carry the blood, which it is stashing in baskets and suspending from each end of a bamboo pole for ease of transport. It is why it is late. Kankabaty waited some more, yet the mosquito did not return home. She asked again, 'When will your boss come home, dears? It is getting very late.'

This time the middle missus answered her. She said, 'The rice husk burns in a pan, the winnow fans, a corner is occupied by the sire.'

Meaning, to collect blood, the boss has entered a human's home. The human has lit rice husk in a pan and fanned the flames with a winnow to create a raging fire. The room is filled with smoke, and the boss is trapped in it. To protect itself, it has occupied a corner of the room where it has concealed itself. It is the reason why it is late. When the smoke dissipates, it will emerge from the house.

Kankabaty fell quiet and waited for a long time. Then she said again, 'What, ho, mistresses? The boss has not returned. How much more late will it be?'

Now, the oldest missus spoke. She said, 'Crack the bite fat, thwack and splat, likely is dead, the sire.' Meaning, perhaps the boss had alighted on somebody. Seated on their person, he had taken a fat bite out of them. The man swatted the boss, and the blow may have killed him.

'The boss is dead.' Hearing thus an inauspicious pronouncement, the youngest queen took offence. Said she, 'You have a big mouth. Let the boss come home. I will tell him, if you die, your oldest will be at peace. The boss will put lime and shoeblack on your face, shave your head, pour rotten milk on your pate and duly bid you riddance.'

Boss Mosquito

The three wives-in-law began a fresh quarrel. Raktabaty began crying loudly. A pandemonium broke out in the mosquito's home. At this juncture, arrived the boss mosquito. Witnessing the loud exchange of bitter argument, the shouting and the remonstrations, it felt simultaneously disgusted and furious.

The mosquito said, 'I can nary take this anymore. Due to your quarrel, neither crow nor kite can bear to rest on the bough nearby our house. Neither Lady Luck nor Laxmi, the wealth goddess, stays at a place where there is such infighting, and in the taluka, the men's blood dries in their veins. Often do I wish to hang myself or swallow poison, indeed suicide is the outcome clearly written in the book of my fate. Only the other day did I have a narrow escape. I had chanced to alight on the skin of an opium eater. How bitter is his blood's taste. I had to throw away one proboscis full of his blood. Rinsed my mouth many times to get rid of the poison. Say I to myself, "In vain did I take pains to save myself from accidental death since I have little wish to continue living in the face of your daily bickering."'

Thus did the mosquito censure his wives until his temper settled down. When he was calm, Raktabaty came and sat on his lap.

Raktabaty said, 'Dad! My Stale Water is here.'

The mosquito asked, 'What on earth, now, is Stale Water?'

Raktabaty's mother answered for her daughter. She said, 'My dear, it is a human child. It is sitting here since evening. Raktabaty has exchanged vows of friendship with it. The girl has been weeping ever since it arrived here. Says she, "I am an honest woman who has lost her husband. Nakeshwari has gobbled him. I will go to the village, find a doctor and make him well."

'I said to her, "My child, wait a bit. Let the boss come home, we will discuss a solution. You are Raktabaty's Stale Water, we will take good care of you." Yet, Raktabaty acquiring Stale Water and being happy cannot be abided with by your two other queens. They now wish to adopt the human child. On this count, they have showered me with many an abuse. Well, I propose before you, since my staying here is no more of any consequence, do drop me off at my parents'. Thenceforth, live happily with your queens. Since I am but a thorn in your flesh, let me take your leave.'

The mosquito said, 'Where is the girl?'

Raktabaty's mother said, 'Yonder, outdoors.'

Raktabaty said, 'Dad, come with me. I will show you where my Stale Water is.'

Raktabaty and the mosquito both took flight. They buzzed themselves to the spot where Kankabaty sat, pale-faced and teary-eyed.

Raktabaty said, 'Stale Water! Look hither. Father comes to see you.'

Respectfully, Kankabaty arose and joined her hands in greeting. Keeping all of her in the frame, the mosquito went and settled on the tip of a monocotyledon stalk while Raktabaty, too, alighted on another stalk next to it. Kankabaty remained standing, hands joined, before the mosquito.

Most humbly did Kankabaty say: 'My sire, I am but a girl in distress. I am without a guardian. In this mysterious garden, I am on my own. I am an honest woman who has lost her husband. I am the sorry Kankabaty. My dearest husband is taken by a ghost. Please rescue him at my instance. Hereby I seek your refuge.'

The mosquito asked, 'Whose property are you?'

Kankabaty said, 'Sire, I was previously my father's property. In childhood, human girlchildren are their father's property. The father has the right to sell them or give them in charity. The blind, the destitute, the elderly and the ill—whoever he chooses will be sold or given that property. Before the child attains full knowledge of the world, the parents sell her and are pleased to believe themselves relieved of responsibility.

'Such is the custom that prevails amongst us. My father has sold me to my husband at the price of three thousand gold coins. Today I am the property of my husband whom I have lost and having lost the care of whom wandering the forest alone and woebegone. Therefore, while I was earlier my father's property, I belong to my husband now.'

The mosquito said, 'Not really. I did not ask that question. I only asked which mosquito it is whose property you are.'

Kankabaty replied, 'Oh dear, who is the mosquito that is my master? Of this, I know nothing of.'

The mosquito said, 'Oh dear. Raktabaty, your Stale Water, I gather, is a grief-crazed madwoman, yet with no knowledge of the world. If she cannot answer my questions correctly, how on earth am I supposed to help her?'

Raktabaty said, 'My sister, Stale Water, hear the questions my father asks of you and answer them correctly.'

The mosquito said, 'Hear me, oh human child. The men and women you see in India are all the property of mosquitoes. I am sure you have run away from the gentleman mosquito that is your master. And that is why you are keeping his name a secret from me, lest I return you. Yet, fear not, child, answer me truthfully. I ask you—which mosquito do you belong to, who sits on your skin and partakes of your haemoglobin? What is his name? What is his address? How many wives is he married to? Who are its children? How many are boys? How many girls? Does he have nephews and grandchildren? Do his friends and relations exercise any ownership on your person? Are you joint property or a singular one? Are you shared with different mosquitoes owning different parts of your body, such as your arms and legs? If you are shared property, where are the mortgage papers? Did any middleman or clerical agent prepare the affidavit or was it the court registrar, the *ameen* themselves, who arrived in your house to sign it? Answer all of my queries accurately. This is because I intend to buy you for myself. There is no dearth of humans in our taluka and a great abundance of human blood there is none to partake of. You, on the other hand, have exchanged a vow of friendship with my Raktabaty—you are her Stale Water—hence it is that I desire to buy you. If I do not, then the mosquitoes that are your masters may file a lawsuit against me in the court. They might even win the lawsuit and take you away from here. Then my Raktabaty will be extremely sad. She will weep incessantly in consequence. One more advice do I have. Indians should not thus travel from village to village. Indians need must sit at home in their respective villages. Only then will there be no dispute amongst mosquitoes over property and estate. Each mosquito can then enjoy their own property in peace and happiness. We will soon devise a way to ensure that. In this moment, reply to my question. Answer me the name of your mosquito-master.'

Kankabaty replied, 'My sire. Truthfully do I say I know not the name of my mosquito-master. That humans are owned by mosquitoes was unbeknownst to me till this very date. That humans are distributed, shared and sold by and amongst mosquitoes was also unknown to me. I even did not know that mosquitoes had names. Tell me, pray, how it is that I will apprise you as to which mosquito is my master.'

The mosquito now became enraged. Its eyes grew red and bulged by the force of its fury. In a sarcastic voice, it said, 'No, honey, I believe that you know nothing. You are a babe in the woods. You have never even seen a mosquito on your body. Those mosquitoes you do not know. You have never spoken to them. You pretender. All you know is going about crying wolf, in the guise of an honest woman who has lost her husband.'

Hearing the mosquito's remonstrations, Kankabaty started crying. Gazing at Kankabaty, Raktabaty winked once. The message behind the wink was—'Stale Water! Do not cry. My father has a quick temper. He is already enraged, your tears will make him angrier still.'

What Raktabaty predicted indeed took place. Seeing Kankabaty cry, the mosquito grew angrier. It said, 'What a tedious girl you are! You know only to weep and wail. All the questions I explained you failed to adequately respond. Now see if you are able to or not answer me correctly this one enquiry. There are crores and crores more of humans roaming this wide world. What is the purpose for which they have been created? Just spell out this single answer.'

Said Kankabaty, 'Why have humans been created on this earth? Why, I really don't have a clue to this answer.'

The mosquito said, 'This girl is indeed foolish and, on top of it, raving mad. She is extremely ignorant. All Indians are foolish and they are completely bereft of common sense. Why, my Raktabaty is a mere child, but she is a lakh times smarter than this human. Tell me, my dear child Raktabaty, why have Indian humans been created?'

Raktabaty said, 'Why, Father, it is only so we can take a drink of their blood.'

The mosquito said, 'Did you hear the correct answer? Do you know now the express purpose for which Indian humans have been put on earth?'

Kankabaty replied,'Yes, your highness. Here now I stand informed that all human creation is for to make the meal of our mosquito brethren.'

Said Raktabaty, 'After all, Dad, my Stale Water is nothing but a human kid. All mosquitoes know that humans have brains, but no intelligence. The foolish amongst us are called humans in the pejorative sense. Everyone says, "Don't speak of that mosquito as one, he is not mosquito, but human." So how can my Stale Water be expected to be as smart as we are? Spare her, Dad, scold my Stale Water no more.'

The mosquito said to itself, 'Truth has been spoken. It is pointless to ask any more questions to this human kid. I, myself, need must take the initiative to investigate.'

Then the mosquito said, 'I say, girl, tell me the name of your village, will you? I do hope you can at least answer this present question.'

Kankabaty replied that the name of her village was Kusumghati. It immediately sent out its servants and associates to Kusumghati with the instruction that Kankabaty's masters be summoned to a conference. The messengers reached Kusumghati, and after a thorough search and many enquiries, came to know that three mosquitoes were the rightful owners of Kankabaty. They were named Gajagand, the Elephant-Cheeked One, Brihatmund, the Large-Headed One, and Bikrittund, the Warped-Lipped One. Raktabaty's father was Deerghshund or the Long-Nosed One. The messengers learned that Kankabaty's owners lived on a sal tree named The Sky Faced.

The messengers found the address, and narrated all to Kankabaty's owners. They wasted no time in accompanying the messengers to Deerghshund's address. Thereafter, after much argument and bargain, Deerghshund bought Kankabaty for the price of three *chhatak* of human ichor. Having fulfilled the transaction, it said to its daughter, 'Here, Raktabaty. Take your Stale Water. This human child is ours now, from this day forth it is our property.'

Addressing Gajagand, Brihatmund, Bikrittund and all other mosquitoes present, Deerghshund said, 'Gentlemen of the Assembly! A grave danger is here threatening all our existences. Till date, by feeding on Indians' blood, mosquitoes had been leading their lives happily and peacefully. India is surrounded by the black waters on three sides while on the other, there are gargantuan mountain ranges. Just as animals are kept inside a paddock, so, too, we had kept Indians enclosed with the help of these natural fences. By staying in India, Indians so far had remained at our service and humbly donated their blood for the purpose of our nourishment. Not so any longer. Today, some of them are waging attempts to cross the high seas and conquer the mountains. That if they behave thus and deprive us of their blood, they commit a great sin is common knowledge. Yet whatever be the reason, the travelling of Indians from one village to another has become more frequent. For instance, just this very evening, a human kid arrived at my door from Kusumghati. That human kid had been your property. Today your property has escaped; tomorrow mine will run away. If humans travel from one village to the next in this way, the consequences of such tourism becomes plain to everybody. One of the outcomes of travel and tourism is acquisition of new learning and enlightenment. Yet if Indians travel and become enlightened they will no longer remain in our control. Commerce and other exchanges will result in greater wealth for them. They will then buy mosquito nets and devise other technologies to deny us our daily meal. Hence I say, let us find a way to bar Indians from foreign travel and stop them going from village to village.'

Deerghshund's speech was greeted with tumultuous applause. Everyone agreed that Deerghshund was a very prudent mosquito; that Deerghshund had the most acute foresight, that none could match Deerghshund's wits and learning on the face of this earth. They acknowledged that it was imperative to find a way to stop Indians from travelling between villages. After much research and consultation, the mosquitoes decided to invite the brahmins to pass an injunction for only then would the humans follow such an order. Or else, they would pay no heed to the stipulation. Having agreed on this agenda, the assembly of mosquitoes sent out invitation cards to all of India's scholars and learned men. When they arrived, Deerghshund addressed them and asked them to research the scriptures for citations confirming the proposal. The experts wasted no time in conducting a seminar and passing the said injunction. As per the injunction, in Kaliyuga, it was banned for the human to travel at all from one village to the next. If one did so, one committed a great sin for which one would be made an outcast right away. For there was no atonement prescribed in the scriptures for this particular trespass. The question arises then that what would Indians do in Kaliyuga instead? To Indians in Kaliyuga, what the scriptures prescribe sounds like so:

Sadakritanjaliputabyangshukahpihitekhshanah.
Ghorandhtamasekripesantubharatvaasinah.
Pibanturudhiranchaisangyabantomashakabhuvi.
Adyaprabhriti bai loke bidhiresprabartitatah.

Meaning, roughly, during Kaliyuga, Indians, having placed blinkers on their eyes, will join their eyes and remain seated inside their dark well-like homes, while the mosquitoes and their uncles would continue to suck out their lifeblood. Having thus received a suitable arrangement made after their very hearts, the mosquitoes were no doubt pleased. The brahmins took their payments and left for their respective residences. The mosquito guests, too, flew homeward.

The Dwarf

Deerghshund, the mosquito, said, 'Raktabaty, my child, from this time on, this human offspring is yours.'

Raktabaty said, 'Beloved Father, this is my sister. With her have I exchanged the solemn Stale Water vows. My Stale Water is in trouble. Nakeshwari has gobbled her spouse. Poor Stale Water has spent herself crying. Do what will lead her to her husband then.' The mosquito wished to update itself on how Nakeshwari came to eat the husband. Kankabaty complied; and supplied him with all the information that was to be had.

After much rumination, the mosquito said, 'Seeing as you are my Raktabaty's friend, Stale Water, I have begun to feel kindly towards you. Hence we shall not feed on you. We shall try and feed you instead. We shall do our best to lead you to your husband. Kharbbur Maharaj is a human who lives in my taluka. I have been told that he knows of many medicines and magical chants. If there is no rain, he can chant an incantation that pierces a hole in the firmament. If it is about to hail, he can say a chant to stop the ice from precipitating. If any elderly woman passes by him, he can correctly spot if she is a witch or not. Ghosts are known to run for their lives as soon as they spy him. There is no one on earth as learned as he is. He is certainly the one who can rescue your husband from Nakeshwari's clutches.'

Said Kankabaty, 'In that case, mister, let us not waste anymore time. Let us go to this gentleman at once. The grief of my husband is burning my soul and has robbed me of my eyesight. Only if he lives will I stay alive. Else, I shall sacrifice my pointless life.'

The mosquito said, 'It is late, you are tired and the taluka is not nearby. Yet, wait. Let me summon my young brother, we will all mount his back and go to Kharbbur Maharaj presently.'

So saying, the mosquito sent for its younger brother. The brother arrived in a short while. Addressing it as 'Haati

Thakurpo', the mosquito women paid it their respects and began ribbing it good-naturedly.

Raktabaty said to Haati Thakurpo, 'Uncle! I have got myself a human offspring. I have exchanged my Stale Water vows with it. I love my Stale Water so much, and my Stale Water loves me equally.'

Kankabaty was astonished. How can a massive elephant be the younger brother of a mosquito? Yet, so it was. Inside the forest, it was called 'Haati Thakurpo' by everybody.

Raktabaty's father said to the elephant, 'Hear me, Brother, I am in great distress. Raktabaty has exchanged Stale Water vows with a human girl. That girl is wandering the roads in tears. Raktabaty is a kind soul and close to tears herself. Hence I have decided to rescue her husband for her should it be within my capabilities. Now only Kharbbur Maharaj can help us in our mission. Therefore, I wish to see Kharbbur right away; yet the girl having walked great distances and shed so many tears is completely exhausted. She will be unable to make the hike to the village. Will you then permit us, Brother, to climb onto your back and you can take us to the village? We will be ever so grateful to you for your kindness.' The elephant agreed. Kankabaty then paid her respects to the mosquito women and bade them farewell.

Thereafter, Kankabaty embraced Raktabaty. She said, 'My sister, Stale Water, you have done me the greatest favour. Never shall I forget your love and your kindness. Should I unite with my spouse, we shall meet again. Else, goodbye forever, my dearest friend.' Raktabaty's eyes welled up with tears that fell one by one on the dewy ground.

The mosquito and Kankabaty climbed onto the elephant's back. The elephant ambled forward. The night passed. Very early in the morning the trio reached Kharbbur's home. They found that the moon was smiling seeing the sight of Kharrbur's face which was morose. The moon's smile rendered all of Kharbbur's magic and powers, spells and incantations, hymns and chants, herbs and medicinal plants fruitless. The mosquito, Kankabaty and the elephant reached Kharbbur's door. Seeing the mosquito at his doorstep, Kharbbur became animated. Joining his hands in greeting, Kharbbur said, 'Sire! What brings you to my house so early in the morning? Usually it is that your much-awaited visit takes place at eventide. Have you then come on a social call with your relatives? Is that why you have brought your younger brother with you so you can load its back with a cargo of ichor?'

Said the mosquito, 'Not at all, not at all. I have not come on a social visit but there is a purpose to our meeting of which I shall inform you presently. For now, I wish to know what is the reason that causes you to sit alone with a morose bearing? It is wrongful to stay depressed and with a sad disposition. I have forbidden you humans many times from suffering depression. If one is not happy, one does not generate enough haemoglobin to make blood, and what blood there is feels also tasteless. If you do not keep joyful and eat nutritious, energy-giving food, what is the point of us sitting on your bloodless persons? If all of you commit such wrongful deeds daily, how are we supposed to take care of our dependants and families? Are you not even a little bit fearful that if your mosquito masters who sit on your bodies are unable to feed on a decent amount of blood they might take offence and be angry?'

Kharbbur said, 'Master! You speak rightly. Of that I have been losing weight I am aware as I know that, if it does not find a decent amount of tasty blood in my body, sire will be angry. Yet I have no recourse, for my wife's torment is the cause of my present state.'

The mosquito asked him, 'Wherefore? What is the matter? What kind of torture is that your wife inflicts on yourself?'

Kharbbur replied, 'Master! In our home, man and wife are forever engaged in dispute. We even take our fists to each other twice or three times a day. The unhappy fact is that while I am three hands tall, my wife's height is seven hands. When we fight, the wife takes her big *nagrai* shoe and rains blow upon blow on my head. She herself remains mostly out of my reach and my blows leave her unaffected. Thus it is that I am always defeated by my wife. From the effect of her blows as well as from the resulting depression have I been losing weight and haemoglobin. Thus you have every right to be angry. But I have no recourse. It is not my fault.'

Said the mosquito, 'Oh yes? Is that the case? Well, then, here is an idea. Today you go to battle your wife with an elephant as your mount.'

So saying, the mosquito lent Kharbbur the elephant. Kharbbur went inside the house mounted on the elephant's back. Once inside, he began quarrelling with his wife. The quarrel soon escalated to blows. Seated on the elephant, Kharbbur rained blows on his wife to his heart's content. Today, the wife's strikes did not quite reach Kharbbur. When the battle got intense, the mosquito's happiness knew no bounds. Having no hands, it could not applaud, having no nails, it could not rub them against one another, and yet it danced a hopscotch lifting one leg or two and crooned Narad's name in a buzz in order to egg on the warriors. Soon, the wife had no choice but to surrender and Kharbbur was gratified. Blood flowed vigorously in his arteries and veins. Sampling it, the mosquito said, 'Bravo! You are sweet and succulent.'

One hundred thanks did Kharbbur pay to Mister Mosquito and asked it the purpose of its auspicious visit. Mister Mosquito related Kankabaty and Nakeshwari's account before him.

Hearing it all, Kharbbur said, 'There is no need to worry. I will rescue this lady's husband from the clutches of Nakeshwari. All ghosts, demons and witches are afraid of me. Please take me to Nakeshwari's chambers. Let me, too, sample for myself how mighty she might be.

The mosquito said, 'Let us then begin our journey. Now, speaking of journeys, it is time all human journeys come to an end. All of you think nothing of boarding ships to Rangoon and Vilayat and have begun to visit distant lands now, haven't you? Not to speak of boarding trains and travelling from continent to continent! Just wait until the new injunction is promulgated and then you will feel the pain.'

Kharbbur asked it, 'This time, the scripture interpreters have banned travel now, have they? Cannot we even step out to collect our herbs?'

The mosquito replied, 'Not at all. This time the ruling is such that you cannot take but one step out of doors. Everyone must dig a deep well inside their house, put on blinkers and sit inside it. If you leave the well or take off your blinkers, a sin will have been committed. You will be punished and ostracised and must spent the rest of your life as an outcast. For the sin is no minor one, but a great one per the scriptures. Indeed, a very great one it is. Well? Haven't we got you now? You thought nothing of boarding ships, taking trains, doing studies and manufacturing mosquito nets, now, did you? What will you do now?'

Kharbbur said, 'Your kind are the great masters. What scriptures you make we needs must follow. You propose and you shall dispose. There is nothing on earth you cannot accomplish.'

The mosquito, Kankabaty and Kharbbur climbed onto the elephant. They went into the forest. It was almost the second *prahar* of the night when they reached the mountain.

The Young Ogre

When the monster, Nakeshwari, caught hold of Khetu, he became moribund and lost consciousness. He was even unaware of Kankabaty having been dispensed with by Nakeshwari through a single exhalation.

Having rendered him nearly lifeless, Nakeshwari said to herself, 'I haven't eaten well in a while. Thanks to the blessings of my favoured deity, such a delicious meal has arrived in my castle. If I eat alone, I shall not be able to derive the full pleasures out of such a meal, hence let me invite my maternal aunt to the feast.' So that the meal would not putrefy by the time the aunt arrived, for the moment, Nakeshwari spared Khetu, leaving him unconscious instead.

Nakeshwari left the castle to bring her aunt. Nakeshwari's aunt lived far away, across the thirteen rivers and seven seas, over on the other side of the Land of the One-Legged. It was long indeed before Nakeshwari reached there and subsequently returned to the castle, accompanied by the elderly woman.

Being elderly, the aunt had no teeth. Seeing Khetu's tender flesh, she became overjoyed and slavering.

Feeling Khetu with her fingers, the aunt said in admiring tones, 'Yippie! Such excellent flesh. I am old now, let the one-legged men's flesh that is wiry as a rope be cut into slabs and grilled over a coal fire. Meanwhile, chop off the fingers of this boy and make a dry dish out of it, cook some of the rest of him in sour sauce and keep; we shall relish it for two days, as it won't spoil easily.'

Interrupting this experienced counsel came a loud racket from outside the doors. An elephant's trumpet, a mosquito's buzz and human chatter entered the castle from outside the mountain. Nakeshwari took alarm and she said, 'Oh dear Auntie, all's lost. There's many a slip between the cup and the lip, they say. The wench must have got herself a warlock.'

'Let's go, then,' said the aunt and, legs apart, the two stood at the gate of the tunnel.

Beside the mountain, near the entrance of the tunnel, the mosquito, Kharbbur and Kankabaty climbed down from the elephant. The elephant seemed to be in a pleasant mood. Ofttimes it gathered the dirt on the ground with its trunk and gave itself a dustbath. At other times, it swayed its honker and swung its mass from side to side. The mosquito, Kharbbur and Kankabaty entered the tunnel. While exiting the tunnel and entering the castle, they had to pass under Nakeshwari and her auntie.

Upon gaining entry, the three found Khetu almost at death's door. The young man had no consciousness. It was uncertain that he was even breathing. Kankabaty fell at his feet, took them in her bosom and started a lament. Kharbbur took his pulse, pried open his eyelids and examined him through various means.

In the end, Kharbbur said, 'Kankabaty, do not weep. Your husband is still alive and will be well soon. I am about to cure him of this ailment.' So saying, Kharbbur began chanting a spell and blowing one hundred puffs into the orifices of Khetu's body. He made him inhale the smell of crushed herbs as well. But all to no avail. Khetu lay there as insensate as before. Not once did his eyelids move, not a finger did stir in his body. Astonished, Kharbbur said, 'What did go wrong? Not ever do my incantations fail to take effect. Even in modest measure, they are wont to produce an outcome. What is the reason then that all my herbs and spells have fallen flat this evening?'

Kharbbur was a worried man. Much as he pondered, he could not arrive at a good guess.

At last, he said, 'My master, the mosquito! Let us all step out together and find what is afoot.'

The trio left the castle again. Kankabaty had lost all hope. She thought had Khetu been destined to live he would have in this moment. The chance she now had of claiming his remains and subsequently sacrificing her own life at his feet kept her going.

Once out, the trio re-entered the tunnel, Kharbbur in the lead. Carefully, Kharbbur combed his immediate vicinity—left, right, back and forth, below, above—in each of the ten scripted directions—until close to the castle he cast his eyes up and saw the pair of demonesses standing feet apart at the exit of the tunnel. Smiling to himself, he ruminated, 'Well, then, aren't you clever little demonesses?'

Now, Kharbbur began chanting his incantation from inside the tunnel. Under its influence, the demonesses were forced to take to their heels. Entering the castle, Kharbbur began striking the floor with his tongs and duster and reciting his spells again. In a few moments, Nakeshwari appeared magically in Khetu's body. Khetu became a speaker, that is, through his lips, the demoness began communicating. Using various mantras and medicine,

Kharbbur repeatedly asked Nakeshwari to leave Khetu alone. Nakeshwari refused, roundly. Said Nakeshwari, 'This man has committed a great crime. He has stolen the wealth in my protection. Therefore, I am not ordained to let him go, and I shall certainly feed on him.'

Then Kharbbur began chanting spells that caused pain to Nakeshwari. When Nakeshwari was unable to bear the pain, she agreed to leave, and yet, would not do so even after making promise after promise. Seeing through her deception, Kharbbur became annoyed indeed. His eyes grew red and his lips trembled in pique. Then he said, 'Now then, you won't leave so easily, will you? Well, let's see if you leave in this very moment.' And he brought a pumpkin, placed a vermillion mark on it, cast a spell to make it a magic pumpkin and then got about severing it into two halves in sacrifice. Placing the magic pumpkin on a pot shard, he raised his sword over it and heaved. At that very moment, Nakeshwari cried out in a desperate voice, 'Save me, save my life. Do not strike; do not cut me in two halves. Hear me, for I say the truth.'

Kharbbur said, 'Go on then. What is it that you wish to say? Why aren't you leaving the poor man alone? Speak or be forever cut into halves.'

Nakeshwari said, 'If I leave this man, you will not stand to gain. The patient will die right away. For, I had taken the life force of the patient, placed it inside a colocasia leaf and tied it to the top of an ice apple palm tree, thinking to make a sauce out of it upon my aunt's arrival. Well, the wind has blown the leaf with the life force in it off the treetop. And the tiny ants have eaten up the life force. Now, tell me, where can I get life force from for to bring the patient? Hence, say I, if I leave, the patient dies.'

Kharbbur made out his charts and calculations to confirm that Nakeshwari had indeed spoken truth. Said Kharbbur to himself, 'Aren't I in trouble now? How can I solve this new problem? None can lend the specific life force that belongs to each one.' After much contemplation, Kharbbur ordered Nakeshwari, 'Go to the spot and find the tiny ants that ate up Khetu's life force.'

Nakeshwari looked for the ants inside fissures on the stone, cracks in the ground, holes on tree trunks and all other possible places in the vicinity of the ice apple palm. She could not find them at any of these places. Big ant, red fire ant, black spider ant, the odorous house ant, whomsoever she met, she and her aunt asked, 'My dears, have you seen the way the tiny ants went?' In vain, though, since none could answer them. The aunt had joined forces with her niece seeing she was in trouble but now the old woman started huffing and puffing, and her leg ached. Then she said to herself, 'Heaven help me now! How I am being punished for lusting after a two-legged man's flesh!'

After much casting about, Nakeshwari met a carpenter ant. Nakeshwari asked the carpenter ant the whereabouts of the tiny ants. The carpenter ant said, 'I know of the tiny ants. Having licked up sweet human life force from a colocasia leaf under the ice apple palm, the tiny ants wiped their mouths and were bound for home. A suited booted frog dressed like a British sahib arrived and, one by one, gulped them all.'

Nakeshwari reported back to the castle with this news for Kharbbur. He immediately sent her forth once again to look for the frog. Nakeshwari cursed her predicament. She said, 'Well! What an irony it is that after having snatched away my meal from my lips he has assigned me to a job that will take it further from my grasp and I must expend myself performing it!' Yet what option did she have but this? If she did not obey him, Kharbbur would chop the pumpkin in two and Nakeshwari's neck would be sliced open at the same time. Nakeshwari combed the forest. She looked in every grove, every foot trail, every pond and every hill. Still she could not trace the amphibian. Returning empty-handed, Nakeshwari said to Kharbbur. 'You can thrash me if you wish, or slash me, but I am unable to find the object in question.'

A great consternation seized Kharbbur. He put on his thinking cap and began meditating. After much meditation, he took a fistful of mustard seeds and cast a spell on each. Then he scattered them forcefully on the ground in front of him. The magical seeds imbibed power from the stars above and rolled with great energy all over the earth, crossing country and village, valley and ocean and dale, until they reached the cool pit in the dirt right beside the old lily pond in which the frog was fast asleep. Making tiny perforations on the frogskin with needle-like precision, they climbed atop the poor ambhibian. The frog's fancy hat fell off its head. It began screaming in pain and desperation.

The mustard seeds slowly pushed the frog out of its hole and began directing it towards the castle. They nudged it inside the tunnel until at last, standing at its exit, the frog knocked upon the castle door.

The mosquito opened the door to the frog. The frog made its way to the chamber where Kankabaty and Kharbbur were seated. One look, and Kankabaty knew it was the same frog she had met some time back. The frog, too, recognised Kankabaty as Kankabaty.

Said the frog, 'Aren't you that pretty little mademoiselle I met the other day? Honey, did I not speak kindly to you? Why then did you go forth and tell everyone where to find my half-a-rupee? This is unacceptable, my dear. Shame on you for doing it. Do you not know better than to speak of wealth before pickpockets? Especially, before this flat-torsoed pickpocket? Everyone, please divide what remains of my half-penny amongst your admirable selves, and let me go in exchange. Hey Mister Flat-Torso! I see that these mustard seeds are your disciples. Please be so kind as to bid them dismount from my head. They are giving me a terrible migraine!'

Said Kharbbur, 'What do we care for your ha'penny? This girl is known to you. What terrific distress she is in you are perhaps aware of. That sickly young man on the bed is no other than her husband. He has come under the assault of Nakeshwari. Nakeshwari had taken out his life force and hidden it on the top of an ice apple tree. A gust of wind had brought it down. Get it expelled from the bellies of the tiny ants and save the life of Kankabaty's husband. If you expel just the ants from your own belly, it will suffice and the mustard seeds will let you go.'

The frog said, 'Verily do I know this girl and I am willing to do what will be in her good.' So saying, the frog stuck its finger into its throat and attempted anti-peristalsis but failed. Kharbbur then went on to feed him some herbs, yet the frog would not throw up its dinner.

Said Kharbbur to self, 'Here I come upon a fresh riddle. Now, what is the answer?'

Checking the frog's pulse with his fingers, Kharbbur thought, 'At last, have I got my enemy, the moon, on the wane.' This brought the moon with its nasty smile back to his recall. It also made him remember that the moon's primary root was the perfect antidote to digestion, as soon as it consumed it, the frog would upchuck its stomach's contents.

Addressing the mosquito, Kharbbur said, 'Your grace. There is no remedy on the face of the earth to induce vomiting in this frog. There is only one such medication in the universe, however. The moon you see in the sky carries it. Only if you skin its primary root and grind it to a paste, mix it well with the dust of seven peppercorns and feed it to the frog, will it vomit up the ants, else there is no avail.'

Hearing these words, the mosquito became depressed. Kankabaty felt all hopeless and disheartened.

Said Kankabaty, 'Dear gentlemen, you have spent considerable energy in the assistance of this lost soul. It all went to waste, for no fault of yours but one of my destiny.

My luck has run out completely. Who can travel the skies and sever the primary root of the moon? No mortal can accomplish this task. The root will not be obtained, and my husband will not be saved. Please return, therefore, to your respective homes. Do not bring yourself to further grief on my account. Thanks to you, I got the corpse of my husband and I shall content myself with it. I shall take refuge in his lotus feet and breathe my last. Please go home, everyone.'

The mosquito said, 'While it is true that I can fly a great distance, even I cannot go as high as to access the moon. For that singular reason, all our efforts are about to prove fruitless. My poor little dear girl, Raktabaty, has been holding out for me to make this mission a success. How can I return home without an excuse?'

Kharbbur said, 'Do not be completely disheartened. Here's an idea. Can you find the young of an ogre? In which case, mounted on its back, it will not be difficult to soar to the sky. An adult ogre will not serve the purpose, for it cannot be tamed. An ogre baby will be just right.'

The frog said, 'I know of a spot where an ogre has birthed a child. I can tell you how to find the place. Yet, tell me, pray, how will catch the young of an ogre? The ogre will swallow all of you in a single bite. On the other hand, let us suppose, you do catch him by trickery. Who then will mount the ogre's child and go to the sky? There is a life risk involved in going there. An intrepid soldier patrols the sky. He may be deaf in both ears and cannot hear well, but it is said he is very intrepid and doubly dutiful. The denizens of the sky live in fear of him. All day and night, he roams up and down the sky. If one falls in his clutches, there is no escape. Hence I wonder, who it is that will go to the sky to bring the root of the moon?'

Kankabaty said, 'None of you need to worry on that account. If I get an ogre's young, I will mount him myself and make the trip. I have no reason to fear. If I fall in the clutches of the soldier of the sky, he can do nothing save take my life. What worse harm can he bring me? I have vowed to give up my life for my husband anyway. Hence why should I fear for it?'

It was thus decided that an ogre's young would be caught, and the frog gave the others the directions to the hill and the hole beside it where its nest was located. The mosquito said, 'We must lay a trap to catch the ogre's child.'

It was agreed that the frog and Kharbbur would hold the fort and sit watch on Khetu while the mosquito, Kankabaty and Haati Thakurpo would leave to catch the ogre.

Before departing, Kankabaty took the dust of Khetu's feet and placed it on her crown.

Yet again, the mosquito said to Kankabaty, 'Are you sure, Kankabaty, that you will be able to climb as far as the sky? That you won't take fright?'

Said young Kankabaty, 'Fright! Why would I take fright amongst all people? If I can touch the sky but once, let me see how the moon protects its principal root from my grasp. Let me see, too, how many swords and shields that deaf soldier in the sky has that he can successfully resist the might of an honest woman.'

Star Bride

Seated elsewhere in the castle, Nakeshwari and her aunt overheard the plan to catch an ogre child. They began to confer together as to how it was they could play spoiler in a way such that neither could Kharbbur lay the blame at their door and nor would their prospective meal—Khetu—fly from their grasp.

Said the aunt, 'Alas, I am old, and have lost my appetite for most of the good things in this world. Yet this is the age when one wants to taste such delicate flesh. It was only our good fortune that such a dish landed in our lap, and yet it is about to get away.

Nakeshwari said, 'Dear Aunt, why don't you heed my advice? Why don't you sit in your basket and rise to the sky. Once there, whitewash the whole sky with quicklime. Do it so that there is no patch left to coat. Take your glasses with you. If you whitewash the entire sky, the wench won't be able to find her way through it, neither can she see the moon and nor can she bring home its primary root. Having made this conspiracy, the aunt went and sat in her basket. The basket soared like the whirlwind and Nakeshwari's aunt coated the whole sky with calcium oxide.

Exiting the castle, the mosquito saw a big drum lying about in the tunnel. It took the drum along with itself. Emerging from the mountainside, Kankabaty and the mosquito mounted the elephant, and the three made their way to the forest where the ogre had given birth. It was past evening when they came to the ogre's pit where it had made its nest.

Glancing at the sky once, the mosquito said, 'I say! What's the matter today? It's evening, and yet why is the moon not in the sky? There are no clouds, yet where are the stars? Why is the sky so waxen?'

The big ogre was sitting guard on its young inside its pit. It was dark and the forest was deep. From afar, the big ogre smelled Kankabaty.

With a blood-curdling cry, said the big ogre from the pit, 'Yowl, howl, growl, do I sniff there a human soul? Who are you all and why do you come this way?'

The mosquito shouted back at the top of its voice, 'Who are you, yourself?'

The ogre said, 'Who else do you think? I am the ogre!'

Said the mosquito, 'Oh yes? Who do you think we are then? We are the rogres!'

The reply unnerved the ogre. It said, 'Good heavens! I should not have underestimated. O-p-q-r, o is for ogre, while r is for rogre, this puts you three rungs above me. Yet, hang on, let me confirm this, clear your throat, dear, let me listen to your cough.'

The mosquito struck the drum and it made a booming din.

Hearing the sound, the ogre said, 'Holy heavens! Is this the sound of your cough? It gives one the shivers, makes the ear ring. You are rogres, indeed.'

The ogre, however, had a suspicious disposition. Even after receiving such irrefutable proof, it did not completely believe the mosquito. Hence it asked again, 'Well, then, show me what kind of rogres you are. Drop a lock of your hair into the pit so I can see it.'

Hearing these words, the mosquito uncoiled the roll of fat cable lying on the elephant's saddle and dropped it into the pit. The ogre picked it up in its paws and examined it carefully. After a while, it said, 'Oh dear heavens! Is this the hair on your head? If it is so long and thick, you, yourselves must be tall and stout indeed. It will be hard for me to overpower you.'

And yet the ogre did not fully believe the mosquito. After some reflection, it said again, 'Well, then, if you are rogres, drop a louse from your head inside the pit, let me see it.

The mosquito said, 'Kankabaty, dismount quickly.'

To the elephant, the mosquito said, 'Brother, now, brace for it!'

So saying, the mosquito caught hold of the elephant and pushed the mammal into the ogre's nest. Hitting the nest, the elephant wrapped its trunk around the baby ogre.

'Screech! Screech!' The baby ogre's screams rocked heaven, earth and the netherworlds, while seeing the gargantuan proboscid-louse, the ogre lost its wits in fright. It said to itself, 'Your head-louse has captured my baby, I only hope that you don't follow it into my nest and catch me.' With this thought in mind, it abandoned its baby and flew off into the night.

The mosquito and Kankabaty then walked to the rim of the pit.

The mosquito said, 'Kankabaty, climb on the back of this creature. Rise to the sky atop this offspring of an ogre and return with the root of the satellite. Once you come back, we will return this ogre's baby to the nest. That is because it is still an infant and needs to suckle on its mother's teats for sustenance. If we keep it, on the other hand, to what end will that be? Whatever is right should be done, but I dearly hope you can stay safe from the intrepid soldier of the skies. It is reputed that he is fearsome and powerful, keep an eye out for him while you ascend.'

Looking skywards, the mosquito then commented, 'Yet, Kankabaty, I have a strange feeling. It is long past moonrise time, and yet I have neither seen the moon nor the stars. But there are no clouds in the sky. Instead of dark clouds, the sky is white in colour. I fail to follow it a single bit. Perhaps, you will know when you ascend. Take very good care while you there, Kankabaty; we will wait here until you return.'

When Kankabaty mounted the baby ogre and steered it upwards, it began to fly swiftly. It was not long before Kankabaty found herself right next to the sky.

Once next to the sky, Kankabaty realised that it was entirely covered in quicklime. Kankabaty wondered, 'How can it be? Who has coated the sky with this chemical?'

Kankabaty could not find the road to enter the sky. In whichever direction she turned, she saw nothing but a coat of lime. She traversed the entire length of the sky from one end to another but did not see an opening. All was whitewashed. 'In a queer predicament I am, indeed,' thought Kankabaty. 'How is it that I will rise above the sky?'

A despairing Kankabaty continued her search. After much seeking, she suddenly spied a perforation in the firmament. The bride of the stars was peeping through that gap. Kankabaty approached her. Seeing Kankabaty, the star bride hid herself, then re-emerged and peered again, fearfully.

Said Kankabaty, 'Hello, Star Bride. Do not fear. I am a girl, too, like yourself, so you needn't be shy either.'

The star bride replied, 'Who are you, my dear? You speak so sweetly. For a while, now, I have been observing you wandering about. Hence did it occur to me to ask you, what are you looking for? Yet I am a bride; isn't it indecorous for me to open a conversation, and with a stranger in the nighttime? It will send out the wrong signal. Talk softly, my dear. My children have just gone to bed. If they wake up, they will not go back to bed, but will wail and disrupt the peace.'

Kankabaty said, 'Star Bride, my dear, my name is Kankabaty. I am an honest woman missing her husband. I am looking for a way to enter the sky. What's the matter today? Why can't I find a way? If I can enter your domain, I can save my husband's life. Please show me inside. I will be forever in your debt.'

The star bride replied, 'I see. Well, my dear, this evening, an old monstress came here and slopped whitewash over the whole sky. No wonder, then, that you cannot see your way. But don't worry. Let me steal around my house and open the sky's back garden gate. Through it you can then take your entry.' So saying, the star bride quietly opened the back garden gate of the sky. Kankabaty slipped in and rose above the firmament.

Intrepid Soldier

Inside the sky, Kankabaty tied the ogre's lead fast to the branch of a floating cloud. Then she set off on foot across the wide field of the sky. All around her, she witnessed stars of every colour abloom illuminating the night. Far ahead of her, like a giant wheel, the moon was sat on its throne.

When Kankabaty entered the sky, the moon received the bad news that for to cut its primary root, a human had arrived in its realm. Spade in hand and madwoman-like, a female human was in this very moment rushing towards itself. The moon took alarm and trembled in fright.

The moon thought, 'Why on earth did I have to be the possessor of such pulchritude? Is it not the cause of so much pique and spite? Had I not been pretty, none would have attempted to cut my primary root. As it is, I must handle Rahu's malfeasance and now if humans begin to cause trouble, how do I live in peace? Had I a neck, I would surely have hanged myself. Yet I have none, for my cursed body is like a damned wheel and nought else. How am I to blame then for not hanging myself? Where do I place the noose?'

Making various expressions of regret, an anxious moon sent for the intrepid soldier of the sky. The sky warrior was certainly valiant in every aspect, only somewhat feeble in hearing and hence a bit deaf. When being spoken to, he needed to be shouted at to be able to hear the speaker.

When the soldier arrived, the moon unburdened itself. It said to the soldier, 'A human is coming to sever my primary root.'

The soldier thought the moon was speaking with mouth wide open only to disparage him for his poor hearing. He became quite annoyed. The soldier said, 'Hang on. Close your mouth a little. Don't crack up into two trying to stretch it.'

This time, through narrower jaws, the moon repeated, 'A human is coming to sever my primary root.'

The soldier said, 'You don't have to speak so secretively! Are you planning to rob anyone that you are whispering? If indeed you are doing so, please give me my share.'

The moon said to itself, 'How hard it is to speak to a soldier, indeed! He takes offence at anything and everything!' To the soldier, it, however, said, 'Oh no, I did not ask to rob anybody. I will not go anywhere to rob anyone. I say, a human is coming to sever my primary root.' At last, the soldier heard what he was being told clearly.

Said the soldier, 'Is a human on its way here to sever your primary root? Well, then, let them do it. What is the big deal?'

The moon said, 'You are the watchman of the skies? Won't you protect me?'

The soldier replied, 'What if my own main root gets severed in the process? Will you help me?'

The moon said, 'If you don't do anything to rescue me from such utter danger, why do you accept your salary?'

The soldier answered, 'Don't you talk about it! I am not nearly paid enough to do this job. If you like, I will resign, go to earth and become a police constable. They will rush to employ me seeing as I am a famous and intrepid soldier.

Besides, they don't sever primary roots over there. Once there, after all the rioting and troublemaking gets over, I will catch a couple of poor souls going about their business and present them in court. Well, then, I must take your leave before the human arrives. I don't want them to drag me into this mess.' So saying, the intrepid soldier departed from the scene rather quickly. 'Let what will be will be,' said the moon, and it slipped a little lower in its chair in resignation.

Having fastened her ogre to a cloud, Kankabaty strode quickly across the sky-fields towards the moon. A rumour began to spread to the effect that a human has arrived from the earth to collect the main roots of all citizens of the sky, be they young, elderly, or adult of either sex. The sky-dwellers each rounded up their children, went indoors and bolted their doors. The stars which bloomed in the forests and groves, and moors and gardens, had no means to escape, so they turned down their brightness. The moon, likewise, could not leave because, being on duty, it could not abandon its post, or else it would have to pay a fine commensurate with the time it deprived the world's denizens of light, so with a glum face and sorrowful gait, it slowly followed its familiar trajectory. In due course, Kankabaty arrived in the moon's presence.

The moon said to itself, 'Oh dear! I see that I am about to lose my primary root. I only hope the human does not kidnap all of me in its place. What if they say, "What a beautiful moon, let me make a bundle of it with my sari and carry me away?" There lies no sense in putting up a fight. Let me shut my eyes, hold my breath and play dead. The human will deem it pointless to take home a dead moon. They will then leave me alone.' Thus resolved, the clever moon shut its eyes and held fast its breath.

Seeing the moon pale, morose and still, Kankabaty thought, 'Woah! Did the moon just die? Did it die out of fright from seeing me come to remove its primary root? Oh no! How pretty was the moon! How pretty the moonlight on full moon nights! These will now be no more. From now on, it will be new moon forever. How the people will reproach me when I go back to earth!'

But after examining the heavenly body carefully, Kankabaty said to herself, 'Not really, no. The moon is still alive. It has perhaps fainted in fear. All to good effect, seeing as doctors first anaesthesise their patients before they saw off their arms and legs. So it is well that the moon has, of its own accord, lost its senses. I do not need its advice to take its main root. But I shall not sever the root. Then it will not recover and will really be dead. I need only a *tola* of the root's skin; let me remove that amount and leave.'

And so Kankabaty circled the moon, found its main root, took out her knife and began to skin the root.

The moon withstood the pain as best as it could for a short while, and then its stamina failed it. 'Oww!' It cried out. 'It hurts so.'

'Have no fear,' said Kankabaty. 'I am almost done here.' Kankabaty quickly removed a *tola* of skin from the moon's principal root.

Then the moon said, 'Will my skin grow back again?'

Kankabaty replied, 'No doubt, it will. Do you think it will remain the same always? Just slap some wet mud over it, then the evil eye won't cause the wound to go septic.'

The moon said, 'What if the wound does go septic?'

Kankabaty replied, 'Should that happen, put some fried flatbread and ghee on it.'

The moon said, 'Are you a lady doctor? Do you know how to heal gums? My gums ache a lot.'

Said Kankabaty, 'I am not a lady doctor. But despite my few years, I have seen and borne a lot. Thus, I have taught myself a few cures. Your gums will never get well. Tell me, do people's teeth stay the same all their lives? Just think back and estimate the number of years you have been around. Just when was it that you had arisen out of the great ocean? There is no point wishing to be a young moon again, now, is there?'

The moon said, 'I do not want to be a young moon. I have plenty of young moons at home; bless them so they each have a long life, then one day you will be left counting the many moons in the sky. In every direction you look, there will be a moon. Even now, my children say to me, "Father, on new moon nights you feel too exhausted to rise from bed in the evening, why don't you send us to rise on your behalf? I refuse their offer, saying it is a long way from one end of the sky to the other. Being young, they will be unable to complete the round."'

Kankabaty asked the moon, 'How old are your kids then?'

The moon replied, 'My oldest, a girl, is just like a bell-metal dish with a raised edge. It shines brightly. Even if you scrub it with tamarind your dishes don't shine as bright. The middle son is like a bronze drum. Besides, there are a lot of other children. The youngest is still a baby and a bit dark-complexioned. Didn't you, humans, wear a glowworm on your foreheads in the old days? The girl is just as big as that. Even if she is dark, my princess, she is enchanting. When she grows up, and rises as the dark moon, the earthlings will say, let not this attractive beauty set, for if she does, the whole world will be covered in leathery dark. Yet, let that be, tell me now how do I cure my gum ailment. I can eat nothing for fear of toothache. I love drumsticks, yet cannot chew them. If you have any remedy, please give it to me.'

Said Kankabaty, 'Well, moon, why don't you accompany me? Thanks to your root, my husband will be well. He can take you to Calcutta where he lives and where the dentists are. They will extract your bad teeth and fit you with dentures.'

The moon took fright again. It said, 'My primary root is sore. I don't think I can roll as far.'

Kankabaty said, 'Don't worry. I will tie you to the edge of my sari.'

The moon became very frightened then. It thought privately, 'This has gone just as I had expected. Why did I open the conversation? I should have kept my eyes shut and played dead.'

To Kankabaty, it said, 'My gum is all well now. You need not worry and take pains. I am quite heavy and you will be unable to carry me. Go now. If you are late, your family will worry for your safety.'

Kankabaty replied, 'What did you just say? That I will be unable to carry you? When I lived with my parents, I took metal plates to the riverbank that would be bigger than yourself. Why don't you wait and see if I can carry you or not?' So saying, Kankabaty spread out the edge of her sari on the sky-field. She would put the moon on it and wrap it all up next. At this very moment, the wife of the moon, Ms Moonlight, arrived at the spot, trailed by the children, weeping loudly and writhing frantically. The moonlight's cries about cracked open the sky-fields. Kankabaty's ears rung from the cries of the moon's children.

Weeping, the moonlight said, 'Dear husband, the intrepid soldier told me that a human will sever your major root, but why would they do that? Have I thrashed rice on their breast that she has turned an enemy? If I am about to be widowed, then I curse her, so shall she be. She will go on to sustain herself only by feeding on the brains of her father and her brother.'

The moon's children pulled the edge of Kankabaty's sari and pleaded, 'My lady, don't cut our father's primary root. Don't take him away with you.'

The youngest child of the moon, the one that looked like a glowworm, alternately wept and raged, and called Kankabaty names, 'You, blackface, you. You unfortunate soul. You sister-in-law consorting with the brother-in-law.' It also scratched Kankabaty and clawed holes into her skin.

Kankabaty became both injured and flustered by its exertions. She said, 'Dear Moonlight, restrain your daughter, my dear. She is clawing the skin off my arms and body.'

Moonlight answered, 'Oh, but surely. I will certainly restrain my daughter while you wreak havoc on my family! What have I done to you that you feel thus entitled? Why would you sever my husband's main root and kill him?'

Kankabaty said, 'No, my dear, I have not killed your husband. I required just a tiny bit of the root and I have scraped it from the surface only. There has not even been a lot of bleeding. Why don't you ask the moon? Afterwards, your husband said his tooth was loose. So I thought, let me take him to Calcutta, get him well again, and then send him back to the sky. But let us forget it, my dear, just stop your children from clawing at my skin.'

The moonlight, however, felt reassured by Kankabaty's reply. The moon's children, too, stopped wailing. The moonlight said, 'If you are done with your work, then, go home. In your terror, business has come to a standstill in the sky. All sky-dwellers have shut themselves up at their respective homes. Everyone is scared out of their wits.'

Kankabaty said, 'It is true my mission is over, but I need a few stars to take home. There are no stars on earth. Here, there are so many beautiful stars, all shining and a-light. I wonder if I could pluck a few of them. My ogre is fastened to a cloud-bough a considerable distance from this spot. Can I get a porter to carry them for me?'

The moonlight said, 'My dear, no one will step out of their home for fear of you. Where will you find a porter? All shopkeepers and businessmen have shut their establishments; every market in the sky is now closed. The streets are deserted. Only I am out and about, but for the sake of my family.'

While the discussion proceeded in this vein, Kankabaty spied an odd fellow hiding behind a cloud and peering about with a suspicious look on his face. Kankabaty thought, why don't I ask this person to carry the stars to the little ogre? Thus resolved, Kankabaty beckoned him. She said, 'I say, can you hear me for a moment?'

As soon as Kankabaty said these words, the man took to his heels. The more Kankabaty went towards him, the farther he ran away. Kankabaty said to herself, 'How fast is this man! Indeed, he runs like the wind.'

Kankabaty would not have caught up with this man had he not by gift of providence slipped on a mound of cloud and fallen flat on his face. As fast as he had fallen, he tried to rise, but Kankabaty had reached him and caught hold of him when he was upright.

Touching the man, Kankabaty realised he had no flesh nor bone. His body was as light as a feather. With the help of two fingers only, Kankabaty picked him up. She brought him close to her eyes and after looking at him carefully found that his body was built up of just two, or perhaps four palm leaves. The body was made of one. The arms were made of palm leaf and so were his nose and mouth. A pair of outer garments was thrown over the leaf. Kankabaty was befuddled.

Kankabaty asked the man, 'Who are you, then?'

The man replied, 'I am the intrepid soldier of the sky. Why do you ask such a silly question? Who else did you think I was, then? Now, let go of me, I shall go home. Don't press me so with those fingers of yours.'

Kankabaty said, 'Is your body built of palm leaf?'

The intrepid soldier said, 'What else do you think it would be built of? Brick and mortar? Lime and concrete? You seem to have travelled widely, haven't you heard of the palm-leaf soldier during your travels? In this whole world, who does not know me? Whenever they see a valiant man, they compare him to me. Now leave me be, I shall go home. What an unholy mess this root cutting business can be, indeed!'

Kankabaty finally understood that the palm-leaf soldier in the fairy tale that she had been told many-a-time in her childhood lived in the sky and not on earth. And it was he who was also known as the intrepid soldier of the sky.

Kankabaty then said, 'Now, look here, intrepid soldier. You must perform the task that I assign you. Or else, I will never let go of you ever. I will pick a bundle-load of stars from the sky. You will have to bear the bundle and walk some paces with me.'

The soldier had no choice but to be enlisted in the task. Kankabaty's sari could only hold so many stars. Kankabaty wondered, 'What could I use to tie the lot of them?'

The soldier said, 'Do not worry. Let us go to the old woman of the sky. She sits under the burflower tree and spins many weaves on her wheel. Let us borrow from her a cotton towel.'

Kankabaty and the soldier went to the old woman of the sky and asked her for a towel. With much griping and many a grumble, the old woman of the sky handed them one. Now Kankabaty set off plucking stars from the sky field. She picked and chose many a half-bud, half-blossom and full bloom, all perfectly shaped and in dazzling colours. Throwing them together into the cotton towel and tying it into a bundle, she placed it on the soldier's head.

The soldier said to himself, 'In my long employment in the sky, I never did have to perform a porter's job. It is fortuitous that the sky dwellers have all locked themselves indoors today. Or else, had I been seen carrying luggage, I would have died of shame.'

Carrying the bundle on his head the soldier walked ahead. Kankabaty followed. In a while, both arrived at the spot where the little ogre was tied. Taking the bundle from the soldier's head, Kankabaty said, 'I do not need your service anymore. You are free to go home.' As soon as she said these words, the soldier broke into such a dash that within moments he had vanished. Said Kankabaty to herself, 'Palm-leaf soldier indeed! No wonder he can run so quickly.'

Bundle in hand, Kankabaty mounted the ogre and began her descent to earth.

The Honest Woman

Upon returning to earth, Kankabaty wasted no time making her way to the rendezvous where the mosquito and elephant had been waiting for her. Both were beside themselves with joy when they heard that she had been successful in obtaining the root. After dropping the little ogre back in its pit, Kankabaty and the mosquito climbed atop the elephant and the three set out for the castle inside the mountain.

Reaching the castle, Kankabaty submitted the root of the moon in the hands of Kharbbur, who weighed it carefully, added seven peppercorns and ground the mix to a paste. He fed the paste to the frog and it began vomiting copiously. The amphibian emptied out all contents of its stomach, and then it said, 'Hereby I believe what I had eaten as a tadpole squirming about in the pond is also come out of my belly, wherein there is absolutely nothing left.'

Inside the pool of the frog's vomit were the tiny ants. Kharbbur picked them out painstakingly; then, with a pair of minuscule forceps, he began extracting the life force from the ants' stomachs, one by one. When all the ants had thus been processed, Kharbbur cried, 'Oh no! What is to be done? What shall we do with so little of life force? This is so meagre it is good as useless.'

Kharbbur became depressed, and the mosquito, too, looked disappointed, the frog started weeping, but Kankabaty held her silence. In their respective invisible states, Nakeshwari and her aunt had observed all and felt satisfied at the outcome. Presently, Kharbbur poured out the life force that he had collected into Khetu's nostril. With a start, Khetu sat up in bed.

Khetu said reproachfully, 'What a deep slumber was I immersed in, Kankabaty! Why did you not awaken me? See, how late it is now in the morning!'

Said Kankabaty, 'If I could, I would certainly have awakened you, my lord.'

Khetu looked about himself. He saw Kankabaty's eyes were wet, and Kharbbur, the mosquito and the frog were also unsmiling. Khetu asked Kankabaty, 'Kankabaty, my dear, why are you weeping? Who are these gentlemen?'Kankabaty made no reply to his questions.

After reflecting a bit, Khetu spoke again. He said, 'I remember all. Since I had not the herb in my hair, Nakeshwari had taken me. O' Kankabaty, were you the one to fetch these gentlemen and cure me? If that be the case, then why are you crying? I am now well, after all, aren't I? I am well, although my head aches very slightly. Let me lie down once more. Kankabaty! Will you be so kind as to massage my head lightly? My head is splitting now. I feel as if I am breathing for the last time. Dear all, please take care of my Kankabaty. Please reach her to her mother's. Dear God, here I come.'

Khetu breathed his last. Everyone bowed their heads and sat in silence. No one spoke and tears flowed all around. Only Kankabaty remained calm and unruffled. When some time had passed, Kharbbur said, 'The party is over. All our efforts went in vain. There is no resort anymore. When the colocasia leaf fell from the ice apple palm, most of the life force inside it was blown away by the wind, and only a little was consumed by the ants. How long could a human sustain himself on it?'

So saying, Kharbbur burst into tears of frustration. The mosquito wept, too, while the frog took out a handkerchief from his pockets and wiped his cheeks with it. Outside the mountain, the elephant raised a dust storm with its trunk to mark the mourning of Khetu's passing. Only Kankabaty made no gesture, neither did she weep. At last, said the mosquito, 'Darling, rise. There is no point grieving. Let us arrange a funeral for your husband. Then I will accompany you to Raktabaty. Seeing Raktabaty, you will feel much better.'

The mosquito, Kharbbur and frog then began consoling Kankabaty upon her loss.

Kharbbur said, 'The material world is transient, my dear. Life itself has no certainty about it. The one here today is gone tomorrow. Rise, my sweet one. After your husband is cremated, stay with Raktabaty for a few days. Then we will take you to your mother's abode.'

Kankabaty said, 'Gentlemen. You have been my friends in need, and I am in your debt. You left no stone unturned to save my husband. That your efforts did not pay off is only due to my poor fate. God will bless each and every one of you. Since you have performed so many favours for me, please perform one more. Each of you, please return home. I have submitted my life at my husband's feet. This body of mine is now bereft of meaning. I will burn this meaningless body along with my husband's to ashes. To that end, please make the arrangements.'

The mosquito chided Kankabaty. It said, 'Shame on you, darling, for even thinking of such a course of action. There are hundreds of honest women alive who do not have husbands. They usually adopt celibacy and spend their time in the service of others.' Thus did Kharbbur and the frog, too, reason with Kankabaty to get her to abandon her deadly plan.

'Auntie!' called Nakeshwari. 'Yes, dear,' said the aunt. 'They are planning to cremate the man, Auntie. We will get nothing but ashes.'

'Yup,' said the aunt.

Nakeshwari said, 'We have the wench to thank for. Let us do such that she, too, meets her end.'

So saying, Nakeshwari appeared in her perceptible form before Kharbbur and the rest of the party.

Said Nakeshwari, 'So you all are planning to take Kankabaty home? Listen here and listen well. We, the monsters, will not stop you from carrying out your intent. Yet this is India, the world's most pious country. Indians are the most pious of peoples. If someone, in grief or despair, makes known their intent of accompanying their husband to the pyre but once, they must follow through. Or else, the taint will land on their father's and mother's families each, and the parents and relatives all needs must hang their heads in shame. The person herself will be henceforth fallen, and anyone who speaks to her or is kind to her will be considered fallen, too, by one and all. Hence I say to the master, Kharbbur, and Mr Mosquito, we have no objections to your taking Kankabaty home. But I will certainly report this to your relatives. Your relatives are not atheists such as yourselves. They will consult the scriptures. Then I shall wait and watch where in the country you end up fixing up your children's marriages successfully.'

Hearing Nakeshwari's words, the mosquito felt alarmed. It knew it must give Raktabaty away in marriage in the near future. What if it failed to find a suitable groom for Raktabaty? So it turned to Kharbbur and it asked him, 'Is it true that Indians observe such a rule?'

Kharbbur replied, 'It was so indeed so many years back. But no longer. The British have banned the custom of *sahamaran*, co-morbidity.'

Nakeshwari said, 'Well, the British did ban the custom, but do you know what the young and educated Bengali men believe today? They believe in restarting old customs in the name of Indian pride. They have gone stir-crazy in the name of throwing their grief-stricken mothers and sisters into the burning fire. And we, monsters, heartily support them in their mission.'

Kharbbur said, 'I personally do not care what becomes of me. I will not abandon Kankabaty. If that leads to my being tagged fallen and being cast out by my family, then so be it. But send this innocent girl to a fiery death? I shall not abide by it.'

Said the mosquito, 'I agree with Kharbbur. I shan't be a coward. I shall take Kankabaty home.'

Said the frog, 'I agree with the mosquito. Let humans be cowards. Not I.'

Said Nakeshwari, 'I see you know little scripture. You have not the sense that you are about to fall into great impiety. If this lady does not burn, she will have to atone for it through the *prajpatya* path, and even then she cannot go home, but must spend as an undertaker's woman the rest of her days.'

Kankabaty said, 'All of you are arguing in vain. I will certainly be honest and accompany my husband and not be dissuaded. I shall certainly give up my life. Please do not entreat me to live. I will not be able to fulfil your entreaty. Please make all arrangements for the pyre. I have one more wish. I wish my pyre be set up at the very spot where my mother-in-law was cremated in our village.'

Seeing Kankabaty's firm resolve, everyone, however reluctant, agreed to help. The mosquito said, 'If you are so resolved, Kankabaty, to perform this strenuous mission, then let me send for my family. Let my wives and Raktabaty come and bid you goodbye.'

Kharbbur said, 'So, too, will I. Let me send the news to my wife as well. Let her bring with her the objects required for the rite. Let me also send for the barber and the priest, and the drummers.'

The frog said, 'I, too, will call my relations and acquaintances and have them attend the funeral.'

Nakeshwari said, 'Auntie! We should not be left out. Mount your basket, I say. Go and invite all the female spirits of the earth. It is not every day that a sahamaran is held, especially in this day and age. Spirits of all ages, children, adult and elderly, will be mightily entertained.'

All climbed atop the elephant with Khetu and Kankabaty. When they reached the cremation ground at Kusumghati, it was one *prahar* in the night.

A grand pyre was set up at the spot Kankabaty pointed out to the assembly. At this juncture, arrived Raktabaty and her mothers as well as Kharbbur's seven-foot tall wife with the items required to observe the co-morbidity rite. She also brought with herself her children, sons and daughters both, and her relatives. She was accompanied by the drummers, the barber and the priest. The relations of the frog and the elephant, too, reached there. As did innumerable ghosts and spirits who came at Nakeshwari's request. That night, the Kusumghati cremation ground thus did indeed witness the strangest assembly of man, spirit and beast, and became crowded with visitors. A weeping Raktabaty fell into the bosom of Kankabaty. Said Raktabaty, 'Stale Water mine! Where do you go now without me? I will not have it.'

Kankabaty said, 'Do not cry, Stale Water. I remain an honest woman by accompanying my husband. Now we will certainly attain heaven. Therefore, do not stop me. I understand your grief, Stale Water. But I have no choice. Happiness on earth is not written in my fate. Permit me to go, Stale Water, with my husband and to the heavenly kingdom. I bless you so that you marry a mosquito prince and raise a wonderful family. And that an unfortunate soul as myself does not enter your life again even as an enemy.'

Kankabaty produced the bundle of stars and handed it over to the mosquito's daughter. She said, 'My dearest Stale Water, string three necklaces with these stars. Take one for yourself and keep aside two for me. I will later tell you the purpose of those.'

Those assembled proceeded to lift Khetu's corpse and place it on the pyre. Heaps of rice were offered to his spirit. The barber chopped off the nails of Kankabaty. He shattered her bangles. Women jostled and fell over one another to collect the said pieces. It is believed that if spirits possess anyone, a piece of an honest woman's bangle worn around the neck drives them away.

Kankabaty removed her iron *noa*-bangle and took a bath. Kharbbur's wife dressed her in a length of blood-red taffeta. With a roll of red thread, she tied a bottle of red lac dye to her wrist. She then stuck a series of decorative combs in her hair and covered her forehead in vermillion.

Thus attired, Kankabaty rinsed her mouth and, sesame seed, water and a blade of grass in hand, sat east-faced. The priest had her repeat this vow.

'On this day of Bhadra, which is the third of the dark fortnight, I, Ms Kankabaty Devi, hope to live in heaven with my husband for as many years as there are kingdoms in the body of man, as the lady, Arundhati, was revered in heaven along with sage Vashistha. Let my mother, father and father-in-law be purified of their sins. Till the day the fourteen Indras rule, may the apsaras sing our paean. Let me be blissful with my husband. If my husband has committed the sins of ingratitude or a brahmin's murder, let him be expiated of them. Having made these wishes, I ascend my husband's pyre.'

The priest made an offering of water and sesame seed to the sun and invoking the chief of each of the eight kingdoms had them bear witness to Kankabaty's act. The words he uttered on behalf of Kankabaty were these:

'Hail the chiefs of the eight kingdoms, the sun, the moon, the winds, the fire, the sky, the earth, the water, my own spirit residing in my heart, death, day, night, evening, as well as faith—witness me ascending the burning pyre of my husband and following my husband to eternity.'

After this vow had been duly said, Kankabaty tied popped rice, round sugar drops in lieu of molasses, and cowrie shells to the edge of her sari and began circumambulating the pyre and strewing with one hand the goodies onto the ground. Young children present there rushed before one another to collect these, especially the popped rice, which if left on the bedding is believed to ward off bedbugs.

One of the female attendees approached Kankabaty and asked for a bit of the vermillion on her forehead. It is believed that if this vermillion is placed on the forehead of a wayward woman, she will inevitably mend her ways. After seven circumambulations had been completed, the priest had Kankabaty repeat the *rigmantra*. Then Kankabaty took the two strings of stars from Raktabaty, climbed atop the pyre, put one of them around the neck of Khetu and placed the other around her own neck. She lay down on the pyre next to her husband.

The attendees tied her to the pyre with freshly cut bark of a deciduous tree. Then they lit the pyre. Having lit the pyre, they began dropping big bundles of cane, wood, hemp and jute on the incipient flames. The drummers began playing a beat so loud that everyone's ears rang from the din. Swiftly spread the flames, and reached high as the sky.

Kankabaty slept. It was a slumber of pleasure. It was a peaceful slumber.

Epilogue: The Profound Slumber of Peace and Pleasure

The naturopath said, 'The sleep that you observe now before you is NREM sleep. The stage of delirium has passed, the pulse is steady, please ensure there is silence in the house. The patient should not be awakened from her sleep.' So saying, the naturopath left. Lost to the world, the patient slept on. The residents of the house spoke in whispers and not even an ant's steps could be heard. Only the mother sat vigil. Frequently, she placed her own hand under the daughter's nostril to check if she still breathed or did not.

The mother had neither eaten nor slept for twenty-two days. She had fought the god of death tooth and nail to save her daughter who was as precious to her as her own life. Whenever the daughter, in excitement of delirium, sat up in bed, the mother consoled her. The mother's gentle words would turn down the flame of delirium, if only for the time being.

The daughter sleeps. Her eyes are shut fast. Fever and fast worth several days have rendered her thin and her colour listless, yet still her beauty shines forth and persuades its beholder that the world is indeed magical. Only the mother now gazes at and savours that rare beauty.

Night turns to morning. After morning comes midday. Still, the patient does not awaken. Only the mother sits by her and keeps vigil. Until the sister comes to the room, and quietly goes to sit by the mother.

The patient's lips moved a little. She spoke some words indistinctly. The sister brought her head close to her lips to discern the words, but failed. The lips moved again and the patient spoke some more words. This time, the mother understood what was being said.

Said the mother, 'My poor baby! Saying Khetu's name, she has all but spent herself. It is all she has been saying these past few days. If only I can join the two pairs of their hands in matrimony would I now be guilt-free.'

The mother's tender voice entered the daughter's ear. She woke up completely and slowly opened her eyes. With an expression of wonder, she then began looking about. The mother said, 'If partial, the delirium has persisted. The gaze isn't normal yet. My child has been unable to recognise anyone over the past nineteen days.'

The sister said, 'Kankabaty! Do you recognise me?'

Softly said Kankabaty: 'Yes, you are my oldest sister.'

The sister asked again, 'Tell me who this is then.'

Kankabaty said, 'The mother.'

Tanu Ray entered the room. He said, 'Kankabaty, my dear! How are you today?'

Kankabaty said, 'Very well, Father.'

Tanu Ray sat by Kankabaty and stroked her arms and the top of her head affectionately. Then he left the room.

Kankabaty wondered, 'I see that my mother, sister and father have accompanied me to heaven. I had not enjoyed my father's affection on earth. Today, in heaven, did I have the good luck to partake of it. The house in heaven, too, is the same as the one we lived in on earth. Yet, what of the one who died with me? Where is he now?'

Kankabaty waited for him a long time, but he did not come.

So Kankabaty asked her mother, 'Mother, where is he?'

The mother said, 'Who do you mean?'

Said Kankabaty, 'The one that was tiger.'

'The delirium is not partial. She is yet not making sense,' the mother said.

The mother's words triggered a bout of reflection in Kankabaty. She realised her body had weakened and also began recalling the train of past events. Kankabaty said, 'Mother, have I been quite ill?'

The mother said, 'Yes, my child. It has been twenty-two days since you have not risen from bed. You had been unconscious. We had no reason to hope that you would live.'

Kankabaty said, 'Mother, I have had a strange dream. The events in the dream are so vivid in my memory that they have made me believe that they occurred actually. Many thoughts are crowding my mind. Of them, I cannot discern which ones are true and which ones are without basis. Hence, Mother, I wish to make of you a few queries. Dear Mother, is it true, for instance, that Janardan Chowdhury had lost his wife?'

The mother said, 'That is true, my dear. That is the root cause of all trouble, I should say.'

Said Kankabaty, 'Mother, is it true then that there was politics over the consumption of ice?'

The mother replied, 'Yes, my child. That was the pretext on which the neighbours slighted Khetu's mother.'

'Where is she, Mother?'Kankabaty asked.

The mother said, 'Here she comes, presently. Why, all the daylight hours she has been spending by your bedside. It is she who loves you more than I. If only I can turn you over to her care, I will be free of my misery. The husband has agreed, so has everyone, now all that is left is for you to get well.' Kankabaty understood that Khetu's mother dying was only in her dream.

Kankabaty said, 'Following the politics, I fell ill, did I not, Mother? And then, Mother, I went to the riverbank and sat on a boat, isn't that right, Mother?'

The mother said, 'Heaven forfend, my dear, for you to do such a thing. You have been bedridden since that date.'

Kankabaty said, 'Mother! Many a strange dream have I dreamt that I am at a loss to recount. Assuredly, it is both amusing and, at the same time, sad to recall them. I dreamt, dear Mother, that I broke out in hives and went to the river to slap water on my chest and arms. Then I took a boat and went to the middle of the river. The boat sank. The fish crowned me their queen. Then, I spent a few days in the hut of the milkmaid. From there, I went to the cremation ground. Thereafter, I returned home. After one year, a tiger came to our house. I accompanied the tiger to the forest. Then I met so many people, monstresses, the frog and the mosquito. I climbed up to the sky, saw so many strange sights and had so many adventures that they all seem real to me even in this moment. Well, Mother, what of the politics? How has it unfolded?'

The mother replied, 'That has been resolved since. When you had been ill, about eight or nine days back, there was a sudden death in zamindar Janardan Chowdhury's household. The zamindar lost his favourite grandson. Janardan Chowdhury had been extremely fond of him.

'The zamindar was beside himself in grief. At the same time, Gobardhan Shiromani, too, fell dangerously ill. In our home, we were then struggling to put up a fight against your illness. Janardan Chowdhury began to see sense. He sent for Ramhari. Ramhari came to the village from Calcutta along with his family. He had a long talk with Janardan Chowdhury. Next, Ramhari went to Niranjan and called him over.

'Ramhari, Niranjan, my husband and Khetu met at Janardan Chowdhury's manorhouse. Janardan Chowdhury said, "I must have been crazy to wish to marry at such an old age. Because of me, Niranjan left his paternal abode, while Khetu, a youngster, I tormented to no end. Since then, have I suffered losses in every direction. Sandeshwar has embezzled money and been jailed. Gobardhan Shiromani has been struck by paralysis and is on his deathbed. At this age, I, too, had to suffer this terrible bereavement. The life of the daughter of this gentleman here might not be spared either."

'Then did he beseech and entreat Niranjan to accept the return of his estate until the latter relented. Niranjan now lives in his old home. Janardan Chowdhury showered many blessings on Khetu until he forgave him.

'Our old man, too, is no longer the same. He is today full of affection, kindness and righteousness. Misfortune is often known to bring about such a change of heart. Your older brother, too, has reformed himself. He has learnt to respect me. When you were ill, Khetu, his mother, Ramhari and Seeta, all worked very hard to make you well. Now that you know all, let us not speak anymore, lest you fall ill all over again.'

Kankabaty remained convalescent for a long time. She took a while to regain her former health. Seeta was the one who kept her company during these days. Kankabaty recounted before Seeta all the events of her dream. Seeta repeated them to her mother, the sister-in-law repeated them to Khetu, and thus all the men and women of the entire neighbourhood came to be familiar with Kankabaty's dream. After hearing her story from start to finish, Seeta was in great pique.

Said Seeta to Kankabaty, 'All the stars you wore yourself and gave to your Stale Water. You never thought of keeping a single one for me. Truly, you do not love me, do you; the one you love is your Stale Water. I shan't speak to you anymore.'

Kankabaty became well and strong as before. She began seeing Khetu for short intervals when he came visiting. Once, Khetu had gone to Kankabaty's house. There was a mosquito flying in the room. Khetu caught the mosquito in his cupped hands, took it to Kankabaty and said to her, 'Hey, Kankabaty, come and see if this mosquito is not your 'Stale Water'. Alas, poor Raktabaty hasn't seen its Stale Water in such a long while. Perhaps, it is lonely and has come to see her.'

The embarrassed Kankabaty fled from the room in shame. From that day onwards, she avoided appearing before Khetu whenever he visited her home.

One day, Niranjan said to Khetu, 'Khetu, my boy, I have heard of Kankabaty's dream. What a strange dream it is. But do not mock it, my boy, for what a dream is not even I cannot certainly say. Oftentimes do I feel that our lives, and hopes and beliefs therein, and our joys and sorrows, are as insubstantial as a dream. Verily is this magical universe unfathomable. For, a single object herein is not completely known to any of us.

'For instance, have a look at the book in my hand. What is its true nature? Isn't it a sum of its properties that are perceived by our senses? We see through our eyes that it has length, width and colour. We feel through our skin its hardness, and through our nose sniff its smell. If we like, we can lick it with our tongue, too, to measure its taste. But beyond this we cannot know this object. Had our sense organs been constituted differently, everything on earth would have appeared different. For instance, this book is black and white now before my eyes. If I have jaundice, it would assume a yellowish shade.

'Thus are we all navigating a dream-like world created on the basis of our five senses.

'Hence why should we laugh at Kankabaty's dream? The way the external world is built by our senses, so, too, her dream world was created by the sensory perceptions she collected while sleeping. From beginning to end, Kankabaty is present in her dream. It is comprised of nothing but what Kankabaty sees, hears, says or feels. The mistakes that are expected of her are present in the dream, as well.

'For instance, a mosquito's proboscis is not a nose. Yet elsewhere, the lady of imagination, herself, has played some jokes with Kankabaty. Whatever it is, one has no choice but to accept the dream as a mysterious one. I am personally surprised as to how Kankabaty composed the Sanskrit verse that comprised the injunction given by the mosquitoes. It was a long time back that I had written it. After a few days, I threw away the piece of paper in which I had noted it down. Perhaps, Kankabaty had picked it and read it up.'

After Kankabaty had recuperated fully, an auspicious date and time was chosen from the almanac and Khetu and Kankabaty's marriage was duly solemnised. Because it came in the wake of much strife and sorrowing, the people of seven villages derived great satisfaction out of its successful completion of whom none other than Janardan Chowdhury was the foremost.

Old age and his phlegmatic tendencies had not been constraints for him to spend the entire night of the marriage at Tanu Ray's. Informing no one, he had secretly ordered an enormous quantity of ice from Calcutta and, during the brahmin-only feast, had said lightheartedly, 'How is it right that only the bridegroom keeps cool by taking ice? That shan't be; for we, too, will partake of the same, and refresh ourselves.'

The villagers, who had never seen ice before their eyes, marvelled at the sight of it. Everyone enthusiastically took a little bit of it home as a return gift.

During the feast of the shudras, Gadadhar Ghosh drank three pitcherfuls of ice water. He then chewed almost a *ser*'s worth of the saw-sharp sheets and consumed them.

Giving away Kankabaty to Khetu's mother, Kankabaty's mother said, 'My revered sister! Here, take charge of your Kankabaty!' In that one moment, none on the face of the earth was happier than the two women. Did Khetu's mother then not ritually welcome Kankabaty into her home and hearth? Did Khetu not then turn all bashful and refuse to look anyone in the eye during the rite? Did Kankabaty then not cover her face with a one-hand overhang of her sari's edge and be just like the proverbial banana bride? Did a child then not take advantage of the overhang, and slipping its face underneath the veil, whistle in Kankabaty's ear and run away? There is no real need to answer these questions. But do you know, dear reader, what Ramhari's wife, who is Khetu's boudidi, did during the welcoming of the bride? She caught hold of Khetu's ear and twisted it good and proper. Do you know what Khetu said after his ear was boxed? He said, 'Go on, Boudidi! Aren't you a shameless creature?'

What did the neighbourhood wives, who witnessed the scene, then reply? Kamal Bhattacharya's old widow, known as Gran, screeched, 'The son of a gun takes ice. Off with his ear, my darling, tear it right off his head!'

What happened next? Khetu made pots of money. He had lots of children. Tanu Ray loved playing with them. When other neighbourhood children beat them during play, he was seen gesticulating wildly while quarrelling with their grandmothers.

And next? Now, how is it right for you, my reader, to keep asking this question? Within no time, this little book has assumed considerable girth and thickness. Not sure if I will get my value for ink and paper in returns, I end here. Suffice to say, my story, too, ends at this point. For, this is the moment when its proverbial green shoots are severed and devoured by the ruminators. And that, in itself, has given rise to the filing of many a complaint and griping.

Glossary

1. Calcutta: Headquarters of the East India Company since 1773 and capital of British India until 1911. Capital of the Indian state of West Bengal till 2001 when its name was changed to Kolkata.
2. Age of Consent Act, 1891: Sparked by the death of an eleven-year-old Bengali girl, Phulmoni Dasi, due to forced intercourse by her 35-year-old husband in 1889, this law raises the age of consent for sexual intercourse for all girls, married or unmarried, from ten to twelve years, the violation of which is to be deemed statutory rape.
3. *sahamaran*: Literal meaning co-morbidity, it refers to the Hindu custom of widows burning themselves to death on their husband's funeral pyres. Banned by the East India Company since 1829 via the Bengal Sati Regulation. Also known as Sati, the literal meaning of which is 'The Honest Woman' but nomenclature-wise which is paradoxical since the act involves abandoning the continued pursuit of excellence, service, love, duty and other values and virtues which constitutes all of life's greatest sins of omission.
4. *habisya*: A widow's custom-mandated diet of rice prepared from sunned grains with a serving of ghee or clarified butter made from the milk of a buffalo or a cow.
5. Gajune Bamun: The brahmin who, unsupervised by his peers, conducts the Shiva worship rituals on behalf of mixed-caste ascetics during Gajan, the week-long Shiva festival that takes place in the last week of Chaitra.
6. *Harisankeertan*: Paean in praise of Vishnu, the lord, in his various incarnations and forms, sung to the accompaniment of bells and brass cymbals (*mandira, knaasi, khanjani*), it belongs to the kirtan genre of devotional music.
7. Kaviratna: Jewel among poets, a courtly title for litterateurs
8. Ekadashi: The eleventh day of either of the fortnights between new and full moon days, and vice-versa; it is a day when widows are mandated to observe special rituals ostensibly meant for purification of the soul.

9. Hindu Widows' Remarriage Act, 1856: Drafted by Lord Dalhousie and passed by Lord Canning before the Indian Rebellion of 1857, it legalised the remarriage of widows in all jurisdictions of India under East India Company rule.
10. *sinni*: A delicious mix of bananas, jaggery, honey, camphor, milk, flour, ghee, raisins, nuts and other condiments offered to the Bengali, Hindu-Muslim deity Satyanarayan, also known as Satyapeer, after being prepared by the brahmin priest by his own hand.
11. *awnna*: Grain
12. *namabali*: A shawl imprinted with the name of the lord god
13. *Varnaparichay Part One*: The first book of a two-part primer of the Bengali language written by Ishwar Chandra Vidyasagar in 1855
14. The Shiva: A phallic icon representing the Hindu god, usually in stone
15. Khetaa: Pejorative for Khetu
16. kulfi: A cup of frozen and sweetened milk
17. memsahib: A European-origin woman
18. mohur: Gold coin first introduced by Sher Shah Suri who ruled between CE 1540 and 1545. It was last minted in British India in 1918.
19. Shuk: A male parakeet; feminine known as Saari
20. kingkhap: Banarasi silk
21. *lauta*: A small pot for personal use is frequently called the lauta in northern India. In Bengali, it is referred to as the *ghoti*.
22. samsara: The cycle of birth and death; also the material world
23. babu: An Indian clerk working for the British; also an English-speaking Bengali male
24. *tiki*: Also called the shikha in chaste Bengali, it is the tuft of ritual hair maintained by brahmins on the crown of their heads and is considered the seat of their powers.
25. The Ramayana: One of the two great Indian epics

26. taka, aadhuli, aana, siki, paisa, kada: A taka or Indian rupee equals two aadhuli; sixteen aana; four siki, each equalling four anna; one hundred paisa (paise); and 256 kada.
27. *byanger aadhuli*: A frog's half-penny; a poor man's last belongings
28. taluka: An estate purchased directly from the government or the landowner (zamindar)
29. *chhatak*: A unit of measurement five hands long and five hands wide; a measure that weighs five *tola*, a sixteenth of a *ser*, or the fourth of a *paua*
30. Kalikaal, Kaliyuga: The last of the four yugas or Hindu epoch, each measuring four million and three hundred and twenty years, the others being Satya, Treta and Dvapar, respectively
31. *thakurpo*: Literally, son of the lord, it is typical form of address for the younger brother-in-law used by brides in a Bengali household.
32. *haat* or hand: One hand or haat is typically eighteen inches long.
33. *nagrai* or the *naagra*: Pointy Rajasthani leather shoes
34. Narad or Narada: Vishnu acolyte who loves setting off quarrels between gods and mortals
35. *chachchari*: A dry, spiced, mix-and-match dish of leftover fish, leaves and vegetables
36. *ambal*: Sour broth
37. chutney: Sauce or condiment
38. *khokkosh*: An ogre; a lesser monster. The *rakshash* being the greater one, the ogre in this story is a *khokkosh* only.
39. *Hnau Mau Khau Re*: What the cry of the ogre (or any monster) sounded (sounds) like. Literal meaning: Yowl, howl, growl, do I sniff a human soul?
40. *dhak*: The Bengali drum
41. Rahu: One of the nine major celestial planets in Hindu astrology, originally a demon and king of meteors. In

severed form, it is the sibling of Ketu, and is said to cause the eclipses of the sun and the moon. The north lunar node is its astronomical equivalent.

42. *tola*: A unit of weight equalling 180 grains troy or 0.375 ounce troy, viz. 11.7 grams

43. *knasi*: Cymbal made of bronze or brass, also known in Bengali as the *mandira* or the *khanjani*

44. *shaali*: Literally sister of the wife, pejorative denoting a casually promiscuous woman

45. *talpataar sepai*: Palm-leaf soldier. Metaphor for a feeble-bodied bigmouth with delusions of valour.

46. *prajapatya prayaschitta*: A vow of penance to be observed by a brahmin if they smell liquor unknowingly to atone for the sin believed to have been so incurred. The sinner performing the *prajapatya prayaschitta* 'shall eat in the morning for three days, then in the evening for three days, then for three days food got unasked, and for the next three days he shall not eat.' (*Manusmriti*). It is in fact a lighter penance or sentence of punishment.

47. *noa*: Iron bangle usual among Bengali wives

48. *khanda*: molasses, used to prepare srikhanda, viz. a medieval Indian sweet made from unfermented milk and no sugar believed to be the food of the (Hindu) gods

49. Cowrie: A mollusc shell earlier used as a denomination of currency. Fifty cowries equal a *kada*. Eighty cowries equal one pana, sixteen panas make a kahan; ten kahans equal one taka or rupee.

50. *ser*: An obsolete unit of dry volume. In 1871, it was defined as being exactly one litre.

51. Brahmanbhojan: Feasting of the brahmins

52. Shudrabhojan: Feasting of the shudras

53. *Notey gaachhti mudolo*: The young sapling of my tale has been completely devoured by the ruminating animal. A saying in Bengali literature denoting the end of a story.

Rostam and Bhanumati

Humpbacked Husband

Many years ago, there ruled a king in the country of Iran. The name of his only offspring was Bhanumati. The king and queen both loved Bhanumati more than their very own lives, which they could gladly lay down for the sake of her happiness. But not only the parents, everyone else, too, was charmed by her excellent beauty and talents. And thus did the entire citizenry love Bhanumati over and above its own respective mundane existences.

Bhanumati grew more and more each day, and like the splendour of a blossoming lotus lights up the whole lake and its fragrance is borne by the wind in every direction, her loveliness illumined all of Iran, and the reputation of her good qualities spread across the nation's borders to foreign shores. The king sat on the job of fixing her a marriage alliance. One day, he told the queen, 'My dear lady, Bhanumati is the apple of my eye. I love her more than my own life and cannot bear to lose sight of her for more than a single moment. If I marry her, I must send her off to her matrimonial home. But I cannot live without her.

Fortunately, she is a child yet. Let a few more days go by, and then a match can be arranged.'

The princes of various kingdoms weren't updated about this plan. Having heard stories of her beauty and merit, all of them began to covet the prospect of her hand in marriage. They dispatched messengers to the king's court with their prayers. Yet, Bhanumati's father did not accept a single proposal. To the messengers, he said, 'My daughter is not of marriageable age. At this stage, I shan't give her hand in marriage.' So saying, he sent away the envoys.

During those days, the kingdom of Nishapur was being ruled by a mighty king. He was not handsome at all and was old to boot. The beard on his chin was white in colour and seven hands long, but worst of all was his deformity—the fact that he was a hunchbacked man. Yet, although he had not been blessed with a good appearance, the king did have in his possession a lot of charms; he was, in fact, what is known as a wizard or magician. He knew many magic charms and more incantations. With the power of these, he could turn day to night and night to day. He could shape-shift from man to animal and vice-versa. Ghost or djinn, giant, demon and fairy, he brought under his thumb with the help of these spells. Pixie and phantom alike spent their waking hours anxious of being the focus of his terror.

He wished to marry young Bhanumati. Said the hunchbacked king to himself, 'While it is true that I am dull-complexioned and have a seven-hand-long beard, which is white as hemp fibre, and I bear a hump as round as an

English pumpkin between my shoulders, I will nevertheless cover Bhanumati's person with ornaments. When she receives the jewels, she will forget her parents and hold only me as dear to her. For such is the way of the world.' So decided, he sent forth an emissary to Bhanumati's parents. Yet, just as the news of Bhanumati's beauty had spread far and wide, so had news circulated about the hunchbacked king's spellbinding talents. When the diplomat arrived at the Iranian court, at first the father felt quite irritated. Said he to himself, 'Just have a look at his ambition! It is of a dwarf reaching for the moon! His beauty is enough to make a grown man faint. What gives him the audacity to ask for Bhanumati's hand in marriage?'

While the king's initial reaction was such, he took fright the very next moment. He was well aware of the hunchbacked king's magical powers and was afraid he would harm Bhanumati if offended. Yet, how could he, in good conscience, marry her to this ugly and evil suitor? His heart did not accept the idea, and he conveyed to the envoy of Nishapur exactly the same message that he had given the others. Besides, he showered him with precious gifts, and with sweet words, bid him farewell.

When the messenger returned to Nishapur and gave the humpbacked king the message, he was furious. He said, 'Shan't they marry Bhanumati to such a suitable boy as I? Well, then, I shall teach them a lesson.'

And so resolved, the Quasimodo visited his master to consult him. Deep within the woods, the master had erected a castle wherein he lived. Having reached its doorstep, the hunchback said, 'Sire! The king of Iran has snubbed me rather badly. He has a daughter named Bhanumati whom I had wished to marry. But he refused the match on grounds of my kyphosis and seven-hand-long flaxen facial hair. The king of Iran must be punished. I do not wish to slay Bhanumati, for I shall marry her in the future. But as of the present, pray tell me how to get back my own and go one up on them.'

The master smiled and said, 'Why worry? Take home this ring. Somehow or the other, reach it to Bhanumati. When she puts it on her finger, she won't lose her life, but there will be a great spectacle. It will result in the king and queen's utter misery. They will then fall at your feet and beg you to marry Bhanumati.'

The crook-backed king returned to the palace with the ring. Once in court, he sent for the chief jeweller in town. When he arrived, he said to him, 'I am placing a tranche of pearls and precious stones as well as valuable ornaments from the treasury in your custody. Take them and travel to the Iranian country. Go to the residence of the Iranian king and sell them at nominal prices. But whatever be the sale proceeds, make sure that this ring that I give you is worn by the princess herself. If you are unable to have her put it on, I shall decapitate you and the members of your family.'

So saying, the king handed him the ring and a consignment of jewels and jewellery from the treasury. With his heart beating in trepidation, the jeweller took them and reached Iran country. After reaching Tehran, he began selling these to ordinary citizens dirt cheap. It gave rise to word of mouth that a jeweller had arrived from an unknown country and was selling his wares at negligible prices. Gradually, it reached the ears of the king's ministers. They went over and purchased many items from him. Presently, the king came to learn of the jeweller and sent for him. Now, the jeweller began producing the finest diamonds, emeralds and pearls and showed them to the king. The king made a lot of buys and dispatched the jeweller to the inner quarters to see Bhanumati and the queen. The queen and Bhanumati bought several ornaments. After the sales were over, the jeweller took out the ring and showed it to the young princess. Bhanumati was amazed by the shape and shine of the diamond-set ring. Praising its craftsmanship with vigour and excitement, she enquired about its price, when the jeweller said, 'This ring is invaluable. You are the princess, hence if you but put it on your finger for once, I shall be gratified immensely.' After paying the jeweller his various monies, the princess took the ring and donned it.

The Skull's Laughter

Next day at dawn, there was an outcry in the king's palace. The king and the queen fell apart in grief. The entire city went into mourning. The reason being, rising from bed, everyone found, with the exception of her face, the whole body of Princess Bhanumati had turned to straw. Have you not seen the straw figures that sculptors prepare while building clay idols of the goddesses? So, too, were Bhanumati's bosom, her arms and her legs. Only her face remained of flesh and of blood. With the mouth located in it, she could speak and have her meals. With her limbs, she could even rise and sit up in bed, but she could not use them for walking.

The king and queen wept bitterly, but how could their tears help Bhanumati? Presently, they summoned doctors and healers and got her treated per prescribed practice. The doctors arranged for Jhalemel and the healers got Mahadev dust, but there was no improvement recorded. Bhanumati remained a straw woman as before. The healers took a long time pondering her pulsebeat but could not diagnose the cause of the metamorphosis. In the end, the king took recourse to the ministrations of spellcasters and got them to treat Bhanumati. Many a slap of the broom did thus fall on Bhanumati. Many a puff of magic breath did she also have to endure blown over parts of herself, yet there was not the slightest change in her state. Then the king brought over the wizards who had the power to summon spirits. The ghosts tramped all over the floor of a darkened room. They consumed two *ser* worth of milk and three *ser* of sandesh. They spoke in rhinal sounds, too, and named herbs and condiments, but it was to no avail. Bhanumati's corpus stayed composed of naught but straw. Finally, having exhausted all resources, the king circulated a chunk of gold through the country precincts. Prize in hand, his men paraded the countryside, crossing city and village accompanied by the drummer boy who called, 'Princess Bhanumati's body has turned to straw save her face. Whosoever can restore her will be rewarded with a half of the kingdom and her hand in marriage. Bang, bang, bang!'

With the hunk of metal, the king's drummer toured one village to the next, but no one dared to stop him by touching the piece. For, if a human body suddenly turns to straw, it is not easy to restore it. Many craved the prize as well as the princess and the kingdom's part ownership; but this condition is undocumented in the medical books, neither has its cure been named therein.

Today, many in Iran are Muslim by faith. Yet in those days, the people of Iran worshipped the sun god and fire (just like Hindus), and brahmins, too, lived in that country alongside citizens of different beliefs. In a certain village of the country, therefore, lived a woman of brahmin origin. Her husband had passed on, leaving her with a male baby. The woman worked hard to raise her boy. His name was Rostam. Today, he had stepped into adulthood, being eighteen years of age, although he hadn't yet made an income. Mother and son, thereby, scraped by barely, fasting for days on end frequently.

One day, there being no grain in the cellar, the pair fasted per usual, but seeing his elderly mother go hungry, the son felt indeed aggrieved. Next morning, said he to her, 'Mother, often have I pleaded before you to grant me permission to go abroad and earn money. While you have always denied it, this fast has been one too many. I can bear to see you suffer no more. It is my duty as a son to look after you and if I fail to fulfil it not only shall I be cast into perdition but will also be known as a spineless coward. Hence let me go immediately to foreign lands and make some money. I shall return with it and the two of us shall thenceforth live happily.'

Hearing his argument, first of all, the mother was beside herself with worry as she was about her own inability to be separated from her son who was as important to her as life itself. But then she submitted, flattered by his attentions, and loudly weeping, bid him farewell.

Rostam had been trained by an old Brahmin. He had read several scriptures in the Avestan language and in Sanskrit. He was also powerfully built; hence it was that at the request of her neighbours that his mother had named him Rostam. Breaking a bough from the beech tree, he prepared a cane and thus fortified against danger began walking. Since there flourished many businesses in the capital, he went in the direction of the city, thinking it would be easier to find employment there.

On the way, however, he spotted a farmer thrashing his cow cruelly. The cow's fault was that it had fed on some grain from his cropland. For this crime alone, he had tethered the animal to a post and was raining blows on its back incessantly. Trapped as it was, it had no choice but to silently bear the full force of the assault. Tears of pain flowed from both its eyes. During that time, a crow was engaged in deterring the farmer by flapping about, trying to peck him from one side and then the other. The plight of the cow had provoked pity in its soul but not in that of the farmer.

Seeing the animal suffer so, Rostam approached the man quickly, and politely asked him to desist. The farmer hurled abuses at him in return and began beating the cow with renewed fury. Rostam lost his temper. Picking a rock-like object from the ground, he flung it at the cultivator. The object did not find its target, but the grower became seized with terror. His eyes bulged and his limbs trembled and quaked. Letting out a grotesque shout, he lost no time to make himself scarce. Rostam was astounded because try as he must have he could not figure out the reason behind his reaction. He drew near the spot where the thing lay and found that it was no stone at all but a human skull. Seeing Rostam, the head bared its two sets of teeth and cackled ominously.

Saadi and Tara

Rostam was surprised to learn that what he had first viewed as a stone was a skull instead. He was even more surprised to hear it laugh. But when it began to speak next, he was beside himself with bafflement.

The skull said, 'Serves him right for torturing the poor cow. I have taught him a lesson indeed. Seeing my fearsome visage, he has lost his wits. He shan't repeat it again. Yet, tell me pray, what might have come about of you had I not been in this place? The evil farmer would surely have taken your life.'

Rostam brandished his cane and said, 'With one blow of this cane, wouldn't I have smashed his head? However, say I, who are you? Never before in my life have I known a fleshless, bloodless, severed head to talk in sentences!'

Said the head, 'I am the son of a king, and the crow pecking the farmer is my sibling. Our younger uncle has slain our father and turned my little sister and myself into a crow and a human skull, respectively, through the power of magic. All day we are cursed to be this way, but when evening falls, we are restored to our human forms.'

Rostam asked him, 'What kingdom are you prince of, and what is the name of your uncle?'

Said the defleshed, desiccated human head, 'My father had been the king of Nishapur. My uncle has occupied his throne after having murdered him. It is he who has also put the hex on the two of us. Perhaps, you have come to hear of the hunchbacked king of Nishapur. Well, he is our younger paternal uncle.'

Rostam asked the skull, 'Is there no way I can rescue the both of you?'

It said, 'When the farmer was beating the cow brutally, you mistook me for a rock and picked me up to hurl me at him. Owing to that single action of yours, you, I and my kid sister have acquired a lot of virtue for which you shall be rewarded and we, too, shall be set free.'

Said Rostam, however, 'Poor am I, and cowardly. I cannot take care of my only mother. How can I expect to incur blessings and how ever shall you be free?'

The skull replied, 'The name of the princess of this land is Bhanumati. My uncle has turned Bhanumati's body into straw with his magic. The king of Iran has circulated a hunk of gold promising to marry her and give the half of his kingdom to the one who heals her. Go and catch hold of the gold hunk. We shall return in the evening and tell you how to restore her to her old form.'

Bidding goodbye to the head, Rostam began walking again. It was not before he reached a village where the king's men and the drummer boy were present. Said the drummer in a booming voice: 'Princess Bhanumati is now a straw girl. Whosoever can make her well will be rewarded by the king with her hand in marriage and a half of the country.'

The road milled with bystanders. Everyone gaped as they heard the proclamation but none dared to touch the gold hunk. Pushing the crowd aside, Rostam stepped forward and placed his hand on it. The people were astonished. Everyone wondered as to how a young brahmin would cure Bhanumati.

The king's soldiers immediately sat him on a speedy horse and took him to their ruler. Glimpsing his looks, the king thought, 'This young man is a good match for the place of my son-in-law. Yet, how can he make Bhanumati well again?' Publicly, he said to Rostam, 'Do you promise to cure my daughter knowing that the famed hakims, vaids and rozas have failed to?'

Rostam replied, 'Yes, your majesty. I am certain I shall be able to cure her highness.'

The king said, 'If so, I shall marry you to her. I shall also gift you one half of my administered realm. Should you fail, have no doubt that I shall order the executioner to cut off your head.'

Rostam said, 'Yes, your majesty. Your will shall prevail. If I fail in my assignment, you can do as you please with me.

Now permit me to bring some medication for her highness.'

The king commanded him to proceed and, leaving the king's assembly, Rostam started walking again. Soon, he reached the moor where he had found the farmer beating a cow and met the skull and the crow. He saw the skull resting inside a hole in the ground, and the crow perched on a nearby bough. Knowing that both would attain human form after dark, he, too, sat there on his haunches to wait.

The sun set slowly. When darkness had fallen, a sixteen-year-old boy and a ten-year-old girl suddenly appeared before him. Due to lack of illumination, Rostam could not make out their features fully, but from what was visible, he felt enchanted. Said he to himself, 'Verily are they royal offspring. Such grace does not arise from common households. Why, I wonder how their uncle could bear to torment this handsome pair in such a nasty manner!'

The brother and sister sat down on either side of Rostam. Said the prince, 'See? We are now in human form. Our meeting is the result of the Almighty's mercies. My name is Saadi, and she is Sitara; Tara, for short. I cannot say how the princess' body has turned to straw and the way to restore her. Tara, however, had learnt some magic from the midwife. She will give you the information.'

The Second Ring

Rostam glanced askance at young Tara. Said Tara, 'After you left, I flew to Nishapur. There, I have learnt all that transpired. Our uncle had proposed to marry Bhanumati. Bhanumati's father spurned him. To avenge himself, our uncle has, with the help of his master, turned her body to straw. Only our uncle's master can make her well.' Rostam asked Tara, 'How can I find the master? Besides, what assurance do I have that he shall help me if I do locate him?'

Tara said, 'Go first to Nishapur. There are eight gates to that city. The northern one is called the Samarkand Gate. There is a tall cedar tree just outside it. If you excavate the ground at its foot just a little, you will find a sharp-edged falchion secreted beneath it. It belongs to our father, and Shamsher is its name. There is a deep wood not far from Nishapur. Having erected a castle amidst it, the master resides therein. Once you reach the door of the castle, knock on it with the help of Shamsher. The door will fall open of itself and you will arrive before the evil wizard or the master. Yet, he shan't be able to harm you if Shamsher is clutched in your fist. In fact, he will cower in fear at the sight of Shamsher. That is when you will ask him how to break the spell on Bhanumati, and if he declines to assist, threaten him.' After providing him with advice in abundance, the siblings said goodbye to Rostam; and at the northern gate of Nishapur, he did unearth an invaluable, koftgari-style, diamond- and emerald-encrusted, fierce sword. A two-day walk in the northerly direction took him to a thick grove, which fearlessly he did penetrate and advance through until, a great distance traversed, he sighted a well-fortified castle whose bastions touched the firmament. At this point, a furious wind blew through the forest. It whistled through the branches of trees that seemed to call out in time, 'catch him; take him down' and so forth. Yet Rostam did not tremble. Boldly, he stepped up to the gate and hammered on it with Shamsher. The blows reverberated through the iron door with the sound of thunder. On the seventh strike, the door fell open and Rostam stepped through.

He did not have to wander about for long. The master was seen hastening to the door having heard the pounding. Seeing his vicious mien, however, Rostam, for the first time, felt fear in his heart. For, the master had a pitch-dark complexion, wizened body and bloodshot eyes. It gave him a monstrous appearance. Petrified, Rostam stood rooted to the spot.

Said the master, 'You wretched one! Identify yourself. How dare you bang on my door? Hang on, I will change you into a monkey and release you in the grove this very moment.'

So saying, the master took a fistful of dust, muttered a spell over it and threw it at Rostam, crying, 'Wretch! Be a monkey, momentarily!'

The power of Shamsher protected Rostam from the spell. He stayed as before, in human form. Raising the sword, he now rushed at the master and made to decapitate him. As soon as the master caught a glimpse of Shamsher, he shuddered and his calves began shivering. Falling at Rostam's feet, he started pleading, 'Let me live. Do not slay me. I shall do just as you bid me to.'

Said Rostam, 'Alright then! I shall not slay you for the time being. But if you do not tell me how to restore

Princess Bhanumati to her former body, I shall cut your throat instantaneously.'

Hearing this, the master said, 'The hunchbacked king of Nishapur is my disciple. I am his teacher. He took a ring from me and gave it to Bhanumati. The spell in the ring turned her into a straw-woman. I shall give you a different ring. If you put it on a finger of her right hand, she will be flesh and blood once more.'

Then the master placed a ring in Rostam's palm. Having received the ring, Rostam proceeded in the direction of Tehran city. Reaching the king's assembly, he addressed him, 'Your majesty! I shall cure her highness, Princess Bhanumati, no later than today. Take me to the princess.' The happy king took Rostam to the inner quarters of the palace. Everyone entered the princess's chamber where she lay on the royal bed. Rostam approached her bedside. He took her straw right hand and slipped the ring onto her finger. As soon as he did, the silage that comprised her body burst into flames.

Bhanumati was aflame. Pandemonium broke out in the king's palace. Courtiers and servants ran to pour pails of water on her to extinguish the blaze. Rostam was at a loss to figure out the cause of the disaster. Trembling and dumbstruck, he stood there petrified for a few moments. But the very next instant, he came to his senses and, fearing that if he remained in the palace he would be executed, ran away in the melee as those around him were busy rescuing Bhanumati.

Bottle of Potion

With a pop, Bhanumati's body ignited into flames. Everyone around her got busy dousing them. Finding himself unobserved, Rostam escaped from the palace.

The courtiers brought pales of water and extinguished the fire. Bhanumati's life was spared, but her nose, tongue and ears had melted. Wondrously, her straw arms and legs weren't affected by the blaze. Yet her facial features that were of flesh and blood were destroyed.

The king was furious. He said, 'A con artiste had come by, coveting the princess and the throne. Bring him before me directly. I shall put him on a spike and sever his head.' But Rostam could not be traced. Exiting the king's palace, he ran breathlessly. Even after leaving the precincts of the city, he speed-walked for a great distance. It was dusk when he reached the moor where he had met Tara and Saadi.

As soon as it was dark, the skull and the crow, i.e., Saadi and Tara, reverted to their human shapes. Rostam narrated before them the events of the palace. Having heard him out, Tara said, 'The master has tricked you. He did not give you the right solution for Bhanumati's problem. He gave you the ring which would cause her to light up in a fire and burn to death. He thought if Bhanumati died, the king would have you slain. Then you can no longer threaten him with the sword Shamsher. That said, is Shamsher with you? The sword Shamsher was tucked in Rostam's waist and, placing his hand on it, he replied in the affirmative. 'Yes,' said Rostam, 'Shamsher stands with me.'

Tara said, 'Very well. Return to the master anon. We shan't slay him now. Do not slay him until Bhanumati is well again. Intimidate him with the falchion and procure the method to heal her from him.'

Before the sun rose the next morning, Rostam said goodbye to Tara and Saadi, and began his journey. Presently, he reached the master's grove, and the trees of the grove began cackling in the wind. Rostam was unafraid and, reaching the fortress, he struck the door with his falchion seven times like before. The door fell open, and stepping inside, he began to look for the master but could not find him. After a long lookabout, he found himself in a dark chamber, which was filled with fossils of animals, roots and barks of trees. In that secret chamber sat the master before a furnace, lit with the help of bellows, preparing a magic potion in it.

Rostam walked in and straightaway caught hold of the master's ponytail. With the hair in his fist, he turned his head up and raised his falchion to sever it. Overcome by fear, the master fell at Rostam's feet. Joining his hands in prayer, said he, repeatedly, 'Do not slay me. My work is not done yet. I am researching a potion that shall make man live forever. When I successfully make it, I shall give it to you. I beg of you. Do not slay me.'

'I hardly believe you,' Rostam said. 'You gave me a fake ring and arranged to have me slain instead, didn't you? I shall certainly kill you.'

Begging and beseeching, the master said, 'I swear I did not trick you. I gave you the correct medicine. But I cannot say why it did not bear results. Why don't you relate to me what happened exactly? Do not slay me without my having wronged you.'

Said Rostam, 'The ring you gave me I had slipped onto a finger of Bhanumati's right hand. As soon as I did, her straw corpus burst into flames. I did not wait to see what happened next. I ran away from the palace. I do not know if she is dead or alive still.'

Said the master, 'Bhanumati is still alive and not dead. I have figured out why she caught fire. Had you removed the ring on her left hand before putting the one on the right? It is the one that I had given to the hunchbacked king of Nishapur.' Rostam said, 'No. I hadn't removed that ring.'

The master said, 'In that case, for this mishap you are to blame. Why did you have her wear a new ring without removing the old? Let that be; for now, I am giving you a special potion. At first, you shall remove the ring from the left hand of Bhanumati. You shan't remove the one on her right. Then you shall wet her body with this medication. If you follow all these steps, Bhanumati will regain her original form and will be flesh and blood again.' So saying, the master handed Rostam a small glass bottle. 'If Bhanumati doesn't get well this time around, I shall return here and cut you down,' threatened Rostam and he left the master's castle. Rostam began his walk back to Tehran. As soon as he reached the capital city, the king's soldiers captured him and took him to their ruler. At the sight of Rostam, the king was beside himself with rage and ordered his execution.

Joining his hands in entreaty, Rostam said, 'Your majesty, do not slay me. For, if you do, you stand to gain nothing. If I live instead, your daughter will return to her former state. The last time around, I had made a mistake, hence the mishappenstance. I have the right cure with me now. If it does not do her any good, you can do with me as you please.'

Rostam's assurances somewhat calmed the king who, accompanied by his courtiers, led him once again to the princess' bedchamber. Once again, Rostam stood by the princess' bed. He had not been aware that her nose, ears and tongue had been disfigured in the fire and the hideous transformation of her face that once had a moonlike beauty pained and frightened him in equal measures.

In the end, he slipped out the ring sent to Bhanumati by the hunchbacked king from her left hand. He did not remove the new ring from her right digits. Then, he soaked her body with drops of the liquid that he had carried in the magic bottle. As soon as the droplets fell on Bhanumati's body, it turned to flesh and blood again. Bhanumati got back her human shape, but her nose, ears and tongue did not heal. Sans them, the sight of her face revolted all.

The Winged Horse

The king was pleased to see Bhanumati's straw body turn flesh and blood once again. But glimpsing the state of her nose, ears and tongue rendered his pleasure bittersweet.

Addressing the king, Rostam said, 'Your majesty! Do not fret. I shall arrange for a way to restore Bhanumati's face to its previous glory. Wait for me. Before long shall I return to you.'

Rostam bid goodbye to the king and made for the moor. Reaching the moor, he camped there until nightfall. At night, he met Saadi and Tara and narrated his progress to them.

Hearing his account, Tara said, 'There is only one way to restore Bhanumati's nose, ears and lapper. If the master magician's nose is severed and its blood smeared on Bhanumati's nose, ears and tongue, then those spots will get healthy again and regain their old look.'

Said Rostam, 'Howsoever afraid for his life, the master will refuse to come with me of his own will. I have to use force. He being light and desiccated, I can carry him so far. But how can I cover the entire distance to the palace?'

Tara said, 'The day I flew to Nishapur, I met the midwife who had been my foster mother and she told me about Shamsher, Bhanumati and the way to rescue us. And, Saadi. She had also mentioned your winged horse. When our uncle slew our father and turned us magically into the crow and the skull, we were babies and our foster mother could do nothing to help us. She said the other day that Saadi has come of age and hence the time has arrived for us to be saved. I am not sure if I can explain how, but Saadi, give your winged horse to Rostam.'

Glancing at Rostam, Saadi said, 'Tomorrow at daybreak, call my winged horse with this verse:

"Gold-hoofed winged horse most enchanting,
O' rising god, prithee, come galloping!"

As soon as you utter this spell, the winged horse will come galloping to your side. My father had gifted it to me with great affection, hence you shan't lash him. Wherever you wish to go, the horse will take you. Mounting his back, you shall fly to the magician's castle, and then, catching hold of him and placing him under your groin, you shall repair to the capital of Iran.'

'You have been working relentlessly for my cause for so long. How is it that I can restore you?' asked Rostam.

'Do not worry on that account,' Tara said. 'From your deed will arise the path to our restitution.'

The next morning, when Saadi and Tara became the skull and crow again, Rostam called the winged horse:

'Gold-hoofed winged horse most enchanting,

O' rising god, prithee, come galloping!'

As soon as he uttered the spell, a handsome horse appeared in the air before him and landed on the ground. The horse was green with four gold hoofs, which were decorated with precious stones. Rostam climbed onto its back and focussed on the magician's castle. Immediately, the horse began to fly through the sky as fast as the seven winds blew. Before he knew it, Rostam was inside the castle, and before he had dismounted and gone a few steps, met the master magician in front of him. Wasting no words, he lifted the master in his arms and proceeded outdoors. The master's body being light and desiccated, it was child's play for him. Without exerting himself, Rostam brought him to the horse and mounted it. The master had been caught unawares at this frightening turn of events. Nonplussed, he did not try to struggle or extricate himself.

Mounting the horse, Rostam willed it to go to the capital of Iran. The horse flew like the seven winds and reached the court of the king of Iran. The courtiers were clearly surprised to see a winged horse, Rostam and the master magician standing before them. Rostam requested the king to have the master magician put in shackles. The master was immediately bound hand and feet at the king's orders. Thereafter, Rostam narrated to the king why he had taken the master prisoner and no doubt the king was surprised to learn it. Dragging the master in chains with them, all went to Bhanumati's bedchamber where Rostam produced a sharp knife and cut off the nose of the magician. The wound on the master's face bled blue in colour and, taking the blue blood, Rostam smeared some of it on the princess' nose, ears and tongue. Immediately, Bhanumati's appendages regained their earlier form and look. She now became completely well. As before, her beauty illumined the palace. The king, queen, ministers and nobles, and all the citizens of Iran country were afloat in an ocean of happiness. Said the king, 'I shall marry you to Princess Bhanumati within the night.'

Thinking of the plight of his mother, Saadi and Tara, Rostam pleaded to postpone the wedding.

The king said, 'You have done me a great service. We should not delay this auspicious job. I shall marry you to the princess before daybreak.'

The noseless magician was thrown behind bars by the order of the king. Thereafter, with great gusto, he set about making the wedding preparations. Since he was king, his orders were executed immediately and soon all was placed at the ready. The highways were sparkling clean and the doorways had new leaf hangings. The citizens decorated their homes and a carnival began comprising dance and music.

When evening fell, all of Tehran lit up with strings of lamps. The hour of the wedding was nigh. The guests took their seats in the hall. The bride and groom, the king and the priest, too, occupied their respective seats. The wedding was but about to begin when the marriage hall was hit by a gust of wind. The gale effaced the lamps and raised a cloud of dust, which caused the darkness to become inspissated. Yet, no sooner had the storm appeared that it dissipated. When the lamps were alight again, it was found that, with the exception of Bhanumati, everyone else was in their respective spot. A search was mounted. All night it continued but proved futile. No one could figure out whereto and whosoever had taken Bhanumati.

Bhanumati Runs Away

While there was no clue to her disappearance, the king and queen were convinced as were the citizens that it was all the work of the hunchbacked king who had spirited Bhanumati away. Reassuring the king, Rostam said, 'Your majesty! Do not fret. If I could defeat the hunchbacked king's master and capture him, I can no doubt beat the king as well and rescue

Bhanumati from his clutches. I am going out in search of her. I shall return in no time.' So saying, Rostam left the palace.

Bhanumati had indeed been taken by the hunchbacked king. Flying through the air at the speed of the seven winds, he whisked her away to Nishapur and locked her away.

Repairing to his private room, the hunchbacked king first took a nice bath with soap. Then, to appear beautiful, he powdered his face. It began to look somewhat like a burnt aluminium pot smeared with quicklime. Make-up done, he put on a pure silk suit laced with gold embroidery. Now he began to resemble the fruit of the palmyra palm peeled out in places. Thereafter, he poured copious quantities of expensive perfumes liberally all over his body. In the end, he slipped out a plain hat from a box, put it on, looked in the mirror and smiled to himself. He then folded it up and placed it inside his pocket, replacing it with a matching embroidered silk hat on his head.

The hunchbacked king headed for the room in which Bhanumati had been secreted. There was a bed in the room, on one end of which she sat weeping inconsolably. Tears flowed from her eyes incessantly and wet her bosom. But when the hunchbacked king entered the room, she wiped her cheeks upon his sight and, with rage writ on her face, said, 'You wicked man! Why have you brought me here? My father will come here with his army and slay you. Drop me home if you fear for your life.'

The hunchbacked king said, 'Shame on you, friend! Why are you so angry? I have brought you here to do you the honour of marrying you. You shan't find a groom more suitable than myself.'

Said Bhanumati, 'To think that I shall marry you! You humanoid, you! Have you no shame? Why don't you look in the mirror for once? I am not about to die that I shall accept you. To think you have oiled your seven-hand beard for my sake! Scoot, now! Skedaddle!'

The hunchbacked king said, 'I haven't oiled my beard but put itar on it. If you don't marry me willingly, I shall force you to consent. Let me, too, see who comes to your aid. I am not afraid of your father. I shall blow him away with a single puff of my breath.'

Bhanumati said, 'If my father is unable to help me, the one who has cut off your master's nose will rescue me and serve you punishment.'

The hunchbacked king had been aware of the news that his master had been imprisoned. He had planned to first marry Bhanumati and then arrange for his deliverance. He was infuriated to learn that in the meantime he had been mutilated. He caught hold of Bhanumati's left hand and pulled it in the direction of the door. He said, 'Come on out to the corridor. I shall call an assembly and a priest and marry you on the spot. Then shall I see who can take you away from me.'

Bhanumati struggled to release herself and, with her right hand, scratched the hunchbacked king on his face and tore at his seven-hand beard. Parts of it came apart in her fist and fell all around her like so much flax. The beard had been cultivated with much care by the hunchbacked king. It began to come out in bits and pieces under Bhanumati's exertions. The hunchbacked king felt afraid. He thought he would lose his darling beard in its entirety if he engaged in a tussle with Bhanumati. So, he released her hand, and he said, 'Hold on. I shall send some beardless men to escort you.'

The angry king left the room, and Bhanumati shut the door, lifted the bolt and put it in its slot. Having put the bolt in place, she returned to sit on the corner of her bed. Her glance fell on a plain hat on the floor. During the struggle, it had fallen there from out of the hunchbacked king's pocket. Sitting on the corner of the bed, Bhanumati took the hat in her hands, turned it over and examined it. Finally, she put it on her head. Well, to begin with, Bhanumati was none other than a young woman. Being a young woman, then, even amid danger to her life and future, she could not be expected to act out of character, now, could she? There was a big mirror in the room. To see how the hat complimented her looks, Bhanumati went to stand before it. But wait a minute! When she went to stand before the mirror, Bhanumati's reflection did not fall on it at all. At a loss, she began to think, 'This is surprising indeed! A while ago, I had seen my reflection in this glass. Why does my image not show in it?' Bhanumati slipped off the hat and immediately her reflection appeared in the mirror. She put it on again, and it disappeared. She repeated the cycle a few times and then said to herself, 'I see. This here is a vanishing hat. People wear it to conceal themselves. The ability to render people invisible is the hat's property.' Carefully holding the hat, Bhanumati went up to the bed and sat on it. Presently, the hunchbacked king and his men began pushing at the door. Since the bolt was in place, they could not open it effortlessly. Yet, for how long can a door withstand magic? Using a spell, the king opened the door in no time. Simultaneously, Bhanumati placed the hat on her head. Entering the room, the hunchbacked king and his beardless men could not find Bhanumati. All were nonplussed. The hunchbacked king realised why Bhanumati could not be spotted. He said to his men, 'Close the door, quickly. Bhanumati is in this very room. Look for her by feeling your way through every nook and cranny inside it. Even if we cannot see her, we are sure to touch upon her presently.'

Rescue

Yet, before this order was spoken and the door closed, Bhanumati had sidled through it avoiding contact with the hunchbacked king and his beardless men. The king's men first searched the whole room thoroughly touching every object. They could not locate Bhanumati. Then they hunted for her all over the palace. The hunt proved fruitless. The hunchbacked king's palace was surrounded by an orchard and gardens. Exiting her room, Bhanumati went and hid herself inside a Spanish jasmine bush in one of the gardens. This was why the king's men failed to catch hold of her and she could not be found. Blind with rage, the hunchbacked king sent out his men in all directions. He set the infantry and cavalry, indeed all four wings of his army, after Bhanumati.

Rostam, on the other hand, had made for the moor straightaway after leaving the Iranian king's palace. It was almost daybreak when he reached the point of his rendezvous with Tara and Saadi. Luckily for him, both were still in their human shapes when he arrived and he unburdened himself before the duo.

Said Saadi, 'This is the job of our uncle. There is no doubt of it. However, you can defeat him with the power of the sword, Shamsher. When it is morning, summon my horse. Speed is of essence. Mount him and go to Nishapur. I cannot advise exactly how you will accomplish your mission, just do as is warranted.'

Agreeing with Saadi's suggestion, Tara added, 'Do not slay our uncle. He may have wronged us a thousand times over, but he is still our elder. But go to our foster mother after you rescue Bhanumati. It is time for us to be restored to our original shapes. Our foster mother will tell you how to break the spell.'

Before long, it was morning. Rostam summoned the winged horse:

'Gold-hoofed winged horse most enchanting,
O' rising god, prithee, come galloping!'

As soon as he uttered the spell, a flying horse appeared in the sky before him. Momentarily, Rostam arrived in Nishapur on its back.

Bhanumati spent the night in the Spanish jasmine bush. When it was morning, her hair come awry, she felt the need to straighten her coif and removed her hat. Standing at a first-floor window, the hunchbacked king spied her in the thicket, but the next moment she had donned the hat again and vanished out of sight.

Stealthily as he could, the hunchbacked king entered the garden and crept towards the flower bush. He came to the spot where he had last seen Bhanumati and began feeling his way around it. A preoccupied Bhanumati sat under the bush.

Distracted by her own thoughts, Bhanumati failed to see the hunchbacked king until suddenly his hand was on her back. It was too late. Desperately, she tried to run away, but her hat caught in the branches of the thicket and slipped off her head, rendering her visible. The hunchbacked king grabbed her by the hair and tried to drag her back into the palace. Bhanumati bit him and scratched at him. Taking offence, the hunchbacked king decided to kill Bhanumati by slashing her neck. With his left hand grasping her hair, he unsheathed the sword with his right from its scabbard on his waist. Raising it high in the air, he was about to bring it down when Rostam arrived on his flying horse and, with the back of Shamsher, smote mightily the right hand of the evil king. The sword fell from Quasimodo's hand and, dismounting, Rostam caught hold of his seven-hand long whiskers. Raising Shamsher, said he, 'Miscreant! Who can save you if I decide to cut you down?'

The hunchbacked king was aghast to find Rostam carrying Shamsher. Fear overtook him and caused him to quake in his shoes. He said, 'Where did you find the sword Shamsher? The fairy, Minak, had given it to my older brother.

I looked for it high and low following his death. It must have been Tara's lowly foster mother who had secreted it. If you so wish, you may slit my throat. I shan't protest it.'

Rostam did not cut down the hunchbacked king. Nor did he slit his throat. He confined him to a chamber under watch. He put Bhanumati in a room, too, and a well-appointed one, asking the servants to service her every need. Then he travelled to the foster mother and asked her about the means to rid Saadi and Tara of the curse they had been suffering. The foster mother said, 'Burn the hunchbacked king's seven-hand beard and smear its ashes on their bodies. Then they shall be free.'

Rostam returned to the hunchbacked king's palace, asked Bhanumati to sit astride the winged horse behind him and returned to Tehran. The king and queen of Iran were overjoyed to reunite with Bhanumati. Rostam, on the other hand, repaired to the moor where he picked up the crow who was Tara and the human skull who was Saadi and transported them to Nishapur. He put them up at the foster mother's home and returned to Tehran again to pick up the master. Thereafter, he took the master to the hunchbacked king's room. The master was an ugly man, and having lost his nose and ears made him look ghastly. Upon seeing the master, the hunchbacked king wept in regret at his disfigurements. Rostam said to the hunchbacked king, 'Do not fret. You will soon join him in his misery. You are already deformed with a hump. Your seven-hand beard was your only pride and joy. Today, it shall be shaved.'

The hunchbacked king fell at Rostam's feet and said, 'Cut my throat but do not cut my beard. All my magical powers are vested in it. I have grown it with so much loving care. Alas! My darling beard will be gone today.'

The hunchbacked king wept aloud, but Rostam did not pay any attention to him. He called the barber over and cut the king's beard. Then he set it on fire and spread the ashes on Tara and Saadi, who regained their human shapes instantaneously. Rostam put Saadi on the throne of Nishapur. Saadi began to look after his subjects as if they were his own offspring. He did not execute his uncle but threw him in the dungeons with his master for company. Rostam returned to Iran in a few days. Meeting the king there, he said, 'Your majesty. I have given life to Bhanumati. Hence, her I do not desire to marry. However, I shall be obliged if you fix her alliance with the king of Nishapur, Saadi. He is my friend.' The king consented to his proposal. With great pomp, the marriage was solemnised. Rostam, on the other hand, had been enamoured of Tara's beauty. He loved her more than he loved Bhanumati. That was the reason why he had declined to marry Bhanumati. After a few more days passed, Rostam and Tara got hitched. A new kingdom was crafted out of one half of Iran and a part of Nishapur's precincts. It was named Samarkand. Rostam was crowned king of Samarkand. Rostam began spending his days comfortably in the company of Tara and his elderly mother. So did Saadi and Bhanumati.

Glossary

1. Nishapur: The Fair City of New Shapur, or Neyshabur, in northeastern Iran is a legacy of Iran's pre-Islamic history. With a 4.5 lakh population, it is, in fact, the second largest city of its Razavi Khorasan province. Nishapur, or Abarshahr, was founded in the third century by the Sassanian Shapur I but, according to Zoroastrian belief, it is 7,500 years old and, as per Ferdowsi's *Shahnameh,* then ruled by the Pishdadians, a line of mythological kings. These kings are said to have descended from the 'first human'. His name was Keyumars and he is also known as the Zoroastrian Adam. In the mid-seventh century, Nishapur fell to Rashidun forces without struggle but went on to become one of the greatest cities of the Old World.
2. Jhalemel: A herbal digestive
3. Mahadev *churna*: Dust of the hemp leaf (*Cannabis sativa, Cannabis indica*) the medicinal property of which includes removal of stress and anxiety. For consumption, mixing with milk or yoghurt shake is the recommended way.
4. Avestan language: Historically known as Zend, it is the language in which the Avesta or the Zoroastrian scripture is written. While the Younger Avestan language was spoken in the first millennium BCE, the Old Avestan language was spoken in the second millennium BCE. Old Avestan is quite similar in grammar and lexicon to Vedic Sanskrit.
5. hakim: A physician using traditional remedies in Muslim countries
6. *vaid*: A physician using traditional remedies in Hindu countries
7. *roza*: Exorcist
8. koftgari: A metallurgical technique originating in central Asia of inlaying weapons, such as swords, with jewels and gold
9. Winged Horse: The mythical horse with wings, also known

as Pakshiraj, king of birds. Unlike a unicorn, it lacks a horn in the middle of its forehead and, speed aside, has no magical characteristics.

10. satchazari: Traditional Indian brocade made of real gold and/or silver embroidery. There are several styles of zari work, such as *zardosi, gota, tilla, kataoki bel, mukaish* and *kinari.* The use of zari was popularised in India during the Mughal era. Surat in Gujarat is the world's largest producer of zari. In Bengali, it is often truncated to only satcha and spoken as such. In the original text, when the hunchbacked king goes to meet Bhanumati in captivity for the first time, he puts on a satchazari suit.
11. Minak: The name of a peri or fairy; also, a village in northern Iran

The Alchemist

Backstory

Anyone who can perform miracles by dint of uttering a spell is called a magician or a sorcerer. Whether or not magicians do exist in this world I shall not discuss in this text. But the majority of those who go as one are deliberate cons; they trick people to make a quick buck. Many an ascetic and wandering saint, at least ones purporting to be so, have betrayed the trust of their victims by promising them gold. They appear at the doorstep of a home and say to the householder, 'Bring me your silver—utensils, currency and jewellery—I have chemicals and a charm that shall turn them into gold.' Hoping to become rich overnight, the master of the house would entrust all his valuable objects with the ascetic who would collect them and leave, never to be seen again.

Yet, the ones who cheat people never do well. The dishonest need must suffer consequences. Right from boyhood days should one resolve never to speak a lie, never do what one believes to be false, and never perpetrate fraud. Mendacity and deception are the habits of the vile and the degraded. The Almighty punishes liars grievously for their wrongs.

To give you an example of how the liar incurs the Almighty's wrath, let me tell you a story. It is a completely true story. The protagonist of this tale had acute intelligence and was armed with daring initiative and versatile knowledge. Yet, at the start of his life, he had said a few lies. Hence, even though he was gifted with every quality, he could not lead a successful life. Instead, misery and despair cast their doom and gloom on him for all his days. The day he died was the day he got his freedom from this fate. Therefore, one must forever be vigilant as to never pass a falsehood through one's lips, commit an act that is less than honest, or even indulge selfish thoughts and feelings within one's own psyche.

Everyone wants to make money and enterprise is man's eternal quest. There exists a long-held fantasy, nay belief, that it is indeed physically possible to turn lead and mercury to silver and make gold from iron and copper. If a paisaworth of copper can be turned into gold, its owner makes a profit of ten crisp bucks. It is why, since the ancient times, humans have been striving to do the same. In the old ages, so many in various countries had devoted their lives to this task. The techniques they applied in their endeavour are collectively known as alchemy, and to narrate the successes and failures of this science is a separate subject. Today I shall refrain from discussing the same. Today I shall recount before you the story of Johann Friedrich Bottger. In his youth, he had trained in alchemy, which means he had expended his efforts to achieve the same end.

Bottger was born in Prussia, which is presently part of the German nation, 217 years ago in CE 1682. He apprenticed at a hospital at the age of twelve. As a child, he had a fascination for the study of chemistry. In those days, chemistry and alchemy were one and the same subject. Bottger used all his leisure hours in alchemic research. In plain English, this meant he experimented the reaction of iron, copper, etc., with various compounds to see if they could be converted to gold. These tests he carried on non-stop for several years on end. Seeing his sharpness and extraordinary knowledge, the owner of the hospital began sponsoring his laboratory work. After some years had passed, Bottger announced that he had discovered the means to prepare gold. To sample the truth of his statement, a demonstration was arranged for in the presence of his employer, the owner of the hospital. No one knows how but that day Bottger presented the owner with the desired result. To trick spectators, phoney ascetics are known to typically deploy similar ruses. One needs to place some gold in a pipe and seal its ends with beeswax. The pipe appears as a cane to the onlooker. Next, they have to light a fire, put some bogus items like sulphur, ghee and so on in a cauldron placed over it, and then make a big show of stirring them, turning these over and over on the flames with the cane. The heat of the fire melts the wax, and soon the gold is deposited into the bowl. Soon, the sulphur and the ghee evaporate and the yellow metal is all that is left. The charlatan gains the trust of the homeowner who thinks, 'Yes, this ascetic can indeed produce gold.' I cannot say for sure if Bottger had adopted this methodology to fool his employer, but he and the witnesses present indeed fell for his hoax and believed that he had discovered a way to turn base metal into gold.

Word spread that a man in such-and-such hospital could create gold and crowds began to collect at the gates for to catch a glimpse of him. Soon, the king heard the news and summoned Bottger. Bottger appeared in court with a gift of gold and declared it had been prepared from copper by him. It was a period when waging wars had depleted the treasury of Prussia. The king himself was an avaricious man. Overjoyed, he thought he had hit the jackpot and ordered him to be imprisoned in a faraway citadel where his task was to prepare pots and pots of gold to replenish the king's treasury.

Bottger was crestfallen. Not only would he lose his freedom, but he was also now likely to be found out and hanged. If worse punishment awaited him, he could not say. He fled to Saxony even as the king sent his horsemen on his trail. At the borders, the Saxon king gave him asylum in Dresden. The horsemen caught up with him, but he evaded their clutches.

As I write this account, Andrew Carnegie does business in the United States of America. He had begun his life as a child labourer. As an adult, he is a steel tycoon and a billionaire. From his great wealth, he has donated to charities a total sum worth ₹75 crore, which is 75,00,00,000 rupees when written in figures, to various public institutions, dividing the money among them—two crore rupees to a hospital for the care of the impoverished, a crore meant for students at an orphanage, another crore to a library, and so on and so forth. Evidently, Mr Carnegie has exhausted his personal desire for money, for it is a rare man who is indifferent to the pull and pursuit of its accumulation.

The lust of money has haunted mankind from the earliest times, and none can easily get rid of it from their mind. Two hundred years back, the kingdoms of Saxony and Poland shared the same ruler. Even though he was a ruler of lands, this king, too, was needy for money. Funds were required to clamp down on the rebellion raging at the time in Poland. Therefore, when the Saxon king heard that 'gold-maker' Bottger had fled Prussia and was seeking refuge in his kingdom, he took delight at the thought—'here's the end to my worries, now I can have gold to my heart's content'—and immediately welcomed him to his capital and put him up in a stately mansion right next to his palace. Ordering his employees and servants to give him the royal treatment complete with lavish meals and gifts of valuable raiment, he ensured that he was kept under watch at all times, with guards accompanying him when he stepped out and keeping an eye on him when he didn't. From the bedroom to the dining hall, at all hours of the day and night, the vigil was kept, and he was never let out of sight. Bottger wondered if indeed he had landed from the frying pan to the fire, seeing that the very danger he had had to abandon his homeland for now threatened to swallow him in his new place of residence.

Meanwhile, the Saxon king's presence became necessary in Poland to suppress the rebellion, and he had to rush there without seeing Bottger privately as he had desired. Hence, upon reaching Poland, he wrote him a letter that could along these lines be paraphrased—'Money has come to be of essence. Making gold, therefore, is no longer optional. Please let me know as to how it is that I can accomplish the same.' To his employees, the king said, 'Torture the man until he obeys my wish.' The king's men began tormenting Bottger in painful ways.

Denouement

At long last, a persecuted Bottger produced a small glass bottle filled with a reddish extract of unknown origin and handed it to the king's men. He said, 'Give this to your king. Say to him that with a pure heart and mind cleansed of evil thoughts, he needs must enter a secluded vestibule. In the chamber, he must prepare a bonfire on which he must melt iron, copper or any other metal. Once it is in molten state, two or three drops of this liquor must be added to the liquefied metal, which will turn into gold right away.' As such, an invaluable substance could not be entrusted with a messenger or porter, the prince himself rode out with the bottle. Archers, infantry soldiers, gunners and horsemen escorted him just the way a small army accompanied the horse of Ashwamedh. At the appointed hour, the prince and the king entered a lonely apartment. With extreme care, they poured three drops of the tincture onto the molten metal, but there was no reaction. The copper stayed copper, and the king was befuddled. He fell into deep depression. 'It must be the drink, and the secret pleasures that I had joined in last night. It poured water on my whole project,' he decided in the end. So saying, he said his prayers, went to church and gave enormous amounts of money to padres to devote to organising ecclesiastical events. When these events had taken place, he considered his sins expiated and again conducted his experiment. He lit a fire and melted copper in which he added the magic liquor. Alas! This time, too, the exercise failed to bear results. Try as he did, the copper wouldn't change. It retained its old characteristics and the king at last became enraged.

The king said to himself, 'The bloke knows how to do the job, he is only playing the fool. He must be tortured until he blurts his secret.' Torture was a commonplace form of punishment in the Middle Ages. In medieval Europe, there prevailed gruesome torture techniques and instruments. Tongs were used to extract the victim's teeth one after another, the rack to break every bone of their body all at once and pokers to inflict burns all over them. The pain was so excruciating that the innocent would confess to thefts they hadn't committed, and harmless old women would swear that they had indeed been witches. As the king took offence, Bottger himself came to the realisation that it was time for him to leave. Pulling the wool over his sentries' eyes, he escaped the mansion and furiously rode for three nights and three days. At last, he reached the kingdom of Austria, where he began eking out a humble existence.

Bottger was asleep one night somewhere in Austria when Saxon soldiers came and took him back to Dresden. This time, he was not kept in house arrest but thrown behind bars inside an impregnable fort where the angry king arrived to see him and, addressing him, irately said, 'My treasury has been empty for months and the soldiers have not been paid in many days. You are under orders to make some gold. If you refuse, I will certainly hang you until you are dead.'

The truth, as said before, was that Bottger did not know how and had committed perjury either to cheat others or to save face. Consequently, he failed to carry out the king's command. The king did not hang him but he did not let him out of jail. Several years went by. The Portuguese sailed to India, China and Japan in the meantime, followed by Hollanders, French and Englishmen. They began doing brisk business exporting luxury goods from the Orient.

Some Europeans had sent home fine china vessels. China crockery is highly elegant and of excellent quality. The Chinese use a variety of white earth to make tableware and decorate it with designs painted on with red and blue dye. When burnt in a furnace or over an open flame, a translucent glass called ceramics is generated. Coming in different shapes and patterns, the bright and glossy white ceramic bowls and dishes were delightfully pleasing to the eye, and in Germany, Holland and England began selling for a price higher than that of the yellow metal.

When this transpired, a well-wisher of our hero said to him, 'Bottger, my dear friend! No one will believe you if you say you cannot produce gold. The king believes you can and are only being mischievous in hiding the know-how of the process from him. You have incurred the royal wrath. It is looking increasingly likely that you will remain imprisoned for the rest of your days. You are an erudite man, well-learned in chemistry. China today is commanding a price higher than that of gold. Why don't you devise a way to turn out ceramic vessels, which the kingdom can export and earn revenue? Perhaps, the king will be pleased then and release you from captivity.'

Bottger took the advice of his friend. He began experimenting with various types of clay. The king assisted him in his work. Under his royal orders, raw material arrived from various corners of the western world and Bottger began crafting the bowls and casting them into the furnace. Yet, try as he did, he failed to construct even the inexact verisimilitude of china vessels. A type of red clay had been procured for the purpose of making the cauldron in which to prepare mixtures of compounds and elements. Bottger used it to fashion a pot, burnt it and discovered that he had hit upon a way to make a class of red ceramic vessel. He produced a whole batch of vessels and gave them over to the king with hopes that these would yield high profits in the market. But since the original ceramics that had caught the fancy of people were white in colour, these, sadly, were not valued comparably.

Bottger began researching means to produce white ceramic vessels in earnest. The king, however, would not free him from his sentence. Humbly and regretfully, the chemist wrote long mails to the king. In one of them, he said, 'Your highness! I have devoted my life to your service. Day and night, I work with your prosperity as my aim. For this, I seek no remuneration. All I beg of you is that do not cage me any longer. Give me freedom. Release me from jail. I give you my word I shall not escape. As long as I am alive, I shall work for the welfare of your kingdom and your people.' The king did not heed his request. His mornings Bottger spent surrounded by the king's guards. Nights he passed locked up in his cell.

Nevertheless, Bottger continued with his tests, trying out techniques with various types of ingredients. Burning the midnight oil, he worked. If, after a hundred and more failures, a single attempt succeeded, he would have considered himself fortunate. But with all of Germany's diverse earths and stones, he failed to produce Chinese porcelain.

In *vilayat*, it was de rigueur among the members of nobility to wear long locks of artificial hair or wigs, to be precise, and Bottger was no exception to the routine. It was also customary for wigmakers to dust their hairpieces with white powder to increase their visual appeal. One day, Bottger observed his wig felt heavier than usual and enquired of his companions as to the possible reason. One of them replied, 'Today they have applied to it the dust of a new clay.'

Bottger sent for the clay that had been used to dust the wig and, when it arrived, he was fascinated. Hope arose in his bosom and he said to himself, 'Perhaps this is the clay that will bring an end to all my experiments.' And his intuition proved correct. For that was exactly what happened.

Kaolin is the name of this white clay. In India, it is found in the districts of Santhal Parganas, Bhagalpur and Munger. The king ordered for an enormous quantity of kaolin from the spot in Germany where it had been first procured from. He also established a huge factory to produce china crockery, vases and utensils. To his neighbouring kings, he said, 'Fine china is being manufactured in Dresden. No longer is it necessary to pay import duties to anyone else.' Evidently, the king had smelt an opportunity here and was fully in favour of an enterprise that was due to bring him more profits than trading gold would ever make. Yet, it was not enough to know what earth yielded porcelain. One had to process it with several compounds and ingredients. Due to his mastery of chemistry, Bottger was the one to invent the same. He also finetuned and supervised the manufacturing methodology from start to end. The king became the possessor of vast wealth, thanks to him. All the same, he did not promote him to a high position in the factory. Nor did he release him from prison. The king forever treated Bottger as his private slave. Bottger was miserable and took to drinking. But ingesting copious amounts of alcohol did not do good to his health. Bottger died a broken man, still young at thirty-five. Had he not spoken a few untruths in his salad days, he would not have met such a vicious fate.

Glossary

1. Ashwamedh: A horse sacrifice ritual practised by Vedic-era kings who first let the animal roam after issuing an open challenge for anyone to stop it, waged a battle with the one who did and, if victor, declared themselves sovereign of the territories thus traversed. Subsequently, a yajna or sacrifice of the horse was performed with the chanting of hymns and lighting of the sacred fire.
2. Hollanders: Natives of Holland, which specifically is the dominant coastal region of the Kingdom of Netherlands, which contains the cities of Amsterdam, Rotterdam and The Hague and whose elevation is lower than the sea level. In most countries, the words, Holland and the Netherlands, are used interchangeably, but in January 2020, the kingdom has officially dropped its support for this practice.
3. *vilayat*: Originally a Turkish word meaning a province or administrative division; under the Caliphate, the term came to refer to any constituent near-sovereign state. However, in Urdu and Hindi, it has come to refer to any foreign country. In Bengal, its corruption, *bilat*, once loosely meant European, but now exclusively alludes to Britain. Interestingly, even the British borrowed it to invent the term Blighty or Ole Blighty for their homeland after coming in contact with the Bengalis, its first usage being traced back to the Boer War which took place during the turn of the nineteenth century into the twentieth.

The Legend of Raikou

Introduction

Save the people of Europe, North America and Australia, all other races are headed for a fall. A long time ago, a French scholar named Courvoisier had written a note that can be paraphrased thus: 'Just as mankind builds a house by putting one brick on another, so, too, the races that have placed one examined, and thereby confirmed, truth on the foundation of another and conquered the mysterious sciences have gone on to advance in wealth, prestige and might, and rule the universe. The ones that disregarded the new sciences have been rendered into slave races.'

The Muslim races, such as the Arabs, Turks and Tatars, were once the jewels of this earth in terms of physical valour, while the Chinese were invincible in crafts and engineering skills, but all these races are on a steep decline for having ignored the new sciences. In the East, only Japan has embraced this new knowledge base and powered by it attained great supremacy, indeed played the role of the entire Asian continent's saving grace. We, as Indians, are especially proud of Japan's accomplishments. Japan is not only the friend of our king, but is also our disciple. Not only Japan, my hunch is that even the Sinhalese were born of our Bengali ancestors. In ancient times, Hindu traders took the sea route from Bengal and Odisha and reached Bali, Cambodia and other islands and nations. Evidence of their achievements are still present in these places.

Since for many a reason I have come to be convinced that Hindus had sailed to Japan and settled there as well, maintaining good relations with their government bodes well. It is our duty to learn where it is on a map, and how the people there live and behave. I have written a few essays on China and Japan before and today I shall broach the subject from a different angle. There are many folktales circulated in Japan. In every society, parents and grandparents tell little boys and girls such tales. What stories do Japanese grandparents tell their little ones? Let me give here an example.

Monster Shuten-douji

The emperor of Japan is called the mikado. A thousand years ago, an emperor named Murakami occupied the office of mikado of Japan. In the Japanese archipelago is a district called Sumiyoshi. During the rule of Murakami, a great terror of monsters prevailed there. A cruel king of monsters named Shuten-douji built a fortress in a forest of the district and began to live inside it. Accompanied by his associates, he raided villages of the district and began slaying their cattle, buffaloes, sheep, goats, horses, donkeys and other pet beasts.

Finally, he tasted human flesh and began to pick up man, woman, boy, girl and the elderly indiscriminately and feeding on them. At first, he imprisoned the humans and made them serve him as slaves. Once they grew fat, he cooked them and consumed their meat.

The Japanese are drinkers of a type of hard liquor known as saké. Monster king Shuten-douji was drunk on saké all the time and in his intoxicated state it was hard to sate his hunger whether it was with human soup, human stew, human fry or human sauce and dips. For this reason, the king of monsters took his soldiers on daily hunts in one nearby village or another and abducted whosoever they could find. Needless to say, panic spread like wildfire and the oppressed residents of the surrounding villages abandoned their homes and fled to faraway lands. Yet the scarcer became the game, the wider the wicked monsters extended the ambit of their hunting, preying upon towns and cities as well. The entire district of Sumiyoshi turned into wilderness and the adjacent districts, too, began feeling the heat.

With his empire on the brink of destruction, anxiety struck the mikado. The emperor was an old man and lacked the strength to fight monsters. Not that it would have helped him if he wasn't. For Shuten-douji was a master of sorcery and deployed magic and the power of illusion to catch and slay humans. Even among monsters, none was his equal in the dark arts. Such were the circumstances that the emperor became completely despondent. Worrying that his empire was lost, that Japan was destined to be bereft of citizen and human habitation, and that its future was of a desert to be infested by monsters and ruled by an evil king, he began to shed tears incessantly.

Raikou of Minamoto

One day, the emperor was seated on his throne surrounded by his courtiers, friends and commanders. A messenger arrived with the news that the evil night crawlers had burnt down close to a hundred villages and taken the residents to their fort. Upon hearing this report, the emperor broke into loud laments, cursing himself for his inability to rescue his subjects and expressing his deepest despair in pitiable words. Resting his cheek on his left palm, he shed bitter tears, and he said, 'O' woe upon me who does not have the strength to save the life of his sons, his very own subjects. Alas! In this vast empire, is there no one who is valiant enough to slay the monster king and save his countrymen and women?'

The courtiers heard the emperor's wish but all the brave soldiers and commanders kept mum looking steadily at their own feet. No one could summon the courage to take on the sorcerer. The young chief of the Minamoto clan of braves was present in court at the time. Yorimitsu was his name. He had been visiting from a distant district for the purpose of diplomacy on behalf of his people. While Yorimitsu remained his given name, he went on to gain a reputation of a heroic spirit and became known as Raikou to ordinary Japanese people. Hence, in this account, he will heretofore be referred to by his later name. Raikou was a youngster of seventeen. He was handsome and agile. His complexion was of the wheat cultivated in the Ganges plain; he had full cheeks and almond eyes slanted upwards at the corners; and his hair was jet black. His physique had the ductility of Ramachandra's when he had visited King Janak's court at the time of the breaking of the great bow. If a bolt of lightning covered by petals can be called tender, Raikou's muscularity possessed the very same characteristic.

Having heard the emperor speak, Raikou stood up, folded his hands and submitted, 'Your Majesty! Please permit me to go forth. I shall battle the clan of monsters and exterminate the last of them.'

The emperor cast one glance on his youthful half-blossomed bud-like body and said, 'My dear son, I salute you and thank you for your initiative. But, my boy, I cannot, in all good conscience, assign you to a task that even the bravest of my warriors have no stomach for.'

Most humbly did Raikou offer again, 'Your Majesty! The Minamoto warriors are forever willing to sacrifice their lives for their nation. If I can indeed defeat the monsters in battle, I will have saved my country from a grave crisis. On the other hand, should I fall in the battlefield, I will attain what all mankind desires, a place in God's heaven, straightaway.'

The emperor tried dissuading him in many ways, but Raikou remained firm in his resolve and pleaded to be allowed to embark on the mission until the emperor gave up and said, 'Alright, my dear boy, if you are so determined to take this journey to fight the monster, then I, too, will accompany you with my army. On no account can I send you to fight the terrible monster all on your own. I may be an old man. In which case, I shall sacrifice what remains of this life for my nation and my people.'

'No, Your Majesty,' replied Raikou. 'Your company or your soldiers will prove to be of no help. The monsters fight a battle of illusions. It is impossible to overcome them by pure physical strength. We must trick them into submission. I will pick exactly three braves from the Minamoto clan and, with them by my side, will proceed to fight the monsters.'

The emperor was left with no option but to accede to his request. Having said goodbye to him, Raikou went to the temple and said his prayers to the deities. Then he and his companions donned the garment of ascetics. The mountain ascetics in Japan are known by the name of *yamabushi*. The *yamabushi* wander the hills with no belongings. Being seers, they are not harmed by humans who feed them and otherwise try to ingratiate themselves to them. Raikou and his companions took a slingbag with themselves in which they placed their iron armours and a pair of scimitars each. Thus prepared, they set out for the monsters' fortress.

The farther they proceeded on their journey the more complaints about harassment by monsters began to reach their ears from the mouths of the local people. Entreaties to desist from continuing their journey were also made. All said, 'The miscreant has no regard for holy men nor ascetics. Once you fall in their clutches, there is no hope, for they will certainly make a meal of yourself.'

'But we gladly accept these circumstances,' Raikou said. 'We do not mind dying, for we shall either slay the monsters or be slain by them. Is it not better to die by the sword than grow old and degenerate?'

Thus riposting, the quartet toured the places in their path and presently, after crossing many a city and village, entered Sumiyoshi district. Here they began to see signs of terror wreaked by the monsters and meet thousands of fugitive people. Said they, 'Shame on yourselves! Are you going to meet and be eaten by the monsters we are leaving behind our ancestral land for? Do no such thing, pray! Why give up your precious lives? Stop now, go home.'

Needless to say, Raikou was not impressed. He and his companions advanced on their way. Soon, the sight of gutted city and countryside began to greet them. Presently, they reached a village where every home had their floors covered in human blood. Neither man nor animal breathed in the far vicinity of them, but the travellers stopped there for the night, rested and, in the morning, resumed their progress. Since they met absolutely no one from this point on, they understood that the monsters had succeeded in converting this once-bustling settlement into a virtual desert, but they walked on over forest and wood, hillock and mountain, and swam through river and lake, going hungry now for days until they came upon a rocky scrubland below a mountain range. In the distance, on one of the scraggly peaks could be seen the monster king's tall fortress, but the young men had been enfeebled by lack of food and tiredness, and they sat down right on the spot.

At this point, on one of the nearer peaks, the group spied an old man with a body as of molten gold sporting a long white beard and white dreadlocks. The old man descended from the mountain and stood before Raikou. Seeing his fitness and pleasant mien, Raikou decided he was no ordinary soul, and he and his men paid loving obeisance before him.

In very gentle tones, the old man asked them, 'My children, who are you? Where are you going through this dangerous land infested by monsters?'

With folded hands, Raikou replied to him, 'Sire! Yorimitsu is the name of your slave, but elsewhere people know me by the name of Raikou. Your slave is the chief of the Minamoto warrior clan, and these are his relatives and friends. We are bound for the fortress of Shuten-douji, king of monsters.'

The old man said, 'Raikou, my son, I am very pleased to have met you. I am not human but the deity of Sumiyoshi district. Not just humans, even my subordinate village deities, not to speak of I, myself, have been oppressed by these wicked beings. As all have fled the country, there is none left to offer us even a flower at the end of the day. We are starving from lack of worship, and losing weight, have turned into bags of skin and bones roaming the streets. But without the help of a human with extraordinary courage and a pure heart, we cannot pierce the monsters' web of illusion. My son, you are just the one we had been looking for. We have spent long months waiting for your appearance.'

Raikou said, 'Father! If that be the case, bless us so we can breach the fortress and finish off those miscreants.'

The district deity said, 'Raikou, my son, you shall not be able to defeat the monsters by physical strength alone. You will trick them into death. When you enter the monsters' fortress, I shall accompany you invisibly. My village deities shall assist you as well. For now, camp here and spend the night as our guests. Have food and drink, and regain your strength. In the morning, you can resume your trek.'

Sooner than he had spoken these words did a splendid castle appear where he stood. Entering the castle, Raikou and his companions sampled a variety of delicacies and were sated before retiring for the night on costly bejewelled bedsteads covered with milk-froth-white linen.

When it was morning, the district deity reappeared and said, 'Raikou! For your protection and the success of your mission, I give you two strange objects. These will come to your aid in the opportune time. First, this golden hat I give you, which you shall wear under your turban just above your head. As long as it is on your head, the monsters' arrows, spears and swords will be unable to injure you. Even the sorcerer's magic will not harm you, and you shall be safe. Next, I give you this drug. The king of the monsters loves his saké, and you shall mix this dust in his drink. After consuming it, the monster will become feeble and fall asleep. That is when you can slay him most conveniently.'

The district deity also gave Raikou some more advice regarding the habits of the monsters. Then he led the way through an impassable mountain trail for a great distance until, late afternoon, the band of brothers reached a large lake. Here, the district deity bade them goodbye and vanished on the spot. Raikou and his companions walked along the bank of the lake in the direction of the fortress. After going some distance, they found a fast-flowing stream emptying itself into the creek.

Further along the way, Raikou saw a young genteel woman weeping on the riverbank. The garment she had on was soaked in blood. Raikou spoke to her and learned that her parents and siblings had become the food of the monsters, while they had kidnapped her and made her a slave. She, too, would be eaten by the monsters after a few days.

The blood on the woman's garment had come from the humans the monsters had slain on that day and cut up and prepared into dishes. The woman had come to the river to wash it off her person. Having told him her story, the woman forbid Raikou from going on to the monsters' fortress, but he, in turn, prevailed on her to show him the way to the citadel.

Finally, Raikou and his mates reached the enormous iron gates of the castle. The fort on the hill was surrounded by high bastions, below which flowed a canal wherein many had perished in the watery depths. It was indeed unthinkable to enter it without permission from the inmates. At the entrance to the fort were many numerous giants with grotesque visage. They had been posted there to guard the castle. Some had the face of a pot, some others the tusks of an elephant, some had snake-like ears while others had eyes like burning plates. Human hearts would be wont to start palpitating at the sight of them.

Hence when four members of this species suddenly appeared at the gates, the guards were surprised, indeed. Unsurprisingly then, when Raikou announced, 'We are travelling ascetics, we request hospitality for the night from your master', they were beside themselves. They could no longer hold back their laughter and broke into freakish howls of mirth as they joked with each at his expense. One of them dug his fingers into Raikou's skin and put them inside his mouth to indicate, 'Tonight we shall derive the greatest pleasure from feeding on your tender flesh.'

Paying no attention to their mockery, Raikou appealed to him again and again to carry his message to the master of the fort. In the end, one of the giants entered the fort and informed his king, 'Your Majesty! Four tender-fleshed tasty morsels have appeared from none-knows-whence at the lion gates.'

The monster-king ordered the ascetics be presented before him without delay. Inside the fort, Raikou saw Shuten-douji seated on a lion throne and surrounded by many more monsters who were armed with various weapons and stood by just below his pedestal. They were hideous, indeed, but Shuten-douji's structure and body shape was so ugly as to be almost indescribable. Suffice to say that the sight of him was enough to make mortals faint and fall to the ground. But Raikou and his companions belonged to the Minamoto clan and had been trained not to be fazed. Upon seeing the terrible king, they were not alarmed but showed him respect due to a leader by performing the *kouchou*, that is prostrating themselves before him on the ground and touching it nine times with their foreheads. Then the king asked them, 'Who are you and whence have you come from?'

Raikou replied, 'Your Majesty! We are ascetics. We do not reside in homes. We are ordained to spend our lives travelling from one holy destination to another. It has been a few days since we entered this district. We have met no one since then. Today we spied your castle and have arrived at your door. We pray that your highness will grant us shelter for the night. The poorest of households donate us a fistful of rice, so we expect Your Majesty will not be constrained to give us a small amount of the grain and a bed.'

Smiling nastily, Shuten-douji said, 'Willingly or not, many a human come to our castle. I shall welcome you exactly the way that I treat them.'

Hearing his words, all those present broke into loud laughter. They understood perfectly well how the ascetics would be cared for. Many a mouth watered at the thought of feeding on the young men.

To his followers, Shuten-douji issued a direction: 'Bring forth the tastiest dishes prepared at my residence today. By the book shall I take care of my guests today. Today we shall all sit together and share a meal with them.'

A feast was cooked. From indoors and outside the castle, the monsters gathered and sat in a file one next to another. As a mark of high regard and respect, the monster-king sat

Raikou and his mates to the right and left of himself. The waiters placed a covered bowl before everyone. The others removed the lid and began their meal.

Removing the cover, Raikou found a human head and two human feet on his plate. There was blood still oozing from the head. The plates of Raikou's companions bore similar items. The monsters were feeding exclusively on human flesh. Seeing the revolting contents of his plate, Raikou did not show the least alarm or distaste. Pretending as if they enjoyed human heads as part of their daily meals, they attacked the food with gusto, although even at that instance they did not in fact take human flesh. Tearing pieces of the meat they brought it close to their lips before secretly dropping these into their respective slingbags. This foiled the monster-king's plans to poke fun at their disgust and misery. He had expected them to be shivering at the sight of their meal, which did not happen. He was quite surprised at the calm demeanour with which they, despite being human themselves, dined on human flesh.

Presently, Raikou said, 'Your Majesty! Our appetites are satiated today, thanks to your kindness. Never have we ever partaken in such delicious fare in the span of our entire lives. Little do we have the power to return this favour of yours. Nevertheless, having travelled far and wide, and in foreign lands, we have come to learn of Your Majesty's fondness for the saké. As saké is brewed from rice grains, it does not have a pleasant odour. We have a substance with us that, if mixed with it, will turn it into a tasty and fragrant drink. It will then be no less in flavour than the nectar drunk by the gods in heaven.'

All day and night, Shuten-douji and his cohorts would drink saké and remain in a frenzied state. Yet the saké was a pungent drink; it did not go easy down the gullet. When he heard that it could be chemically transformed into an appetising beverage, he was delighted. He immediately ordered the ascetics to turn the foul-smelling saké into a sweet and flavourful alcoholic nectar.

Dance of the Monsters

Japan experiences cold winters and hence the dinner hall of the fortress had been appointed with a fireplace on which Raikou asked for the iron wok full of saké to be placed. As the saké started boiling, Raikou added to it the narcotic dust given to him by the district deity. When the dust had been mixed well, Raikou asked for the wok to be removed from the fire and served out the drinks. Sampling it, the monster-king found it sweet as nectar and delicious to the taste. Whosoever drank it got thirstier. So, they drank the liquor by the cupful and filled their stomachs to their heart's content. But Raikou and his companions did not touch the liquor, and seeing as they were ascetics in disguise, none asked them to partake of the same.

At the outset, after having drunk the narcotic liquor, the drinkers experienced euphoria. A blissful Shuten-douji ordered the dancers to be brought before him. Now, the cruel king had kidnapped daughters of rich men and engaged them in performing music and dances for his entertainment. Once their utility was over, he fed on them and appointed a fresh batch of performers. It was the same with the gentlewomen appointed as cleaners and maids. The dancers did their moves while the monster-king clapped to the beat. Presently, he rose from his seat and joined the girls. His cohorts followed suit and the hall, which had initially tinkled with the sound of bells on the feet of the human danseuses, resounded with the thud of monstresses' feet. Among Raikou's braves, Sadamiti was a fine dancer. To keep the monsters occupied, Raikou asked him to join the dance. Sadamiti became a runaway hit with the monsters.

As they danced, the monsters drank incessantly. Soon, the narcotic took effect, and they began to feel listless, weak and disoriented. Monster-king Shuten-douji had drunk the most and was the first to fall. As he hit the floor unconscious, he was picked up by his cohorts who rushed him to a bedroom and returned to join the dance. It was not long, though, before, one by one, the giants lost their sense and consciousness. The floor was covered with inert bodies of snoring demons.

Raikou entered Shuten-douji's bedchamber with his companions. He saw the monster-king lying on a golden cot with several gentlewomen at his service. One massaged his feet. Another waved a hand fan. Yet another carded her fingers through the monster-king's woolly hair. The prisoners had seen Raikou and his braves break bread with the monsters. They had gathered that these were monsters themselves, albeit in disguise, rather than ascetics. Therefore, Raikou spoke to allay those fears, and he said, 'Do not fear us. We are humans just as yourselves. The emperor has sent us to rescue you.'

So saying, Raikou and his mates took out their armours and scimitars from their respective sling bags. They put on the armours. With their razor-sharp weapons, they were about to behead the giants, when inside the bedchamber appeared the district god who raised his finger and asked the group to tarry. He said, 'Raikou, my son. Hold on and hear my warning. The monster has many powers. He will not die as soon as you decapitate him. His severed head, severed arms and severed feet will severally fight you. You cannot win a battle against severed organs. Hence, take this rope. Bind the monster fast to the cot and then cut him to tiny, little pieces to ensure death.' The district god then handed Raikou a length of magic rope. Raikou and his mates used it to tie the sleeping giant fast to the bedstead. Then, raising his scimitar, Raikou severed the head of the giant with a single blow. The room was filled with a thunderous yell.

Unfortunately, Raikou had failed to fasten the head of the giant to the bed correctly with the magic rope given to him by the deity and as soon as he cut it off the torso it rose up to the ceiling, bared its elephant-teeth and, grinding those with a terrible din, cast itself furiously at Raikou's head. Raikou's iron helmet shattered to pieces with a single bite of these teeth. Raikou's head, too, would have surely met the same fate had it not been for the golden hat that they could not pierce through and thus it was that the article saved his life.

At this time, Raikou's mates were not merely standing by. Among them had been Suna, who was a bosom friend of his. Before this adventure, he had assisted him in many a battle, fighting by his side. Once it so happened that a giant named the spider-demon had begun to terrorise the people of a certain village. It was with Suna's help that Raikou had succeeded in decimating the colossus. Another time, the demon had the body of a spinning wheel. Casting himself into the sky, he spun his way speedy as a bolt of lightning, landing in one country one day, and in another the next, leaving a trail of havoc. Then, too, Suna had helped Raikou eliminate the monster.

Raikou in Danger

When the monster-head failed to bite Raikou in the head, it descended to its chest level and tried again. Though his chest was protected by the armour, it was not magical and, therefore, penetrable by the monster's teeth. Raikou was brought to his knees by the disembodied head. His sword fell to the ground. With both hands, he held fast to the head, and with all his might, attempted to keep it away from his skin. But he failed to do so. The teeth were about to perforate it and slice open his heart, killing him, when the district god suddenly appeared in the room and loudly exclaimed, 'Suna! What are you waiting for? Save Raikou's life.'

Suna glanced in Raikou's direction. It took him a fraction of a second to understand his predicament and another fraction to slice the head in two halves with one powerful blow of his own scimitar. He went on striking the head until it was chopped to bits and had no power left in it. Once again, Raikou made a narrow escape.

While Raikou and Suna were engaged in battle with the head, the monster's severed arms and feet had been straining to free themselves with the might of an elephant in heat, but the divine rope did not yield. Hence the limbs raised the cot to the ceiling again and again and tried to bring it down on their adversaries. But the head of the monster had been severed from the body, which had become bereft of sight. So Raikou and his braves could easily dodge the furniture's rampage. Once the head had been destroyed, every time the bed fell on the floor with a crash, they slashed at the headless body with their swords, and, ultimately, the concerted effort of the quartet resulted in it being hacked to smithereens, in the same way. Thus did the evil monster-king Shuten-douji meet his end at the hands of Raikou and his peerless braves.

Victory

The commotion coming out of the bedroom finally awakened the other monsters as well. They armed themselves and quickly appeared on the spot. Within seconds, Raikou and his braves were engaged in a fierce battle with the monsters. As luck would have it, the battle took place in the narrow confines of the bedchamber, hence it was possible for a few to take on multitudes standing at the door of the room.

The monsters could not surround the four from all sides. They had been weakened by the drink and had also lost their wits. Even so, the battle raged through the night. Just at daybreak, the last four monsters fell, overwhelmed by the injuries inflicted on them by Raikou and his friends.

Some of the young women at the monster-king's service assisted Raikou and his team in battle. Others sat in the far corner and wept or fainted at first challenge. Once they won the battle, Raikou and his companions consoled these women. Then they requested them to give them the directions to the prison. The prison was at the foot of the fort, some distance away. The women took the warriors there through a secret tunnel. Reaching the prison, the warriors found two more giants standing guard and immediately waged a battle. This time, however, they defeated them shortly, and tied them up to take them alive and present them as trophies to the emperor.

Inside the prison were many men and women who roared their joy and approval of Raikou. The young women then took Raikou to a cave. It was the place where the monsters murdered their victims before feeding on them. The ground there was wet with human blood and skulls, bones and skeletons lay about with abandon. Enraged at the sight, Raikou ordered his men to immediately take the lives of the two captives and the last monsters were beheaded.

Raikou's mission was now completed. He collected the treasure from the monsters' fort, gathered the erstwhile prisoners together and commenced his return journey to the capital. The deities, too, accompanied them, in seen and unseen shapes. The sun did not shine fiercely but gently warmed their tired bodies and brightly lit the way. A fragrant breeze blew and fruit-laden trees bent their boughs. The spring was abundant with cool water for the party to quench its thirst. From the firmament, the local deities covered them with flower showers. Once they passed the wilderness of lonely Sumiyoshi and crossed over into populated lands, such an uproarious welcome did they receive that it does not bear mention. Nor does it to describe the emperor's relief and gratitude that he expressed upon meeting the young hero. The citizens lit rows of lamps in their own homes for several nights at a stretch. Celebrations continued for all those days. In the end, the emperor called over the court poet and asked him to compose a song recording the deeds of Raikou and his braves and inscribe it in golden ink. This story is drawn from the very same narrative.

Glossary

1. King George V: Grandson of Queen Victoria, grandfather of Queen Elizabeth, the former king of the United Kingdom ruled between 1910 and 1936
2. saké: Japanese rice beer served warm and typically drunk from small porcelain cups called *sakazuki*. Ironically or not, it is deemed one of the world's healthiest beverages and is said to have carcinogenic properties. 1 October is World Saké Day.

When Vidyadhari Lost Her Appetite

Rosy's Envy

Said Rosy the maid, 'Now, look here, Vidyadhari! On our master's fair countenance, stop putting lime and shoeblack. Our master, Neelambar Ghosh, is a renowned advocate. Can you name a single person who does not know his name? It is sullied if you are seen around the neighbourhood bumming a piece of jaggery off the grocer, sponging a bit of syrup off the confectioner, accepting a helping of green banana curry from Mrs Roy; in short, touching everyone and their aunt for this that and the other all the while being in his employ. Why, let alone the master's, your activities make our own heads hang in shame. If only from the pain of your mooching, we can't even raise them to talk to others.'

Vidyadhari smirked. 'You lot see my fault in everything, don't you? The lady prefers my company to others' and that is what is attracting your jealousy. I have been suffering from a lost appetite; nothing I eat appeals to my taste buds. My meal is of a sparrow. I have become thin as a rope from starvation. Without musculature, how will I work in another's home? Hence, I strive to feed myself a fistful of rice, with a bit of tamarind paste or a chip of jaggery. I am impecunious. Where will I get the money to buy rossogolla, sandesh and other goodies? The grocer is fond of me, so he gave me a small portion of jaggery the other day. The confectioner, too, is well-disposed, so he lent me some syrup in a sal leaf cone. Why does it bother you so badly?'

Pitem the manservant spoke up. 'Lost your appetite, my foot! The brahmin cook fills your stone dish to the brim, even so you need two or three refills. If this be its manifestation, then had your appetite been active, you would have eaten horses from the barns and elephants from the stable. Many a mansion have I given my service to, many a maid have I met while working therein, but a shameless mooch like you I swear I have not set my eyes on. What say, brahmin, does not this tramp alone consume the rations of three?'

Sidem said, 'Well, Vidyadhari, it is not a good habit to talk to neighbours in a way that shows the master in poor light. I work hard in the kitchen and I serve you myself. You, of all employees, get the biggest portion of the greens. Tell me, my dear, how come is your appetite absent?'

Rosy chipped in, 'If you so can't keep your gluttony under control and desire to sample sandesh, why don't you buy them in the legitimate way? You say you are impecunious and you don't have any money, but do you expect us to believe you? You sport a thick gold armlet and fat gold beads. How many times have you told me that you placed 600 rupees in a pot and buried the vessel in the earth under the floor of your bachelor bed in the outhouse? All in all, you have got the jackpot—one thousand rupees. Ever since I was widowed, I have been working in people's homes. I don't have one thousand cowries, let alone rupees. Pitem here, he has been a waiter since he was a boy. How much money has he accumulated? Sidem the brahmin mortgaged land to get married. Till date, he has been unable to pay his debt. But his daughter has grown. Perhaps, he can sell her and fulfil it!'

Vidyadhari responded, 'In this wide world, who is there that I can call my own? Certainly, no one I can depend on for a square meal. No doubt, I must save what I earn and strive to augment it with gifts. What do you worry for? You have a brother and a nephew to ask after you in your time of need.' That's when Sidem observed, 'While you say to all you are wasting away, the truth is that you are fat and if a fly lands on you, it will fail to find a footing.'

Vidyadhari raised her voice to its shrillest pitch. 'You slighted me. May your wife expire, may your daughter meet her death. May your shameless dream of selling her to make your fortune be shattered to smithereens!'

Sidem the brahmin said, 'There you go! Pitem and Rosy, do you think I said anything to merit such an outburst from a tramp? Does she need to be so proud of being a servant, even if she is a personal maid of the lady? But wait. Whenever the lady says she has 308 ailments, her heart is beating fast and her head is spinning, Vidyadhari humours her. That is the secret, after all, behind why she is the lady's favourite. Now if I spill the beans, she won't last here for two more days. For instance, tell me, tramp, while making tea for the lady the other evening, who put her paw in the sugar bowl and stuffed her mouth? We have all got ourselves a pipe each to drink by making a hole in the milk skin to one side of the pan. None of us take more than a mouthful or two each. Who was the cat that lifted the whole layer of skin and cream and ate it? Who was it that removed the eggs from the belly of the carp while cleaning it in the morning?'

Rosy spoke, 'In earlier days, we shared equally amongst ourselves the rice and pulses we saved. Now, you are keeping them all to yourself and won't give us any. How is that a fair deal? Aren't we, too, in this service industry? The other day, they delivered wet black grams and grated coconut pulp from upstairs to make green banana curry. You consumed one half of all that by yourself. And then one morning, they delivered fresh jalebis to the house for the lady. You removed their outer petals and collected them. Then you ate each and every one of the petals. Did it occur to you to say, "Why, Rosy, you, too, eat one or two of them?" Why didn't it cross your mind to say so? Don't we have mouths, too, and bellies? Or is it that you think we have no desire for gourmet food?'

Thus, it was that the four servants engaged in a fiery war of words in Neelambar Ghosh's kitchen. The trio of Sidem the brahmin, Pitem the manservant and Rosy the maid was to one side, and Vidyadhari alone was to the other. How long could Abhimanyu last before the seven great warriors' fusillade? Presently, Vidyadhari had no choice but to accept defeat and leave the field to the victors.

Purusottam's Good Luck

Tears flowing, Vidyadhari ran upstairs to her mistress and complained loudly, 'My lady! The brahmin says you are not ill and have been joking. Your heart doesn't race and your head doesn't spin. You have been spending the master's money out of mere caprice. You haven't lost your appetite; if a fly lands on you, it can't find a footing.'

The lady of the manor said, 'Really? Why, the audacious wretch, he has forgotten his station, hasn't he?'

Vidyadhari said, 'My dear lady, I, too, would say the same. Said I, "My dear brahmin, you must not speak ill of the boss. All eight *prahar* of the day, I am with the lady. How can I give you a count of the illnesses she is suffering from? It is purely on account of my care that she is surviving." My lady, as soon as I uttered these words, the wretched brahmin began making such vile allegations against me that they don't bear repeating. The master's favourite manservant, that wretched Pitem, and the barren Rosy, they, too, joined him. They are all jealous that you are my mistress and just a little fond of me. Yet, my lady, please find another maid. I will no longer be in your service.'

The next day, Mr Neelambar dismissed Sidem the brahmin from duty, and gave Pitem and Rosy a piece of his mind each.

Vidyadhari used her contacts to have appointed in his place a different brahmin. This brahmin bore an appearance that belonged to a man in a million. His face was large, but it was longer than it was broad. His complexion though was a shiny black. But his entire face was pockmarked with small pox scars, so it was difficult to figure out just how dark or fair his skin really was. His cheekbones were so high that his eyes next to them seemed like deep wells. Located between them, the nose was high and long to boot. The mouth was as large as a lake, and if he smiled, frightened onlookers lost their wits. The colour of his hair and eyes were that of copper and howsoever much he oiled his mop its texture stayed rough as always. The brahmin's name was Purusottam and Utkala Kingdom was his country.

Since the quarrel, Vidyadhari had stopped visiting the grocer and the confectioner for treats. Two days after Purusottam had been employed, she said to him, 'My dear brahmin, don't presume that I am an ordinary maid. See my gold beads, and my gold armlet. How fat it is, the armlet. To top it all off, I have kept a pot full of money worth 600 rupees buried under the floor of my private room. I have no relatives on any branch of my family. But I won't live long. You see, I have lost my appetite. Every day, my eyes burn and I feel feverish. I don't much desire to live either. Death will bring my lonely life a measure of relief. But Yama, the god of death, has forgotten me. Still, if I commit suicide, I won't go to heaven, so I don't attempt it. Or else, I would have been long gone—having either overdosed on opium or hanged myself or drowned in the river. That be the case, I won't live long either. I wish that following my demise a well-born person such as yourself gets to enjoy my jewels and my money.' Her words buoyed Purusottam's spirits. However, he said, 'No, my dear, you will live long yet. Your illness is not that hard to cure. Bequest or not, I will look after you as I would look after my own mother and take care of you if you are in need.'

'Oh, you don't have to take care of me for long,' Vidyadhari continued. 'I know my body. It will fail me, soon. Besides, I don't have an iota of desire to live anymore. The money I will bequeath to you. Our master is a barrister; so, I very well know how to make out a will. You simply have to write it on a piece of paper that you wish to bequeath so-and-so all your jewels and money. If I do that, you will automatically receive everything. Only, keep this a secret, will you?'

Purusottam agreed. From that day forward, he began ladling out all the greens and fish on Vidyadhari's plate. Pitem and Rosy got nothing, so they began grumbling. But they dared not complain loudly for fear of reprisal from the master.

In four–five days, Vidyadhari brought over a piece of paper and handed it to Purusottam. On it was written that he would be the one to receive all of Vidyadhari's property. Purusottam confirmed from his sources that such a piece of paper was indeed called a will, and it was by means of it that people conferred their property to another.

Purusottam's heart filled with contentment. From that day onwards, he asked the milkwoman to daily deliver an extra *paua* of milk solely for Vidyadhari. From that day on, he purchased cheese curd sweets from his own wages and began feeding them to Vidyadhari.

One day, Vidyadhari said, 'I have no more time. The *kabiraj* said, "Dear Vidyadhari, you are getting frailer by the day. Indeed, you are as frail as a bird. There are dark circles under your eyes. At most, you will live for three more months." Said I,"Dear sir, I don't have a passion for living. I just can't bear the pain of my illness anymore. If I poison myself I will be barred from heaven. If you are kind enough to add some to my daily medication, you will earn my blessing." The *kabiraj* said, "No, my dear, that won't be necessary. Don't you worry, though, your pulse is so weak. You have at the most three months to live."'

Purusottam gave her a onceover. If earlier she consumed a stone dishful of rice, now she consumed two dishes of the grain. Leave aside wasting, Vidyadhari was getting larger and larger by the day, partaking as she did of all the goodies Purusottam plied her with. It had been three months to that day that Purusottam had spent looking after her. He had not sent his salary home for all these months. He had spent it all on Vidyadhari.

Three more months went by. Vidyadhari did not die. Having experienced no dearth of ingredients in the nutrition department, her skin began glowing. Till date, on Vidyadhari's account, Purusottam had spent twenty-five rupees. Doubt cast its first shadow on his mind.

The Praanmugro Tree's Root

The members of Neelambar Ghosh's kitchen were up to their old antics. On one side, it was Pitem the manservant and Rosy the maid. On the other, it was Vidyadhari and Purusottam. The quarrels had resumed in earnest. One day, Rosy addressed Vidyadhari, 'Have you lost your judgement? Just this morning, you went to the confectioner's shop and bought sandesh for the master. Before serving it to him, you let the brahmin lick at it twice and then you, yourself, gave it ten good licks. When did you say to me, "Rosy, why don't you, too, give it a couple of licks?" If one attains something, one's duty is to share it with others. If I am a maid, so are you. Do you know that if you don't share your treat with me, you commit a sin? The Lord God above will pass His judgement. And what of this pockmarked Brahmin, what's the quality of his reckoning? What a face he has, by the way, like a two-and-a-half-foot Setala with a face cut like a diamond shining! The blackfaces could find no other cook, so they turned Jagannath into one instead, and of all beings! Well, then, why doesn't the Lord of the World Jagannath break the hand that is raised to give Vidyadhari things? So you can be a cripple and achieve a full likeness? Death upon us all; may the Lord have mercy!'

Purusottam went to bed with a fever brought upon by Rosy's curses. Meanwhile, Vidyadhari kept losing a little of what putatively was left of her appetite with each passing day. She would say, 'My dear brahmin, I can seem to taste nothing. If I could find some Kheermohan sweets, perhaps I could exert myself really hard and eat but one of them.' Or, 'They are hawking Sarbhaja. I can seem to taste nothing. If I get a scrap of that sweet, maybe I can try and see if I can eat it.' Or, 'Dear brahmin, I have been told there is a sandesh in

Baghbazar, it is known by the name of Aabar Khabo, which means I Will Eat This Again. Perhaps if you can get it for me, my appetite will be restored.' Such were Vidyadhari's many requests, which were now coming daily. What could Purusottam do? Having invested so much money, he was chary of cheesing off Vidyadhari and having it go down the drain. He had no choice but fulfil all of her requests. But instead of expiring, Vidyadhari began swelling into the shape of an oil barrel. Purusottam would look at her trunk from time to time and sigh deeply. One day, Purusottam was sitting with the grocer in his shop. The grocer said, 'Hey, brahmin. Has Vidyadhari the maid who works in your kitchen got back her missing appetite?'

'You ask of the missing appetite of Vidyadhari?' Purusottam responded. 'If earlier she ate one stone dishful of rice, now she eats two stone dishfuls of them.'

'Yes?' said the grocer. 'Oh well.' He sighed. After a short pause, he said, 'Is Vidyadhari's illness getting worse? Has the *kabiraj* felt her pulse beat and said she won't live for long? Well, that happens to be why she comes to me everyday to take a *chhatak* of ghee and to make a concoction a half *paua* of *bataasa* sugar drops by the same token.'

'She pays for them, I suppose?' enquired Purusottam.

'Nope,' said the grocer. 'But she is fond of my son. She has promised to bestow all her worldly belongings on him once she passes. She has made a will in his name.'

It was as if Purusottam had been hit by a bolt of lightning. The grocer opened his fretwork cash box and produced the said document. Purusottam, too, got the version in his own possession and showed it him. The duo realised they had been tricked; Vidyadhari had been luring them with the promise of the gold beads, *anantahaar* and cash, and fleecing them for treats and titbits. They made their enquiries, and it was furthermore revealed that she had given a similar will to the confectioner as well and taken milk, butter and rabri from him. The Odia shopkeeper had been provided a copy of the same document and had parted with puffed rice hunks in jaggery syrup and brinjal fritters. In this way, Vidyadhari had duped many a person into giving her these little gifts.

Ashamed that he had been fooled by someone as trivial as a woman, Purusottam did not share his tale of woe with anyone. But he resolved, 'Come what may, I need to collect my money from this tramp. If I let people know, they will have a good laugh and I will never get back my due.'

How then to collect that money? The path of confrontation being closed to him, he decided to go down the one of deceit.

Purusottam put on his thinking cap. He spent the next two-three days in deep contemplation. Then in the evening, finding her alone, he asked Vidyadhari, 'How did you like the fish gravy I cooked for you yesterday? Is your belly on fire yet?' Vidyadhari replied, wonderingly, 'Why would you say so? What was in the gravy that would set fire to my heart and my belly?'

Purusottam said, 'Nothing so terrible. Except that you told me that you wished to be relieved by death. That if someone poisoned you, they will earn your blessing. Remember, you asked the *kabiraj* for a drug that would have this effect? Said I to myself, "Poor Vidyadhari! She has been suffering so, has no desire to go on living, why don't I administer to her some poison so that she can attain her salvation?" So I ground out the root of our native Praanmugro tree and added some of that paste to your fish recipe.'

It was as if Vidyadhari just took a fall from the blue firmament. With greatest consternation, she uttered these words, 'What say you, you oven-faced lout of a brahmin?'

'Well, you were the one who repeatedly let on to me that you wanted to live no more. If you change your mind now, how can I help it?' Purusottam calmly responded.

Vidyadhari said, 'Snake in the grass! You, infertile Odia Brahmin! Is this what has been on your mind? Alack! My chest! Oh look, how it crackles and smoulders now. Pop and rush, my belly burns. Dear goddess, help me, I die.' So saying, Vidyadhari fell on the floor with a big thump. Tears flowing, she lamented piercingly and loudly, 'There goes my chest, my belly, my belly, my chest, my life spirit. Oh, my lady! Your maid Vidyadhari departs now. Bring me a doctor, quick. Oh, Pitem and Rosy. Come now, my dears. Come on and pitch in to save my life. Oh, dear goddess, holy mother! Save my life, dear mother. I will sacrifice a double ram at your altar. Dear father Taraknath, help me and I will worship you in your temple after reaching it covering the path to it with my prone body every inch of the way!'

Fearing that she would kick up a ruckus, Purusottam covered her mouth with his hand. 'Quiet,' he ordered.

Vidyadhari heaved herself up in a huff at his touch. She said, 'Oh, you son of a barren woman, you are back again, are you? What tree did you say you put the root of in my fish? You think I will be mum? I will go to the police station this very moment. I will have you handcuffed and hanged from the gallows. Hi Pitem! Come here and call the watchman. This barren woman's son has fed me poison. He murdered me to get his hands on my money. Oh dear! My stomach is on fire. Alas, what fate has befallen me!'

'Pipe down,' said Purusottam. 'If indeed you do not wish to die, then I know the antidote of this poison. It is not known to the doctor or the *kabiraj*, mind it. If I am arrested and taken to jail, who will bring it to you? Your fate will doubtless be sealed in that case.'

Vidyadhari said, 'Son of a barren woman! Bring me that drug right away!'

Purusottam said, 'That medicine will cost exactly five bucks. I don't have a single penny in my purse. Where will I get the money to buy it? If you take a small bottleful today, then your life will be spared for the moment. It will take five or six more bottles to flush the toxin out of your system. I am an impecunious brahmin. Where will I get thirty to thirty-five rupees in one go? I would hardly have mixed the poison in the fish had you mentioned earlier that you have no wish to be dead.'

Vidyadhari said, 'Son of an infertile woman! I will give you the money. You save my life in exchange. You are my guardian angel. Save my life, my belly, from this charring plague.' Hand on belly, a weeping Vidyadhari went to her room and emerged. She handed Purusottam five rupees, and said, 'Go, my dear, go. I forgive you your bungle. Save my life in this moment.'

'Have no fear,' Purusottam assured her. 'You will be well as soon as you drink the potion. But speak of this mishap to none. I will return soon. In the meanwhile, sit under the tap in the backyard and have some water put on your head and belly.'

The Elephant and the Turtle

So saying, Purusottam left the manor. Needless to mention that he hadn't administered any poison to Vidyadhari. He had hatched this plot only to collect the money he had spent on Vidyadhari.

Turning the corner, Purusottam got himself a small glass bottle for six pennies. He went to the streetside tap and filled the bottle. Then he got a paisa's worth of soda and mixed it with the contents of the bottle. Thus having prepared a counterfeit, he returned to the residence. He was basking in the certainty that he had gotten five rupees. Now, if only he could follow through for five or six more bottles.

It was twilight when Purusottam returned. Glancing towards the kitchen, he noticed Pitem and Rosy standing conferring in low tones. For the past few months, Purusottam had been denying them their rightful share of fish and vegetables, giving it all to Vidyadhari. So, they had grounds to be angry with him. Now, thinking that they might have heard the news about the poison administration, Purusottam flew into a raging panic.

He did not have to guess for long. Pitem called him over and said, 'Hey, brahmin, you have committed a huge catastrophe. You have administered poison to Vidyadhari. If the cops get a single whiff, they will come immediately, tie you up and take you away. Presently, you will be hanged.'

Purusottam's dark face turned ashen in fear. He protested, 'I didn't really poison her. I only lied to her that I did.'

Pitem said, 'Who will believe you? If you haven't given her poison, then why did you take those five rupees from her for the drug? Why then has Vidyadhari taken leave of her senses?'

An astonished Purusottam repeated, 'Taken leave of her senses? I swear to you I did not give her a drug that might have caused it.'

Pitem said, 'She is very mad now. The two of us could not hold her down. We did try and make her feel a little better. But as soon as she did, she perpetrated a fresh catastrophe. She walked straight upstairs and lay in the lady's big bed. The lady is at the garden tap washing clothes. Upon returning, if she finds Vidyadhari lying in her bed, she will take our hides. The master, too, will return within the hour. All the beans will be spilt. That is probably when he will call the police and turn you over to them.'

Purusottam began quaking. Said he, 'Brother mine, I fall at your feet. Save me from this calamity. Advise me, brother, what should I do to free myself from its clutches?'

Pitem answered, 'We did try, you know. We exerted all our strength but failed to budge her from the lady's bed. Now if you could lift her in your arms and carry her down the stairs to the kitchen, there can be a solution. But if you linger all will be lost. The mistress will arrive at any moment. If she sees Vidyadhari in her own bed, she will have our hides.'

Purusottam said, 'I will go at once.'

Rosy spoke. She said, 'Wait. Hold on. You can't go in like that. As soon as you take her in your arms, she will raise an alarm. Hearing her cries, the lady will come running and the cat will be out of the bag.'

'What must be done then?' Purusottam asked desperately.

Rosy entered her room and appeared with a large sack that she handed over to Purusottam and said, 'Go to the lady's room and slip this over Vidyadhari's head. Then lift her up with both your arms. Take care that she does not remove the sack from her head. Then bring her downstairs. If you can reach her to us, we will talk to her and get her to calm down.'

Sack in hand, Purusottam ran up the stairs without wasting any more words. Swiftly, he entered the lady's room. It was dark now, and the lamps had not been lighted. Whoever was lying on the lady's bed was assailed upon by Purusottam at great speed. He quickly slipped the sack over their head and pulled it down their chest, back, arms and waist. Lifting the figure in his arms, he then lugged it outside the room. The sack-covered figure attempted to scream. But only a rattle and a whimper emerged from the folds of the cloth. It then tried to free its arms. Yet the stubborn Odia brahmin would not give up. He partly heaved and partly dragged the figure up to the staircase. By which time, the figure partially freed its arms from the sack's encumbrance and his chokehold.

The figure now began to claw at Purusottam with both hands, while biting at him through the folds of the sack and kicking out at him with both feet. The staircase became the scene of the prehistoric fight between the elephant and the great turtle. Purusottam was backfooted by the resistance. Though he tried very hard, he failed to bring the figure down the stairs. If he succeeded in moving it two steps forward, it immediately took a step back. And as the struggle raged, who would appear at the foot of the stairs but the lord and master of the house.

To begin with, the Odia brahmin was certainly not easy on the eyes at the best of times. To the master, he now looked like an apparition flailing. This apparition was struggling with another one, all covered in sackcloth. In the presence of this marvellous sight, the master wondered if he had chanced upon a lowlife, a madman or a spirit. 'What on earth is this?' he cried out in bewilderment.

A shocked Purusottam looked in the direction of the master's voice and saw whom but him standing only two steps below him. Right behind the master, holding the lamp stood none other than maid Vidyadhari.

At the sight of Vidyadhari, Purusottam's spirit shrivelled inside him. He dropped the woman inside the sack right on the spot where they had been struggling and quickly climbed down the stairs, slipping past the master. Exiting the door, he left the house for good, never coming back to pick up his clothes or collect his salary. From that day forward, nothing was heard of him. When Purusottam left, Vidyadhari the maid, Rosy the maid and Pitem the manservant all pretended to be idiots. They opined, 'We have no clue why the brahmin performed such a deed.' This is why even Neelambarbabu could not find out much about the reasons behind this extraordinary affair. His belief is that the Odia Brahmin either suffered a bout of mental illness or was possessed by a spirit.

Be that as it may, Neelambarbabu proceeded to remove the sack from the head of the woman, and whose face should emerge from the bag but that of his wife herself! The mistress had fainted by this point. After many ministrations, she regained consciousness. But she began experiencing bouts of hysteria. For six months, she suffered from various illnesses. Neelambarbabu showed her to many doctors and *kabiraj*, spent a lot of money and finally got her well. The family is now passing its days peacefully.

Glossary

1. Pitem: A colloquial variant of Pitambar, meaning the yellow-robed god, used as a man's name
2. Sidem: Colloquial variant of Sridam, referring to a mythical devotee of Krishna, also used as a man's name
3. *prahar*: The traditional unit of time. There are eight *prahar* in a day.
4. *paua*: 250 grams or a quarter of a litre
5. *chhatak*: A sixteenth part of a *ser*, which in metric terms is close to a litre of liquid
6. *Anantahaar*: A style of gold necklace with multiple strings attached to a temple-shaped locket. Translates literally to the endless garland.

Author's Biography

Unlike the general experience in today's age of multi-specialty hospitals, domain specialists and hyper-focussed, mediocre punditry, the turn of the nineteenth century was a time of polymaths and discoverers of pathbreaking ideas. J.B.S. Haldane, a mathematician who later became a geneticist, served in World War I as a captain. He also studied philosophy and the classics, taught biology at Cambridge without a degree, suggested the central idea of in vitro fertilisation, became a Marxist of some distinction, adopted Indian citizenship, wrote comic poetry, served in the Indian Statistical Institute and laid the foundations of the field of biostatistics. Kedarnath Pandey aka Rahul Sankrityayan spent forty-five years travelling the world. He invented the Indian travelogue, was a polyglot and philosopher who moved from Hinduism through the Arya Samaj into Buddhism and finally into the embracing arms of socialist ideology, taught Indology in Leningrad, contributed to the Indian independence movement and straddled the fields of Tibetology, folklore, Hindi literature, drama, lexicography and sociology, which gave him a breadth of vision that continues to astound all. Historian and grammarian Harinath Dey, who died at the young age of 34 years, spoke as many languages! He translated the Rigveda, and Subandhu and Kalidasa's work, from Sanskrit into English, wrote the first English-Persian lexicon, penned 88 volumes on literature, linguistics and Hinduism and was the first Indian librarian of the National Library of India. Yet, save a handful of scholars, how many remember his name?

In the world of Bengali literature, too, the great Jagadish Chandra Bose and the inimitable Rajshekhar Basu pushed boundaries and transgressed borders. Basu was a chemist, while Bose, who pioneered the discovery of radio waves and invented the crescograph, wrote the first Indian science fiction and penned timeless verse. Trailokyanath, who served as curator of the Indian Museum, on the other hand, was arguably the first to study India's industrial revolution in the nineteenth century.

Trailokyanath Mukhopadhyay, who is known as T.N. Mukharji in the British Indian government records, was born on 22 July 1847, in the village of Rahuta, near Shyamnagar in the North 24 Parganas district of West Bengal. He was schooled in Chinsurah and Bhadreshwar. Trailokyanath enjoyed multiple careers. At first, he was a schoolteacher in Daroka (Birbhum), Ukhra, Raniganj and in Sahajadpur, Sirajganj. From 1868, he was a police sub-inspector in Cuttack. Having learned Odia, he then joined Bhagavati Charan Das' *Utkal Subhakari* as editor. In 1870,

Trailokyanath joined the Bengal Gazetteer Office as a clerk. He rose to become assistant director of the Government of India's agriculture department. During India's Great Famine of 1876–78, which had been exacerbated by Viceroy Lytton's policy of exporting Indian wheat and other cash crops, it was he who advised the government that it could save many lives by promoting the cultivation of carrots. This policy was adopted in the Raebareli and Sultanpur districts of Uttar Pradesh.

Thereafter, Trailokyanath went on to join the government's revenue department. He helped in organising the exhibits for the Calcutta International Exhibition of 1883. There, he was reportedly awarded a medal by the visiting Russian tsarevich. He also created a descriptive catalogue of Indian produce, *Hand-book of Indian Products (Art-manufactures and Raw Materials)*, which was contributed to the Amsterdam exhibition of 1883. From 1886, he was assistant curator of the Indian Museum in Calcutta. He fulfilled the duties of this position with distinction and flair. During this period, he compiled another highly valued catalogue, *Art-manufactures of India* (1888). His work thus intersected the fields of economics, geography and commerce. Trailokyanath was quite possibly responsible for organising the Indian portion of the 1886 colonial and Indian exhibition in London at the height of Queen Victoria's reign. In 1896, he retired on a pension and embarked on his literary career.

For the purpose of performing his duties as museum

curator, Trailokyanath travelled to Europe several times. He visited Amsterdam, Cologne and Glassgow and wrote about his travels in English. The 430-page travelogue was published in 1902. Titled simply *A Visit to Europe*, it offers a refreshing view of the continent through the sharp eyes of the outsider:

> We went ashore at Port Said, but as it was in the evening after it was dark, we could not see much of the place. We however saw various coffee houses, small theatres, and gambling shops. The dregs of all European countries gather here; Port Said is therefore noted for its immorality. On the 25th March during night time we left Port Said and entered the Mediterranean. We received fresh passengers in Egypt, among whom was an American Missionary of a certain persuasion. He was delighted to see a magnificent crop of heathens on board the vessel, and he at once set to commence his harvesting operations.[1]

As a writer, Trailokyanath was an inventor and interlocutor of various literary genres. His most critically admired work was his first. Though a surreal fantasy with elements of speculative fiction, *Kankabaty*, published in 1892, nevertheless retained its qualities that made it suitable for children's reading, and it was praised for being successful

1 Mukherji, T.N., *A Visit to Europe*, https://archive.org/details/in.ernet.dli.2015.121324. Accessed on 22 December 2022..

only as such by Rabindranath Tagore who clearly did not want to mention its other, more exciting, aspects. An early magic realist, Trailokyanath also wrote tragedy and social drama wherein he provided his reader with a clear-eyed and empathetic perspective on the society of nineteenth-century Bengal. Sadly, Trailokyanath's most famous work, *Damrucharit* (1923), published after his death in 1919, ended up reducing his reputation to that of a clever satirist only. The defeatist Bengali establishment and talking heads feel vindicated by and thereby share an inordinate fascination for this genre.

For instance, very few are aware that Trailokyanath was an essayist, too. His *Bharat Barshio Bigyan Sobha*, 1903, has now attained the status of a rare book. It must be mined for historical and cultural information by interest readers. He also compiled the first volume of *Bangla Vishwakosh*, a Bengali-language encyclopaedia, with archaeologist and social historian Nagendranath Basu.

Some of Trailokyanath's stories contain frequent mentions of *ganja* (marijuana) and *chandu* (opium). In 2009, Tapas Majumdar, his fourth-generation relative, wrote in *The Telegraph*:

> Trailokyanath was nothing if not versatile. Many years later, he would be giving evidence before the International Opium Commission on the different kinds of addiction to opium and the consequences. He was considered by the English to be their expert on